1

Taming the Wilderness Historical Fiction Series

Night Flight
Caravan

JOANN KLUSMEYER

innovo
PUBLISHING

Published by Innovo Publishing, LLC
www.innovopublishing.com
1-888-546-2111

Providing Full-Service Publishing Services for Christian Authors, Artists &
Ministries: Books, eBooks, Audiobooks, Music, Screenplays, Film & Curricula

Taming the Wilderness
Historical Fiction Series for Adults

Volume 1

NIGHT FLIGHT
&
CARAVAN

ISBN: 978-1-61314-718-4

Cover Design & Interior Layout: Innovo Publishing, LLC

Printed in the United States of America
U.S. Printing History
First Edition: 2021

Contents

Things can just rock along, and nothing is done about a potential problem until something slaps one in the face. It happened that way to Eben when he saw the in-laws of his deceased son reach out for his 5-year-old granddaughter. Reality struck with deadly force. She must not be reared in a bootlegging family. Drastic needs took drastic measures, and it must happen in secret—actually, in the dark of night.

It might have been just cold feet, but it took something powerful to influence the move made by some Nebraska families one cold winter day. The urge, however, moved a lot of people in the same way: hence, the Caravan.

Night Flight

One

Roberta stood in the garden, covering her eyes to shield them from the last rays of the bright, late-February sunshine.

She and the soon-to-be-five-year-old, Alecia, had been harvesting some of the last of the winter turnips to store in the root cellar and perhaps make into pickles to vary the late-winter diet. It would soon be time to break ground for the new planting.

Blinking against the sun, she felt her lungs tighten and her muscles cringe at the sight of two wagons heading up the hill toward the mountain farmhouse. Taking the little girl by the hand, she led her toward the house and toward the trouble, whatever it was. Two unexpected wagons in the mid-afternoon could be only one thing… trouble.

Apprehension mounted as she recognized her brother's horse, Dancer, being led, riderless, beside the first wagon. She felt the tingle of her scalp tightening with fear.

With a mountain woman's continuous attention toward preparedness, acquired during her twenty-two years of life, she dusted the loose dirt from her apron and held it ready. At a raised palm from the driver of the first wagon, she wrapped her apron before the face of the child, turning her and hurrying her away from the dreaded scene.

"Papa," she called to the man working in the barn. "Would you go see to the wagons out front? We're takin' a little stroll."

The older man walked as rapidly as his years permitted toward the approaching vehicles, and the little girl looked up at Roberta with questions in her eyes.

"It's all right, honey. We'll go see if we can find where old Cockle Bonnet hid her nest. She's likely gonna be bringin' in a new family any day now."

Reluctantly, the little girl allowed herself to be drawn into the search for the hen's nest. It was necessary for Roberta to occupy the child until the first of the preparations were made at the house. Ten or fifteen minutes should be enough. Meanwhile, her mind raced in many directions. How bad was it… what to do about it… and what to do with the child? These were decisions more immediate than the location of the nest of the brooding hen.

"Honey," she addressed the girl, "let's go see Grandpa Ned."

The child's small hand tightened in hers as she instinctively hesitated. The wide, blue eyes looked up into Roberta's.

"Just for a little while, darling. I'll be comin' back to get you 'afore suppertime. Can you do that?"

"Why?"

"Big Papa and I have some things to do."

"I'll help…."

"No, darling, not this time. But I promise I'll come to get you. Now, don't be cryin'. Grandpa Ned won't like to see tears in your eyes. Make a big smile. That's my girl!" Roberta encouraged with a forced smile of her own.

They walked down the steep hill and picked their way over the brook, stepping then on a path of flat stones. The trail rose immediately up a steep hill to the mountain cabin. On the porch of the cabin sat an old man, his eternal jug beside him, but he seemed in possession of his wits.

"Brought the girl, eh?"

"For a while. I think she'd like to see the new puppies. I'll be back to get her before supper. Bye, now."

Roberta loosed her hand from the girl's reluctant one and stepped away. After a pause, Alecia walked on toward the porch where the old man sat.

Roberta's heart pounded as she turned and retraced her steps down to the brook and up again. What would she find waiting for her?

Not good, that was certain. Her father was standing at the crest of the hill, watching for her.

"Bertie, I waited too long. I know'd it was time to be leavin', and I didn't go. Rob paid the price."

"Really bad?" A cave-in at the coal mine could mean death or dismemberment, or it could be only a cloud of black smoke to add to the rest of the blackness of the coalmine. For the one escaping loss of life or limb, the inevitable result was a layer of coal dust in the lungs and a cough that followed the miner to his grave.

The old man walked along in silence. His daughter insisted on an answer.

"Papa... was it bad?"

The question was too much. Like a mighty cedar tree that crumbles to the earth when a forest fire has burned away its roots, the old man sunk to his knees on the ground and bowed his face into the dirt, sobs tearing themselves from the bony frame. His daughter fell to the rocky path beside him and wrapped him in her arms.

"No, Papa! No! It can't be!" But she knew it was and pulled herself to her feet, drawing the old man after her. She squared her shoulders, resolutely marching toward the mountain cabin... toward the men who stood waiting with heads bowed and hats in hand.

Dreams must play themselves out, and even nightmares continue to force themselves into the thoughts of a night. So must the actions of the day continue, but there is a difference. A new life appears each morning as the nightmare fades, but the ravages of an actual day can leave torn lives to be dealt with forever.

Some years ago, her strong, beautiful brother, the laughing Eldon, three years older than Roberta, had been brought home in the wagon, barely alive, and a week later he was buried. He was stolen from her by the coal seam that ran through the mountain and beneath her own cabin.

Now her twin brother, Robert....

Both her brothers... gone... and only she was left with her papa. It was indecent, somehow, for the child to die before the parent. Especially the beautiful Eldon, and now the quiet, sensitive Robert, her childhood playmate and the sharer of confidences over her whole life. Gone.

It was truly startling, the speed with which thoughts can race through the head. Between the sight of the flock of chickens, scratching in the backyard, and the shape under the sheet spread over the bed, a million thoughts had whirled… and uppermost among was the hope (prayer?) that Papa had been wrong, and Robert had only been severely hurt. Hurts can be healed.

But that was not to be. The white sheet covered her brother from his feet to the top of his head, extending up and over the unruly mop of red-gold wiry curls.

The dreadful weight that had been whirling in her head now suddenly dropped with terrible finality into the pit of her stomach. Gone… first Eldon, whose death had also taken her frail mother from the grief of it all… now Robert, her soul mate. And one other thing. Her mind thumbed its way through the pages of her thoughts, searching for another date. Two years ago it was, counting from last December, that the only man she had ever loved had walked away from the mountains and from her.

But, like nightmares that cannot be stopped, this day must be lived through, and she lifted the corner of the sheet to look at the mangled body of her twin brother. There was no time for tears, as there was Alecia, Robert's daughter, to be thought of.

From the barn, she could hear the hammering of nails into the wood, and it drummed into her mind the necessity to make plans for Alecia. She had promised to go get her, but that would mean the child would be brought into the house. She would see a sight that would bring nightmares into her dreams as long as she lived. For the child, losing her mother at three was something that could be dealt with, because she still had her father. Now he was gone, but she must eventually be permitted to see him, or she would think he had gone away and left her because he did not love her. What to do…?

A discrete tap at the door told her they had arrived, the women folk of other miners, and they had come to help her through the next days. Just as she and her mother had gone to others in the time of their loss. Just as they had come when Eldon….

She opened the door and wordlessly permitted the silent forms, clad in work dresses, aprons, shawls and bonnets, to enter. Words were unnecessary, and there was nothing to be said that had not been already said over and over and over.

Large, comfortable Annie McDougal, who had buried a husband and son, placed a leather-skinned, calloused hand on Roberta's arm as she looked into her eyes. No words were necessary.

"Annie…?" Roberta pled, uselessly.

"What, sweetheart…?" The arms spread wide, and Roberta was pulled toward the pillowy bosom. The tears she had pushed aside now found their outlet, drenching the fabric of Annie McDougal's wool shawl.

When the sobs died away and she was able to speak, Roberta whispered. "Annie, his little girl, she's got'a see her pa. You know? To give her a picture in her mind to look back on? Can you…?"

"Yes, honey, I can. Now you go tend to your papa. He's not got youth like you got, and it'll hit 'im hard this day and likely harder tomorrow."

Roberta slipped away and joined her father in the kitchen.

"Papa? Papa? I wouldn't be botherin' you, but I got'a go get Alecia. I promised."

Wiping his eyes, the old man nodded. "Yes. You go on."

Two

So soon the eternity had passed, and they were in the cemetery.

Roberta stood with her father as the last prayer was spoken by the preacher and those in attendance had gathered around the three of them. The little girl hid her face in the front of her aunt's dress. Words of intended comfort were said as the trio climbed into the buggy. The horse moved out onto the road, leaving others to the filling and leveling of the grave.

"We're leaving." The old man made the announcement as though discussing the weather.

"What, Papa?"

"It's time and past time. We're leaving."

"Papa…" Roberta glanced knowingly toward the attentive ears of the little girl, and her father nodded his understanding.

"Yessirree, we're leavin' that cemetery, 'afore the road gets dusty from all them other buggies."

The little girl looked at the ground and grinned at the joke. "Aw, Big Papa, there ain't no dust. This here ain't summertime!"

"This ain't summertime?" He pretended surprise.

The small fist pounded on her grandfather's sleeve. "No, Big Papa! It's wintertime."

"Oh," he exclaimed. "That must be why I'm wearin' a coat!"

"Big Papa! You're so silly!"

Leaving, huh? The word had stuck in Roberta's ears. Old Eben Carlile had often spoke of leaving; in fact, he had brought it up just about once a month since his wife had passed on. Virginia Carlile, never strong physically, had been the force that had held Eben together for the greater part of his 56 years of age. She had been his link to the rugged mountains around the cabin, but his tie to the rocks and trees had been severed when she was put in the ground.

Roberta knew about links. She'd had some of her own. One link had been severely weakened when the man she loved had walked away, promising he would come back for her. It had not happened.

When the little girl was tucked away in bed, Roberta joined her father around the miniature parlor stove. The weather was unseasonably mild, but a small fire had been laid to take the chill off the room. Fresh coffee filled the parlor with a fragrant, roasted-nut smell. The coffee was made from the package of coffee beans brought by neighbors, along with the other food, to the laying-out. A friendly mountain custom.

There was talking to be done.

Roberta sat on her mother's small sewing chair and looked at the flames in the miniature stove. Her father spoke.

"South. That'd be the place. Around water and boatin', like there's plenty of, over to the river. An old man could find jobs a'plenty."

"Jobs, Papa?" Did she have to remind him of his 56 years? Remind him that he was not strong and young anymore? Did she have to mention his accelerated decline since her mother's death?

"Little girl, your old pa, he ain't done in yet. They's fishin' net mendin' to be done and cleanin' and calkin' the leaks in the boats. Old man like me, he'd find job's a'plenty. Us three that's left, it wouldn't take too much to take care'a us."

"You thought this through, Papa? Like what to do with the place here? You think there's some kind of a rush to get on the road?"

"Bertie, child, think on it. For you and me, likely there'd be no rush. For that youngen in the next room, we're down to days, the way I figure it."

"Days?"

"Days," he uttered with finality. "The Doughertys, they might not be no swifter in the head than the average box-turtle, but it ain't gonna take them more'n a week or so, and they'll see that with her pa gone, we ain't got no more legal hold on that little girl than they got. That happens and they'll be here to get 'er."

The horror of the thought silenced his words, and Roberta felt her stomach muscles clench like the steel claws of a wolf trap. A panorama of scenes flashed through her mind of robberies and other unsolved crimes that seemed to point toward the Doughertys, of the frequent jailing of their male members and the shy little Letha who often slipped away and climbed the mountain to play with her when they were children. Also among the vivid pictures were those of the grownup Letha, pregnant with Robert's second child, staring into Roberta's blue eyes with her own gray ones, sharp as steel knives.

"Somethin' happens to me, don't you let 'em take my little girl!"

"Hush, up, Lee! You're gonna be fine. It ain't like this here was your first baby!"

But Letha had been insistent. "Don't you be tryin' to jolly me out'a what I got'a say. YOU KEEP MY LITTLE GIRL! I got'a hear you promise me."

Roberta did, and she remembered those words again as she had stood beside Robert at the grave of lovely Letha and the baby that she had not been strong enough to bear.

She glanced at the old man as he stared into the fire, its orange and red flames reflecting against the tears on his face and in the moisture pooled in his swimming eyes. "I ain't lifted a gun agin no livin' human, and I ain't aimin' to start now, so what's left for us is to get out. Don't say nothin' in front'a the girl, but you get together in your mind what you got'a take, as much as'll go in a wagon, and you leave the rest to me."

"But, Papa…."

"Hush, child. The less you know of it'll be the less you'll say. Likely there'll be times you'll be sayin' to folks what you and me'll do, but this here's a time that I say what's to be done. Sometime this week, you take 'er across the valley one more time, to see the youngens over there, but don't be leavin' 'er alone."

"Sure, Papa…."

There'd be no sleep for her tonight. With a pencil and paper, she walked around the room, checking what could be removed without an explanation to the girl. It wouldn't be easy.

"Bertie, child…."

"Yeah, Papa…?"

"Likely be easier to do your plannin' if you was to know we'll be leavin' in the night."

"Night?"

"For a fact. The through-train to the south goes past here at one fifty, barrelin' on down the valley less'n it's been flagged. Station don't open at night. A body wantin' on that train got'a do the flaggin' hisself."

Well, yes, that would make the planning easier. Alecia could be put to bed, and there would be time to load up if she had her list made up already.

"Papa, how're we gonna get all our plunder on that train, this bein' only a flag stop?"

"Bertie, child, that ain't your worry. You figure out what'll go on that wagon and I'll tend to gettin' it off."

Put like that, it would be simple. So she started the list. Boxes. Trunks. Her mother's sewing rocker. Alecia's stuffed bear that had been made by her grandmother, and the rag doll she herself had made for her last Christmas. Their clothes, the dishes, the....

"Papa, the parlor stove?" Likely not, but she was hopeful.

"Put it in. It hardly ain't much bigger'n a stewpot."

She paused in her list-making as a memory stabbed her. The jar! She couldn't leave without the jar. A glance at the window reminded her of the full moon, furnishing plenty of light, but still, Papa would want her to light a lantern. Then he would want to know what she was doing.

He still stared into the flames, so Roberta went to the lean-to kitchen and moved a few pots, making a fair amount of noise. What man noted any sound that came from the kitchen?

Easing silently through the door, she hurried across the yard and down the path toward the outhouse. Stopping halfway, she walked toward the large oak. Clearing away the leaves with her hands (Papa wouldn't like that! Snakes can hide under leaves), she felt the reassuring hardness of the glass jar with the tight-fitting zinc lid. The coins inside whispered, clicking metallically against each other.

Cradling it carefully in her apron, she took the jar into the kitchen and set it inside her soup kettle. That took care of that.

"More coffee, Papa?"

"Might as well. Still got a lot'a thinkin' to get done."

Three

Early in the morning, Eben Carlile paid a visit to his neighbor on the next farm.

"Eli, you always had a hanker to add my farm to yourn; what'll you give me if I was to sell?"

"What'll you take?"

"A two hunnerd dollar bill. But if'n you'll do me a favor, I'll split that two hunnerd half in two."

"What'd the favor be?"

"It'd be that you don't say nothin' about this for a week, givin' me time to get away."

"Why'd it need to be kept a secret?"

"The Doughertys. I find myself needin' to get away, maybe earn a little hard money, and I had me the idea the river'd be a place to do it."

"The river?"

"Yeah, down to the south where the fishin' is. Figured they'd be needin' a old codger like me to kick around and do the dirty work. Need a way to take care'a my girl till she gets herself a man, and there's the least'n to be thought on."

"Not gonna leave the little girl here?"

"Think on it, man! Bertie bein' the only ma she's knowed, and now her pa's gone? It'd be shameful to leave her, though likely she'll be a peck'a trouble. Maybe later…."

Elias Weatherby nodded his head knowingly. Good of Eben to take on the responsibility of a youngen—and her hardly out of diapers.

"Tell you what. I'll take you up on that if you can make a trip into Hilltop first thing in the mornin' to sign the papers. You'll be gone in a week? Well, this place'll miss you."

"Aw, not much, 'n there'll be the comin' and goin' for visits, the youngen still havin' kinfolks here."

Elias nodded again. "What about your farm plunder? What'll you do with it?"

Eben chewed on a straw and spat the broken end onto the ground. "This and that. Got a place to get rid of some of it on west'a my place. Got'a deliver it today. Gonna be some of it left around up there. Anything still there when we leave, that'll be yours."

Elias nodded. This was turning out to be a good day.

Eben returned to his cabin and inspected the practically new wagon stored under a shed out of the weather. Good paint job. Color of a grasshopper, and they'd teased Robert when he brought it home.

He inspected the undercarriage. Wheels been kept greased. His son had bought himself a good wagon, Eben had to admit, and the span of bays he bought at the same time drew a second look most anywhere they went. Likely he'd paid too much for the wagon and horses and for the new clothes he'd got for the little one out of the money from selling his place. Leastwise, he didn't seem to have any left.

Eben rubbed the hay dust off the shiny paint and sighed. When Robert's wife died, that should have been the time to leave the mountain, but change is hard, especially when a man is past 50 years old and he's bone-tired of life. Then, too, there was Roberta, still thinking that young man would be back. Everyone else had thought so, too, but things happen. Young men get themselves killed, or there could have been a dozen other things to keep him away.

Anyway, two years was long enough to wait, and Eben didn't have to be hit over the head to know it was now time to go. Time and past time. Elias was getting a bargain, but Eben did not have the luxury of months to shop for a buyer, and now he needed to load the wagon.

A few plow points and a strong shaft, buckets, a roll of lightweight rope, axel grease, part of a roll of wire. On and on, picking up this and that, Eben was occupied until noon.

Over dinner he told his daughter, "Gonna be headin' west with stuff I thinned out. Could be late gettin' back."

At her raised eyebrows, he added, "Takin' the grasshopper."

So Robert's wagon was to be sold. She nodded. "You have to, Papa? Sure, and it's best, I reckon."

Alecia forked green beans into her mouth. "Big Papa, grasshoppers make wings out'a their legs and that's how they can hop or fly."

"Who told you that?"

"Grandpa Ned."

Eben buttered a biscuit and wondered why people lie to a child when the truth would be easier told. Well, that would stop in five days.

He left the yard with the bays pulling the green wagon, and the saddle horse was tethered behind. Roberta glanced at it with a bit of regret, but Papa had decided, and she hoped he was doing the right thing.

Eben watched the gait of the horses ahead of him. Good, even gait. Not excitable. Robert was a good judge of horseflesh. You could tell by watching them that they had set Robert back a pretty penny. Still, there should have been a little something left from the sale of his place.

At the edge of Pinetop, Tennessee, the old man stopped in front of a hardware store, buying two full sets of side clamps for holding cleats to a wagon. At the lumberyard, he selected ten tough, springy strips of wood, two very large canvas tarpaulins and two buckets of heavy oil, which he stowed in the wagon beside the tar.

On to the livery stable he went to conduct his final business.

It was dark when he left Pinetop and near midnight when his tired saddle horse climbed the hill to her warm stable and hay. The two hounds, Pete and Pokey, were left behind him at the livery stable.

"Papa! I was about to get worried. I been loadin' into the wagon, figurin' if we was needin somethin' to ride, we could use the buggy. I was thinkin' what I'd use to cover the stuff, Alecia askin' questions like she does."

"You done good. Don't be concernin' yourself. I took care'a it. It's covered with a canvas I picked up."

"Our buggy, Papa? What about…?"

"Don't you be worryin'. I got stuff disposed of the best I know'd how."

Four

Then it was the last day.

The roosters had hardly finished crowing when a light tap sounded at the door. Roberta left her biscuit dough to answer it. There stood old Annie McDougal.

"Come in. You alright, Annie?'

"Right as rain. All exceptin' my old ramblin' brain. Could'a give you this at church next Sunday, but like as not, I'd'a forgot it agin. Then, too, the sight'a it could'a plowed up grief best left to deal with in private."

"What is it?" Certainly it must be important, as it brought Annie up the hill almost before daylight.

"It's this, honey." She drew a handkerchief from her apron pocket. "It was at the layin'-out that I looked at that young man, whilst I was a'combin' that curly hair, and I said to myself, 'Annie, they's a little girl in there that lost her papa, and what'll she think later when she tries to remember what he looked like?' So I got me the scissors and clipped some of them curls. Then, when I got'a 'em home, I tied 'em in little bunches, so's they'd not muss up when they was put away."

The gnarled old hands tugged apart the knot in the cloth square and spread it on the table. There, laying on the cloth, was a pile of red-gold curls, likely enough to fill a teacup. How had she been able to cut so much hair and have it not show? And what a loving and thoughtful thing to do... to think of the future that way. And of Robert's little girl.

"Annie, I got no words to thank you."

"Sure you have. You just said 'em. Now I got'a be getting' on."

"Wait. I got a present for you. You bein' such a friend to my mama, I want to give you something that was a thing she liked."

Roberta reached up to the wall and took down a picture. It was a scene painted on glass, its vivid colors depicting a bird nest and a pair of bluebirds hovered around a trio of open mouths. She was surprised to note the square of unfaded wallpaper behind the picture. The bright square blazed out from the faded roses of the paper. Annie noticed it, too.

"But you'd not want...."

"I want you to take it. That's what I really want, and when you look at it, think of my mother." She would have liked to have said 'think of us,' but Papa had said to TELL NO ONE.

"Well, honey, if you're sure... and thanks."

And Annie was gone. Roberta tied the rosy caramel-colored curls, the exact shade of her own, into the cloth and tucked it into the jar, then hesitated. No, the curls might get squashed... yes, it was the place for them. Right there in that jar with the coins left over from the sale of Robert's farm. He'd told her, "Bert, you take this and hide it. In the mine like I am, there'd be a chance some day I won't come out. The money's to take care of my little girl."

The glass jar was wrapped in a cloth and buried in the trunk full of clothing.

After breakfast, Roberta suggested, "Let's go see Grandpa Ned and the cousins."

At Alecia's hesitation, she added, "Then we'll look for that nest old Cockle Bonnet hid out."

As the girl played with the other children, her cousins, Roberta fought for words to say to be polite to the old man. Words that would not involve the future of Alecia, but it was not to be.

"Losin' 'er pa'd put the lassie in a new light, us bein' kin the same as you. She could just as well's to be here with other youngens to play with."

Roberta forced herself into calmness. "That's the truth. 'Course, that'd be a thing for you and Pa to be settlin'. I ain't got no say in the matter." Tension made her breath thin and thready.

The man picked up his jug, took a gulp, and set it down again. "Speck the thing to do'd be to leave 'er here tilst the talkin' got done."

Think, Roberta, THINK! "You know, that' be a good idea, too, 'cept for one thing."

"What'd that be?"

"That girl, she's got so spoiled to her stuffed bear to sleep with, likely no one'd get a wink'a sleep for her caterwalin'. We shouldn't'a let a kid get that'a'way."

That wasn't a lie, was it? A whole lie? Sure, she slept with the bear, but certainly she wouldn't cry for more than a minute or two if she didn't have it for a night. However, she might find other reasons to cry.

The old man was considering his options… getting his way or losing sleep from the crying child. Sleep won.

"Wal, I don't tucker to spoilin' a kid, but that can be took care of. Bring the blasted thang on over when you bring her."

Roberta sighed and nodded. "Sure thing."

"And don't you be thinkin' to forget about it, neither. You and your pa'll both know I got ways'a makin' somethin' happen."

Roberta nodded again. "Like I said, don't you worry none. Pa'll make sure nothin' happens. He ain't wantin' no trouble." She wasn't certain she convinced the old man.

In the late afternoon, Roberta poured warm water in the washtub by the stove and set Alecia to taking a tub bath. Who knew when her next one would be? As the little girl splashed, soaped, and poured water from one cup to another, her aunt and grandfather stood in the kitchen and talked.

"You 'bout ready?" he asked.

19

She nodded. "Poor little thing's tired. She'll be asleep by seven. Give me four hours after that and I'll be ready to pull out." She fingered her list, twisting it apprehensively.

"Good. You tell me when she's asleep, and I'll move her to the buggy."

"Buggy? But I thought…?"

"Don't think. Pack. All I got'a do is wait for the fire to die down and take the stove. You're fixin' food right now?"

"Don't I always? Fixin' to make more biscuits right this minute. Don't reckon they serve food on the train."

"I reckon not."

Then they were ready, and the lanterns were lighted and hung on the buggy and also on the side of the wagon. The horses knew the trail, and the wavering light from the kerosene lanterns was enough. Roberta sat in the buggy beside the sleeping girl, waiting while the fancy parlor stove was cleaned of ashes and wrapped with canvas to be stowed in the buggy.

Now that her part of the preparation was finished, Roberta devoted herself to the many puzzling things her father had done in the last few days, not the least of which was his refusal to confide in her.

Apparently someone was going to take care of the place here; maybe the neighbor. She had never ridden the train before, but it was a puzzle to her how so many loose, unboxed pieces could be shipped on the train without being crated and how much would it cost, all told.

Then, there was the living expenses until Papa found work, and Robert's jar of coins would likely be needed to see them through. If it was enough. It would have to be.

Finally Eben came out of the house, closing the door firmly behind him. The light of the lantern glistened on a row of shiny metal pieces that had been attached to the wagon. What had Papa put those on there for? Come to notice it, that was not even Papa's wagon! Newer, maybe.

Oh, of course! It was borrowed! Whoever he got it from would go to the train station and pick it up tomorrow! Very clever of him.

"Move out," came the signal, and Roberta moved her buggy onto the trail. The sound of crunched gravel and the flicker of the lantern light behind her told her they were truly on the way.

Alecia slept soundly on a pallet at her feet.

Five

The trail to the valley was as familiar to Roberta as the back of her hand, so she was free to think. Prickles of excitement tickled her scalp. Frightened though she was to make such a move, there had been no alternative choice. Like the children of Israel at the Red Sea with the Egyptian chariots behind, there could be no turning back.

And there was Ned Dougherty. As soon as he realized Alecia was not being brought to him, he would be at the house. He would follow the trail the wagons made. He would ask where they had gone, where their tickets had been bought for… surely Papa had the tickets!

He would follow. Whereever the town was, he would be there! They would not be hard to find… and they could not watch Alecia every minute… and what if Papa had to use the gun as he had threatened? Would it really be murder?

With each passing minute, fear churned up more acid in her stomach, and nausea fought against her tight throat muscles. She should have insisted Papa talk with her so she could help plan. Maybe it was not too late. Maybe they could go the other way. A train went north at four, about two hours after the southbound. Maybe they could change their tickets. She'd ask Pa when they got to the station.

The scant moonlight indicated a break in the trees up ahead. The road would be easier, now, and in just a few minutes, they would get to the train station.

The station was totally dark. Papa pulled around her on the empty road and shouted, "Follow in my tracks." He rolled the wagon wheels up the gravel road up to the door of the dark and empty station and then on across the bumpy train tracks. Alecia roused, and Roberta reached down and patted her arm, helping her settle into sleep again.

An empty wagon was sitting in the yard… their old wagon. Eben pulled up beside it and then on around and motioned her to follow. Then he stopped. While the two vehicles waited, the old man stepped down and went to the empty wagon. Picking up the tongue, he strained to push it backward, checking to see that it was settled in the gravel tracks he had just made. On his way back to the loaded wagon, he dragged his feet through any stray tracks that he could see.

"Bertie, you follow me now, and we're gonna make all the miles we can twixt now and after while, when the trouble commences to break loose. Don't you be thinkin' on nothin' 'cept followin' me and takin' care'a the lassie."

Roberta nodded, biting her lip to keep back the words. Papa was in charge. He had even dropped back into the old Scottish word for girl. When she was small, she was called a "lassie", but somewhere along the way it had changed. So now it had changed back. Papa was doing what he thought had to be done, as he always had, and a small smile of pride played about her lips, and her scalp tingled with the very excitement of it all.

The moon shone on the gravel of the Tennessee road as it climbed to the top of the mountain toward the town of Pinetop. Below them echoed the whistle of the train, its drivers clickity-clacking against the track. The sound became louder, then softer, and then more and more faint as it headed south without the Carlile family aboard.

It was clear, now, that Papa had thoughts of catching it somewhere else, but if so, Pinetop was certainly the long way around.

Light was breaking as the wagon pulled into Pinetop. Papa waved his lantern and was answered by another waving light. In minutes, they pulled up beside Robert's "grasshopper," now hitched to the team of bays stomping and jiggling their harnesses impatiently.

"Pull on up ahead," came the command, sounding loud in the silent streets.

"Move on," came Papa's voice. "Get on around there. Whoa. Hold it! Whoa, there!"

The two men worked between the wagons for a short time, then Papa handed the man something and told him, "Much obliged, friend."

"Thanks and good luck to ye. I'd be thinkin' ye'll need it."

Her father came to her buggy.

"Bertie, lass, you follow on, and I'll be pullin' both wagons till we get where we got'a use the wheel brakes. Then you'll be havin' to drive a wagon and we'll pull the buggy. Don't waste time sayin' nothin' yet. You'll get answers 'afore this day be gone."

"Sure, Papa." She waited until the double wagons were on the road, and she clicked her horse in behind them. There'd be an answer before the day was gone! He would be good to his promise.

Six

In the still, cold air of the mountaintop, the only sound was a distant early rooster and a snort from one of the bays until she heard the command, "Git on along, there! Pull out, there!"

A shiver trembled through the caravan as the first wagon broke into a roll and the bays leaned into their traces to draw the Grasshopper after them. Roberta clicked to Dancer, the carriage horse, and the buggy moved along behind the wagons onto the road. The moon had waned and only a band of pale stars remained along the western sky. Sunrise came early on a Tennessee mountaintop.

Handling the reins was second nature to Roberta, leaving her free to think. The Grasshopper, in the road ahead of her, had been totally transformed by a canvas covering stretched over bent strips of wood. The ends of the wood had been tucked into metal cleats attached to the side of the wagon… cleats exactly like the ones on the gray wagon that pulled it. Evidently, Papa intended to cover that one, too. Well, that should make the traveling more comfortable, wherever it was they were going.

The current weather was mild for late February, but a brisk wind whistled through the buggy now that they were clear of the trees and the protection of the valley. Alecia was almost hidden within the heap of quilts in the floorboard of the buggy. Maybe she would sleep a while longer. Roberta herself shivered with nervous apprehension. She would have used heavier wraps if she had known she would not be boarding the train to the south country. It would be good to know the reason Papa had felt he could not confide in her.

And Alecia. She'd just have to stay wrapped in the warm quilts until they could stop.

The black silhouette of the trees was giving way to the gray of winter dawn, and the woodlands were dotted with the deep green of pines and cedars. The road was following the ridge of the mountain as long as possible, but, sooner or later, they would be forced to go down the hill. She pulled her scarf tighter against the cold, pushing from her mind the comfort of something hot to drink. Coffee… or even tea. Maybe there would be time to make some when they stopped.

A stab of golden light flashed onto the top of a pine tree as the road turned north. Sunrise! A break in the roadside cover permitted the golden light to flash on the side of the canvas cover of the Grasshopper.

The road ahead disappeared into the trees. They were going down to the valley.

Grasshopper moved to the side of the road, and Roberta reined Dancer in behind it.

"Bertie, lass, we're changin' out. We're hookin' the buggy to the Grasshopper. You'll take the other'n and wait till I pull around."

"Dancer?"

"Gonna cut 'er loose and lead her on a tether. Them bays won't even know they got the weight'a the buggy hangin' on 'em. Now, you know the workin'a them brakes, and they been tightened. You need'ta get you more wraps agin the cold."

"Papa, we got'a get Alecia out'a here. She'll wake up and be scared bein' alone. And I wasn't knowin' she'd need her heavy coat. It'll take a bit'a time to get it out'a the trunk. And, Papa, somethin' hot'd be good, and maybe a bite... she'll be hungry."

"Got'a wait. There's a place part way down where we can pull off and be hid. With the rigs we got on the road, we'd be remembered by anyone that come by."

"Remembered?"

"That'd be apart'a what you'll know later. I regret to do this to ya, but it was my best thought."

Roberta climbed into the front wagon and dug through the top layer of small things in the trunk. Wool scarf, Alecia's coat and soft bonnet, thick stockings... no, the stockings could wait. They'd just wrap her up in the quilts.

Papa struggled to lift the sleeping girl wrapped in the quilt. She was growing so fast! The transfer to the new bed hardly aroused her, and she sighed back into sleep.

Partway down the hill, the green wagon pulled from the road into a turnout that was almost totally hidden by the screen of last year's leaves on the blackjack oaks. The cessation of motion aroused the little girl, and she sat up, rubbing her eyes. Roberta straightened her own stiff legs, flexed her cold, stump-like feet, and stepped down to the ground.

"Morning, baby!" Roberta greeted the little girl brightly. "We went for a little ride, and now we're gettin' breakfast."

Within minutes, the metal legs of the tripod held the container of steaming coffee. Warmed, left-over biscuits with butter and plum jelly made up breakfast. They sat as close to the fire as possible and began to eat.

Roberta spoke to the girl. "Alec, honey, you're gonna have to help me drink my warm coffee so your insides don't turn into icicles."

Steaming coffee was a miracle! The little girl sipped from the cup, then Roberta sipped, and the only other sound was the crackling of flames. It was clearly time for Papa to speak.

"Wouldn't'a done it this'a'way if there'd been any other direction to go. We made a promise to the lassie's ma, and that promise gonna be kept. Me a'sayin' we had tickets on the southbound was a smoke screen, but it weren't no lie. I got tickets in my pocket. Jist didn't say we was a'gonna use 'em. I made arrangement to get the empty wagon picked up, and come time it's been seen that we didn't go south, we'll be long gone."

"But, Papa, the job on the river…?"

"I thought about it and it would'a worked. Had reasons to think up another plan. If I'd'a gone south, it'd be good as long as I could work, but then after that, there'd be nuthin' for my lass and lassie, being in a strange place and nuthin' to go home to."

"Nothin' to…?"

Papa shook his head. "Ain't no goin' back. Had this in mind and mostly planned out, way back 'afore the cave-in. Hadn't said nuthin'; waitin' till the plan was clear in my head. Shouldn't'a done that. I hadn't ought'a waited. Should'a said somethin'. I done wrong to both my boys."

The fire crackled under the kettle, and Roberta poured the black, boiling brew into his cup. "You could'a told me, Papa…" she chided gently.

The old man shook his head sadly. "No. If I had, you could'a been put in position of havin' to lie about the plans. Best I could say to you was to take everything you wanted. Sayin' I was leavin' the dogs with someone was true, bein' they was took to Pinetop."

"Papa, are we aimin' to hide out in the timber and in winter time? 'Cause Alecia…."

"Ain't hidin' out, exactly. It's gonna be worse'n that." From his pocket he took a tattered, many-times-folded scrap of paper and handed it to her. She glanced at the black words on the yellowed paper that had turned her life into such a confusing direction: "FREE

LAND… Oklahoma territory… quarter section. South of Cherokee Outlet."

"What is this, Papa?"

"We're a'goin' to a place called Oklahoma. We're'a commencin' a trip'a more'n 500 miles, and I figure we'll be on the road the better part'a two months. I know you didn't git to do the preparin' you would'a if you'd know'd. I regret that, but I done the only thing I thought was safe for the lassie."

"Papa, it says here it'll be a race to see who gets there first to get the land. You thinkin' we can run?"

"I can try. Chances are I'll not win the land, but there'll be work I can do, and you and the lassie, you'll be in a new place with new people, and there'll be a place for you. Likely, I can't leave you nuthin' when I go, but I can leave you in a place where you can do for yourself."

Roberta nodded. This would take some thought, and she sighed deeply, buttered another biscuit and handed it to Alecia. "We'll be needin to stop at a store. Peanut butter'd be nice, maybe eggs to go with the bacon I got under all that stuff."

"Thought we might. We'll get on down the hill and be in a townsite 'afore nightfall. Gonna put the cover on that first wagon to make it warmer. Only take a minute, if you'll put out that fire and load up the cookin' gear."

And they were on the road again.

Whatever was Papa thinking? Oklahoma? Such a strange and foreign-sounding word!

Alecia's words broke in on her thoughts. "Where are we a'goin'?"

Hmmmm. What could she say? "Well, honey, first off, we'll go for a long ride. Then Big Papa wants us to go to a place called Oklahoma. 'Course, it'll take a long time."

"All day?"

"More than that. It'll take a lot'a days."

That gave the little girl something to think about, so she sat under the shelter of the canvas covering and watched the scenery go by.

Roberta studied the outline of the canvas cover of the wagon before her. It made a snug hideaway over the crates and boxes containing her choice of what to bring. And now it was time to plan. Food. Where did she put the few glass jars of fruit and the canned sausages she thought would be sustaining them until Papa found work on the river? Peaches and blackberries and several jars of jelly. That jelly would be handy. Also, the sausages… maybe a dozen jars left from the butchering last fall.

The metal bins in which she kept flour, sugar and cornmeal were less than half full. The baking supplies she had packed had been wrapped in tea towels and put in the water bucket. Likely it was a good place for them until she needed a water bucket.

How would she be able to bake biscuits over a campfire? Well, she had a number of miles to figure it out. She had no potatoes or eggs. How did one cook without potatoes and eggs? She had packed several pounds of dry beans, but how could she cook them for the more than three hours or so it took to get them tender? A lengthy soaking might cut down the time.

Alecia watched the scenery, pointing to a particular tree until they passed by it, then picking another one in the distance, pointing to it. Roberta watched her, thinking. What would a little, almost-five-year-old girl do while riding in a wagon for a month… maybe two months?

On the heels of that thought came another.

Bathing! Where was the washtub that doubled as a bathtub, but then, where was the building that was warm enough to take a bath in? Where were the soap and washcloths? Obviously, there would need to be a search for necessary items and a re-pack to make them handier. It might even take several days to work this all out.

She glanced at the little girl whose hands were now in her lap and whose head nodded with the movement of the wagon. Roberta reached toward her and pulled her close, her head pillowing on the quilt over their legs. The little girl sighed, nestled more comfortably, and slept.

Roberta was free to think again. Papa always—at least for the past several years, and certainly after her mother's death—discussed their business with her. Why the drastic change? Why couldn't he have told her about Oklahoma? Didn't he trust her? But then, what good would it have done, as what he did was the only right thing to do? They had promised both her mother and then her father that Alecia would not be allowed to go back across the valley for longer than a few hours to play with cousins. So they were doing the only thing that was safe, and what did it matter how it came about?

Think about food.

Two skillets! That's what would work. The biscuits could be put in the smoking hot iron skillet, and the other skillet of the same size would be put upside down over it. When they began to rise, both skillets would be turned, together, to allow the biscuits to brown on the other side. Of course, that would make only nine biscuits, barely enough for one meal. So while they were packing up after the meal, and while the fire still burned, she would make two more batches of biscuits for later. Maybe not the best idea, but it would be something they could fill up on and be better than nothing.

Beans. The next stream they passed would furnish the water, and they could be put to soak. She may just as well see how it worked when they made the first camp.

Sleeping. The little canvas shelter above her had drop curtains on both ends, likely shutting out a lot of the nighttime cold. What if it snowed or sleeted, or a driving wind with rain came down? And the horses, how could they stand the weather? Well, the first thing was to get the beans to soaking.

Seven

The beans had plumped in the water taken from the mountain stream, and they now bubbled and rolled in the pot suspended from the tripod. A pile of dry wood lay beside the fire for adding before the blaze died down. The rich aroma of the sausage grease she had added for seasoning drifted about the camp.

"Papa, I ain't wantin' to criticize or second guess your plans, but I keep wonderin' why it was that you couldn't'a said to me, private, that it wasn't south where we was headed. I'd done a better job'a havin' somethin' to eat."

Eben Carlile sighed and watched the flame as darkness fell around them. "Bertie, lass, it was this'a'way. I know'd it'd be a thing you'd want to know, and if I'd'a told you, you'd'a thought in your mind whether it was best for the three of us to travel that far, and me of the age I am. You'd'a thought this'a'way and that, comin' up with the best plan for the three of us, and you would'a likely argued in favor of the south river town, bein' easier on me.

"I couldn't let you do that, 'cause then if I finally argued you down and we come on, and something happened to me, you'd be forever blamin' yourself for not arguing stronger. I had it in my head that we'd be makin' this trip, bein' the only way open to us. And you wasn't to be tempted to try to change me, or accidently let a word slip as to where we was headed.

"Me, I done decided this was the last big decision to make on my own, that you and the lassie'd be the only ones considered. If'n I was able to do what I wanted to, we'd make it together, and I'd see you settled. Think on it and you'd know, if we was to go south it'd be no time till it was found out what river town it was we went to and where we was at.

"This'a'way, we'll be long and gone and not found. I consider it to be a idea sent by the Good Lord and consider myself to be at fault for not actin' on it sooner."

Roberta stirred the beans and listened thoughtfully.

Glancing toward the nodding girl, he added softly, "Knowin' Ned since we was boys together, I know there ain't no way he'll let this pass. He's got'a mad streak that grows inside'a him, takin' away his good sense. I let slip words about the south, and actual bought tickets at the station, but didn't mention no town. Searchin' around down there, that'll take him time, givin' us more of a start. That empty wagon'll add to the truth of it.

"Time he figures we went toward Pinetop, he'll hear we was headed for St. Louie, to the river front. If he don't find us there, he'll maybe try Memphis, and by then we'll be half past Arkansas. The way I figure it, us crossin' the Mississippi River'll see us safe. They's a network'a roads through them mountains, and he can't check 'em all. That's the best I could figger, and I'm lookin' to the Good Lord to make up whatever I lack."

Roberta added wood to the fire and nodded, satisfied. Whatever she must do for their comfort, she would do. Papa had certainly done the best he could, likely the best both of them could have done. The simmering liquid had begun to smell like beans, the staple food of her family for generations.

Eight

They were on the road before daylight, and early morning found them entering Glen Hollow. A general store, a gristmill, and a blacksmith shop that advertised hardware all lined up the sides of the graveled street. Houses dotted among the trees on the mountain slopes extending upward each direction. Roberta pulled her wagon to the side of the road behind the Grasshopper.

"Bertie, lass, you think on what you need from the general store, and I'll step over to the blacksmith's."

Potatoes, eggs, a jar of peanut butter, matches, flour and meal. Other things could wait for a larger town. A sudden impulse made her add a stick of peppermint candy.

"Them candy sticks come two to the penny."

She added another one and handed the coins to the clerk. Stowing her purchases, she settled in to wait. A fifty-pound sack of chopped corn was added to the Grasshopper's load, and a second trip brought two sheets of metal mesh and a small iron box that were tucked in beside them. Seeing Roberta was waiting and ready, Eben climbed aboard and yelled, "Git on up, there. Move out!"

"Git on up," she encouraged, and her team followed. She broke the candy stick in half, giving one piece to Alecia and returning the other to the sack. She was rewarded with a smile, and the little girl sucked the sweet, offering licks to the rag doll and the stuffed bear. Lifting a tiny, empty, toy teacup to her lips, she pretended to have a tea party.

Roberta made a decision. At the first town with a Five and Dime, she would look for something to help the little girl pass away the time.

Riding along left a lot of time to think. Her mind wandered back to the major unsolved mystery of her adult life. Her Danny left the mountain, and he did not return. Why?

Danny Dunbar had been almost a second brother, as he spent a lot of time at their house playing with her twin brother, Robert. Then, when Alecia's beautiful mother began to cross over the valley to get away from her family, Robert's attention was taken, and he married Letha Dougherty a week before he was eighteen. That was when Danny began to look on Roberta as more than a playmate. For Roberta, life was perfect. Robert was her soul mate, and Danny was her love.

Then, as a man with a family to take care of, Robert was forced into the coal seam that honeycombed the mountain. Dark, dirty and dangerous it was, but a man took care of his family. Even the loss of his brother could not take away the necessity of earning a living somehow, somewhere.

Danny's parents, however, refused to permit him to go into the mine. Other than the mine, there was no employment that would support a family, and he could therefore not afford to marry. The mountain farms grew enough food to sustain a family, but there was no place to earn hard cash for certain necessities.

A year passed and then another. Danny's restlessness became acute, and it reached a climax at about the time her brother, Eldon, was pulled from the cave-in.

It was directly after Eldon's funeral that the Dunbar family began to talk of resettling somewhere in the west. Being a good and obedient son, Danny had agreed with his parents that it was his duty, as the oldest son, to help see his parents and younger siblings settled before he went on with his own life.

"I'll be back," he had promised. "Shouldn't take no more'a a few months. I'll be back for you, and we'll find a way to get married." So what could she say? If he had been other than a devoted and loving son to his parents, he would not have been the man she loved.

So he had gone, and her wait had begun. She knew there would soon be a letter… but there wasn't. The letter did not come. A few months passed, and Danny did not come. Danny, the name so much a part of her that when her mother had sung the old Scottish ballad "Danny Boy," her little-girl mind had thought her Danny was the subject of the song.

After the months of waiting, she began to be looked at by community's available, eligible men. Being twenty, an age at which she would seem to have been married, she was looked at by men who were older, perhaps who had lost a wife, men who had children to care for. And she had considered this one and that one, but… no….

Then Robert's loving wife had taken to her bed with a difficult pregnancy, and Roberta had begun to "help out." There was Alecia to care for and the everyday duties of the household to be done.

It was then that her brother's wife had begged her, tearfully and hysterically, to make certain her little girl never crossed the valley. The place on the other mountain was too hard to escape once a body got mired down into it.

Roberta had tried to reassure her. "It's just your tiredness a'talkin', and when that baby gets here and you get up, you'll be seein' to your little girl yourself."

But Letha was not to be comforted. When her time came, she fought valiantly, but lost the battle, taking with her the baby son who was not old enough to live without her. In despair, Robert had sold his farm and moved his daughter back to his father's house.

When he had handed Roberta the money from the sale of his house, he had told her, "I know you're knowin' the danger'a the mine. My little girl's ma didn't want her to cross the valley, and I don't either. You're gonna promise me you'll see that don't happen."

Roberta had taken the money and wanted to say, "Hush up, Rob! There ain't nothin' gonna happen to you," but she couldn't make her mouth form the words. Eldon's funeral had been too recent.

And there was still no letter from Danny. It had been a long year, and there had been no message at all.

Seeing her still unmarried, more men looked at her... other men with families that had no mother, but she now had Alecia and did not feel that she was free to look around. But even more than that, everything that was within her still waited for Danny.

Then it was two years, and she knew Danny would not return. Each day in the mountain cabin seemed to move into the next day, and she cooked and cleaned, and she and the little girl looked for old Cockle Bonnet's nest, trying to locate it before the old Dominecker hen appeared in the barnyard, clucking to call her newest cheeping brood around her.

And now Robert's body was brought home, and circumstances had again wrapped themselves around her, propelling her forward into this gray-painted wagon behind the plodding horses, the paint and the black, wondering what would be for dinner.

Biscuits and peanut butter and a bowl of canned peaches. It would be necessary to open a jar of something, as she needed an empty jar in case she got a chance to get a little milk for Alecia. Maybe at a farm house...?

Papa had told her he wanted to be on the road each morning as early as possible, allowing them to make their miles and stop earlier in the afternoon. That way the horses could rest and graze on the dry remains of last summer's grass. At Pecan Hollow, he had announced at the general store that he had "picked up stakes and headed out to improve his luck. Heard things was good up St. Louie way." It did not hurt to leave a false trail.

From the edge of the little town, he had actually turned north, using up precious time to appear to be headed for St Louis on the Mississippi before turning south again. Well, he should know the habits of Ned Dougherty after all these years. Best to be safe.

So an early stop would allow her to heat the beans.

The winter sun had passed the treetops when he pulled into a grove of trees that would screen the wagons from the road. From the Grasshopper, he took the metal box and the sheets of mesh. Fitting them together, he formed a table-like platform and set it over the flame.

"Your stove, lass. Figure that'll hold them biscuit skillets and the bean pot. Likely'll even cook a baked 'tater, come time we want'a try it. This here box might be an oven, but then again, it might be just a waste'a money. It was the onliest thing that blacksmith had already made up that resembled a oven."

Roberta studied the iron box. That could be the answer to baking cornbread. She had decided she would have to make cornmeal skillet-cakes to go with the beans, but this should work. With all he had on his mind, it was so good of Papa to think of her difficulty at cooking over a blaze.

And the good weather still held.

Nine

Butkin Corners was just ahead. "Corners" meant a crossroads, and it likely meant a bigger town. It could mean a Five and Dime.

It did. Roberta spent precious coins for a color book (with a box containing 6 crayons) and an ABC book. And she bought a fly swatter for the many insects attracted to their cooking fires.

Between Butkin Corners and O'Reilly, Alecia looked at her book and learned to repeat:

"'A' is for apple that grows on a tree.

Some are for piggy, and some are for me."

She carefully studied the colorful picture around the words. A fat pig walked on its hind legs, making her smile at the ridiculousness of such a thing. The pig wore a little blue jacket and a smile and carried a basket of apples over its front leg. In the background was an apple tree with the ground beneath it covered with apples. A small girl in a pink dress gathered apples in her basket.

It absorbed the child for several miles, and she repeated the little verse over and over. Roberta made her save the crayons for the supper stop when the jiggle of the wagon would not mess up the pictures.

They pulled into the edge of Memphis, Tennessee and took their place in the ferry line to wait their turn. She bought two quarts of milk in glass bottles, a loaf of bread and a package of cookies for their lunch as they inched forward toward the river.

Boredom finally put Alecia to sleep, and Roberta was glad for that when she looked down into the swirling, muddy water of the Mississippi River. The horses skittered and danced and had to have their blinders attached to their bridles and be led by the handlers. Comforting words came from the experienced men on the ferry, and kind hands patted the animal's noses and ears to comfort them. And she crossed into the state of Arkansas.

Papa did not fare so well. The handlers brought across the Grasshopper with the buggy attached, but, on the next trip, Dancer reared, wall-eyed and terrified, climbing the air with her front feet. No amount of effort by Eben calmed her, and she was finally put into a whole-head blinder and enclosed in a box-stall, its sides pulled firmly against her ribs. Huffing and heaving, she danced her way across the river, hoofs beating a staccato on the deck, totally unable to respond to Eben's calming voice. Nervous ripples played down her back and foam formed on her chewing lips as the ferry finally jerked into its chains and was pulled against the bank.

Strain showed in Eben's face as he led the horse away from the river, but it seemed all in a day's work to the handlers.

How could he have known the horse would react so violently at the sight of the river? With all the rivers ahead of them, this could present a problem.

They spent the night at the edge of Memphis, the wagons headed west. From late afternoon until the dusk had turned into blackness, Eben spent the time preparing the canvas covering over the wagons. Not trusting the tarpaulins to be totally waterproof, he carefully painted the fabric with oil to expand and tighten the fibers, then followed with a light coating of diluted tar. Now the tan of the covering had become a dull black. Pounding the lid back on the bucket, he tucked it into the bed of the Grasshopper, intending to apply a second coat when this one settled in.

They prepared for an early start the next morning, and the weather still held. Potatoes were boiled, then browned in a skillet with crumbled sausage to be eaten cold for tomorrow's midday meal.

Between Memphis and O'Leary's Gap, Alecia learned:

"'B' is for ball for the baby to play with.

'B' is for ball that the dog runs away with."

The picture showed a small child seated in the grass, watching a puppy run away with a blue ball. "Take the ball back to the baby, Puppy," she instructed the picture. "You have to let the baby have a turn."

There was no reason to stop in O'Leary's Gap, so the caravan rolled on through the small town of seven houses, a store and shed advertising wagons for sale. Before they made the midday stop, the little girl learned:

"'C' is for chicken, with flappity wings.

It scratches for worms and wiggly things."

The picture showed a hen surrounded with downy, yellow chicks running this way and that, scratching.

"Bertie?"

"What, precious?"

"What happened to old Cockle Bonnet?"

What, indeed! "Darlin', that was one of them things Big Papa took care of 'afore we left home. One of the neighbors likely got her already and took her to their house."

"Her babies, too?"

"I'd think so." *I hope so*, she told herself.

"This picture don't look like old Cockle Bonnet. I never saw a mama chicken that was yellow like the babies."

Roberta studied the picture. "You know, honey, I don't think I ever did, either."

"We could look at another page," she suggested hopefully.

"No, sweetheart. We'll save that for tomorrow. Play with your doll for a while, and then you can take a nap."

Reluctantly, the girl put the book aside and picked up her doll. Hugging the soft body of the toy, she stared absently out at the slowly passing scenery. As the wagon jogged along, she lifted her thumb to her mouth and began to suck. She hadn't sucked her thumb since she was two.

They were only five days on the road with more than fifty to go.

It would help if she and the girl could walk beside the wagon for a way. Constant sitting was not good for Alecia, or for herself, for that matter. But someone had to drive, and there was no one to do it but her. She sighed and watched the rumps of the horses moving before her, drawing the wagon slowly along.

The weather held until midnight. The first gusts of wind tore at the flaps of the canvas cover, banging them stiffly against the wooden ribs. Eben sat up from his sleep, considering his next move. The horses had been tethered in the grove of trees, the best and only protection he could give them.

As the gusts of wind strengthened, he left the Grasshopper and went to the gray wagon, easing himself past the flaps. In the light of a flash of lightning, he saw the two figures sitting closely together.

"You two doin' alright?"

"Reckon so. It's just the strangeness of it all and the sway'a the wagon in the wind."

"No problem to that, and you got no need to be scairt. The wagon can't turn over 'cept with a twister."

Then the rain started. Loud drops beat against the canvas cover hardly two feet above their heads. Alecia edged closer to her aunt and pulled Roberta's arm more tightly around her shoulders. The drops fell faster, beating a tat-tat overhead, drowning any words that might be said.

A lightning strike caused a whinny from the horses, then another whinny. Thunder rolled down the valley, crackling and popping. Finally, weariness claimed the girl, and the adults sat waiting wordlessly for the storm to pass.

Dawn broke, clear and cold, with the wind whistling past the corners of the canvas. A fire was out of the question. The food box held only leftover cornbread and a jar of water.

The protective grove contained four horses. Dancer was missing.

"You got'a look for her?"

"'Speck I'll look for a while. Can't afford to take too much time lookin' when I don't have no idea whereat she'd likely be."

So Papa disappeared into the screen of trees and Roberta was left with her pounding heart. The cold, wet wind of eastern Arkansas whipped around the wagons, and she was free to think and make decisions. She would not again be caught without food.

She spread butter on a piece of crumbly cold cornbread and handed it to the girl while she herself waited, listening. A crunch in the gravel nearby startled her, and she peeked out of the canvas into the liquid brown eyes of Dancer. The horse snorted, shook her head, and lined herself up with the shafts of the buggy.

Roberta crawled from the wagon and called out in the direction of the trees. "Papa, she's back! PAPA!"

His answer came from behind her. "I'm here, lass. Been followin' 'er, and 'er seemin' to be tryin' to get back."

Seeing her lined up with the buggy shafts, he exclaimed, "Well, I'll be! I think that horse's feelin left out, bein' led along with the tether. Could be I should put her in the harness." So the left-hand bay had an easy day on the tether.

At Lone Grove, Arkansas, they stopped at the general store, where Roberta bought a tin of crackers and two flat cans of sardines packed in oil. Wrapping them in a quilt, she buried them under the plunder in the green wagon. That was one thing that didn't have to be cooked when a fire couldn't be started.

Between Lone Grove and Marshall, Alecia learned:

"'D' is for dog, with a waggley tail.

See how he digs with a shovel and pail?"

"Look, Bertie! This here dog don't know how to dig like old Pete and Pokey. He's got 'im a shovel and no hands to hold on. He ought'a dig with his paws like a real dog. Bertie, where is Pete and Pokey?"

"Honey, they went to stay with some friends in the town."

"Dog friends or folks friends?"

"Both, I'd think." *I hope.*

Between Marshall and Grapevine, she learned:

"'E' is for egg, and it sits on a wall.

He better hang on, if he don't want to fall!"

"Lookie, Bertie, this egg's got hands!" And she learned:

"'F' is for fish, all foolish and fat.

He'd better watch out for the paws of the cat!"

A round glass bowl held a gold-colored fish, and a yellow kitten looked down in the water at him. The little girl studied the picture.

"Bertie, how come that fish to be in that jar and not in the river? How did he get in there?"

"Someone put him there."

"Why?"

"I reckon they thought he'd look good there."

"Then why don't he?"

"Swear if I know, honey. But that was a good question."

"'G' is for glass, all shiny and round.

I think it would break if it fell to the ground."

They lowered into a valley. It had to happen soon, and there it was just up ahead. A river, or more like a creek. But Dancer leaned forward and planted her trim hooves firmly into the mud and pulled, drawing the wagon along. Climbing out on the bank, she leaned into the traces, her hooves slipping only slightly as the wagon cleared the water.

So far, so good.

"'H' is for hat, to wear on my head.

Its ribbons are blue, and its tassels are red."

"Bertie, that's a funny lookin' hat."

"You're right, darling."

Ten

Eben had a lot of time to think. The storm, light as it was, gave him pause to consider. Alone on the road with the lass and lassie and the threatened loss of Dancer were something to think about. That fleet-footed, lightweight animal was to be the transportation in the "run" for the new land. From here on, Eben would manage to be near a town, or maybe a farmhouse, when he stopped for the night. Even if it meant stopping before he had planned to. He had their safety to consider.

Over the jiggle of the wagon, he studied the tattered map. A hundred and fifty miles into Arkansas, he would come onto the Arkansas River. He could follow that landmark the rest of the way across the state and all the way to the Oklahoma border before the wide river must be crossed. The longer he could avoid it, the smaller the river would be when that time came. Wouldn't it?

There would be likely several ferry crossings. The thing that worried him more, though, was the tributary streams joining the Arkansas, and they would likely be wide and deep, and some might have to be gone around. That would add time and miles.

So it was only three o'clock when they stopped at a farmhouse. There was no way to know how near the next one would be, and the chilly March evenings were short.

Basket over her arm, Roberta walked to the farmhouse, the little girl holding to her skirt. This looked like a good place to replenish her egg supply.

Wiping her hands on her apron, the mistress of the house exclaimed, "Oh, honey, I wouldn't be sellin' you no eggs, and us with layin' hens a eatin' us out'a house and home! You just come on in here and… I swear that little old basket'a yourn won't hold enough to bother with. Ain't you got somethin' bigger? No matter, I'll find somethin'."

"But we…"

"Now I know, bein' this early, that you ain't started to cook your supper. What you're gonna do is stay and eat with us and we can have us a good visit. Your little girl, she can play with our youngens."

"Oh, we couldn't…."

"Sure you could. Food we got lots of, but folks to visit with, they come few and far between. Here you are, right by our house and you can't go nowhere till morning. You got other youngens? Your man, he tendin' the stock?"

"All we got is my Papa, greasin' the wheels. He…."

"Never mind. I'll send my man out to help and bring 'im back. Better yet, them animals can be turned into the barn, onto the hay. MARVIN! COME HELP THIS HERE TRAVELER."

Beef stew with colorful vegetables steamed in the thick bowls. Lightbread and butter, foaming glasses of milk and supper cake, rich with eggs and sweet with bee tree honey, graced the huge kitchen table. Alecia laughed with the three Smith children, played and squealed, and listened as Roberta read the ABC book to the four of them.

The five horses lined up at the manger and ate rich hay in the warmth of the barn.

At dawn, they pulled away from the house with full stomachs, dozens of eggs, fat golden sweet potatoes and a sack of corn for the horses. The Smiths only accepted money for the corn because Eben had said he would not take it if he could not pay, and they needed it.

The color book with only a few pictures colored, along with the six crayons, was left for the Smith children.

Marvin and Ellen Smith stood at their gate and waved until they could be seen no longer.

As soon as it was light enough to see, Alecia learned:

"'I' is for ice cream on a hot summer day.

If you don't eat it fast, it will all melt away."

"Look, Bertie. Them kids in the picture got ice cream, and there ain't even no snow to make it with. How'd a body make ice cream when there ain't no snow?"

"They get the milk cold with pieces of ice."

"Off the river?"

Hmmmm. "Well, maybe. I guess they could."

"'J' is for jam that I spread on my bread.

Sometimes I would rather have jelly instead."

The picture showed a girl with a slice of bread. A jar of jam and a jar of jelly were on the table. Alecia giggled. "That girl, she don't know that it don't make no difference what she eats, that'll it still be good."

At the town of Three Springs, Roberta went to the Five and Dime for a new color book and crayons, and as she turned to leave, she saw the toy china dishes. Alecia had a single, well-used toy teacup to use for her tea parties, but this set had four plates and saucers and four darling little cups with tiny, delicate handles. The teapot had a precious little curved spout and a tiny lid. The cream pitcher and the sugar bowl completed the set, and it was just too charming for words! Also, it cost twenty-five cents. Far too much for a toy, but she could not tear her eyes away from the beauty of it.

From deep within her came a childhood longing for this precious toy. As she would have reluctantly turned away, Alecia reached an exploring finger toward the tiny cup, looking up at Roberta with her slate-blue eyes, silently pleading with her aunt from under their curled lashes.

Inside her mind, Roberta formed the words, "Robert, your money's gonna get a special thing for your little girl. I don't care if it costs nigh as much as a sack of corn for the horses."

As Roberta reached for the tea set to buy it, Alecia jerked back her fingers, knowing she mustn't touch what wasn't hers. As they walked together back to the wagon, the little girl skipped ahead, carefully ignoring the wonderful object in the sack. It couldn't possibly be for her. But it was, and her voice had no words to respond to the wonder of it all.

Roberta spread a tea towel over the wooden lid of a trunk, so the jiggle of the wagon would not topple the teapot. The doll and the bear had a tea party that lasted all the way from Pocasset to Edinburgh, pausing only long enough to learn:

"'K' is for kite that sails on the wind.

With a string on the front and a tail on the end."

"Can we have a kite in Pamoma?"

"It's Oklahoma, and if they have any wind, we can have a kite."

They camped alone outside of Middletown, remembering the good times at the Smiths. The campfire heated the oven to bake the orange-gold sweet potatoes, served with chunks of rich yellow butter, skillet cornbread, and fresh milk.

Eleven

March in Arkansas was mild until the rains came. The bedding now felt clammy and musty, and Roberta longed to hang the quilts on a clothesline to whip in the sunny breezes, but what she got were ten days of drizzle to be endured.

They now followed a small river, and the early stops at river towns allowed fish to be added to their diet. Most of the tributary streams had ferry crossings, and Dancer swam docilely across when tethered to the ferry. Another problem passed.

Roberta began to feel the tug of longing for the end of the journey. The routine of living was now set, and she found her mind projecting ahead. Oklahoma… new land with no house. New people. When her thoughts drifted back to Tennessee and Danny, she forced the memory from her head. Papa was right. It was time for a new start in a new land.

And Papa… he stood straighter, and his steps were quicker. Only three weeks gone and he seemed to be tireless. One evening, after checking the wheels of the wagons and the feet of the horses, he sat with the scrappy maps he had picked up here and there and all the notices of the land run. No two maps were alike, and he mulled them over, comparing and calculating days against miles and the weather against rivers to be crossed.

Roberta thought of food and ways to dry their underthings that she washed in the streams. Alecia played with the toy dishes. After the little girl was asleep in her quilts, Roberta opened the box to admire the dishes, and one of the tiny cups was missing. A search through the bedding did not produce the delicate little cup, so she made a mental note to be careful where she put her foot until it was found. Then, on a sudden hunch, she felt into the quilts for Alecia's hand, and, peeling her small fingers from around the missing cup, she returned it to the box, smiling. "Robert, I'm glad I paid all that money. You'd love to see your little girl a'playin' with them dishes."

And Roberta rolled along the road, searching among her thoughts for pleasant ones, trying to ignore the still-sensitive wound made by Danny and the lackadaisical manner of the small girl in her charge. She had already made peace with her father's decision... Eben had done the only thing he could do, and, given all the facts, she would probably have done the same. So what was left?

The only home she had ever known was the four-room hillside house with the lean-to kitchen and the added lean-to parlor built three steps below the level of the main house. The parlor had been a thing of pride for her mother, being a place where ruffled curtains and plumped cushions could be kept from the dust of open windows and the wear and tear of everyday use. Her sewing chair had been there and Papa's rocker. A library table which held their few books, lined up between store-bought bookends. The family Bible held a place of honor, and when given permission to bring what she chose, the books were a first thought. A collection of her mother's favorite pictures were hung on the wall that was covered with the wallpaper decorated with pink roses. The fancy wallpaper would have been a foolish extravagance, except that it brought her mother so much pleasure.

And there was the parlor stove. Designed after the huge, efficient potbellies that graced every house in the mountains, the parlor stove was small, shiny, and surprisingly efficient except in the dead of the winter. Her mother had undergone a fair amount of ribbing from her sons as they split wood chunks into pieces small enough for the stove. They had teasingly referred to it as her "toothpick burner" or the "splinter stove." The second thought Roberta had had, after the books, was the desire to bring the impractical stove along into the unknown. A bit of home and a lingering pleasant thought of her mother.

In the manner of all other dutiful daughters, Roberta had taken her place in the kitchen and the garden, well-acquainted with the uses of the scrub board and wash tub, the wood-fired cookstove, the pressure canner and the bevy of flatirons needed to make dress ruffles flounce properly and force the collars of Sunday shirts to stand up board-stiff. These necessities of civil existence were all beside her in the gray wagon.

For while still in the pain of her grief from the loss of her brother, she had been obliged to select, from what had been her whole life of twenty-two years, only those possessions that could be fitted into a wagon bed four feet wide and ten feet long. The sudden necessity of this selection had overshadowed her grief, postponing it to a more convenient time.

It was now convenient, and, like the mountain mist settling thickly in the valleys, her thoughts of Robert and what his loss would mean to her cut into her heart, still sensitive from the loss of Danny. Papa had been right. It was time to get away from the land that took away those they loved.

So now she traveled west. The chill of March in the Arkansas mountains had become second nature during the past weeks. She wore her heavy coat from morning to night, except when the winter sun was able to shed a little warmth in the afternoon. She had dispensed with washing clothes, except for their underthings. Her mother would have been horrified at the thought. But then, how dirty can one get sitting on the buckboard all day?

She still planned meals, but instead of her well-stocked cellar and farmyard to select from, she mentally inventoried her provisions, hoping to get an idea for something different. When the urge became too great, she bought this or that in the small town stores. Fresh in her memory was a recent purchase of onions. Whoever heard of not having onions close at hand, and if not that, where would one buy them? She seemed almost surprised that the country store stocked a few scrawny specimens. And after that, it seemed strange that one would pay actual money for something so common as an onion, but how was she to cook without them? Nothing added the flavor of an onion to the cooking except the real thing. So even the lowly onion became food for thought as the wagon rolled along.

Then there was Alecia. Roberta had no desire to mention the thumb-sucking to her father. For a four-year-old to be restricted to the range normally permitted to a toddler, namely that of the four by ten rolling-box wagon bed, was it so surprising that the child reverted to toddler behavior? She played with the china dishes, her doll and bear, and the color book. She was happy to learn the verse or two in the ABC book, and she "read" them to herself over and over. But she seemed, well… it was hard to put a finger on it. Dull? Lackadaisical? Bored? Perhaps all of these. She ate well… or, at least, fairly well for a child with no exercise. And she didn't complain. And if she did complain, what could Roberta have changed to make things better?

Then her thoughts passed on to her own life. Danny was no more, and the part of her life she had reserved for him must be filled with something. Papa didn't put it in actual words, but she could tell he hoped they would be moving toward someone to fill her need, someone who could be found in the great unknown before them. Someone to fill the vacancy left by Danny.

Well, maybe… and she would try to keep an open mind. Continuing to moon over Danny was not going to bring him back. She would try, but it would be a long time before she would not dream of the solid, stocky build that was Danny, the red-gold hair and the fledgling beard he was attempting to grow back when he left the mountain. Little boy freckles on rounded cheeks had become tanned skin on his broad cheekbones and on his high, intelligent forehead. The green eyes of the little boy had turned to a deep hazel, almost topaz, as he turned toward the sun. But they changed to the murky, brown-green of a mountain trout pond when he moved into the shadows.

The knobby knees of the little boy had filled out into the strong, solid legs of a Scottish laddie from the old country. His arms had muscled out, and the bulges strained against the fabric of his Sunday shirt. All in all, a fine figure of a man, and the remembered sight of him was certain to be a hard thing to purge from her mind.

But here she had occupied at least three miles going over his good points, as if she must re-convince herself. In fairness, though, this was the first time she had thought of him today, and here it was, late afternoon. It was almost time to try to think up something to eat, but first. there was the little girl.

"Alec, honey, bring your ABC book and come sit by me." At least, learning the rhymes provided a small stimulation for her mind.

"'L' is for lamb that plays in the sun.

It likes to jump and to gallop and run."

As the little girl repeated the lines of the rhyme as she pointed to the words, Roberta's thoughts drifted to the man at the reins of the bays. Papa was taking the trip well. In fact, he seemed to look a lot better than he had those last months on the hill. Likely, the knowledge of what he was going to have to do had pulled him down… that, and the drastic change it would mean for his family. But that was over and done now, and he seemed to be doing well.

Twelve

Eben held the reins loosely. The bays plodded along the two tracts of the road that stretched out before them, moving ahead without any direction from him. Where else could they go except straight ahead? To make his daily goal of twenty miles, it was necessary that they set their own pace. If he had put the gray wagon first, pulled by the paint and the black, they would have continuously tried to quicken their steps to get to wherever they were going, and would have to be continuously slowed to a maintainable speed. However, the mixed pair on the second wagon, traveling behind, they were forced to move along with the speed of the steady bays.

Then there was Dancer. Eben would like to keep her on the tether. She was too light for serious pulling, and she put a strain on whichever of the other animals he teamed with her. She was a strange one, and she hated to be left out. If only there was someone else along (Robert?), then she could be ridden, and she would feel she was part of the team, but there was no one. So when they came closer to the line, the Indian Meridian of Oklahoma, he would try to ride her of an evening to let her get the feel of him. He'd do that before the day of the run for the land and perhaps he would have a chance at winning a claim… maybe….

When he had left the mountains, Eben had felt like Moses at the banks of the Red Sea. He was reluctant to go forward but disaster was close behind. The flight from the mountains had been one of desperation, but after crossing the Mississippi, it had gradually turned into an adventure. At least, it had for him. He was not sure the lass and lassie were faring so well, but there were things to be endured, and this might be one of them. Certainly, his beloved daughter knew how to endure… she had endured her share.

It had been a relief to find Arkansas so well settled. The merchants in small towns and the farmers plowing in the fields had been equally friendly and happy to give direction or advice. It was often necessary to ask which all-weather road led to the next town west and whether any unpleasant surprises were likely.

Sometimes there had been no road that was totally "all-weather," but so far, they had been blessed with conditions that had not held them back. Some days they had not made his goal of twenty miles, but his plan had left some room for setbacks. One had to build flexibility into one's plans, and when one had done his best, the rest was up to God. Wasn't it?

He was careful to give thanks for the help God gave him. When he was a little fellow, he enjoyed hearing his mother tell the story behind the choice of his name… Ebenezer.

"It was your Grandmama, son. She was the one to want to give you that name. A great one to trust in God, she was. And she was one to remember Samuel in the Bible and how he was led to a new place by the Good Lord, and he wasn't even seein' the end of his journey, but he wasn't one to tease the Good Lord into lettin' him see the whole of it.

"Then, there was the time when he had gone as far as he could see the way of, and he thought it was time to say something to God. He gathered stones and build a pillar of 'em, and he named the pillar Ebenezer, because that was his people's word for meanin, 'Lord, it was only by Your strength and direction that I was able to come this far.' He know'd the Lord was smart 'nuff to know he was meanin', 'Lord, you got me out here and I don't know why, but I belong to You, and so it'll have to be You as takes me on.'

"Your Grandmama liked the way old Samuel in the Bible done that. She had come to America in the ship with her family from the old country. Things was bad back in the highlands, and someone was always tryin' to overrun the good Scottish families, them a'tryin' to raise their families and serve the true God.

"Then it got to be more'n could be stood, and they got tired'a the sight'a the lassies a'starin' out over the hills and glens, seein' nothin' but the purple haze'a the heather plants. Too many laddies had come back from the wars 'hind the beat'a the drums, 'stead'a blowin' on the pipes.' Too many bairns had no papa, and too many more of 'em didn't get no chance to be born.

"Then it was that your Great Grandpap took a'hold on the idea that it was God tellin' 'em his work was done in the hills'a his home and that he was to leave the highlands. Took 'im a while to convince the family, and not all of 'em was ever tuned in to the idea. But then, not everyone that left the land'a Egypt had the moxie to cross over Jordan to the land God made for 'em.

"So your Great Grandpap gathered his own family, and your Grandmama was jist a shirttail girl at that time. Her brothers was bigger, (them as was left after the spears and arrows'a battle took their toll) and there was some cousins and neighbors that took it on theirselves to tag along. There was families that had no money for the ship steerage fare, but they pooled together and got passage for the strongest son, hopin' he'd find a way to get the rest of the family on along after 'im. Most times he did.

"But there was your Grandmama, and her a wee girl, but she lived through the storms and starvation on that ship, and it bein' one that took a lot of wee bairns to their grave. She stepped off onto the land in the new country, healthy as you please, and this here is her story to tell, and it goes like this as she told it to me."

At this point young Eben would settle comfortably down at his mother's knee to enjoy the oft-told story that went like this.

"It took some years and some walkin', but the family was led to these here mountains. They know'd it was the doin' of the Good Lord, else how could they'a found good strong lands like they'd left behind in the old country? The thing they missed was the heather, all bloomin' purple, but what they found was good huntin'a animals that was free for all, and they wasn't jailed for poachin'.

"They didn't find none'a the King's salmon in the streams, the fish the common folks in Scotland wasn't to eat, the King thinkin' the salmon was too good for common folk. Sure, and there weren't no salmon streams in the new country, but the mountain pools fairly thrashed theirselves dry with the brown trout. All the sunshiny pools sparkled with orange punkin-seed perch.

"There weren't no grouse in the heather, 'cause there weren't no heather, but there was geese'n turkeys, ducks'n doves. There was meat a'plenty and the laddies grew strong.

"So it was that the time come that the uppity folks from the old country was sorry they let everyone go (mighty near like old Pharaoh in Egypt), and they come over in the ships to make war and take back the country your Great Grandpap had found by bein' led by the Good Lord. When the strong laddies knew they might lose the good life they had, they was quick to sharp up their swords and tune up their pipes."

Tears had formed in his mother's eyes as she continued. "They left these here mountains a'pipin' the notes'a 'Scotland, the Brave', jist like they was a'goin' to fight in the old Country.

"The rest'a the folks stood there, the old folks and the lassies, so proud their hair fair stood on end, and ripples'a good feelin' crawled along the skin'a their necks and arms. The old men, rememberin' the battles they saw, bowed their heads in thanksgivin' that it wasn't the old country bein' fought for. Every ma and pa of them boys, they wasn't thinkin' on their sons a'comin' back 'hind the drums. They was a'thinkin' these highland laddies'd be comin' back, a'pipin' and a'struttin' with pride that they was permitted by the Good Lord to fight for this good land He give 'em."

She sniffed and continued, "Well, it weren't no easy thing, that war. Up in the mountains, we didn't hear too much, and what it was we did hear, it weren't too good. There wasn't nothin' we could do 'cept wait and have faith that the Good Lord'd take care'a the laddies. After all, it was the Good Lord what brung us here.

"We waited and watched, and all the lassies looked out over the blue mountains. There weren't no purple heather, but wherever laddies goes to war, lassies will wait and watch. Then we waited, and I was there waitin', and there came the day we heard the sound'a the pipes, fair to make our scalps tingle. It weren't the sad sound'a the dirge, keepin' rhythm to the feet'a the Clydesdales. It were the lilt'a the Scottish ballads, singin' about love and dancin', and shoutin' for the joy'a livin'.

"We listened, not hardly' darin' to breath, lest the sound of it die away. We stood on our porches and by our gateposts and listened, feedin' our souls on them sounds, like we fed our mouths with tater pie. The old men swallered lumps in their throats for the gratefulness of it all.

"The folks, as had watched their laddies go, now had tears in their eyes. They listened to the notes, and the tears rolled down. Every ma was certain that a sound she heard was made by the son'a her womb, and likely she was right. A ma knows these things.

"Then them laddies, when they know'd themselves to be in hearin' distance, there was a pause and then the sound thundered up the hill and down the valley, and it was the notes'a 'Scotland, the Brave'.

"Your Grandmama, she said old men fell to the ground and kissed the rocky soil, mamas sobbed into their aprons, and the lassies, they began a'runnin'.

"Them lassies, they wasn't fooled by the mountain echos, makin' the sound seem to come from all sides. Them lassies knew where the laddies was, and your Grandmama, she was one of 'em that ran the fastest. She pulled her skirt tail up over her arm and ran down the hill to meet the sound."

The storyteller sighed with the memory. "Sure enough, your Granddaddy was one'a them pipers, like she knew he was, and she grabbed onto 'im and held 'im, givin' him no room to finger the notes on the bagpipe. It didn't matter none, though, 'cause he was laughin' too much to do no blowin'. And it wasn't long till there weren't no more music, every one'a them laddies bein' held like your Granddaddy was.

"And the big thing of it was, there weren't none of the laddies that left that there mountain that didn't come back. There weren't no funeral dirge to dampin' the eye on that day.

"There were a party with laughin' and dancin' and eatin' good food, like you never saw the beat of. There came a spate'a weddin's that followed, and come spring, your Grandmama had herself a little girl."

Here the story paused, and the little boy, Eben, knew it was time to yell, "It was you, Mama! You was the first baby to come out'a them weddin's."

Then the story could continue. "Yessirree, I was the first'a them babies to get born, and they thought to call my front name Faith, bein' what they had that my papa'd get hisself back from the fightin' so's I could be born. Their next baby was Joy, 'cause that was what everyone had. They had more girls, and they didn't get to use the name they was savin' to give to their first little boy."

The small boy could restrain himself no longer and shouted, "It was bein' saved for me. That's what it was!"

Then his beautiful mother would hug him and smile and say, "It's the God's truth. That special name was being saved for a special boy, and your Grandmama, she said these words to me: 'We was in a land, and we was called out by God to go where we didn't know no one. We crossed the water and climbed the mountain and here we are. We are like old Samuel and we need to build us a monument sayin' we know it was on account'a the guidance and grace'a the Good Lord we got this far. Even if we don't know what it is out there ahead, we know the Good Lord brung us here, so he must still be with us.'

"Then she says to me, 'Faith, honey, this bonny bairn God gave to us is better'n any pile'a stones. This boy, he gonna be our Ebenezer, tellin' God we're grateful he brung us this far.' So we did, your pa and me, we did what your Grandmama said, 'cause you was our Ebenezer, too.'"

The Grasshopper rolled along behind the swaying rumps of the bays as it traveled the Arkansas roads. The reins lay loosely in his calloused hands, his thoughts still strongly on his mama and his grandmama in the mountains and of they faith they had in him.

He slumped forward tiredly on the buckboard seat of the wagon. What a sorry pillar of strength he had become! The woman God gave him and both his strong laddies were now a part of the mountains behind him. Before him was the great unknown. He was not afraid except for the lass and lassie riding in the gray wagon behind him. Truly, he had not stood up to the strength of his name.

But God now seemed to be giving him new strength. Truth be told, he felt better than he had all winter, moping about the farm, waiting for spring so he could break the garden and plant the crops.

He did have a fear, though. As he passed through the little town of Humble, Arkansas, he had inquired, as usual, of the road ahead.

"Wish't I could give you good news," the man at the blacksmith shop had said. "It ain't that the roads can't be got through, it's more like it'll take a fair length'a time and you bein' in a hurry to get where you're a'goin'. Follerin' this here river, like you been doin', that was a good plan, only it ain't a'gonna work for the next spell'a days.

"You got yourself a lake a'comin' up, one we call Piney. Got a river a'comin' in it, keepin' it full all the time. In the dry weather, it ain't no trouble to wade through them little bayous comin' in at the edge'a the lake. Onliest thing is, we been havin' a spell'a wet weather.

"It'd be my guess, ya'll find the ground a mite boggy. I'd say to backtrack and go out around, if you was to have a lot'a time, which you say you ain't. I'd say to stop and wait for the dry, only we likely got more wet a'comin'. The thing I'd say to ya now is that I don't know what I'd do. Looks like you got good hoof stock, and could be you'll pull on through. Could haft'a off-load some of your plunder... you know, the heavy stuff?"

Eben had listened, dread grabbing his chest with the feeling that he was coming down with a case of the pneumonia. He pictured the lowland lake being fed constantly by a mountain river and, in the springtime, by a network of small rivulets, each of them creating a muddy delta to be pulled through. Not good. He could wait a few days, but the chance of more spring rain in the mountains was likely, just as the blacksmith had warned.

He'd just give it some thought and talk to the Good Lord about it. He had no doubts that the Good Lord heard and answered prayers, but he sincerely wished the Good Lord would be plainer with His answers. It would be good if God's answers could be written down on paper, so he could study them the way he studied his maps.

Well, this had seemed the only way open to him, and he had taken it. There was no chance now to turn back. However, there was another option. Ned Dougherty would never find him here, and he could stop. He could find a place among these good people and provide well for the lass and lassie. He could do that, but he knew in his heart he would not, so rather than ask the Good Lord what to do, he had best ask for help in getting done the thing he knew he had to do.

His sleep had been fitful. Roberta, apparently sensing his dilemma, was silent as she stirred the oatmeal, adding a large chunk of the butter that she had purchased at a farmhouse a few miles back. He watched as she set the cereal off the flames and added a handful of raisins, stirring them into the pot. She slid the pan of biscuits from the cast iron oven and poured a cup of milk for the lassie. Breakfast was served.

While they ate, thunder rolled ominously overhead. Neither he nor Roberta commented on it, as though their silence would make it harmless. He watched, however, as his daughter skillfully mixed more biscuit batter and slid it in the still-hot oven. By the time he hitched all the animals, she might have a chance to bake two more pans of bread. The lassie sat watching, a shawl pulled around her against the dampness of the morning. Her eyes drooped listlessly. Not surprising, really, considering it was hardly natural for a four-year-old to sit quietly mile after tedious mile.

This was one of the mornings that Dancer insisted on being in the traces, and it was easier to give in than to struggle with the headstrong filly. He'd let her take a turn and then, when they reached the delta mud, he would switch out. It would be safe to let her pull with the paint, now that the ground was level, and let the black have a rest and be ready for the hard pull later.

Daylight should have been broken by now, but the black clouds lowered and the thunder still rumbled. Distant lightning flashes seemed to be getting closer, and if they must turn north to go around Piney

Lake, they would be moving straight into them. *What to do, Lord? Wait or go on?* If the Lord heard the question and agreed to answer, the message did not get through to Eben, and the horses continued to be harnessed, and the biscuits continued to be baked.

It was still dark under the clouds when the wagons pulled onto the dirt road, and they were hardly up to speed when the first showers hit. The crackle of the large drops against the hardness of the tarred canvas made speech impossible—not that there was anything to say. Eben turned his team into the advancing storm and Roberta followed. Alecia crawled into the shell of the canvas and pulled the shawl around her.

It was clear that the good weather was no longer holding.

Thirteen

Eben kept the bays at a slow pace, rounding every turn with care as he watched for the delta mud. He heard the first mountain stream before he saw it. Gushing from the side of the mountain, it pounded against a large flat rock and spread into a sheet of water at least thirty feet wide as it crossed the road. From the appearance of the water, the road had a rock bottom, and that would keep the water shallow.

Halting the team, he pulled on his hip-length gumboots and walked into the muddy flow. Just as he thought. A flat rock guided the water into Piney Lake, and it would be safe to pull the wagons on over it.

Cautioning Roberta to take it slow and hold back on Dancer, he moved into the water with the bays. The rock bottom held, and both vehicles were safely drawn up into the road. So now on to the next one.

The rain shower had let up, but the black clouds were still lowering. There must have been a downpour in the mountains, because they could hear the roar of the next creek as it tore, swirling, against the trees and rocks. At a turn of the road, there it was before them, at least fifty feet across. It was certainly at flood stage, judging from the height of the water on the trunks of the sycamores.

"Papa...?"

Eben walked back to the gray wagon.

"Papa, you don't think we...."

"Lass, we either fjord the creek or we stay here. Either way, it'd be a judgment call. Weather could fair up, and this'd run down in a day or two. We got no way'a knowin' what's up in the mountains pushin' on down. Or we could pull on through. I figure the bays'll make it, but I can say whatever we got settin' on the wagon floor, it'll get wet with the seepin' in. You might want to look toward pilin' up what hadn't ought'a get wet."

Roberta sighed as she watched her father walk away. She surveyed the plunder, trying to decide what she should move to the top. Really, there was not much she could do, and she'd just have to hope that nothing was completely ruined. If she started shuffling things around, she would wake Alecia. The longer the girl could sleep, the longer she, Roberta, did not have to look into that "lost puppy" face. So she waited while her father walked the road, moving back and forth, carefully assessing. Then he came to the wagon.

"The road's gone bad, alright. Bottom's out and the current's dug holes. I worked out a way, though, and here's what we'll do. I'll take the bays on over. They'll do good. Then I'll come back and ride Dancer over. I don't want you a'tryin' to go across, you not knowin' where the holes are. Time I get Dancer tied up, I'll come and hitch on the black and drive this'n across."

Roberta nodded. What else could she do? She heard her father call to the team. "Git up, there. Move on out. Gee up! Gee! GEE! Move on!"

The black canvas top of the Grasshopper and the square top of the buggy slewed this way and that as the wheels took the uneven roadbed beneath the water. Roberta waited and watched as the strong, heavy-bodied bays strained to pull the loaded green wagon up from the tight suction of the mud and water. She held the reins and waited as she had been instructed. She did not have long to wait!

As the buggy wheels cleared the muddy water, Dancer reared her head, whining loudly, then she plunged ahead into the seething loblolly of mud before her. Roberta startled up, yanking back on the rein to stop the filly, but with a toss of her head, the horse caught the bit in her teeth and headed into the water.

"Back! Back! BACK! Hold it!"

She screamed at the top of her voice and held back on the rein, bracing her feet on the endgate of the wagon, but Dancer's teeth held fast. The paint dug his hooves into the slick mud to no avail. Dancer was determined to pull her wagon across the water. By herself if need be. The black horse, tethered to the back of the wagon, tried to hold back, but with only a halter, he could add no strength.

Down the slope and into the water rolled the wagon, heading straight for the opposite bank. Eben stared with horrified eyes.

"STOP!"

"I CAN'T! SHE'S GOT THE BIT IN HER TEETH!"

Moving as fast as the swirling water permitted, Eben sloshed toward the wagon and the straining Dancer. Roberta loosed the rein, as any direction from her at this point would be useless. It was then that the paint horse stepped into the first scoured-out hole.

The struggle to regain his footing pulled against Dancer's harness and she lost all her footing and went down in a froth of foam. The water closed over her body, leaving only her head above. Letting loose on the bit, she screamed and whinnied, kicking wildly. The force of the water turned the wagon's direction down stream toward the edge of the lake, only a few yards away. The frightened filly must be stopped.

Eben had reached the flailing feet of Dancer and, grabbing her sodden mane, pulled himself astride her neck, tightening his knees around her head. With his knife, he slashed at the traces, freeing her from the harness. The horse, loosed from the weight of the wagon, began to swim through the six-foot deep water toward the bank and the bays.

The floundering of the horses had turned the tongue of the wagon toward the lake, crimping it solidly. The front wheels seemed to be floating free but the paint horse had found something to stand on and was remaining still, waiting to be rescued. The black whinnied nervously from behind the wagon.

Alecia aroused from her bed and began to crawl forward toward the buckboard seat.

"Go back, Alec."

"But I wanna come…."

"GO BACK! NOW!"

The little girl burst into heartbroken tears, but Roberta did not look back at her.

"STAY THERE AND DON'T MOVE!"

The water seemed to be getting deeper as Eben returned, swimming the last few feet.

"LIFT THE LASSIE ON MY BACK! YOU STAY PUT!" he yelled above the roar of the water.

Alecia was standing at the edge of the wagon, and Roberta lifted her out and onto the waiting shoulders. Locking her arms around his neck, the girl rode through the water, white as a sheet and silent with terror. Roberta watched as Eben swam back to the corner of the half-floating wagon.

"GET ON MY BACK!"

"NO, PAPA! I'M TOO HEAVY!"

"DON'T WASTE TIME! DO WHAT I SAID!"

Tentatively she moved across the buckboard and lowered herself into the water, putting an arm around her father's neck. How could he possible carry the both of them?

"PAPA, I CAN SWIM!" she shouted in his ear.

"NO! JUST HANG ON!"

She held on, and felt the strong swim strokes of her father moving below her, towing her through the water. As they neared the bank and shallower water, he stood and held her hand as they climbed out onto the soggy road.

"Papa, you...."

"Hush, lass. You couldn't'a made that current, no bigger'n you are and with all your wet clothes, and under the water like you was, you weren't no weight on me, a'tall."

The Grasshopper contained no dry clothing—only the clammy, damp quilts of Eben's bed—but Roberta wrapped them around herself and the girl, hugging her as they watched the continued rescue.

Once again, Eben paddled to the wagon. Astride the back of the paint, he loosed him from the traces and swam him to the bank. Swimming back once more, he loosed the black from the rear and led him to the front of the wagon, looping a line around the twisted tongue.

Roberta cringed as she watched, her mind projecting into what could happen. The crimped wheels had stopped the pull of the current, and if they were straightened, the pull could start again sucking the wagon toward the lake. However, the fighting hooves of Dancer were no longer in the mix... so maybe... She held her breath.

Slowly, the tongue began to come around, the black straining with all his strength and her father yelling encouragement until the tongue was straight with the road and had began to be doubled the other way, bringing the end of it into shallower water. The rear wheels of the wagon, stuck firmly in the mud, still held.

Loosing the line to the tongue, Eben brought the black horse to the bank and sat down and sighed wearily. Roberta thought of many things to say, but she said none of them.

Finally, Eben could speak. "Had a thought for a minute there. I ought'a cut that flighty filly a'loose and let her ride the current down to the lake, and good riddance."

After a full minute of silence, "Papa, can we get the wagon?"

"Well, lass, I'm a'gonna try. But the fact is, wagons can be bought. People can't, and I got you and the little one over. Them horses is what we needed to get us to the next town, and we got them. I'm ready to say a 'thank you' to the Good Lord for that much. Quick as I catch my breath, I'll take them bays over there and hitch onto that wagon. They already know to step around them holes."

Roberta hugged the shivering lump of a girl beside her and watched the wagon settle into the swirling water. She mentally tried to calculate how much was now soaked in the lower layer of their plunder and not only wet, but muddy wet.

Eben added, "Might well's to plan on a camp right here. I got line mendin' that'll take me most'a the night. Had to chop that filly a'loose or she'd'a had you both in the Piney."

Being given a duty cleared her mind, and Roberta began to consider what to do about a camp. Food? Dry wood? Dry clothes… maybe, if the gray wagon didn't get washed away. Alecia leaned sideways and her eyes drooped shut. Roberta nodded her approval. The child could use a bit of escape from the horror she had come through. They all could!

Fourteen

Apparently the storm had passed. The fast-running water became shallower, and the wet and shivering man led the bays back to the stranded wagon. Working under water, he separated the ruined lines and attached the fresh horses. Crawling from the drag of the water, he pulled himself onto the buckboard.

"Git up, there! Move on out!"

The large hooves of the team of bays sought solid footing, and together they leaned forward, moving steadily in the direction indicated by the reins.

"GEE UP! GEE UP, THERE!"

Together they pulled to the right, testing their footsteps, drawing the wagon tongue straight with the road. The sticky mud around the rear wheels pulled them up short.

"GIT UP, THERE!"

Eben shouted encouragement and direction, and the animals pulled, sucking the wheels loose from the clutches of the mud. The wagon settled into the water with all wheels on the soft ooze, and it half rolled-half floated to the other side, leaning with the current of the mountain stream.

He pulled the gray wagon up behind the buggy and loosed the animals.

"Pitch me them quilts in there, will you?" he called to Roberta.

"The bed quilts?"

"Yeah, we got'a cover these horses. They're all shiverin' in the wind, and we can't be losin' 'em, stuck out here, hid from God and everybody."

Roberta stared at him in shock, and he amended, "Shouldn't'a said that. God knows where we are, but He's likely the only one."

Roberta sorted through the quilts, picking the oldest ones and handing them to her father as she was told. With five quilts gone, how would they keep warm, but he was right… they couldn't afford the loss of the horses.

As she stepped across the gear her father had packed into the Grasshopper, her foot slipped on a metal object, pinching her ankle. As she stooped to move it aside, she found herself looking at the tiny parlor stove. Hmmmm….

Setting the three parts of it in place, she looked for the bolts and found them in a can under the ash grate. With chilled fingers, she inserted the bolts in the holes and tightened them as much as her raw, rebelling hands would permit.

The pipe… it should be close by. Where? Aw, yes, there it was. Pulling two sections of it from the other metal objects, she fitted them together. She needed one more to make an angle to carry the smoke from the shelter of the canvas. There!

Now for some wood she could burn, but there would certainly be nothing dry. Picking her way along the muddy road, she peered into the trees. Hmmm, a cave. And it was not far away.

Crawling through the dripping branches, she stepped into the darkness, waiting for her eyes to accustom themselves. The floor was littered… with dry wood! Not much, but enough to start the fire. Feeling around the walls, she found the rest of the wood. Piled neatly against the wall, it was. This cave had been regularly used by people… and there were the ashes of a past fire to prove it.

Back on the road, she glanced at the five horses, all wearing quilts over their backs. Damp quilts, but better than nothing, and they would keep away the chill wind. And there, hunkered on the ground, was another quilt-covered object, sorting twisted lines, laying them out on the wet ruts of the road. He was struggling to see them in the gathering dark.

"Papa…?"

No answer.

"Papa, I wouldn't be botherin', knowin' what you got'a do, but I likely got a good idea."

"What, lass? We could use one."

"I found a cave over yonder, and it's got dry wood. I could build a cook fire in it, or if I had the parlor stove in there, I'd warm it up."

He looked up from the tangled leather strips.

"Parlor stove?"

"Yeah, Papa. I got it together, just find myself needin' a little help on the liftin'."

Eben pulled himself up from the ground and stretched his back, arching it tiredly. Looking toward the green wagon, he exclaimed, "Well, I'll be switched if you ain't. I'll move that over to where you want it. I'm thinkin' we'll be here more'n a day."

"No, Papa, we'll both move it."

"Now, lass, I can…."

"I said 'no', Papa. You done enough for four men already. You help me carry it and I'll be getting' some taters cooked."

The small stove was set into the cave, its angled pipe extending past the cave entrance. Dry wood in the firebox caught, and a warm blaze filled the tiny parlor stove and eventually the cave. Now for the food.

Potatoes were fast, diced in the skillet with sausage and grease. It was time to wake Alecia and get her cleaned up.

"Alec, baby…" she called softly. "Alec? Alecia, are you awake?"

No answer.

Roberta crawled into the wagon and peeled back the damp quilt from the warm body. Very warm body. Her experienced hand felt the girl's neck and her underarms. Fever. Not bad. Yet.

"Alecia, baby? Are you sick? Let's see what's wrong."

"No. I can't get up."

"You can't? Then I'll help you," Roberta told her brightly.

Pulling her gently from the quilt, she gathered her in her arms.

"OUCH!"

"Ouch? What hurt?"

"My sores."

"Sores! Where?"

"All over!"

Gathering damp quilt and all, Roberta carried her through the wet brush to the cave. Someone had rolled flattish rocks into the cave, probably to use as chairs. Sitting on one, she peeled back the bedding to look for the sores. She found them. Red pimples covered the girl's face, neck and torso. Some of the pimples had drained and scabbed over. Probably not measles, but very likely it was chickenpox.

With a sigh, she wrapped the quilt back around the little girl. What the child really didn't need now was a chill. She stifled her first urge, which was to tell her father. But no, he couldn't do anything, and he had enough problems for one day. He'd be in soon, anyway, because it was getting too dark to see.

"Are you hungry?" she asked the child, mainly for something to say.

"Huh-uh."

"Well, then, I know what to fix for girls who aren't hungry."

"No."

Ignoring her, Roberta scooped a few spoonfuls of the fragrant potatoes and onions from the skillet and mashed them in a bowl. From her dwindling supply of milk, she poured the little tin cup half full and set it on the parlor stove.

Papa would be very hungry, and there were still some eggs. Now was the time to cook them. Trudging back to the wagon, she felt around in the darkness, locating the driest garments she could find, the remaining eggs, and a candle stub. The second trip brought two plates, a jar of peaches and the coffee pot. Papa was going to need something hot inside.

There. That would take care of tonight, and tomorrow would have to be a problem for tomorrow. And it would then be light enough to see what was going on.

Adding the warm milk to the mashed potatoes, she encouraged Alecia, "Hmmm, look what we have! Potato soup for a good girl."

Alecia was not impressed but opened her mouth because she was too tired to resist.

It was pitch dark when Eben pushed his way through the trees to the cave. The darkness was held back by the flickering flame of the candle, and the cave was cheerful and almost warm. In addition, there was the wonderful smell of potatoes and onions and the bracing, fragrant aroma of the coffee that filled the low-roofed room.

Eben looked around at what Roberta had accomplished and then looked up toward the ceiling. "God," he told the roof of the cave, "did I ever thank You, proper-like, for givin' me my Bertie lass? If I didn't, then I should'a. She's one of them better things You saw fit to give me."

Roberta watched then ducked her head in embarrassment at this unusual show of verbal affection. "I 'speck you're ready ta eat, now, Papa? I was a'waitin' till you settled down to put on the eggs. I set your coffee over there on that rock."

"Thank you, lass."

"And, Papa…?"

"Yes, lass…?

"You count on spendin' the night in the cave… here with us."

"Well, I…."

"There ain't no talkin' to be done, Papa. This here's a big place'n I brung everything dry I could find, on account'a the horses a'gettin' the quilts. There's your pillow and that knee quilt."

"I thought I'd…."

"No, Papa. I need you in here. This youngen's got herself a rash, likely just chickenpox, but she's limp as a dishrag and ain't a'wantin' to eat. I don't want'a be up tendin' after her and worryin' about you out there, damp and chillin'. I'm puttin' it straight to you and sayin' that you owe this to me. I'm a doin' what I can, but what would we do, me and this youngen, happen you got yourself down? Am I bein' clear?"

Eben nodded. She was being very clear, and she made sense. He had intended to make his bedroom in the Grasshopper, assuring privacy to his grown daughter, but he could understand what she said.

They all needed each other. He'd just make a trip out and make a last check on the horses. A night's sleep in the almost warm and dry cave was a thing to be looked forward to.

Fortified by the hot, tasty meal and multiple cups of coffee, he made his way back out to the animals. All were fine except for Dancer, who was carrying a rear leg. Eben lifted the foot and felt the hoof. Yep, threw a shoe. Carefully he worked his hand up her shinbone and around to the hamstring.

A knot! When his hand touched the swollen lump, the horse shied away, ripples of pain playing about her hip and rump. Not good.

He felt around in the dark of the wagon bed for the bottle of liniment and a cloth… any cloth. The night wind poured down from the mountain, wet and heavy, tugging at his jacket and whipping his still-wet pants against his legs, now numb from cold and weariness.

Ignoring the cold, he poured liniment onto the rag and bound the filly's leg, soothing her with pats and soft words as she flinched away from the pain. Bandage in place, he sloshed more of the pain relieving liquid over the rag. He'd have to see to replenishing his liniment supply first chance he got.

Then, after patting the filly's face and fondling her ears, he returned to the warmth of the cave.

Fifteen

When the coals under the grill no longer shed light in the cave, Roberta stirred them, placing more wood at the edges. If she needed to get up suddenly, she didn't want to be in the dark in a strange place.

Weariness swept over her, and, putting on all the clothing she could find, she curled up beside the little girl. Nothing much could be done until morning. Except dreams… maybe nightmares.

Little Bertie Carlile looked through her cabin window and saw him in the yard. Excitedly following her brother through the door, she shouted and laughed with glee. Danny had come to play!

The autumn leaves had fallen and blown themselves into heaps and drifts, crisp and colorful. The red of the sweet gum's star-shaped leaves was now a deep rust, and the willow and persimmon leaves were butter yellow. The tiny leaves of the black locust were orange circles that decorated the ground like a drift of spring crocus flowers.

The three of them played, running down the hill to fling themselves into the crinkly pile. Then Danny and Robert joined hands for a "buggy ride" game. The object of the game was to stand facing each other, toes touching, and hands clasped. Then both participants leaned backward as far as their arms would permit. In this position, they began to spin around in a circle, taking tiny steps. Faster and faster they spun until dizziness overpowered them, and they fell into a tangled, laughing heap of arms and legs.

Little Bertie watched as the boys whirled and then finally fell, and she threw herself into the middle of the fun and laughter.

"Me, now! Me, now!" she begged.

Danny pulled himself from the pile and grabbed her hands. Joy and happiness poured through her and she laughed with glee… then she knew it was all a pretense. With both hands before her, she pushed him away, knowing within herself that he was not real.

"NO! NO! GO AWAY!" she screamed at him, beating her fists against his puzzled face. "GO AWAY AND DON'T YOU NEVER COME BACK!"

Then he leaned toward her with his strong, little-boy hands and clasped her shoulders, shaking her….

No, it was not Danny. In the dim, early-morning light, she could see it was Papa shaking her, and the bright, crisp October day became a cold, damp cave. Papa was holding her shoulders and Alecia sat up, staring with sleep-blurred eyes.

"Bertie…?"

Roberta was yanked back to reality, and she looked around at the flickering shadows of the cave. Danny had been so real for a minute there, and what happened? Now he was gone again. Was she to be forever losing him?

"Bertie, lass… You ailin'?"

"No, Papa. Just had me a bad dream. Likely the tiredness'a the day settlin' in. Wish't I hadn't woke you; you needin' rest. You go on now, and I'll get back to sleep."

Eben paused, watching her face. Likely dreaming of Danny again. It was truly a puzzle about that young man. Could be that the change of scene would dim the picture of him in her mind, and she would be able to look at other men. Surely….

Finally, with a sigh, he left her and returned to the back of the cave where he had made his bed and was able to drift into uneasy sleep.

The next sound he heard was the jingle of harness rings and the grind of gravel. Horses loose? Wagon starting to roll?

Startling upright, he shed a few layers of covering, enabling himself to move better, and at the door of the cave he met the sound of a human voice.

"Hello, the cave!"

"Hello," he returned as he took his shoes from near last night's coals, turning them over and tapping them together to dislodge any insects they might have attracted. Hurriedly tying the strings, he stepped out.

"Friend, wouldn't'a been disturbin' you none, but it was my idea you didn't know you had a horse down."

"Down…?"

"Flat to the ground. The little filly. Rest of 'em seem to be makin' out good."

"Thanks." That was all he needed! A horse down!

At the road, he saw the stranger had stepped from his wagon and stood over the animal, stroking her ears. "If'n it was me and I could get her up, I'd be walkin' her over to the ferry. Got'a fellow over there, wheelwright by trade, but he'd do a good job on her. I'm a'thinkin' you'd be a stranger to these parts. My name's Jones, like half the county."

"Eben Carlile here. Trekkin' over from Tennessee, headin' for Oklahoma territory."

"Oh, then, man, you got'a see Ben Fry, over to the ferry. This little filly got'a have somethin' done. You want I help you get 'er up?"

"Well, I wouldn't want'a put you out…?"

"No trouble. If you'd take the front, her knowin' you, I'd be seein' toward straightenin' her rump, to get 'er leg straight."

It seemed like a good plan, and Eben reached over the filly's shoulder, his face close to her ear. Tugging her toward himself, he whispered and blew short breaths in her ear. Neighbor Jones had braced his feet against a tree trunk with his back against the horse's rump, pushing and letting back, then pushing again, encouraging her to straighten and stand. Finally, the little horse scrambled her legs beneath her, and encouraging hands on her belly gave her the strength to stand. One step down with the bandaged leg and she jerked it up off the ground.

"Ain't puttin' no weight on it, huh?" Jones observed.

Eben shook his head sadly and tried to think. Clearly, a three-legged horse cannot walk. Bending down, he felt the hamstring, fingering the knot beneath the wrapping. Leg broke? Likely. If that was so, it would take a bullet to finish the job.

Jones stroked his whiskered chin. "Got me a thought. Could be somethin' that'a help. Maybe not. That fellow, Fry, he's got 'im a sling he rigged up for a leg problem on one'a his animals. Wasn't hamstring, but it could work."

"Sling?"

"Yeah, it was a contraption thing that went under the belly and around the flanks, holdin' up some'a the weight. Course, if it's a break, the sling wouldn't be no help. Good lookin' little filly you got, and if'n it was me, I'd be a'tryin'."

Eben nodded. "How far is this fellow?"

"Mile and a half on. I'm a'goin' that'a'way myself. Could say somethin' to 'im."

"Friend, I thank you, but I figure I got'a make the trip over there myself. This here black, he'll take me and I can work out a deal. Much obliged for the help."

Jones waved and rolled away, and minutes later, the black was bridled and waiting.

"Bertie, lass, I'm ridin' the black down the road. Fellow said we could get help. You fix food and do what you can, and I'll be right back."

Alecia still slept, and Roberta stirred the oatmeal in the kettle. There was still plenty of butter, so she was generous with it, creating golden pools on the gray mush. It would be quick and easy and ready to eat when Papa got back.

At the ferry crossing, there was a group of buildings, and several new wagons were setting about. A sign proclaimed FRY'S LANDING. Ben Fry answered the call, still chewing the last of his breakfast biscuits.

"What can I do for you, friend?"

"Got me a horse down. Heard you could help."

"Down flat?"

"She was. Now she's standin' on three."

"Back or front?"

"Back."

"Good. Bring 'er on, and I got'a sling that'll let her get rest and healin'."

"Can't. She won't touch down."

"That bad, huh! Then we'll take the sling to her. Come help me load it on. How far are you?"

"Little over a mile."

"Gator Creek, huh?"

"Gator...?"

"Yeah, them gators ain't 'sposed to be this far north, but it seems they took to Piney Lake, and they ain't wantin' to leave. They like Gator Creek, wallerin' out holes in the road faster'n me and the neighbors can fill 'em."

Eben nodded. "Found it, but the filly didn't listen to me."

Ben Fry nodded knowingly. He knew horseflesh.

"Friend, this here sling, it's a heavy thing, but I got a sled I move it on. Follow me out here, and you can help." Together, they hoisted the contraption onto the platform over the wooden runners.

"Friend, you head on out and get back to 'em, and I'll be comin' on."

At the cave, Eben explained over a steaming bowl of oatmeal. "Got us help a'comin. Dancer ain't doin' too good."

"Is she... will you... ?"

"Don't know yet. Could be bad."

Gulping the last bites, Eben met Ben Fry at the road. He waited as the man slid his hand down the filly's leg, testing along the shinbone.

"Got 'er a dent in her shinbone that I can feel under the wrappin'. Smell liniment on 'er, and that'd be good. That hamstring ain't the big trouble. Bone could be cracked, or jist dented. Won't know fer a day, maybe two."

Eben waited as the man continued to examine the horse. "Lost a shoe but that ain't no problem. Don't seem to be nothin' else a rest won't put right. How did she happen to get bunged up?"

"Well, she was hitched to the wagon and got excited with the water...."

"Man, you had this little old horse hooked to that load? Why, she ain't big enough... to...!"

"Tell that to the horse. I done know it. She was a'givin' me all kinds'a trouble till I commenced lettin' 'er have a turn at the tongue. Bein' flatland down here by the lake, I thought it was a good place to put her on, aimin' to change to the black to pull the fjord."

"Oh... she weren't one to wait on bein' told, huh?"

While he talked, the sling was unloaded and the parts of it set on either side of the filly with the canvas band stretched under her belly. "Now, I'm gonna turn these screws up to take the weight off her back legs. I want her good hoof jist touchin' the ground. You tell me when."

"How long do you figger her to be laid up?"

"Depends. Bone broke… we'll know by the end'a the day. Dented… then we're lookin' at two days, maybe three. Her bein' young, likely two days'll have 'er puttin' it down. Now, what we got'a do is let 'er down every hour fer a minute or two. Don't want to cut off the belly blood flow fer too long. Good thing she'a a filly. She can have all the water she wants, and we don't have'ta be here fer her to get rid of it."

Ben Fry sniffed and looked around. "You got women folks here? I smell cookin'."

"I got my daughter and a little girl."

"Lan' sakes, man, why didn't you say so? They'll be needin' to be took to the house, out'a the weather."

"Well, we been in the weather for a month… come over from Tennessee."

"You don't say! Then, fer sure, they got'a come on."

"Nuther thing, the little one, she's ailin'."

"Sick? What's wrong?"

"Chickenpox, most likely. Broke out strong late yesterday."

A smile of relief wreathed the weathered face. "Aw, man, chickenpox ain't nothin'. Been through that with all four'a mine. The youngen ought'n to be out in the weather, though. What was you a'fixin' to do?"

"Well, till all this happened, I was fixin' to look for a place to stay to get 'er in. What's close around here?"

"The closest place with a name'd be Dardanelle."

"Good. That was where we was a'headed. Big place, is it?"

"Right sizeable. They got everything down there. Places to eat and sleep, and a body'd be able to buy anything he could imagine."

"Two day's afore we could get there, though…" Eben reasoned.

Ben Fry nodded, then his weathered brows lowered over his eyes. "What all was it you wanted in the city, if you don't mind me bein' so nosey?"

"Thought we needed to get dried out. Bottom layer'a both wagons took on water'n the quilts we got was used to save the horses from a chill. My daughter, she needs a rest, and like you said, the little'n needs to be inside. Could be I could take them on and get 'em put up, then come back...."

"Friend, I got me a better idea. All your hoof stock is needin' a rest. I got a set up here better'n any livery and I got rooms to spare in my house. I even got me a shack for hired help, come a busy spell and I get to needin' it. What we're gonna do is this. You gonna get your women folk and all your plunder back in one'a the wagons, and we'll get 'em inside. Then you'n me, we'll talk on how to get you on the road agin. I reckon you didn't take note'a the damage to your wagon wheel. I wouldn't'a 'cept it's my business, makin' and repairin' wheels, along with buildin' wagons.

"Now I'll commence to hitch up while you go see your folks. Which team you want'a take?"

Wordlessly, Eben sighed with relief.

Sixteen

Within the hour, Roberta sat on the buckboard beside her father, holding the quilt-wrapped, droopy girl in her lap. She sighed from weariness and relief. Someone had made a decision and they were rolling. *Thank you, Lord.*

Bosomy Mae Fry met her at the door. "Oh, honey, don't you think nothin' about no dirt. You get right on in here out'a the miserable weather 'afore you catch your death. You ate? Well, you'd be needin' hot tea to drive the cold out'a your bones. I know how it is, livin' down here in this draw like we do. Every bit'a cold wet wind that hits the mountains, it just slides down here on top of us."

A cluster of faces filled the doorway.

"Come on in here, you youngens. This here little girl's spots is just chickenpox, like you all had. Happen she has a cup'a tea, or would she like milk? And we got fresh cookies, still hot. Miss..?"

"Roberta Carlile. Ma'am, we wouldn't want...."

"Call me Mae. Don't you worry about bein' no trouble. My youngens don't get to see no one from one week to the next, and they're fairly itchin' to take your little girl in where they play. She ought'a eat first, don't you think?"

A foaming cup of creamy milk appeared before Alecia, and a handful of raisin cookies were heaped beside it. Without hesitation, the girl picked up a cookie in one hand and the milk in the other.

"Now there's plenty more, if she'll drink it…."

"Well, she…."

"Now for you, Roberta, is it? We got mint tea and raspberry leaf. Mint? Good choice for drivin' out the cold. They's cookies, or bread and butter…."

"The cookies look wonderful. The last ones we had were in Memphis."

At Mae's puzzled look, she explained. "Memphis, Tennessee… over on the border. We come from past there."

"Oh."

The tea and the dry warmth of the room spread over Roberta like melted butter over a hot biscuit, soaking into every pore. Mint tea had never tasted so good, and the warmth of the thick cup comforted her rough, chapped hands. The corner of her eye noticed that Alecia was nibbling on the last of the cookies, and the milk cup was empty.

Mae also noticed. "I'll just get some…."

Roberta stopped her. "Wait, please. She's been ailin' and not eatin' for several days, and I'd not want her upchuckin' on your shiny clean floor."

"Well, likely you're right, though it wouldn't be the first time the floor was upchucked on. We'll let 'er rest, then she'll want more." She turned to address the faces in the doorway. "Now you can take her to play, and see you be careful. You 'member how you felt when you was broke out."

Alecia looked up at Roberta, who nodded. Sliding from her bench at the table, the girl went toward the smiling faces in the doorway.

"Now, honey, my man says you spent the night in the Wagonshed Cave. 'Speck you found the wood, all right. It's was good to build a fire to keep out the gators."

"Gators?"

"Yeah, and would ya believe it? Them lizards that's meant to live down south, they come up here to our lake and stayed. Big old green demons, look like they come straight outta the pit'a hell. They like to wander around and swaller a pig or a chicken that ain't watchin'."

"They go into the cave…?"

"Right regular. Folks around here call that creek "Gator Creek" after the times they been found there. Now about you...."

During the course of the morning, seven quilts were dipped in lye-soap suds and were now dripping on the line. Water was heating on the stove to wash the rest of the things.

"Now, Roberta, I got a room fixed up for you and the girl, and you just act like it's yours while you're here. You feel tired, you go lay down. Your pa'll be fixed up in the shack. It's warm and dry, and I was thinkin', pardon me for bein so bold, but it was my thought you might want a warm bath in a tub..." Mae turned her face away, embarrassed to be so frank with this stranger who was also her company.

Roberta, on the other hand, pictured a washtub with steam rising from the water. She imagined lowering her aching body into the marvelous liquid, smelling the clean smell of the soapy steam. She thought of being permitted to just sit there for five minutes, maybe ten, and then to dry herself, rubbing feeling into skin that had been swathed in layers of clothing for weeks. The very thought of it sent ripples of anticipation up her neck and into her scalp.

SCALP! She could wash her hair. She could dip her head down in the warm soapy water and feel the tingle of soap bubbles against her scalp! She could lather the greasy strings of her hair so the comb could be drawn through without dragging.

Mae's voice cut into her reverie. "Now, honey, if I said somethin' out'a turn, I didn't go to do it. I was just thinkin', if'n it was me...."

"Oh, please don't apologize! I'd like nothing better'n a bath."

Mae's smile beamed. "Then, honey, we'll just go heat that old shack and put on some water. Your little girl, she'll be fine while you take as long as you want. Later on, we'll make a bath for her."

Roberta relaxed in the tub of water and fought against sleep. The warm softness of the foam pushed every thought from her mind. Working the lather into her hair seemed to be such a great gift that she looked up, smiling. *Thank you, God! Sure, it was Dancer with the injured leg that brought about all this pleasure, but all good and perfect gifts come from above, and this bath is perfect. Thank you, God!*

They stayed at the Big Piney crossing for three days. Mae Fry talked and laughed, cooked and entertained as though Roberta was a favored relative.

"Ain't wishin' no bad luck on you, but I wish't you could stay longer. The time goes flyin' past, and me with so much to talk on. You wouldn't want to think on stayin', would you? There'd be work for your pa... and all...?"

Roberta shook her head sadly. "Reckon not. Papa, he's got a bee in his bonnet to get on, and you know how it is when a man gets a idea. But now, to me, the idea'a stayin' here, I couldn't think'a nothin' no better."

Noise, squeals and laughter came from the back room. Who knew what they were playing, but it was obviously a lot of fun. Mae yelled above the racket, "Now you see you be easy with that little girl. Likely she ain't the harum-scarums you are, and we wouldn't want to see her get hurt!"

"Sure, Ma... " And the noise, squeals and laughter resumed.

Late the second day, Roberta scrubbed the red mud from the gray wagon and set her trunk in the corner of it. Around it she put the grill and oven, her remaining food stores and the freshly clean and folded clothing. She spread the quilts to make the bed, tossing the fluffy pillows on it. A day on the clothesline in the sun, weak though it was, did wonders for the moldy, musty smell of the feathers in the pillows.

Sadness and reluctance dragged at her hands as she worked. It would be so good to stay here. Mae... the children... someone to talk to...? But tomorrow night would see them ready to go. First light the next day would see them rolling. Papa said Dancer would be ready.

The wheelwright commented, "Good thing how that filly's healin' up. I was thinkin' it was just a dent but wasn't wantin' to get you hopin' too much. That sling, pickin' up her weight like it does, encouraged her to stand down when she could, gettin' her strength back. Now, if you'd be wantin' to, I could trade out with you and keep 'er, lettin' you take one'a mine. Could be a answer, her bein' headstrong like she is."

Eben listened but shook his head. "Reckon I'll go on with her. Ain't much more she can pull on me now that I won't see a'comin'. Needs to be rode, she does, and it fair breaks her spirit, not bein' used. My son, Robert, that died, likely he spoiled her. Much obliged to you makin' 'er right. It's getting' time I settled up with you."

"Sure, and you'd want to do that. Here's how I figger it. I don't charge like they do in the city, havin' my own place and growin' my food. There's the cost'a repairin' the wheel, the use'a the sling, the food for the horses... that'd come to $5.00, even."

70

Eben hesitated. "Then there's the room and the food, and the help from your missus, washin' and all. Add that in and give me the total."

"Friend, my missus has had the best three days she's had all year. She likes talkin', and I don't half listen most'a the time. And them youngens'a mine, they was fairly starved for another face to play with, and you'd be knowin' that from all the racket they make. Now, about you, I don't know when I've had a better time with no man, 'cept maybe my pa, us a'talkin' of a evening, sharin' ideas. If money was to be movin', it'd likely go t'other way and I'd be payin' you, so you better pay the $5.00, 'afore I start handin' money over to you."

Eben counted out the bills and helped Ben Fry load the sling onto the sled. Dancer leaned her weight gingerly onto the injured leg as the men watched.

"Lookin' good. We'll just walk 'er slow up to the barn and get a shoe on 'er. She'll be right as rain. Pity you don't want to trade out. I sort'a grew a soft feelin' for that little girl."

Eben nodded. He had a soft feeling, too, but he was going to be more careful about leaving temptation in her way.

"Figger you'll be stoppin' at the Fort?"

"Fort?"

"Smith. Fort Smith. I don't get too much actual truth about it, bein' that most folks goin' through here don't come back by. But I hear they got the cavalry garrisoned there, havin' 'em on hand if there gets to be trouble."

"What trouble'd there be?"

"With the folks wantin' land… like you folks. Seems like they're thinkin' there'll be crowds'a folks, and maybe fightin'. I know you'll be lookin' out for keepin' yerself safe."

"They let folks stay at the Fort?"

"Likely not, but it seems a town popped up around the Fort. The river, it loops in on itself, 'afore it starts into the mountains. Inside that bend, it's easier to protect, and them as can moves in close to the cavalry. Leastways, that's what I hear. Anyway, it'd be the place to stock up and rest a mite, if you find herself havin' the time."

Roberta left the crayons for the Fry children, along with the color book with only two pictures colored. It seemed little enough for what they had given her. Three dozen eggs were tucked into the food box along with a whole fried chicken, still warm from the skillet. A cake, richly studded with nuts was beside the chicken, and potatoes ("spring's here, and they'll rot if you don't take 'em") and onions (same reason). And other gifts.

Ben Fry gave last minute instructions. "Now, remember, hang a right at the next fork, and it'll take you up past the deltas. I can't bring up the memory'a nothin' too deep for the filly to wade. From then on, keep your compass bearin' to the southwest. When you bump up agin the river bank, follow it on to the Fort."

"Much obliged, man."

Roberta and Mae wept on each other's shoulders, and Alecia dabbed at her eyes with the ruffle on her sleeve. Coats were put on, and they walked out the door.

Eben took his seat in the Grasshopper and rolled onto the road, the buggy bumping along behind. Roberta clicked her team into action and followed the buggy and the rounded rump of Dancer. She was tethered behind the Grasshopper, walking beside the buggy. It was Eben's idea, partly so Roberta could notice if she seemed to have trouble and partly, it was hoped, that she would think if she was walking beside the buggy, surely she was doing something.

Alecia took her ABC book from the trunk, and by noon she had learned:

"'M' is for mice, who picnic on crumbs.

The two in the picture are very good chums."

"Bertie, what is 'chums'?"

"That means 'friends.'"

"Then how come it don't say that? Look, Bertie. The mice are walkin' on their hind feet carryin' a basket. They couldn't do that, actual, could they?"

"No, baby. Someone just wanted to draw a funny picture."

That afternoon, she learned:

"'N' is for nest in the branch of a tree.

Where a family of birds is happy as can be."

And she learned:

"'O' is for owl, 'Whoo, whoo' he is saying.

The day is for sleeping, the night is for playing."

"How come he plays at night?"

"Well, he has really good eyes, and he can see in the dark. Do you think that would be why?"

Alecia silently considered the matter, then turned to the front of the book, pointing to each word and repeating, "'A' is for...."

Roberta glanced at the girl beside her. The pox marks were fading, and her cheeks had color. The three days rest had done her a lot of good, but where had the chickenpox come from? The Smith children, no doubt. Oh, well, that was one more childhood problem behind them.

Eben faced the early morning darkness with a band of stars showing low on the western sky. Take the right at the next fork... that would take him around the next delta. The bays, rested, well-fed and curried, walked on with their steady pace. The light in the eastern sky that preceded the rising sun now outlined the broad rumps of the team and reflected silver off the loops and buckles of their harnesses. Life was good.

The problem at Gator Creek had been a close one, or so it had seemed. However, thinking back, he remembered the strength pouring into him from above. It was mighty like the Good Lord had Himself a funnel, right up to the sky, and poured strength down through it, flowing it into him... Never a particularly strong swimmer, Eben felt his arms pull tirelessly as he carried the lass and lassie to the bank and as he fumbled in the red water for the buckles to free the paint horse. He had swum against the strong current that came barreling down from the mountain, and reason told him his own strength was not that great.

Several times he had crossed the roiling waters, churning and foaming. Then there was the thing about the rear wheels. Stuck in the mud, they were, and with the heavily loaded wagon swinging free and even with the tongue waving loose, they had held fast. He'd hitched the bays, and they had to pull hard, but they were able to free the wheels from the mud. The strength of the mud had held until he could get into position.

And Dancer. If Ben Fry had not been close, how would she be walking? Even if he had known about a sling, how could he have made one?

"Well, God, I just got this one thing to say. There's been a time, ever since You took Robert, that I was doubtin' that You was able to see me, down in those tall trees of the farm. Seemed everything I touched fell apart, and my mind was a froth'a worries about what to do. Then, when there weren't no way to go, seems like, I struck out west, still not knowin' if You was takin' note.

"It's in my mind to thank You for helpin' me to get my lass and lassie out'a that wagon, but You know'd they weren't in no danger with You holdin' that wagon fast in that red mud.

"Seems like I been kind'a lookin' down at the ground and at the backsides of these bays when I should'a been lookin' up. I'm rememberin' how You shone a light in the face'a Paul in Your book, him thinkin' he was doin' Your work when he wasn't. I know I been thinkin' my problems was maybe Your fault, but they ain't, and I see it now. I just wanted to say this to You, 'afore You think You got'a shine a bright light down on me. I'm hopin' I won't have to be blinded to get some sense in my head.

"Maybe it's too soon to be askin', us still a month'a days and nigh onto two hunnerd miles to go, but it's in my mind that I'll need Your help when the race starts. Likely, I'll need it more'n I did back at Gator Creek. If I still had my Robert, him and that flighty horse'a his, they'd have us a piece'a land, sure enough. But I ain't got him, and I'm still of a mind you want us to go this'a'way, so I'll be askin' for help. The way You poured your strength down in my arms to let me swim, I'm hopin' You'll help me stay on that ornery piece'a horseflesh and show her or me, one of us, the way to go. I ain't got no idea what we're goin' into, but You do.

"Nuther thing, God. If You're still of a mind to listen, would You take note'a that lass'a mine, mopin' and heartsick all this time over that young man? Could you see it in your heart to take the sight'a him out'a her head, so's she can see someone who'll make her happy?"

He followed the bays, and the sun broke free of the mountain, glistening down on the fresh-washed world. Immediately ahead was the fork in the road: the left fork due west, and the right fork going north. Well, sure as shootin' he'd have gone the wrong way, had it not been for Ben Fry's direction.

"God, You still listenin'? I ain't easy in my mind on how I'll find us a place. I know You called Abraham to come to a place You'd show 'im, and You guided Moses through the wilderness. You guided my people when they was swallowed up by other nations, and You put 'em on the eagle ships of the tribe'a Dan and sailed 'em to the highlands. They hadn't no knowledge'a where they was goin', but You took 'em to where they could rest up. You took them same people and put 'em on the tall ships agin and brought 'em to the new country. That weren't all. You took 'em to the mountains so's they'd feel at home.

"Now You can plainly see how I've done gone and left the mountains, headed for the flat land, and I ain't got no inklin' about no direction. All I know to do is follow this here river till You tell me not to and then to get on that flighty filly and ride till You tell me to stop. But I figure I got just about as much knowin' as my people had, every time they moved. They was a time I thought I might not be able to go it all the way, and I'd have'ta be makin' my lass go on alone, but you been givin' me strength. I'm feelin' like I ain't too old, and that I'll live to see my lass safe and happy.

"Nuther thing, God. I'm findin' it lonesome ridin' alone. I'm needin' to talk to someone, and it looks like it's got'a be You. Thank you, God."

Seventeen

The 5th Cavalry, garrisoned at Oklahoma Station, had the mission to patrol the eastern border of the Unassigned Lands tucked within the Cherokee Strip and the Iowa tribal lands extending to the border of the Sac and Fox. The eastern border followed the Indian Meridian line from the northern tribes down to the land of the Potawatomie to the south.

For a land so essentially flat as Oklahoma territory, the eastern border had an uncommonly great number of small creeks and rivers that cut into the banks of the Deep Fork and also into the South Canadian. The mud of the lowlands gave way to a soil made of round particles, and the particles, like marbles, shifted and moved. When a gushing prairie storm swept in from the west, the suddenness of the rivulets and the width of the sheets of water tended to roll the particles along, scouring out streams and gullies. The river called Deep Fork held not so much deep water, but rather its banks arose steeply on either side, and the water flowed deeply within the bed.

Small tributaries joined the Deep Fork, creating their own gullies. The eastern border of the Unassigned Lands cut across these gullies as it followed the Meridian, and there was no way for a stranger to know when he had reached the Unassigned Lands. No one was permitted to enter the Unassigned Lands until the time of the run, and the 5th Cavalry was given the mission to flush out those who slipped through sooner than the date of the run.

Also, how were those who wished to participate in the run to know where the line was? So it was decided the Cavalry would be responsible for the marker flags. From the detachment quartered at Taylor Springs, they fanned out with the flags that were to be pounded into the ground as markers. They were close enough together that a person could stand at one marker and see the one to the north, also the one to the south, and if he crossed over into the Unassigned Lands (and if he was found there), he would be excluded from participating in the run.

Amos Kelvey turned his mount, a fine jumper, southward to check the border for "sooners" who had slipped in and to make certain the markers were still intact. Jonathan McClain followed along behind, as it was determined there would be safety in pairs. Amos, twenty-three and a corporal, had signed on with the Cavalry in St. Louis, Missouri, and Jonathan, a private, hailed from Leavenworth, Kansas. In the course of their assignments, they had a lot of time to talk.

Jonathan wondered, "What do you think'll happen, come race day?"

"Stampede," came the answer.

"Really? You think that many'll find this border? I heard most everyone'd be comin' down from the north."

"Yeah, and there'll be a dozen stampedes up there. Be glad we got assigned to the gullies and washes."

The agile horses sized up the width of the gashes cut into the red dirt and made the decisions as to whether to jump them or scramble down one bank and up the other.

Jonathan again. "Wish't we could get us some'a this land. Don't seem hardly right for the soldiers to be left out. The times we walked this border, I get'a feelin' it's mine. It don't matter to me that it has scrub oak and cottonwood, 'stead'a pines'n maples."

"What would you do with it?"

"Quick as my time was up, I'd go get my girl and we'd live here. She's been wantin' to get married, but her pa wouldn't hear to it, not with me goin' in the army."

"Why'd you join up?"

"Money. There weren't nothin' else to do fer hard cash. The Cavalry don't pay much, but it's better'n I had, and I need money to buy us a place."

"Kid, pull over and dismount. I got us an idea."

At this point the corporal made his own decision. Two hours later the two men were in complete agreement, and their heads buzzed with their individual plans which now… suddenly… seemed to be possible.

Following the Meridian south to Deep Fork, the two young men stood facing the west. Following along the bank of the river, they watched for a describable landmark, and they did not have to go far. Dead ahead was a grove of sycamore trees, their roots extending into the red dirt of a small creek flowing into the Deep Fork from the south. That was it.

With the hatchets they were required to carry, they blazed into the trunks of the sycamores, marking the four trees that were the most noticeable ones. Backing up two hundred feet they turned westward to see if their blaze showed.

It did. Plainly.

"You ain't thinkin' we over did it, are you?"

Amos cocked his head sideways, this way and that, studying the foot-long gashes made through the tan tree bark. The white of the new wood showed plainly.

"I don't think so. It's got'a be seen, and I ain't thinkin' it'll be seen by anyone not lookin' for it. So we got that done, and we'll do yours first, then mine."

The private's eyes sparkled with excitement as he led the corporal through the scrub trees, grapevines and tangles of briars. The nimble horses skirted the low limbs of the blackjack oaks and quivering cottonwoods.

"It'd be here."

"Then let's get started. Do a three-sided blaze, face high, so it'll be seen from all sides."

When a row of trees had been clearly marked, they made their way back to the sycamores, blazing the trail as they went, making sure that every cut in the black bark of the oaks was within sight of the next one.

"You gonna be able to get that girl's brother down here in time for the run?"

Jonathan nodded excitedly. "He can be got to by telegraph. He's got two weeks to get the message and get here and he's been in the same way as me, not makin' no money."

Back at the sycamore grove, the pair headed toward the south, the corporal leading. Like a bee headed for clover, he blazed as he went. Six miles into the territory he trudged, twice crossing the sycamore-filled creek until he began his triple blaze.

Carefully checking his compass, he went due west, blazing for two solid miles.

"Man, how much land you thinkin' to get?"

"One for me and one for my brother. Them two extras is to throw someone off, thinkin' it's been took. Then, too, I said to 'im to watch for maybe someone to help 'im fight off the claim jumpers, once he gets it staked."

The private stared at the corporal, highly impressed. "You was a'plannin' to do this all the time and didn't say nothin' till now. You wasn't gonna tell me nothin'."

"Sure I was. I did, didn't I? I just wasn't wantin' to say nothin' till we was comin' out for the last time. Wasn't really wantin' no one else to catch on. We'll camp here tonight and get on in early so's you can send your wire."

So it was that Amos Kelvey slept well on the piece of Oklahoma land that he hoped would become his.

Eighteen

The two-wagon caravan from Tennessee reached Fort Smith and rested over one day to restock. Eben studied the wares of the hardware store, selecting this and that. He would have taken more, but he was still not certain that he would make it through with both wagons, and if one had to go, a lot of his plunder would go with it.

Roberta checked the food, making difficult decisions. The weight of food was to be considered, but the distance between towns would be much farther, or so they were told. Ever since Gator Creek, Papa had seemed like a new person, taking his rifle into trees to bring back a squirrel or two. Rabbits were plentiful, but would they continue to be? How different was Oklahoma from Tennessee and Arkansas?

Flour, cornmeal, sugar, peanut butter… what would they eat when they got there? Were there stores, and how long would the money last? *Hush up that kind'a thinkin', Roberta,* she chided herself. *There ain't no turnin' back, and remember Moses at the Red Sea... he made it on through, didn't he?*

A wide ferryboat docked at the fort, servicing those heading west. The first wagon was pulled aboard, the bays were attached behind it and a noisy, smoking engine turned the paddlewheels to the western bank.

Next trip.

"Hey, man, we can pull that little old buggy on with this wagon."

Eben looked down at the swirling water. Not so wide as the Mississippi, but still impressive, and as near as he could see, there was no crate for transporting spooked beasts.

Taking his silence as permission, the ferry hands pulled the buggy in behind the wagon and began to attach the horses to the tether.

Eben found his tongue. "Would ya mind to put the paint and the black on the outsides?"

"Sure, man."

Dancer stood calm and docile, staring into the water. Her only movement was the ripples of nervous excitement playing along her back and shoulders. While Eben wondered if he should attend to her himself, a ferry hand reached for her bridle and drew her forward.

She startled slightly when the engine fired but walked between the black and the paint into the water, and she swam when it became to deep to walk. On the opposite shore, the boat pulled into the chains of the dock, and the animals were led out onto the sandy bank of the Arkansas River. Eben let out a long breath as he claimed his animals and paid the fee. *Thank you, Lord. Again.*

Nineteen

April happened in eastern Oklahoma just as the hills of Arkansas changed into rounded knolls sprouting a confetti of many floral shades of wild flowers. Nut trees and stately cottonwoods shot forth their pollen packs to take advantage of the first hungry insects to hatch from their eggs. Birds darted after the insects and crammed them into the open mouths occupying their nests.

Spring rabbits were everywhere, and many of them became stew. Others were browned on the spit over a flame.

A three-day downpour halted the caravan as its passengers huddled, bored, under the shelter, afraid to risk the muddy roads. The horses thrived, however, and cropped the sweet grass as the rain drenched their backs and flowed through their eyelashes. It was a warm April rain, and when it was gone, the sunshine snapped and sparkled off every new-furled leaf. A calico carpet of flowers blanketed the knolls.

Then the knolls became gentle rises, undulating across the landscape. It was mid-April, and by Eben's reckoning, they were less than fifty miles from the marked Indian Meridian, their destination. That was a three-day trip, or an easy four days.

Eben spread his maps before him, studying them while bracing against the gently sway of the wagon. Hand-drawn maps they were, taken from flyers, advertisements and newspapers. Which was right? *God, you see the problem I got here? I judge You're seein' it and fixin' to guide me one more time. And I thank You. One more time.*

It was here they came onto a young man walking, a sack slung over his shoulder.

"Hello, friend," Eben called when he came near.

"Hello to you."

"Went lame. Had to let 'im go."

Eben halted his team. "Friend, I know I'm a stranger, but we seem to be goin' the same way, and I take the liberty to ask a favor. You can ride in the wagon beside me if you want, but it'd be my wish that you ride my filly. She's fair sufferin' to be rode."

The young man brightened. "I could do you that favor, mister. I got nigh onto fifty miles to go, and I was thinkin' I might not make it, havin' ta go a'foot."

Eben loosed Dancer from the wagon and pitched the saddle over her back, cinching it securely under her belly.

"Headed for the land run?"

"Hope to. That where you're goin'?"

So for the next three evenings, the product of Jared's hunting skill was added to the communal meal. He was sixteen and lived a week's-walking distance back to the east. His pa had left for the run and had wired him to hurry on out, being he was needed to stay with the claim while his pa went to register.

He was doing fine until his horse stepped in a gopher hole, breaking his leg. With wet eyes, Jared had leveled his gun to the eyes of his horse, squeezed the trigger, shouldered his pack and headed west. The first day, he ran part of the way but had to give it up. He sorted through his pack for what he could do without, and what he put aside was so little that it made no difference in the weight. To make time, he had slighted his meals and sleep, and he was about dead on his feet.

"It's shore a good thing you done for me, mister, and you, too, miss. My belly was thinkin' my throat'd been slit, or else somethin' would'a been comin down."

"Where're you thinkin' you'll find your pa?"

"He wired and said to come to a place called Deep Fork, and I'd know it by the steep banks. Said I was to go due west tilst I came to the bank and a grove'a sycamores, then follow it to where he'd be waitin'. Said if he was gone, I was to wait somewhere along that river, and he'd be there when he could. All ready I was a'knowin' I wasn't gonna make it."

Eben spread out his maps and traced the marked waterways with his finger. "Deep Fork. There it'd be, comin' kind'a east, then takin' a south turn. I ain't what you'd call expert with the needle, but I been usin' my compass, followin' what it says, and I'd say we'll likely come out near the bend."

"You think so, mister? Then I'd be findin' my pa after all. I'd sure hate to be the cause'a us not gettin' land, the way he's been a'countin' on it and all. And they's eleven'a us youngens."

"Eleven?" Eben repeated, impressed.

"Yeah, four of 'em was twins."

"Four... ?"

"Yeah. Two of 'em's six and two of 'em's eight. Pa was thinkin' a quarter section'd be 'bout right to grow the food to feed us."

Eben nodded. Pa was probably about right.

Twenty

The corporal and the private patrolled the eastern border, riding back and forth on their assigned section of the Indian Meridian.

"You got that message through to your girl's brother, did you?"

"Yeah, but ain't heard back. Hope someone was at the station to get it out to 'im. Him or Pa... someone...."

"Likely they did." Corporal Amos Kelvey of the 5th Cavalry tried to encourage him. "Likely they did, but there'll be no way for you to know till it's over. You and me, we'll be busy holdin' back the crowd, stoppin' them as wants to be here sooner. It'll be them 'sooners' that'll give us the trouble."

"You fer sure thinkin' there'll be that many?"

"Got'a be. See 'em now, startin' to camp back in them trees. Keep edgin' closer, they do, and it ain't for a week yet. Gonna be a mess. Look, Jonathan, right through them trees. There's two fellows tryin' to slip through. We got'a get 'em."

"Git up, there," the corporal instructed his mount, and the obedient horse plunged into the thicket, followed by the roan bearing the private.

Twenty-One

News of the "run" had reached Nebraska. An entire town was on the move. It had been decided, for good and certain reasons, that a small town in that state would move to the new Oklahoma territory. Part of the town, at least, and that part grew until a third or more of the town restlessly planned to be part of the move.

They formed a pact that assured them of a section of Oklahoma land to start a new town. Those able-bodied and adventurous among them would make the run, though it was certain that not all would be able to secure and hold a tract. If more than one was successful, the best tract would be retained, and the other (others!) would be sold and the money used by the town.

It could work.

The runners would operate in pairs, for safety and companionship and also to leave one runner on the tract while the other went to register the claim.

Of the many pairs, the one most excited could have been the Kendall brothers, Chester and Douglas, twenty and eighteen, respectively.

At the border, the six pairs of runners drew lots for position along the Kansas border to wait for permission to cross to the northern border of the Unassigned Lands. This permission was expected to come down on the 18th of April, and by the 15th of the month, wagons, horses and foot runners were twenty deep in places.

Chester and Douglas Kendall drew very short sticks, assigning them to the eastern edge of the strip, barely in line with the edge of the Unassigned Lands, but the waiting crowds were much thinner out there.

In fact, there were whole sections where no one at all was waiting, and it was not even clear where the line was, except for flagged markers here and there.

The young men chose a position and settled down to wait.

"Two days is a long wait."

"It's just one day."

"No, two."

"One. 'Member how we walked all night that first night, then slept and walked some more? Then we roasted that rabbit and came on. We used up two days."

"No, it was one."

"Let's ask someone what day it is."

"Who'd we ask? You see anyone?"

"Reckon we ought'a go on east till we find someone?"

"I ain't no more'n average judge'a distance, but I think we come as far as we can come. We ain't seen hide or hair of a human person for two hours."

"Well, then, let's shoot us up some food. This land here's so flat, likely we could see a rabbit a mile away."

"I'd sooner have squirrel meat."

"You see squirrels where there ain't no trees?"

"Why not? I see a chicken where there ain't no henhouse."

"Where at?"

Chester pointed with his gun, moving slowly as an experienced hunter would. Douglas stood motionless, as would be expected of the one who was not holding the gun.

BANG!

"Got it! Shore looks like a chicken. Prairie chicken."

The hungry young men ran to the pile of feathers.

"Grouse! Even better."

"You 'speck we could find two? I could eat one, just me alone."

"You start a fire and I'll scout around."

He was successful, and in a short time, the bones, picked clean of meat, were heaped on the prairie grass.

"I been thinkin'. You're likely right on the day. There was the part of the day that was the 15th, and then we drew them miserable straws. We know'd we'd have to get movin', and we griped and bellyached till so late, and we was so put out, we couldn't sleep, so we got up and kept walkin'. That'd been the 16th when we saw them five wagons lined up, and we come on a ways and went to sleep… still the 16th. Went to sleep that night, and woke up and made flapjacks on that fire and ate 'em with no butter or honey. That'd been the 17th, wouldn't it'a been? Walked all that day, didn't we?"

"Yeah, and that wasn't today so it'd been yesterday. This here'd be the 18th. Tomorrow, that'd be the 19th. That makes three days to get through the strip. Reckon we'll hear when they say 'go'?"

"If we don't, we can tell noontime when we see it. We been tellin' noon by the sun since we was in diapers."

That settled, the boys leaned back on the new grass and watched the stars as they popped out in the black sky. The call of the grouse woke them before the sun came up.

"We must be in the matin' ground to have all them grouse. Reckon they'd be good as anything for breakfast and us havin' time between now and noon."

"You build the fire this time, and I'll go and get 'im."

The rise of the sun was never more closely watched than by Chester and Douglas on that day, actually the 18th of April, 1889, not the 19th as they supposed. As it reached its exact peak, the boys looked to the right and the left and strained their ears but heard nothing but the grouse.

"Them noisy, loud-mouthed birds, a'chirpin' and squealin'. We couldn't hear the shot if it was made."

A half a mile away, Pa Mosley slept in the wagon as Ma went hunting for the midday meal. She didn't have to go far and leveled her rifle at a bounding rabbit, picking him off in a mid-air leap.

"There it is," yelled Chester, excitedly, indicating the report of the gun.

"I'll be danged if it ain't. I was getting' a'feared we wasn't gonna get the signal."

"Bring out the needle, and let's get ourselves aimed right."

The small, glass-domed instrument nestled in Douglas's square, calloused palm, and the needle quivered, then set point to the north. The boys shouldered their packs and headed south, their long legs eating up the distance.

Twenty-Two

The sun had set on the northern Missouri farm, and old Daniel Dunbar leaned himself comfortably against the broad trunk of the maple. It had been a satisfying day near the end of February, 1889. There had been good winter moisture, and the fertile soil was deep and well-watered. He and his sons had spent long hours preparing the virgin land for its first crop.

It hadn't been easy... cutting through the sod, breaking it apart. The fine network of plant roots had the strength of canvas fabric, and the sharpest of plows wore down a strong team in a few hours. It was a good farm, though, and one he and the boys could be proud of. Not like that one by the Mississippi that had washed out seeds and fences and drowned two litters of pigs. Wasn't no wonder he had gotten it for practically a song, the owner saying he had to head back east on account of sickness. He'd have been sick, for sure.

Well, he had learned, and one wash-away had been enough. He gathered his wife and sons, his livestock and all he could carry and headed out. Sure, that land would have grown a good-looking crop—any year that the crawdads didn't get it.

He sighed and looked around him with the sense of a man who had done well. The women folk had served a good meal, the day was over, and he was free to rest and think on what was to be done tomorrow. This farm wasn't so big as the one on the bottoms, and it had cost mighty near every cent he had. The winter had been close but now the hogs were farrowing, new calves were in the barn and chickens clucked around the house. There was now a bit of money coming in.

In the yard with him were his three sons. There, stretched out on the beginnings of new grass, were Patrick and Errol, their hands under their heads, looking up into the last rays of the early spring sun. Two years ago, when he left the mountains, Errol had been a mere toothpick of a boy, and Patrick had not been much bigger, and they had been part of the reason for the drastic move from the place of his ancestors. The other part of the reason was also within his sight, and he was squatting on his toes, chin on his hand, staring toward the east. He should be resting for the work to be done tomorrow instead of staring to the east, mooning.

As the man watched, his firstborn son, Danny, stood and walked out to the newly-stretched barbed-wire fence, leaning against a post with both elbows, still staring toward the east. The setting sun glistened off his golden hair, bleached by its rays. Danny boy, his mother had called him, and when he became old enough, she refused to allow him to go into the coal seam beneath the mountain.

Danny boy. As Daniel watched his son, guilt spread over him, soaking into his very being like the drenching of a summer shower. It was difficult to justify his actions, and the depth of guilt he felt was becoming unbearable.

When he had left the mountains, he had told his son, rightly, that Patrick could not take his place, and that he owed it to his family to help them resettle. Then he could return to the mountains (though he hoped it would not come to that.)

That was before the farm in the bottoms and the colossal failure of it… along with the loss of some stock and equipment. For the next move, he had needed his son even more, and by then, what he had done had such consequences he dare not admit it.

So Danny had gone with them to the Missouri hill country, though he had made the trip twice to the bottoms to check for a message. It was not Daniel's fault his son's second letter brought no response. It had been duly mailed at the general store. Late spring, it was, and shirtsleeve weather. It had not been until fall that he had discovered the first letter still in the inside pocket of his sheepskin jumper. Nothing could be gained by admitting to his son that it had not been mailed, so he had torn it to shreds, grinding it into the ground with his shoe heel.

Since then, there had been two others mailed, and maybe they got through… maybe not. The mail was retained in the feed store until picked up and taken to the Santa Fe Depot. Anyway, there seemed to be no answers. The girl was likely married and settled in by now.

As old Daniel watched his son, he was no longer able to push away the knowledge that his son had fulfilled his responsibility and then some. Going on twenty-three, he had long been his own man, yet he served, without complaining, the needs of the family.

He looked at Patrick, eighteen now and strong as a bull. Patrick's heart and mind were here on the Missouri hillside, and sometimes on the girl at the next farm. His work in the field was equal to Danny's, and there beside him was Errol. Such a hand as Errol had with the animals, and there wasn't nothing broke that Errol couldn't fix with a hammer, saw and a roll of baling wire.

Guilt smothered the man until he could hardly breath. He was in the wrong, and he must correct that.

"Dan," he called.

No answer.

"DAN!"

"Yeah, Pa."

"Could you come here?"

His son turned away from the fence and came to him, his walk showing no tiredness from his day in the field.

"What, Pa?"

"Son, sit down here by me. I got things to say."

Danny sat down and leaned against the same maple, close enough to hear, but still facing the east.

"Son, we been gone from the mountain nigh two years…."

"More'n two years, Pa."

Daniel corrected his timeline. "More'n two years, now. Know'd you wasn't keen on comin' along, but you doin' it kept the family in good stead. Aimed to release you in the fall, a year ago, and here come that flood and we had'a pick up stakes."

He paused, and Danny said nothing.

"Well, it's come to me now that we got things well in hand, Patrick settlin' in like he has. As of now, I want you to consider you done your duty and then some, and you're free to go on your way."

Danny still sat, staring eastward.

"Son, what'll you do? You're knowin' your ma'd want you to stay here and, law sakes, this farm'd take care'a you along with us, but it ain't for me to make your decision."

Silence.

"Now, son, if you was to want to head back east, you'd be free to take your pick'a any two horses we got. You think on it. Likely that girl'll still be there."

"After two years and no word? A girl like her?"

"Did ya say to 'er you'd be back? Did she promise?"

"Sure, Pa, but with no word, could be she gave out on me. How'd she know I might'n be dead?"

The sharp dregs of his guilt were ground into his heart as the man listened to the despair of his son. What he said was the truth, and what other son would have stayed and worked with the patience Danny had? What had his selfishness done to his son?

"Likely I got no rights in this here, but I wouldn't be givin' up on that girl. This mail, it ain't what you call reliable. Could'a got lost any number'a places. Happen you make a trip back, you'd rest your mind, and you could come back here or go anywhere, just so you'd let your ma know where you was at."

The early tree frogs had begun to screech in the gathering dusk, along with the low murmur of voices as Patrick and Errol conversed.

"Pa…."

"Yes, son?"

"It'd be Babe and Posey I'd want to take, and I'll be gone at first light."

"So soon? Your ma…."

"Pa, I been with Ma, helpin' to care for her for the past more'n two years. At first light, I'll kiss her goodbye and go."

"Sure, son…."

Danny Dunbar lifted himself from the ground beside the massive maple and went to the barn. Sorting out two saddles and other tack, he went to the corral and brought the two paint fillies into their stalls. A liberal amount of grain was dumped into each feed bin.

"Eat up, girls," he advised. "There won't be no more corn for a while."

From the loft of the log barn, he tossed down the saddlebags, two water canteens, a small tarpaulin and an oilskin coat and slouch hat. Packing these things in saddlebag, he went to the house.

His mother sat at the table drinking a cup of steaming tea. Across the table was another cup of tea, liberally laced with top milk, the way he preferred it. Also on the table were neatly folded piles of his clothing, a bar of soap, two towels and a tiny jar of antiseptic salve.

"Sit down, son."

Danny sat. "You know, don't you, Ma?"

"Sure, and it's past time. I been seein' you pinin' to be your own man and your pa keepin' you long past what was agreed. I'm 'memberin' it was me that was the reason for us a'leavin', but here you stand, healthy and breathin', and maybe you'd'a lived through workin' in the mines, maybe you wouldn't'a. Anyway, I done what I done and I still have three sons."

Danny sipped the tea and watched the strength in his mother's face. True, he was alive, and he did not have coal miner's cough. "Thanks, Ma."

"Your pa, he's got money put back. It ain't what your wages should'a been, but it's a fourth share'a what's been made. I'll see you get it. And Danny boy…?"

"What, Ma?"

"You'll find 'er."

"Maybe... maybe not."

"Yes, son. You'll find 'er, whoever she is."

"Ma, I don't know how long I'll be gone, but I'll write you. I'll be wantin' you to know where I am, so's you can be askin' the Good Lord to watch out for me."

She watched him smile to soften the jab at her tendency to over-protect. "You do that, son. At the places you'll be goin', likely the Good Lord'll need help findin' ya."

Danny drained his tea, hugged his mother's shoulders and picked up the piles she had laid out for him.

"Save room in the pack for the side'a bacon and the gravy skillet."

"Sure, Ma."

Danny fitted his gear into the dusty saddlebags and climbed to the loft. This was his place to be alone, and the jumbled race of thoughts in his head had become so intense he needed this time. Lying back on the hay, the tiredness of his workday and the excitement of tomorrow were too much for his brain, and he fell into sleep.

The flapping of the rooster's wings, a prelude to his early morning bugling, woke the young man in the loft. Brushing the loose hay from his clothing, he fed Babe and Posey again and tossed the saddles on their backs. Why did he need two saddles? It didn't occur to him to wonder. The bags were thrown across Babe's back and cinched under her ample belly. His fingers felt for the tension under the straps... if they were too loose, she would be rubbed raw, or worse, she might blister.

The kitchen window was a yellow square of light in a black world. He entered through the back door to the smell of fried pork and potatoes. Beside his plate were biscuits and gravy. Also, stacked neatly beside it was a side of bacon, six eggs, a small jar of jelly, flour, baking powder and salt. A fork, a spoon and a skillet and small kettle completed the assemblage.

"Sit down, son, and eat. These here eggs been boiled, so you eat 'em first when you get started. Now this here jelly ain't much, but see you rinse out the glass and lid and keep it... happen it'll come in handy. I know you'll have plenty'a shot for your Springfield, and that'll make meat, but a slice off that bacon'll make fryin' grease."

"Thanks, Ma."

"Now you sit down and eat and let me look at you, fillin' my eyes for when you're gone. I ain't sayin' that to make you sad. You been more'n a good son, and I had you longer'n I could'a expected to have a boy. Later, we'll wake your pa and brothers to say goodbye, but this here is my time."

She watched as he ate. His sun-bleached hair flopped down over his high, broad forehead in red-gold curls, so like her father's. The shape of his mouth, generous and sensitive, came from her own mother. The broad squareness of his head, and the position of his ears were from his father, a feature that had attracted her to him.

His thick, stocky shoulders were modeled after her idea of what a man should look like, and his capable hands dwarfed the teaspoon as he stirred the tea. All in all, her Danny boy was her reason for living, and the thought of his going away wrenched the very morrow from her bones, but he would never know it from her. She watched him eat, and smiled, cheerfully.

As he finished the last buttered biscuit, she handed him a small sack of coins. "Your pa and me, we wish't it was more, but we know it'll get you started. You pack this gear and I'll wake the folks up."

The eastern sky was becoming pale behind the silhouette of trees as he led the fillies to the front gate and returned to the kitchen. Pa, Patrick and Errol were there. Rebecca, Anne Marie, Carolyn, Lizzie and baby Mary Catherine, just a toddler. He hugged his puzzled siblings and left explanations with his mother to deal with. He hugged his pa and whispered, "Take care'a yourself, Pa."

His ma took his hand and walked with him to the gate. He bent down to let her kiss him on the cheek and he knew she had chosen the dark yard to say goodbye so he would not see her tears. He rode away in the cool dawn breeze, his mother's tears still wet on his cheek.

Twenty-Three

Danny Dunbar rode east into the rising sun and continued that direction all day. The valley of the Mississippi made easy traveling, and he would turn south to St. Louis to cross over. The first night, he was lucky enough to find a cave to keep off the night chill, and the second night he appropriated an unguarded haystack. He had gone to sleep to the sound of munching as Babe and Posey helped themselves to the bedstraw.

Then he was on the banks of the Mississippi. There was no lack of caves and outcroppings along the riverbanks, and at St. Louis, he crossed on the ferry after restocking his provisions. He had not looked at the coins in the bag until he was well down the road but was pleasantly surprised. He knew they were doing well on the farm but not that well. Had his mother added to it from her own stash? Very likely.

He hung close to the bank of the river for ease in traveling until he reached the east-west thoroughfare from northern Arkansas, through the pigtail of Missouri and into Tennessee. As he saw the first marker on a Tennessee road, his heart skipped a beat and a lump arose in his throat. One more night on the road, and he just might make it in.

He remembered the backwoods shortcuts like the palm of his hand and cut across pastures and through thick woodland, down into steep ravines and up the other side, scrambling the horses over tree roots and under low branches.

Just after dark he reached a popular stop-over cave, shared jointly by humans and small animals. As he held the carcass of a young squirrel over the small fire in the mouth of the cave, he considered the morrow.

If he went on in, straight as the crow flies, he would reach Robert's house first, and that would be a good thing. He was suffering with eagerness to see his boyhood friend, and addition, he could bathe and clean up before going on. In his wish to be on the way, he had not washed any clothing, and his own bathing had been sketchy. If she should happen to still be there… anyway, he could find about her from Robert.

The tired horses struggled up hills better suited for monkeys or eagles and pulled out onto the trail to Robert's hillside farm.

He knocked on the door and was met by strangers.

No, young man, they didn't know much about the fellow they bought the farm from. Heard some word that he went to live at his pa's but couldn't be sure.

Sensing bad news, Danny climbed the road to the old Carlile farm. Nothing good could come from Robert selling his farm. Even Danny's lack of a bath was hardly in his mind as his thoughts raced around and sorted themselves, only to re-tangle themselves into knots again.

He paused the tired horses at the gate and looked around. Grass was growing in the corral, and no animals were visible. The house was closed and shuttered.

"Hello, the house," he called, and the echo bounced back, "ooo, ouse."

No answer for a moment, then a chorus of barking erupted from the shed. Out of the swinging door burst Pete and Pokey. Joyfully, the hounds leaped against Danny in the exuberance of recognition. Yipping and squealing gleefully, they escorted him through the gate and up to the door of the empty house.

Danny tested the door. Locked. Loosing the horses in the corral, he walked around and looked at what had been a well-kept farm. The loft still held hay and the kitchen garden had overgrown turnips. At the well, he took the bucket from the hook and lowered it into the water, drawing up a drink. He poured some into the dog's pan, and they drank, then milled around him, seeming to be as puzzled as he.

Well, there were two things he could do. There was Elias Weatherby, whose farm was attached to the Carlile place. Or he could take the path down the hill to Annie McDougal's. He decided on the latter.

Leaving the horses in the corral, he walked down the trail, the dogs orbiting his progress.

"Hello, the house!"

Annie McDougal focused her dim eyes on the young man at the gate, then beamed radiantly. "As I live and breathe, if it ain't that handsome Dunbar lad. Got so good lookin' I couldn't hardly remember who he was!"

Her arm drew him into her house and led him to the table. "Tea'll be ready, and here, start in on these here cookies. Now, if you ain't a picnic to the eyes, just to look at you. Your pa and ma, are they...?"

"They're well. They got 'em a good place in Missouri. Annie, the Carliles...? I come from up there and it's deader'n a ghost. What happened?"

"Sure, and you'd not know, bein' gone. I'll get to what I know first. That Robert, his little wife died, bein' in a family way. He sold out and come to his pa's to get help with the little girl. Then he was in a cave-in and come home in the wagon. Gone."

"Dead...? Robert?"

Annie nodded. "Sorry to say. Well, after the layin'-out and buryin', it weren't hardly days till they was gone."

"Gone… you mean…?"

Annie poured hot water into two teacups and the peppermint aroma filled the little kitchen. "You want cream? Sure you do…" and she poured a generous amount.

"I know you're wantin' to know, and I'll tell you my best thought. You know that little girl, her ma bein' a Dougherty and less than they'd ought'a be, they wasn't nothin' said when her pa was livin', but when he was gone, they put in a fuss for the little girl. You know them two, Ned and Eben, each one of 'em stubborner the other. Well, Ned, he'd be a sight meaner, but Eben, he'd be smarter. Or that'd be my guess.

"Now Eben, he sold his place to Elias Weatherby and let slip that he was goin' down the river fixin' to find work with the shrimpers or somethin'. Well, that Ned, quick as he seen Eben'd pulled out, he headed out down there with one'a his boys. Finally come back without that little girl. Scoured around a few other places and still didn't find 'er."

Annie hitched her cane-bottom chair close to Danny, as though the walls might have ears. "Now here's what I think. I think that talk of the shrimpers was a blind lead. Could be Eben said he'd head out south, when he knew he'd go north. Or west, or even east. Leastwise, he was gone."

Danny sipped the tea and studied Annie's old face. "What'd be your best thought'a what to do?"

"About findin' that girl? Well, when they left here, more'n a month past, she didn't have no man with her, 'cept her pa. You'd want to know that. Now there'd be a lot'a ways to go, 'cept south, and if'n it was me, I'd break into that house up there and look everywhere for a sign. I'd look in the barn and maybe the shed and all. Could be some scrap of'a idea'd come to ya. Eat up them cookies, son."

Danny picked up a cookie and popped it into his mouth. The thread of excitement that had pulled him along had disappeared like a puff of smoke. She was gone, and she could be any of three directions and several in between.

"Son, let me cook up somethin' solid 'nuff for a strappin' fellow like you."

Danny sighed, "Thank you. Annie, but I think I'll take you up on what you said. I don't see no other way."

Annie nodded, thoughtfully. "I'd'a figured that'd be what you'd say. But now I'll say this. Come time you look around and decide, then you come down by here, and let me make you a lunch to get you started a'lookin' for her."

"Well, I...."

"No backtalk. It won't take no time to come by, and your ma'd never forgive me if I didn't do for her favorite youngen."

Her blatant persuasion brought a smile to his face. He had no doubts that what she wanted him to come by for was to know where he was going. Well, why not?

"Sure, Annie. I'll come by."

The pair of dogs escorted him up the path and to the house. He lifted a window and stepped into the house where he had spent so many hours. Unlocking the door from the inside, he let the dogs in, and they were on his heels as he led the tour of inspection.

Kitchen stove was there... no kettles or dishes. Beds were there... no bedding. Trunks were gone, and so were their clothes. He looked in the cellar and saw rows of canned fruit. He selected a jar of peaches and shut the cellar door.

There was hay in the loft but no chopped corn or pig feed. No droppings in the barnyard. One old clucking hen called to half-grown chicks but there were no other chickens.

Back to the house. He stepped down in the parlor, and the tiny stove was gone, and so was their ma's little chair. Dropping into Eben's big rocking chair, he leaned back, trying to think. No effort had been made to clean the floor, so they must have left in a hurry.

They traveled light, but took the stove. He said he was going south, so he was likely going north. Back in the yard, he stood where a wagon would be loaded and looked around. Blown into a pile of leaves and sodden by rain was a yellowed sheet of paper.

Danny straightened out the wrinkles and read, "OKLAHOMA TERRITORY... free land, a whole quarter section... first come, first served." His eyes skimmed through the words, recognizing them as words he had read before. The same flyers had been circulated in Missouri, and he would have been tempted, but he had not been released, and there was Roberta to think about.

In the house, he fired up the cook stove, poured the peaches in a pan and topped it with biscuit dough. Popping it in the oven, he sat down on a dusty chair beside a dusty table and made a mental inventory of what was missing. The buggy was gone and the wagon, but missing items would have made a load, leaving no room for people. He must have gotten two wagons… of course, Robert's wagon. So they were going a long way.

He ate the entire peach cobbler and stretched out on the dusty floor, unmindful now of his missed bath. The dogs didn't care how bad he might smell.

The dogs woke him up at daylight, and he walked down the hill to Annie's. Over a country breakfast, he confided. "I figure you to be right. What'd make sense'd be to go to St Louis. They's lots'a work to be had up there. Be easy for old fellows to get light work on the docks."

Annie sipped her tea and admired the good sense of the young man who agreed with her deduction. "It'd be the onliest thing I could think of. You thinkin' you'll be able to find 'em, there in that big city?"

"Sure, and it may take a little time, but I got time. Thanks so much for the food and the help. You take care'a yourself."

Whistling to the dogs, he mounted Posey, and Babe followed along under the loaded saddlebags. At Pinetop, he stopped to get a couple of quarts of corn. Could be the girls would be traveling hard for a while, and they needed to stay healthy.

The man who sold him the corn exclaimed, "Oh, there's them dogs! Disappeared on me, they did, and I figured they went back home."

"You know these dogs?"

"In a manner'a speakin'. Fellow left 'em with me. I didn't need no dogs and took 'em as a favor. I did some work for 'im."

"Trailer work?"

"More like boardin'."

"Did he take both trailers? I figure…."

"Yeah, an old gray one, and that new green one. You'd know which one."

"Sure. He'd need 'em both, headin' north in February."

"Yeah, but it ain't that far to St. Louie. Gonna work on the docks, he said."

"Yeah, he'll be good at that. Well, I got'a head on out. These bein' your dogs, you want I leave 'im here?"

"Naw, they'd just break loose'n go home."

"Likely. So long."

The jubilant dogs ran circles around the horses as Danny Dunbar headed out across the ridge, preparing to descend into the valley. Now he knew WHAT was going on, but not WHY.

Old Eben Carlile was headed to the Oklahoma Land Rush with a grown daughter and a baby… well, she was a little girl, now. Why?

It would take some thought, and he had five hundred miles to think about it. He'd pace the horses and feed them well. Summer coming on; he could travel long days, and he'd make a lot better time than with a wagon and team.

Twenty-Four

The gathering at the eastern boarder of the Unassigned Lands was growing by the hour. The two blue-shirted Cavalry officers patrolled their one-mile section, making an authoritative presence, passing in plain view of the gathering. Amos Kelvey cut his eyes aside, searching for his brother among the crowd but did not see him.

The good grazing of the spring grass had been worn down by cropping horses and milling feet, so the animals had to be taken east of the lines to be fed, creating a constant milling about. Wagons were unhitched and waiting along the line, most of them not being part of the run. There were three days to go, and already those from the Kansas border were on their way down through the Cherokee Outlet.

Children played games and squabbled, and tired parents began to yell at them and at each other. There was no place to be alone, and everyone labored with the stark knowledge that all the people along the line would be competing for the same tracts of land.

Alecia was glad for playmates, and she had plenty of time to learn:

"'P' is for paint, red, yellow and blue.
If I had a brush, I would paint some on you!"
"'Q' is for quilt to spread on the bed.
I will be warm from my feet to my head."
"How will his head stay warm if it isn't under the quilt?"
"I don't know, honey."
"'R' is for rabbit, all fluffy and white.
Give him a carrot and he'll take a bite."

The small children gathered around her and looked at the pictures while Roberta read the poems, but she was firm about the color books.

"No, Alec. You can't have them till later, reason bein' there ain't enough to go around, and they'd color up all the pictures. You play other games with the children and color when you have to be alone."

A fistfight broke out among the bored, single riders, waiting as restlessly as their horses. The struggle drew a ring of observers, each one quick to take sides.

Someone made too much noise late at night and drew angry words from his neighbors.

A horse drawn sulky, loaded too heavily for its two lightweight wheels, joined the line, being driven by a fellow calling himself Cap Haney. Said he'd come up the Indian Meridian all the way up from the south, and you wouldn't believe the sight'a the folks a'waiting.

The bored men gathered around the newcomer, who addressed his audience. "Fellows, have you looked around you at all these gullies and ditches and that red mud? You 'speck this'll make farm land? Land down south, why, it's deep and dark, especially that by the big river. Good land."

"How come you not to stay?"

"Too many wagons."

"What difference'd that make?"

"Couldn't even get up to the line."

"How come? They wouldn't let you?"

Cap nodded. "Pushed and shoved. They's even been some knives pulled."

"So you left?"

"Yeah, but it's good land down there."

"Why'n't ya go back?"

"No use to."

"That must be how come you come on up here where all the gullies are."

A stiff breeze came up, and the smoke from a cooking fire blew into a neighboring tent. The resident of the tent came out with his rifle cocked. He was wrestled down by two others, and his gun unloaded.

The Cavalry men could see trouble brewing across the line, but their authority stopped at the banners posted along the way.

A tall, dark haired man with a pencil mustache cupped his hands to his mouth and called out, "Could I have ten men come together here?"

"What for?"

"Who do you think you are, givin' orders?"

But several men, actually more than ten, were curious enough to come to him. He looked around into their faces and invited them, "Let's sit down here and talk."

The circle of men was such an interesting curiosity that others joined.

"I'm Leon Baxter, and I'm waitin' here just like all'a you. Got to thinkin', though. Waitin' here with nothin' to do is gonna get us in trouble if we don't do somethin'. It's true we're all gonna be after the same tracts of land, but by the day after the run, we'll be neighbors instead'a enemies, and we don't need hard feelin's movin' around amongst us."

More of the men and some women gathered around, crowding close to hear.

"Talk louder!"

"What're ya sayin'?"

"Hey, man, get up on that wagon tongue so's we can all hear. Somethin' goin' on we need to know?"

The man calling himself Baxter stepped up on a wagon tongue and began again. "I was just thinkin' about after the run, most of us'll have land, and we'll not want to look the left and right and see someone we punched in the nose only yesterday."

A chuckle passed through the listeners.

Cap Haney yelled, "Yeah, and this here land ain't worth no one scrappin' over it. Never seen such hard-lookin' land."

"Where'd you see better land?"

"All down south. They's good land past the river."

"How come you not to stay there?"

"Too many wagons."

"So you come on here."

"Yeah, but...."

"So if you don't like it here, leave."

"Well, I...."

"Hey, fellows! I think there's too many wagons here. One too many. Let's get rid'a this here stupid lookin sulky."

"Let's shove it in the creek."

"Naw, it'd mess up the water."

Cap Haney backed up before the line of loud voices, finally turning to run into the trees. At the sight of his retreating heels, the advancing line of men looked at each other and grinned, then broke into laughter.

"Guess we took care'a that problem."

"Might say we was already neighbors, a'workin' together."

"Want'a do somethin' to this contraption, sure enough?"

"Naw, don't pay it no mind."

"Say, let's us men walk in the woods and scare up some game and have a big do this last night we're here."

"Yeah, and the women could cook up somethin', and we'd roast meat over one big fire, 'stead'a all the little ones scattered everywheres. Startin' now, we'd have time to have all the meat we want."

Cap Haney had not made a reappearance before the men shouldered their guns and marched into the trees. Could be he thought they were after him.

The fire was built up in midafternoon, and the word was passed down and up the line to come to the party and bring what you got. Women who had eyed the strangers in the next camp with concern now began swapping recipes. The men began to discuss the best qualities to look for in a horse (wagon, cow, dog).

Roberta joined in. Her father had said he wanted to be alone a little while, and she had honored his privacy. Then she had seen him walk over to the river, following along its bank heading east. She was mildly curious, but it was none of her business, and, besides, she was looking forward to the party.

Twenty-Five

Chester and Douglas Kendall were headed south. They were well within their self-appointed schedule but were concerned that they saw no other people. They had heard of the huge crowds that would be gathering, and apparently that information had been wrong.

"You sure we're goin' the right way?"

"You mean south?" his younger brother countered.

"Yeah. Could be we're veerin' to the east. You lookin' at the needle?"

"Now lookie here. They's two'a us, one to carry the gun and t'other one got the compass. Allowin' as how you took it on yourself to get the gun, that left me with the needle, and I been havin' it in my hand, checkin' every minute."

They walked in silence for a short way, and the older brother offered in a softer voice, "I wasn't meanin' nothin' by what I said. Just find myself wonderin' whereat is all the people. This here's gonna be the night 'afore the run, and I was thinkin' there'd be them here that we'd line up with. Figured in my head that in a foot race, we'd make out well as most, better'n some."

After a few more steps, the younger brother agreed. "Be no reason to be racin' each other, bein' we ain't after the same piece. Wonder how them others is makin' it?"

"Yeah, and if they got good land. This here don't look like Nebraska, but I'm likin' the look'a the trees. I seen a good bunch'a nut trees and berry vines. 'Course, we ain't there yet."

"I got to feelin' sorry for Manny, wantin' to come on with us. A fellow sixteen, he wasn't wantin' to hang back with the women and old folks."

"Yeah, glad it wasn't me. There's our pa, aimin' to come on with two wagons, and Ma, she says she ain't makin' that trip with a wagon load's youngens and her havin' to mess with all the women stuff she's got'a do."

"And Pa sayin' a wagon and a buggy weren't as good as two wagons...."

"And Ma a'sayin' she'd just stay there in town, thank you very much...."

"And Pa, he says not on his life, and he'll just take the whole bloomin' place, wagons and the buggy and if anybody's got 'im a bicycle, it can go, too!"

The memory of the discussion at home drew such a wonderful mental picture the young men laughed till they cried and dragged their sleeves across their eyes to wipe the tears. It had all been too wonderful, especially since it was younger brother, Manford, who was selected to stay and bring on the other wagon while Ma followed with the buggy.

"Don't know why Pa gets hisself in them fusses with Ma, 'cause he ain't never won out on any of 'em yet."

"And what he wants don't make sense sometimes. If'n he'd'a thought, he'd'a know'd he'd want the buggy, once he got it here."

"And 'member Ma sayin' she wasn't takin' no youngens in the buggy with her, havin' to have it filled up with the food stuff?"

"Yeah, that Manny drew a bad deal. Happen we'll get a chance to make it up to 'em sometime."

"My gut says it's time to be eatin'." Squinting up at the afternoon sun, he calculated, "Seems to be about four… maybe four-thirty, would you say?"

"Could stop to eat, quick as we see somethin' to shoot."

"Squirrels? I could eat two."

"Shouldn't be no trick to get four or five."

With the succulent bodies of the spring squirrels roasting on their green stick spits, Chester suggested, "Spread out that map, will you? I'm recallin' a jog in from the east, once we get past that little river. Got a big river down there, somewhere, they was sayin'. Couldn't'a been that one we just swam."

In the waning light, they studied the map. "This dang thing's been folded till the creases 'bout ate up the marks. See, there's that jog I was 'memberin'."

"Yeah, but we done allowed for that. 'Member? Lessen this needle's gone haywire, we stand might near where we ought'a be."

"But don't it seem strange there ain't no other folks?"

"Yeah, but we got till noon tomorrow to meet up with 'em. We'll make it."

"We could walk on tonight, after we eat."

"Naw, it'd be too dark to see the needle, and you'd bellyache about me getting' us too far to the east."

"I said I was sorry."

"No offense."

Twenty-Six

Babe and Posey kept up a steady pace bolstered by the corn they were given most every night. Small towns appeared along the road often enough to keep the supply going. A stop or two during the day to graze on an exceptionally good patch of green seemed to be enough to keep them going.

The dogs disappeared for an hour or so now and again and could be heard baying through the woods, only to appear with a rabbit, squirrel or maybe a possum. In their gratefulness to see a familiar face and be permitted to tag along, they kept Danny supplied with meat as well.

With singleness of purpose, he had headed west, skirting Piney Lake, wading easily through the water of Gator Creek, and considered swimming the horses through Big Piney River, the stream that fed the lake, but the ferry at Fry's Landing was handy and fast.

At the fork, he took the left road, but the water level was down and he pulled no wagons, so he had no difficulty following the twists and turns of the Arkansas River.

At the fort, he stopped to restock provisions and pick up information.

"Yeah, the folks headin' out to the territory, they mostly come through here, pickin' up supplies. Been a lot of 'em come through. If they all get out there at once, they'll be thick as hasty puddin'. Likely be so close up agin each other a body couldn't stir 'em with a stick."

"You got maps?"

"Sure have. Got four different kinds."

"Gimme one."

"Which you want?"

"Ain't they all alike?"

"Shucks, no, man! If they was all alike, why'd I have four 'stead'a one?"

"No way to tell which is the best one?"

"Haven't yet. Folks mostly don't report back. If'n they did, then we know that'n was a bad'n."

While Danny contemplated his dilemma, the owner of the maps suggested, "Why'n ya take one'a each? Ain't too many folks wantin' 'em no more."

Danny picked up the four maps.

"Say, how come a strappin' fellow like you ain't got hisself out there in time to make the run for free land?"

With a sad smile, Danny answered, "The story'd take too long to tell."

At the Arkansas River, a buggy was loaded on the ferry, and the handlers motioned to the young man with the two horses and two dogs. The man and the dogs rode, and the horses swam behind the paddleboat ferry as it chugged its way across the Arkansas River.

As he rode westward, the hills of Arkansas melted down into the rounded knolls of Oklahoma, which further melted into the rolling flat land. The twentieth of April found him leaving Sac and Fox land, and entering into the land of the Iowa.

Twenty-Seven

Eben Carlile had found the camp too noisy and confusing to have his conversation with God. Having too much on his mind to be interested in the party, he slipped away to spend some time on the riverbank and prepare himself for the next day.

Not being a particularly adept horseman, he had used parts of the last few days to reacquaint himself with saddleback riding, and Dancer happily plunged into the thick trees, gullies and small streams. She was fearless. She also did not allow space for the rider on her back, forcing him to prostrate himself across the saddle horn or be raked off by low limbs.

"God, you knowin' how I am on that horse, I wonder, could You be throwin' a little help my way? Just for myself I wouldn't be askin', but I got them two that I got'a take care of, if I can. If You'll let me stay on that horse, and let me see where one of them survey markers is, I'll be grateful to You the rest'a my life. Wait, God, I wasn't meanin' I'd not be grateful if I didn't. I want to do whatever it is that You want did. I can work for someone else and be glad to. There'll be somebody amongst this crowd that's got money and that'll need help."

Eben waited an appropriate time for God to answer, but it seemed a response was not forthcoming. In the distance, he could hear laughing and singing, and he was grateful. Roberta was part of the festivities, and as this was to be her home... the one he had brought her to without asking her permission, it was good for her to be known.

"Thank you, God, for that good girl You saw fit to give me. I know you'll look out for her. Nuther thing, God, I want to thank You for getting' us here all in one piece. I know it was by Your strength all that happened."

As Eben looked at the water flowing by in the Deep Fork River, he was reminded of the awful time at Gator Creek and the tragedy that had so nearly happened. He looked at the stones lying around him, many of the size of a pancake and twice as thick. On impulse, he gathered a few, piling them into a pile beside the Deep Fork River. Here, on the eve of this most important of days, he needed a tangible object on which to center his faith. The prophets of old were all the time building altars, and maybe God liked that. Samuel had built the altar and named it and praised God that he had been able to come this far.

The little pile of tan stones began to take on the shape of an altar, and Eben continued to work smaller stones into the corners, thinking all the time of God's goodness. He stepped around it to adjust the shape, and a three-foot-wide chunk of turf fell away beneath his feet. It scooted down the slippery red bank of the river, pulling Eben and the altar stones down on it.

What a mess! And it got worse. The clay bed of the river was so slippery he could not regain his footing, and was whirled away into the current.

The river was not so deep that he was in danger of drowning, and he was able to catch hold onto a root protruding from the bank.

Now what?

Everyone was at the party making a lot of noise and couldn't hear him if he called. His first relieved thought was that it would be totally possible to hang on to the root until he was missed, or until the noise quieted down, and then he would yell for help. The injury in his side was almost bearable, and he managed to breathe between searing stabs of fiery pain.

In dismay, he looked around at the stones of his altar, most of them flattened against the slick, sloping bank. *What happened, God?*

James Kelvey, weary to exhaustion, was relieved to see plumes of smoke at last and hear a noise made by humans. It had been a long, lonesome trip across Oklahoma from the fort, and seemingly everything bad that could happen did so.

For safety, he had left his pregnant wife at Fort Smith. It had been his intention to come to the territory after the excitement of the run had settled down and try to buy a lot in town. He had felt it was just not possible to leave his wife at this time. Then he had the wire from his brother to get on the road if at all possible and follow Deep Fork to the markers on the Indian Meridian. He was not to veer from the instructions, not the least bit, and be prepared to wait for the run.

It had not been an easy trip, but he had made it, and here it was, the last day before the run. He had a tired horse, and he was too exhausted to care that he was pushing the poor animal past his strength. He really had to make it to the Meridian today, or all would be lost. Then, too, he needed to have a little rest and be ready to make the run by noon on the 22nd.

Actually finding Deep Fork had not been a problem, as a well-worn trail led to it and it was plainly marked, but following it was a bit harder, and the rutted wagon road he traveled pulled away and went south, leaving him to plunge through the brush and make twists and turns to keep from losing sight of the river.

So now he could see the smoke of a large fire up ahead. He was going to make it after all. He allowed his tired horse to back off and walk, now that the end of the trip was in sight, and, as he glanced again toward the river, he could hear an echoing cry. It sounded like a call for help, and it sounded as though it was coming from the river.

At first he ignored it. He was too tired. Certainly, no one would be in the river. However, it wouldn't kill him to take a few steps over there and see. Dismounting, he walked to the edge of the river, noting where a piece of the bank had caved into the stream, and there, across the stream, was a man holding to a piece of root. Still calling for help, he was.

Blinking his eyes, James reassured himself that he was actually seeing something.

"Help! Hey, can you help me?"

"Sure, man. I got a rope over on the saddle. Hang on a minute."

The light rope sailed over the water, landing near Eben's hand, and with this assistance, he was guided to the bank.

"You hurt, mister?"

"My ankle is all. And a rib sprain, maybe." Eben spoke with more confidence than he felt. If his words could make the injury only a sprained ankle, he could still ride. If it was a hip injury, or a broken rib, the way it felt to be, it was doubtful if he would ride a horse for days.

"Here, fellow, put that loop under your armpits, and I'll pull you up."

James braced himself against a tree limb and, with the last measures of his strength, pulled the man to the bank. Eben gritted his teeth against the pain and allowed himself to be hauled up the muddy bank.

"Much obliged. Name's Carlile. You here for the run?"

"James Kelvey. I'm gonna try, if my horse ain't too wore out from the trek to get here."

"He'll have time to graze and rest. You go on, and I'll make it, now."

"You sure?"

"Right sure. My wagon's right over there."

Scraping some of the mud from his shoes, Eben determined that his ankle was in good shape but not his sixth and seventh rib. Carefully touching along their length, he decided that there were no breaks creating splinters that would puncture a lung. There were only piercing stabs of pain with every breath.

Inching his way to the wagon, he pulled himself inside and lowered his body to the bed. There was thinking to be done. It was totally obvious he would not be part of the run, and it was doubtful he would even be able to drive the team. Roberta would have to help him bind his chest to ease the pain and give it a chance to heal, but he'd wait a while for that. She was having a good time at the party, getting acquainted, and that was something she needed to do. That Baxter fellow had been right; it was important to get along with neighbors.

Lying on his back, he looked up at the ceiling of his canvas wagon cover.

"God," he sighed with discouragement, "I was only trying to raise an altar to You, and I was going to be like Samuel and thank You for bringing us this far and ask You to show us the right way to go. Now that's all spoiled by me not seein' how that bank was… the way it was all washed out underneath. I'm sorry, Lord."

James Kelvey's slow steps led his tired horse toward the noisy party, but before he reached them, he sank down heavily beneath a blackjack oak and closed his eyes. The horse, feeling the slack reins, reached for a tempting clump of switch grass and then another, cropping the fresh green stems while his rider dozed.

Twenty-Eight

The sun was gone, and a ring of stars decorated the horizon as a three-quarter moon shone overhead. Two young men lay on the grass, their backpacks beside them.

The older one whispered, "You awake?"

"Yeah," came the answer.

"I keep runnin' words through my head, tryin' to get the straight of it. I know we crossed over that river, but I ain't fer sure it was the right one. It's hard to know how big is big when it's somebody else that's describin' it. We ain't seen no markers nowhere."

Douglas was irritated. "Now, if you've gone to thinkin' I let us get veered off, I ain't a'wantin' to hear it. I'd sooner listen to the katydids in the trees."

"Hey, don't get yer feathers ruffled. That wasn't in my mind. I know you can read a needle good as me, and you can shoot good as me, too. It's just that things ain't stackin' up right. How come is it that we got to be the only two folks in the world since Adam and Eve? If'n there's more, how come we ain't seen 'em?"

A pause. "I know. Me, too. I keep goin' over and over the things that was said back at the Kansas line. We was to head south on the 19th, and be at the markers three days later. Seemed to me that little old Cherokee Strip was of a size that we'd walk in two, maybe two and a half days, havin' us a half day rest."

"Me, too."

"And here we are, ain't even got to the markers yet. Somethin' happened to size'a our steps, do you reckon? This map was pencil drawed, and I had the thought maybe it wasn't maybe actual the way it ought'a be."

"I thought on that, too, and it's been a worry."

"I get to thinkin', since we ain't neither one a'sleepin', could be that we ought'a be walkin' on."

"You 'speck there'd be light enough to see the needle? I sure would hate to waste match light."

"Well, there's the moon. Ain't as easy to foller as the sun, but we could try. Could maybe foller the moon, and not use the matches except every so far."

"Then what're we doin', sittin' here?"

The moonlight was dim, but the two young men were able to see well enough to keep from tripping.

"If'n it was August, 'stead'a April, I'd be scairt'a snakes, trampin' around in the dark like this. Don't figure them rascals to be too chipper in the cool'a the night. Need the sun to get their joints a'turnin'."

The cicadas buzzed in the trees, and the sound of tree frogs came from every direction. The only other sound was that of soft footsteps and an occasional broken twig or dead limb.

"You reckon we'd see a marker, dark like it is?"

"I thought about that. If'n they was to be tall, with white flags, like up at the Kansas border, I allow we'd spot 'em. Could be they'd be usin' a different kind down here. We'll just have to keep a lookout for anything strange."

The footsteps made enough noise that the small varmints moved out of their way.

"Allow it'd be time to check the needle?"

"Yeah, stop just like you are, so's we'd know the way we was headed. I'll strike us up a light."

The glow of the match shone on the calloused palm and on the shielding fingers. It's flickering flames revealed the black point of the needle pointing into Douglas' chest.

"Still square on the money," his brother pronounced. "Listen!"

A new sound mingled with the woodland noises. It was the unmistakable murmur of water flowing over rocks.

"Well, I'll be danged if it don't sound like water. Reckon it's a river?"

"Was they to be two rivers?"

"Didn't think so, but like you said, that map was hand drawn. Could'a been wrong."

"Let's go."

Within minutes, the two stood on the bank of a small river looking down. The moonlight sparkled on the stream of water below them.

"Don't look like too big of a river, but that could be what they'd call it. Seems real washed out to not have no more water in it than it does. Could be the dry season?"

"Wouldn't think so, bein' April. Could be, though, that this place is a lot different than Nebraska. Well, we got'a get across this thing. I ain't wantin' to have soggy wet clothes till noon tomorrow, and I know what to do."

"Good idea."

With every stitch of clothing removed and tied in a bundle, they crept down the slippery clay bank into the water. It was cold, but n more so than the Nebraska water they had often swam in, so they carefully felt their way along in the chest-deep water to the opposite bank. Leaving their clothing bundles on the grass, they returned for the backpacks.

Sitting on the bank to dry out a little before putting on their clothes, Chester looked around on the ground at the wealth of dry sticks and twigs.

"Say, I got a thought. How's that flour a'holdin' out? I got a hanker for a couple'a flapjacks."

"'Speck we could spare some. I'll stir 'em up and you rake up some sticks to burn."

Douglas removed a strip of fat from their dwindling supply of fat back bacon from the last hog butchering. It was becoming a bit rancid, but it still provided grease to keep the flapjacks from sticking. Within minutes, flavorful smoke billowed up from the skillet, and the first battercake was poured, sizzling, into the long-handled skillet. Jiggling it a bit to loosen it, he took it from the fire, and with a skillful flip of the wrist, the half-done cake vaulted into the air and turned a lazy somersault, then it was deftly caught on its way down.

"This'n got done. You want it?"

Chester extended his hand, on which lay a large oak leaf. With a jerk of the pan, Douglas slid the cake onto the leaf and poured another one.

"Got honey enough for maybe one time. Use it now, or save it?"

His brother made a decision. "Let's use it. Could be we'll see a bee tree, but if we don't, we still need the energy, bein' behind like we are."

"Good thinkin'."

Honey was drizzled on the hot bread, and it was rolled up like a flute. Thinking took a lot of energy, and the two travelers had done a lot of thinking lately, so they sat on the bank of the stream, their bare bodies white in the pale moonlight. They watched the rippling flow of the water and savored the taste of the bread and honey.

"I still say that ain't much of a river, but if'n that's the best they can do...."

"Me, too, but that's got'a be it. I allow we just missed the markers...."

"You dry 'nuff to dress? I seem to be. 'Speck we better be getting' on."

"Yeah," and the pancake cook wiped out his skillet with a leaf, carefully returning the pan and his remaining supplies into his backpack.

In minutes they were on their way.

"I don't know about you, but I'm ready for the sun to come up. I'm tired'a stumblin' along slow. We got'a make up some time."

"Yeah. I can't figger for the life'a me where we went wrong. I'd'a thought we could step it off with the best of 'em."

"Hope we didn't miss seein' nothin' in the dark. Tryin' to look both ways the way we was, likely we didn't make up too much time."

"You think, us bein' a day late, we'll find a place?"

"Maybe. Maybe not. If'n we don't, the others ought'a. Onliest thing is, I had my head set on us bein' the ones to find the townsite. You know how they was thinkin' the place we drawed'd be good. Bein' less'n a half-day's travel to the Santa Fe lines...."

"Yeah, we may not find it, but we both know we done our best."

The bright April sun popped through the tops of the cottonwood trees and shone down on two tired young men who had just crossed over The Deep Fork of the Canadian River.

"Chet?"

"Huh?"

"Wouldn't you'a thought, this bein' the day after the run, this place's be swarmin' with people, thicker'n fleas on a hound dog."

"Hmmmm. Could be there ain't too much call for free land? Hard to believe that."

"Likely there's better land than this, but this don't look too bad to me."

"Be good for row crops. Clear out the stumps and it'd be good grazin'. Always thought it'd be a good job to tend cattle, feedin' 'em out."

"Yeah, this land'd be good for that."

Douglas shaded the compass with his free hand, squinting at the dial. "Time to move in west a little. We been anglin' east. 'Bout five hunnerd feet'd do it."

Together, they stepped off the required distance and again turned south.

"You know, I like this here land. I been lookin' down a'countin' and come up with more'n twenty kinds'a grass. Variety like that, a fellow'd have a beef fed out in no time."

Douglas sighed wistfully. "Yeah, that'd be good. Likely we'd be old men 'afore we got the chance at that, havin' to save up for the land. We ain't even knowin' what kind'a jobs there'll be."

"Yeah, and you know what Pa said about us havin' to maybe hire out to the Santa Fe or to some freighter with a haulin' contract. He thinkin' it'll be while 'afore his wagon buildin' business builds up."

A few minutes of silence. "Yeah, but I sure do like this here land." He walked a few steps ahead of Douglas and stopped so suddenly, his brother almost stepped on his heels.

"Look!"

"What? A snake?"

"If'n that's a snake, it's just been recent cut from a tree. I think we done found the markers!"

"Where?"

"There, see? New cut wood with the numbers painted?"

"Oh. How'd they expect a body to find somethin' like that in all these trees? Seems they could'a put 'em up higher, like on the Kansas border."

"Well, we found 'em now, so let's make tracks."

"Could be we'll get somethin' yet, bein' only a half day late."

Weariness evaporated as their strides lengthened. Ahead of them extended a long stretch of land where limbs had been trimmed back, and, every so often, a stake of new wood appeared.

"How many'a them markers is there? Wouldn't think they'd be goin' both ways."

"If'n they was plannin' to do things different, they'd ought'a told us."

"Stop!" commanded Chester. "Lookie at my finger and follow to that oak."

"Hmmm, a blaze. As I live and breath, they been through here blazin' a trail. Wouldn't'a thought of 'em bein' so helpful as all that. That'll save us a sight'a time. Let's hurry on down this here trail."

By now their steps had quickened into a run.

"Wait, I see a triple blaze. Look at that row'a trees, havin' a slice off the east, west and south sides. They been marked special."

The young men turned to examine the marked trees. "Look at that, stretched out there, a quarter mile or more, all of 'em marked."

"And look at where you're standin'. Look at that little stake with them numbers. Likely somethin' important'd be goin' in here. But on south there ain't no blaze or no stakes."

"What're ya thinkin', that we maybe got here 'afore everything was gone?"

"Could be. Don't know why these places'd be passed over."

"That don't matter. Let's step up off one and see if it's been took."

Together their measured stride stepped off a half a mile.

"Should be findin' a stake close now."

"I see it! Over there! And in all that way, we didn't see no claim stake. See 'em on that other side, but them stakes ain't like ours. Don't matter none, a stake's a stake. 'Speck it'd be best to step the whole quarter section, just to make sure. Wouldn't want'a be laughed at by the town, tryin' to get somethin' someone else's done got. I'll get out the needle."

Chester stood at the numbered stake and looked both ways, his mind a seethe of thoughts.

It wasn't really often that a shocking new idea descended upon him, and the few times it had, it had turned out to be unworkable. This time, with the force of a shotgun blast, a realization penetrated his young skull.

"Doug...."

"Huh?"

"Stop and listen to me. Here we are lookin' at two quarter sections, as has been passed over by other folks and turned down. This here's land we couldn't even dream about on our best night. If'n it ain't wanted by others, why'n't couldn't it be ours?"

"Yeah, we was gonna...."

"NO! Listen to me. You and me, ours. We got our feet planted on what we'd be claimin' for the townsite, and there, yonder, lays one just as good, flat up agin the side'a this'n."

"You thinkin'...?"

"Yep, and it ain't too easy, tired like I am."

Chester rubbed his arms to even out the goosebumps of excitement playing along his skin. Didn't help.

"Just think about it. I know you're too young to sign fer a claim, and me bein' on the edge'a bein' too young, but this is a thing we ain't never gonna see again. We got the chance to do our duty to the town and have us a section, just you and me!"

"Just you and me? Not Pa?"

"'Member, Pa, he's put in for two of them town lots. 'Course if he wanted to live on our land, we'd likely let 'em. Maybe."

Douglas raised both hands to his head and scratched his scalp to ease the rippling tremors of excitement. "Just you and me...."

"Well, by rights, we ought'a let Manny in on it. If he hadn't'a been snagged by Pa to bring on the wagon, it'd been one'a us."

"Just you and me and Manny… a quarter section!"

"They's one catch to it."

"What'd that be?"

"I'd have to manage to meet up with someone from the town and put one'a these in his name and then put ours in my name. Can't one person have two quarter sections… I think."

"Couldn't ya just pick a name somewhere out'a the bunch'a them as come down?"

"Gonna have to think on that. Well, we got these claim stakes we brung that they give us. We'll just have to be stretchin' 'em out to cover both pieces."

"Just you and me and Manny…? We could…?"

"First off, we could string out these claim stakes. Good as these pieces'a land are, could be someone else'd be late like us, and nab 'em off us."

From Chester's pack came the strips of wood furnished by the town planners.

"Chet, break out the rifle. We fixin' to eat off our own land. Lookie through them trees at that grandpappy cottontail."

BANG!

Both young men were tense as bowstrings from nerves. It was frightening to move from Pa's oldest sons to two grown men expected to make decisions.

Didn't matter. Just keep on doin' what comes next, they told themselves.

Claim stakes strung out and pounded in the ground, a large rabbit roasted and eaten, Chester leaned back against a tree and sighed. "I'm gonna take me a little rest, then strike out over to Guthrie to file. Wake me up in a couple'a hours."

Twenty-Nine

Miles away, another young man was forced into a decision. Once made, it was easy to follow. A lot of steps would be necessary to take him to where he knew he must be.

Danny Dunbar, with Babe and Posey, moved across the rolling plains of Central Oklahoma like a planet moving through the sky, orbited by its own pair of satellites.

With him, the two dogs, fit and lean with hard muscles, circled and encouraged him, taking time out to hunt then to forge on ahead. When they were hungry, they seemed to find game. Occasionally they shared their meal with him.

Now that he was near the Unassigned Lands, Danny sought to settle on a plan… not particularly easy amid the swirl of his thoughts. Even combining the main parts of all four of his maps, he was still not able to get a satisfactory picture.

Finally, at the point of exasperation, his thoughts settled down into two plans, and he didn't like either one of them.

There was the shotgun approach, wherein he would move into whatever direction seemed best, asking around and looking for clues. Of course, that could mean that he would be looking for Roberta for the next six months or longer.

The other plan, possibly his favorite, would be to systematically canvas the new lands, feeling certain he would find her sooner or later, possibly in six months or less.

If he used the latter plan, he would start at the north end and head south. Surely they would settle on the first land they found, and it would likely be near the eastern border.

All four of his maps showed the northern river, Cimarron, and one to the south called Canadian. In between was a tributary called Deep Fork, and it seemed to be fairly long, circling around the rolling knolls and finally emptying into the Canadian. If he was to pick a point and decide it was accurate, it would be the Deep Fork.

If he followed Deep Fork before it joined the Canadian, it would lead him to the northern part of the Unassigned Land, and that would be the natural place to start.

The possible futility of this trip weighed heavily on his mind, and sometimes he was tempted to be angry with his father for making it necessary. Then, soft on the heels of the anger was the knowledge that he, himself, had allowed it to be done, feeling his family responsibilities so heavily.

Anyway, it did no good to be angry now. Just a waste of energy.

And this was good land. It was very different from the Tennessee mountains and even from the roughness of northern Missouri; still, it seemed good. From the top of one of the rolling knolls, one could stand and look and see maybe forever, until the trees got in the way. Many things could be done with this land.

His mind projected further.

The decision was made, and he would find Roberta if it took the rest of his life, and perhaps she would forgive him. Perhaps she had found no one else, and if so, there were things he could do, though a life without Roberts did not fit within the cockles of his mind.

He had money, and if it was not enough, he would work. They would settle in this new land among new people and would become a part of them, just as their own ancestors had done in the hill country.

Yes, it was easy to dream ahead as the April sun poured warmth around him, and the wide night sky was friendly with stars.

It was now the 20th of April, and he would not get there in time for the run, nor did he expect to.

Thirty

It was late in the afternoon of the 21st of April, and tomorrow was the day. Corporal Amos Kelvey and Private Jonathan McClain patrolled their stretch of the border with fierce protectiveness. They both had high stakes riding on this run.

The private had seen his girlfriend's brother waiting across the line and had been able to signal to him a bit of encouragement. It would not be seemingly for him to actually call a greeting, as he was on duty.

The corporal had an anxious moment but had, as a desperate measure, gone across the border on the pretext of making sure that everyone was following the rules. As he had looked about, he had seen his brother, James, asleep against the trunk of a tree. If he was asleep, then surely he needed his rest and did not need to be woken up. After all, his brother knew what his instructions were, and from here on in, their combined success depended on him.

He went back to his patrolling, relieved. He had stationed the private at the south end of their mile, and he had taken the north. As he went south, the private would come north and they would pass at the half-mile mark. In this way, they could show more presence, and if either of them was late at the midpoint, it would mean that there was some trouble, and the other one could come to his assistance.

Not that there would be any trouble. No one was going to go through their mile any sooner than the appointed time. Other patrollers could have trouble with their "sooners," but there would be none within their mile.

Thirty-One

It had been a wonderful day for Roberta. The icy sheet of reserve had been broken, and the other women and girls had talked and laughed as if they had been friends for years. Secrets and dreams were shared, recipes were traded and experiences recounted.

One young mother of three had laughingly taken some of the women to look under her trailer at the squirrel skins. There was hardly an inch of the underside of the wagon that was not covered with the golden pelts where her ten-year-old son had hammered them. He had in mind to dry them and have his mother make him a quilt or maybe a coat. If they could keep the squirrel warm, they could do the same for him.

Another had confided, fearfully, that she might be pregnant with her first baby, and how could she ever get through the ordeal without her mother? She had been laughingly told to look around her... and they asked how many mothers would she like to have. They would all be neighbors now, and all she had to do was call, and they would help.

Then, late in the day, Roberta had taken some of the meat and gone back to her wagon, knowing her father had missed the meal. Glancing into the Grasshopper, she saw him stretched out on his bed. Good. He needed his rest likely more than he needed food.

Now at the gray wagon, she still felt festive and excited. The party had given her a special energy. Searching down into her supplies, she reached the sack containing a dozen large, snow-white bars of lye soap. They were one of the gifts pressed onto her by Mae Fry back at Gator Creek, seemingly so many years ago! The whiteness of the soap fairly glistened ("How do you get your soap so white, Mae?" she'd asked. Mae had smiled modestly. "I reckon it'd be the strainin'. When it's getting' thick and close to set, I strain till nothin' hangs in the strainer. Then I use the dark soap that catched in the strainer for overhalls'n things."), and Roberta cut a sliver from one end of the bar of soap. She drew a bucket of water from the river. It was a bit cold, but she did not want to wait to heat it.

Into the bucket she dunked her head, then lathered her caramel red curls into a mountain of foam. The creamy bubbles next to her scalp tingled as they broke, giving her a feeling that she could just fly away. Parties were wonderful, and surely there would be more now that everyone had met.

Hair rinsed and dried, she rubbed out Alecia'a dresses and her own underthings and then went to the Grasshopper to get some of her father's things to take advantage of the leftover suds. He was still in bed. Strange.

As she gathered an armload of dirty shirts, he spoke.

"Bertie, lass, step in here beside me."

Roberta crawled into the wagon. "You not doin' too well, Papa?"

"Not well at all. Seems I took a tumble and pulled a couple'a ribs. I reckon it'll have me pretty well stove up for a while."

Roberta was concerned. "How'd you fall, Papa?"

"Oh, just trompin' around where I hadn't ought'a. I'll live. Only thing is, I'll not be able to ride tomorrow, and the run'll go on without me. Sure, and it's a disappointment, but there was a good chance I'd'a not made it anyway. We still got the other plan, that one bein' I'd work for someone. I figure there'll be plenty to be done everywhere."

Roberta looked into his face as he spoke, and disappointment showed in every line. There had always been the underlying knowledge that he might not get the land, but the thought that he might be successful had pulled him through the long, hard trip from Tennessee.

"Well, Papa, you just stay there, and I'll be back with meat for your supper. There was a lot to eat and we had fun. I'm gonna suds out some things."

Walking away from the Grasshopper, she felt the buoyant joy of the afternoon oozing from her like from a pinhole in a balloon, continuous and unstoppable. She, too, had been pulled forward with the excitement of a new land to plant and to till, to build on and to spend her life on. Poor Papa! Poor herself!

Later, with Eben's sprung ribs bound, Roberta went about straightening her wagon, her regular evening chore. Somehow, in the course of every day, things got in disarray. Tomorrow they would leave the camp, to go where…? Alecia would leave the new friends she had made over the last few days. Papa would…? What would Papa do? This trip had buoyed him up and put new life in him, and now it could all be lost. *What happened, God? We was so sure You was watching out for us?*

Finally, with the little girl asleep, Roberta crept from the gray wagon and walked around it, stepping into the light of the half moon. She could see the flutter of the banners on the border markers. In the distance, she saw the small fire made by the Cavalry officer. One man sat vigilantly beside it. The other one was probably not far away, guarding another part of the line. Well, after tomorrow, they would get to rest a while. No matter which way the fate of the runners turned, their work would be done.

Sleep refused to come to her, so she went to the front of the wagon and climbed up onto the wooden tongue to look around. The horses were close, and occasional snorting and stomping told of mosquitoes and other night things pestering them.

In the pale light, she could see Dancer, head raised, looking toward her. Roberta went to the filly and stroked her face, cupping the velvet chin in her hand. "Too bad, Dancer. You'd'a liked that run, but you ain't gonna get to go. I know you're gonna want to, but you just…" Her whispered voice trailed off. Dancer nodded her head and blew her breath conversationally.

Maybe. Why not? What would be lost?

Moving quietly to the Grasshopper, she reached in and took one of her father's shirts and a pair of overalls. In the light of the moon, she slipped on the shirt and buttoned it up, then stepped into the overall legs. Fastening the buckle on the gallowses, she looked down at herself. Hmmmm… maybe….

A voice from inside the wagon, though spoken softly, startled her.

"Lass…?"

"Papa! I didn't…."

"Bertie, lass," he interrupted. "If you're thinkin' you're gonna fool someone into thinkin' you're a boy, you're gonna have to wrap somethin' around your midsection to even things out a bit."

"Oh, Papa, I don't think…."

"Sure, and folks do what they do. I done what I done, and I'm layin' here, all stove up. Now, you'll do what you do, and that could be goin' on with my plan, or that could mean you go off on your own. You're a woman, grown, and back on the mountain I said I was doin' the last thing I was a'gonna do to you. That bein' to make you come to this place. Now, you and me are equals, and you'll do what you think best."

"Papa…."

"You hear me, lass. Don't you let nothin' I ever said keep you from doin' what you think you ought'a do. But I'm sayin' agin, you better think on changin' your shape if you're thinkin' to fool anyone."

Roberta blushed in the moonlight. Papa had a point.

"'Speck you'll be needin' my straw hat, too. No, if'n you'd take that canvas slouch hat, it'd come down farther on your face. It's right down there at the end, a'hangin' up, and you take it and see what you can do. Now git on out and don't keep me awake no more."

"Aw, Papa, you really think I could…?"

"Ain't never gonna know less'n you try, huh?"

"Good night, Papa."

"Good night, lass."

Roberta sorted quietly through the plunder for the tea towels. They would be just about right. She tried binding three towels around her middle, pinning the ends. Not bad. However, there was still a lot of room inside the overalls. Two more towels would make her look chubby, and that would be good.

The top button of the shirt still allowed the neck of the shirt to hang limply, showing a lot of her neck and beardless chin. Rummaging again, she brought up a scarf of shiny red material that she used to tie up her hair in the winter after it was washed. Winding it twice around her throat, she tied it in a loose bow, tucking the ends into her collar. Good. That helped to take up the extra space in the neck of the shirt.

The slouch hat pulled down snugly over her ears, and the floppy brim hung down even lower, so she could barely see out. Good. If she could barely see out, others could barely see in.

Quietly removing her costume, she folded the pieces together and set them aside, then crawled into the bed with Alecia and went promptly to sleep.

Then it was the 22nd of April, and the Oklahoma sun beamed warmly between the treetops.

Roberta went about her duties of making food. Her father was able to sit up, but any other movement caused great discomfort. It was clear he was not going to be able to make the run.

Near noon, she cleared away the remains of the camp, packing it into the wagons as she had so many times over the past two months.

She spent a while with Dancer, reassuring herself as well as the horse. It had been a long time since Roberta had ridden on a straddle saddle.

"Dancer, you and me, we'll have to take it slow, now. You wouldn't want'a bump me off, would you?"

The horse nuzzled her velvety face along Roberta's jaw. She was really such a friendly little thing.

When others began readying their mounts, Roberta swung the saddle onto Dancer's back, causing the animal's skin to ripple with excitement. Pull the cinches tight, her father had warned. Dancer didn't like them to be tight, and drew in her breath. Roberta held the cinch buckle and waited until the horse was forced to breath, and quickly caught up the slack.

No one looked her way. Everyone had better things to do than to be nosy right now. She'd wait a while before she put on her costume. If she only had a dress with a skirt full enough to retain her modesty, she would dispense with the deception and go as a girl. But she didn't have such a dress.

At eleven o'clock, some riders were already pulling into line, and she sent Alecia to stay with her grandfather.

"You stay with Big Papa 'cause he don't feel good, and he may need you to get something for 'im. Then I want you to lay down on his bed and take a nap, because I got things to do and can't be watching you."

Disappointment showed on the girl's face. Still, it was an important job to take care of one's ailing grandfather. "I'll take my color book and make a him picture."

"You may take your color book if you promise to keep it hid so no one but Big Papa can see it."

"I promise."

It was eleven-thirty, and the corporal was pacing nervously behind the banners. Roberta slipped into the wagon and put on the overalls and shirt. Braiding her hair tightly, she wadded it into a bun and pinned it to the top of her head. The slouch hat pulled low on her forehead and its floppy brim barely cleared her eyebrows.

It was eleven-forty-five, and she stepped quickly from the wagon, swinging herself up into the saddle. What a strange feel it was as the horse walked. She tried to adjust herself to the movement of Dancer's gait.

It was five minutes until twelve, and the Cavalry officer galloped along the line, holding his pistol high. He shouted as he passed, "You will soon hear a gun. Do not run until MY gun goes off. No one will run until MY gun sounds."

Then, in the distance, they heard the faint report of the gunshot. It was instantly followed by another shot, another and another. Then, not more than a quarter of a mile away, they heard another shot, and it must have come from the private's gun.

Instantly, the corporal's shot rang out, and a thin trail of smoke left the muzzle of the gun.

"GO!" he shouted, as though the sound of his gun might not be encouragement enough.

Dancer shied slightly at the sound of the gun, but as the other animals plunged forward, she was eager to join them. She started on with such suddenness, Roberta was forced to lean forward over the saddle horn simply to hang on.

Thirty-Two

Moving as one, the line surged forward.

There was Edward Brown from Missouri on the back of his fastest horse. Behind him, his excited family shouted encouragement, his older sons, ages seven and nine, running after him in their excitement until their mother called them back.

Josh Pettingill turned at the last moment to wave to Dollie, his six-year-old daughter, and allowed a black stallion cut in front of him. "GO! GO! GO!" commanded Dollie's mother, so Josh turned and thundered away.

Cassie Stanfield shouted encouragement to her fourteen-year-old son, who was the oldest of her children. Cassie's husband had been killed two weeks ago, and she wasn't telling how, but she was determined to get the new land. She would have ridden herself, except for her highly pregnant condition, so she stayed in camp with her three other children, leaving the riding to her son, Raymond. He leaned into the wind and guided the horse with his knees, urging him to go faster.

Baxter, the camp peacemaker, rode out with no cheering section behind him. His family was safely parked back in Arkansas.

Maynard Simpson, a crotchety old bachelor, rode a mule, loaded with all his earthly possessions and his own bulky self. The mule, under its load, finally disappeared into the trees.

There were a number of single riders, and several who tried to take their buggies over the rough and rutted ground, only to give up and begin to run on foot.

The Cavalry private, Jonathan McClain, was able to wave to his girlfriend's brother, David, as he headed up the creek, per instructions.

The newlyweds left their horses tied and stood side by side at the line, their claim stakes in their hands. At the sound of the gun, they calmly stepped over the line and drove their stakes into the Oklahoma soil. Then, their own claim secured, they settled back to watch the show.

Roberta had not had a chance to decide on a plan. Until yesterday, Papa had been the one, and only since midnight had she been for certain sure that she would try it. What could she lose? With her own success tied to Dancer's, she had struck out.

James Kelvey, brother to the corporal, feeling some better after he was rested, urged his horse, who was not rested, on to greater speed. He looked around him as his brother had instructed him to do. Certainly, he and his brother would get one quarter section, but if he was able to play his cards right, they might get two, one for each of them.

He was to look for someone young, maybe who might have other family members along who could furnish another name. Now, how in the mad tarnation was he to determine all that with men and horses galloping in every direction? Better he forget his brother's greedy idea and head out in the direction he needed to go.

Dancer the friendly had become somewhat acquainted with the horse ridden by James Kelvey, and they had blown conversationally to each other during the night. They had flopped rubbery lips in a horsey raspberry and waved their heads. In fact, they had gotten on well, amusing each other in the light of the moon.

And now, Dancer saw her friend of last night as he trotted down the edge of Deep Fork River. She trotted rapidly after him, her rider hanging on as best she could.

James scanned the brushy forest for the landmark. Sycamores, a grove of them, would be growing in a small creek. As he spotted the sycamores ahead, he decided to make one last effort at finding a buddy (he really would need someone to help guard against claim jumpers while he made the trip to Guthrie), and he turned to see who was following.

Behind him was a little red-brown filly being ridden by a short, somewhat chubby boy in a shirt that was much too big. No one else was close, so if he was going to pick someone to help, it would have to be this young man. He pulled his horse back for a second to allow the filly to catch up and also to size up the boy.

Hmmm, there was something uncommon about that boy, the way he held himself and the way he rode. Suspicious. That boy was going to have to develop a more manly attitude, or he was going to have a hard life.

"Hey, fellow!"

The brim of the slouch hat lifted, slightly.

"Name's James Kelvey. What's yours?"

"Uh... Rob. My name's Rob Carlile."

Bad voice, too, for a fellow, but James didn't need someone with a good voice. He only needed a name.

"Got a idea where you're goin'?"

"Not yet," came the answer. "Just lookin'."

Roberta had managed to pick up the rhythm of Dancer's gait and no longer had to lean forward. The riding experience of her childhood was filtering back after so many years.

"I got a line on a good tract, and I can help someone in return for a little help to me."

Roberta glanced sideways at this man. Did she actually look like she could be of help to anyone?

He continued, "See up ahead at them sycamores? That'll be where we turn. You got anyone back in camp waitin'?"

"Uh... well...."

"I mean someone who's over twenty one and isn't running. Wife, mother, someone?"

"I got a Papa and a little girl is all."

Little girl! Why this boy couldn't possibly... oops! What was wrong with his brain! One look at those hands and the way they held the reins... and at the tilt of the chin when he turned his head. That was no boy! Maybe, even better than a boy!

"We got'a turn here," he instructed. "Now look way up ahead, where you see the blaze in that blackjack. I'm a'gonna take off runnin' fast, and you follow, close as you can. Don't you lose sight'a me and I can do you a big favor."

Favor! A man could do her a favor! What a thought! But there he was, galloping away, and how dangerous could he be on a galloping horse? Not only that, she could use a favor. If he was telling the truth.

"Come on, Dancer!" Roberta bravely gouged her knees into Dancer's shoulders.

The man on the horse was flying through the trees, dodging this way and that, and she momentarily lost him. "Come on, Dancer!" Dancer answered the challenge.

Then she saw him again. He had wheeled around and seen her, then raced off again. What in the world was going on?

They must have galloped three miles, at least, and she knew she was totally lost if she did not manage to keep up with this man who seemed to know where he was going. Dancer was now wrapped up in the game and was dodging trees and jumping ditches, determined to catch up with her new friend of the night.

Each time Roberta glanced up, there was a newly blazed tree, its white, inner wood showing. Then she saw the man (James?) stop and wait as Dancer galloped to catch up. When she had almost reached him, he wheeled and cut into the trees, and Dancer spun around and followed.

Roberta had quit wondering what was going on and was concentrating on trying to stay on the horse. After a mile, the man and horse stopped. Dancer pulled up beside them.

"Rob? This is it, and I'll be quick. See this row'a blazed trees? There's three claims here in a row. I want a name to hold one for my brother who couldn't be in the run. He'll pay money to someone to do it, and maybe it could be you? Or your pa?"

Roberta looked at the trees and the ground and the row of little stakes with a fancy number painted on them.

"Don't you worry about them numbers. They don't mean a thing, and they're just to fool someone into thinkin' they're taken. Nuther thing, you didn't fool me for long, and I know you ain't no boy."

Roberta looked up, startled.

"It's all right. I ain't out to hurt no one. All I want is a name. My brother, he's in the Cavalry, and he can't qualify for land. He pointed me to these and said, for the use of a name, he'd pay a hundred dollars now and another hundred when he could get the land in his name. Will you do it, Rob…? What's your real name?"

"Roberta."

"Will you? I need to know so if you won't, I can find someone else."

"What you're sayin' is I can have a claim right here and a hundred dollars for the use'a my papa's name?"

"Right. Where is your pa? How come he wasn't the one to run?"

"He got hisself hurt yesterday. A fall or somethin'. I didn't see it happen."

"A fall…?"

"I think maybe he slipped and fell in the river by the look'a the mud on his clothes."

"Fell in the river, huh? I fished a fellow out'a the river late yesterday. Seemed like some kind of a party was goin' on, but I was too tired to care. Heard the fellow call, and I threwed 'im a line and fished 'im out."

Roberta stared at the man, absorbing the knowledge that this man had possibly saved her father's life. The irony of it was not missed by James, and he grinned mischievously.

"Well, Miss Roberta, I think maybe you owe me the use'a your pa's name. I got a feelin' he'll not object neither."

While she hesitated, he continued, "Likely we ought'a go back to the line and bring your pa here. 'Cause I'll be goin' on over to Guthrie Station to the land office and file, and I'll need his permission to declare for him. But first, we'll get these claim stakes pounded in. I'm half afraid to leave… even for a minute."

Roberta nodded. "I can stay. I know what everyone said about claim jumpers gonna be a problem. I'll stay, 'cause I might not know exactly the way back to the line, bein' I wasn't really lookin' side to side. Dancer ain't what you'd call a real easy horse to guide."

"Well, you wouldn't be afraid here?"

"No more'n any place else. The green wagon'd be my papa."

James Kelvey had hardly gone when two young men appeared from among the trees. At the sight of Roberta, one held his rifle where it could be plainly seen.

"Don't you go no further, or I'll be forced to level this here gun at you."

The threat of the gun was backed up by a pair of efficient-looking fists, doubled and held chin-high.

"Don't shoot," Roberta called in her obviously feminine voice.

Eyes widened, mouths flew open, and the gun was lowered.

"You're a… girl?"

Roberta looked down, remembering her costume. The rolled up shirt sleeves had begun to unroll, the baggy overalls hung here and there below her round belly, compliments of several tea towels. She took off the slouch hat, revealing caramel braids over the top of her head.

"Excuse us, miss… We wasn't knowin' it weren't a claim jumper, like folks said'd be by. We was late a'gettin' to the run, but we found two places here that wasn't took. We seen the markers you put along there but we didn't see no one."

Roberta nodded. These young men must be her neighbors, but she didn't remember them from the camp. Of course, there were many camps like theirs all up and down the line.

"Pleased to meet you. I'm Roberta Carlile."

"Kendall's the name. I'm Chester and that's my brother, Douglas. Pardon my sayin' so, but you don't seem to have no gun. I was a'fixin' to cut out toward Guthrie, but my brother, he'll be here and have this gun, and he's a good shot. You wouldn't want no body to get that good place you got. I'm cuttin' out, but you see trouble anywheres here about, you yell, and he'll see to you."

At that, Chester ceremoniously surrendered the gun to his brother and was handed the small, round compass. Douglas shouldered the gun and nodded assurance toward Roberta. "Yes miss, you just yell."

With that, the brother began a march down the row of claim stakes, whistling a tune. Roberta stood alone among the trees and looked this way and that. The birds sang overhead and small lizards scooted here and there. A butterfly lit on an orange tuberose flower and worked his way through the cluster of tiny blossoms.

Was it really over? The run? The activity that had consumed her thoughts for two months and 500 miles? It had been less than two hours ago that she had hesitantly, fearfully donned the ridiculous garb she now wore. It couldn't be over, and she couldn't be standing on what would be her own land. Dancer munched contentedly on the grass clumps, not caring who they belonged to.

Her land. Her's and Papa's. It was what he wanted for her and what he brought her here to get. It was a place for Alecia to grow up. It was a whole quarter section. The young men she had just met would be neighbors. It was all too much to comprehend.

She sat down on a small flat rock, resting her chin in her hand. It really couldn't be possible that it was all over so quickly and the land would be hers. It had to be God's doing. *Why, of course it was! Thank you, God!*

She was still sitting there when the young man with the gun (Douglas Somebody?) came back, stomping through the trees and whistling.

"Hello, miss…?"

"I'm here."

"Oh, there you are. I wasn't lookin' for you to be sittin' down. I was scared somebody'd come by and… Pardon my sayin', but are you gonna have people come to help you?"

"Oh, yes, and I think that must be them, now."

It had been a bit slow going, bringing the wagons through the trees. The gray wagon led the way with James's horse tethered. The Grasshopper followed on, the buggy wheels humping and rolling over rocks and dead limbs.

Both James and Papa eyed the young man with the gun.

"Papa?"

"My name's Kendall, mister. Pleased to meet ya." The square, calloused palm shot out to each of the older men in turn. "And you, too, young lady."

Alecia giggled and hid her hands behind her back.

James Kelvey wrote down the information he needed to have in order to declare the tracts. With a wave, he was off, hoping to make it to the city before the land office would be closed. Maybe it would stay open all night, and he could get on back.

Eben looked at his daughter and opened his arms. Roberta walked into them. "Oh, Papa, we're here. You did the right thing. I was scared for a while, but you did the right thing."

He had no words, only a wide smile. And a lot of heartfelt nods.

Then there were the horses to attend to, and Eben loosed them from the wagons, tying them to a tree. From the Grasshopper, he took the 150-foot roll of barbed wire he had picked up at Fort Smith and strung it around several trees. Stapling it securely to the tree bark, he created the first corral.

"Got us a way to keep the animals from wanderin' all over the place, come dark."

Roberta nodded and sighed. Folks got hungry, and there was always a meal just ahead. She began to look for a good place to set up her grill and oven. Dry wood a'plenty lay all about. There'd be no looking for firewood for a while.

Eben rummaged around in the Grasshopper and located plow shafts and points, and the can of bolts needed to hold the plow together. He set out the box containing the seeds. It would be too late for some things, but if he could find a bit of sun in amongst these trees, he'd get in a row or two of beans, some tomatoes. Turnips would be good; they grew fast. Corn would have to wait, as would a number of other things. He would be too busy to tend to much garden if he expected to get a solid, dry roof over their heads before cold weather.

Roberta wandered over to see what he was doing.

"That plow...? Papa, your ribs...?"

"Bertie, lass, it's only pain. There ain't no break nor splinters to punch through a lung. All it'll be is the hurtin' muscles, and if it gets too bad, I'll get you to bind me up tighter. The Good Lord give us this good land, but here it is almost May, and I ain't figurin' that He'll be wantin' to add on a few extra summer growin' months. I'll plow a few rows in amongst these roots, and afore anything comes up, I'll have these here trees down to let the sun come in on 'em. Gonna be needin' them trees for a cabin."

"Papa...?"

"What, lass?"

"You plantin' taters?"

He shook his head. "Them's one of the things that'll have to wait. I didn't put in no seed taters."

"I got a plan. Them taters Mae Fry gave us, they've done gone to sproutin'. I could chop deep around them eyes when I peel, and chances are they'll grow. Soak 'em, maybe? You think?"

"That'd be good, lass. Go careful with the water. We ain't knowin' yet how far it'll be to get it 'afore we get our well dug."

Thirty-Three

The two members of the 5th Cavalry relaxed under a redbud tree after the tensions of the morning.

128

"Seems like we got through with no 'sooners' a'plungin' through ahead'a the gun. Seems we didn't hear'a nobody else that didn't have no trouble when we was back at the garrison at Taylor Springs." The private chuckled at the prospect of getting to brag to the others that they had no trouble at all, and their section had been guarded securely.

The corporal nodded. "Seems like we pulled through without havin' to use the handcuffs. What I'm thinkin' is it wouldn't hurt to go ridin' through the first few tracks, checkin' just to make sure.

Jonathan McClain, the private, knew what the checking would consist of. The corporal wanted to see if, indeed, his brother had been successful in getting two lots. The private also knew that, no matter how friendly they had become, it was not the best thing for a private to point out that a corporal was doing something solely out of selfish curiosity.

"Reckon that'd be a good thing, to check things out and be sure. We could patrol a way, just to be sure 'afore we started to brag."

Down the blazed trail they went, looking both ways. A lot of activity was going on, both to the east and west of them, and when they reached the triple blazed row of trees, they turned west. Following along the line, they saw a young man patrolling what was obviously his new claim. His gun was against his shoulder as he marched, and a merry tune came whistling through his teeth.

Amos Kelvey turned his horse to go toward the young man, and he saw the remains of the fire. Dismounting, he touched the ashes. Cold. The remains of a rabbit were tossed away nearby. Hmmmm.

"Hey, fellow!"

"Yes, sir, mister."

"This your fire?"

"Mine and my brother's, yes, sir. We got here hungry and shot us a rabbit here on our own claim."

"When did you get here?"

"Not long. We ain't been here no time, hardly. Got us a late start. You thinkin' they's somethin' wrong?"

Amos studied the cold ashes. Up to now, he had a perfect record on keeping out the "sooners," those who slipped in ahead of time. Like the private had said, it would be fun to brag, because it seemed most of the officers had been practically run ragged, chasing down those runners that they had let slip past them. When caught, the "sooners" had to be taken prisoner, and they were not allowed to participate in

129

the run when the actual time came. It was bad, too, because some of them had families here. Of course, they shouldn't have tried to slip through. The rules had been well posted. He felt bad for those folks, but he was, however, a Cavalry officer with a job and a duty.

The private watched him silently, as a private should.

"Fellow, you know what a 'sooner' is?"

"Yes, sir, mister. They told us at the line. If'n we was to get in ahead'a the gun, we'd not get us no chance at land a'tall. We was careful, my brother and me, and we stood on that Kansas line till the shot came, clear and loud. We wouldn't'a done no jumpin' the gun. They was trustin' us not to mess up."

"Who was trustin' you?"

"The town. We was part'a the ones to get to pick the town site. We think this'n here'd be the best; 'course, they's others that might'a done better. My brother, he's gone to Guthrie to sign up."

Amos Kelvey stroked his whiskered chin as he pondered. A town site, huh? Right next to his property, or his and James's if his brother...? Hmmmm. Cold ashes. Brother gone. It didn't sound good.

"You're... sure...?"

"Oh, yes, sir, mister. There weren't no doubt on that, us used to hearin' guns since we was in diapers, we wouldn't be makin' no mistake. And I'd not mind a'tellin' ya, sir, that we wasn't sooner'n nobody. We kind'a played a trick on ourselves, seems like."

"How was that?"

"Well, here we was, thinkin' we was as fast'a walker as most and faster'n some, and this bein' so wooded, like it said on the sheet, we was thinkin' we'd walk and not bother with horses.

"Well, we must'a misfigured, someway, and got behind. Turned out we had'a walk at night two times just to get here on time, and then we was still late. Would'a been worse'n that if there hadn't'a been a moon. Time we got here, we was mighty nigh a'runnin', scared we wasn't gonna get nothin'. We saw them tracts across the way already staked, and we looked nd there wasn't no stake on these. Couldn't'a thought why they'd'a been missed, but we sure was glad. We hadn't even stopped to eat, and there was that rabbit right here on our own land."

Amos looked at the wide smile on the young man and at the cold ashes and the remains of the rabbit.

And thought of a nearby town site. He made a decision in the only direction his mind would permit him. Those ashes were likely not as cold as he had thought, and how long does it take a clever young man to shoot and cook a rabbit? And these young men would be his neighbors.

He looked around and commented. "Looks like a good piece'a land. Glad to find you weren't a sooner."

"Oh, we wouldn't'a jumped the gun. Our pa, he wouldn't hold with us goin' up agin the law. No way!"

Amos did not look at the private as they directed the horses on up the line of blazed trees. Their record was still intact, and they still had bragging rights. Anyway, how cold could ashes be on a warm April day?

His breath came thready with anxiety as he neared the two wagons setting among the trees.

"You folks doin' alright?"

Eben stepped down from the wagon slowly to favor his sore ribs. "Doin' right well, officer. I was gettin' out my plow points to put together a plow. Aim to break ground tomorrow."

"You folks stake this claim?"

"Yes, sir. Truth to be told, this'n belongs to my daughter. That'd be her, back at the cookin' fire. I lay claim to a section farther on down. I aimed to get my daughter's improvement started and then move on down to mine. We doin' anything wrong?"

"How about registerin' your claim? You took care'a that?"

"Oh, yes, sir. Young fellow on the claim west'a us, he's filin' a declaration right now. He was tellin' us how that'd give us a day or two to settle in 'afore we had to validate it. He was tellin' us it wasn't safe to leave a claim on account'a jumpers."

"He was right. You folks got yerselves a gun?"

"Yes, sir. Got three of 'em. I'm a good shot, and my daughter, she's right fair. 'Course there's that young fellow across the way. I'd be willin' to bet he knows how to use a gun."

The Cavalry man in the sharp-looking blue suit smiled and nodded. "Seems you got things well in hand. Good day."

"Good day, sir."

Eben watched him leave, then bent to his work.

Amos Kelvey felt his heart quicken. James had been successful. The plowing would being done on what would be his land in eighteen months, on the date his current enlistment ran out.

As they moved on through the trees, the private found the courage to comment, "We was both of us lucky, wasn't we?"

It didn't matter that there was no answer.

Thirty-Four

The sun was low in his eyes as Chester Kendall pushed himself to go on. A horse would be handy now, and maybe there was someone in the town who could let him have one for the return trip. All day, most of the night, and all day again with only a couple of hours of sleep was just about to do him in.

He blinked his tired eyes and studied the compass. Where was the town of Guthrie? He knew the miles, if the map was right, and he knew the direction. Sooner or later he would be there. One foot, then another, and he leaned forward from weariness.

A little stream flowed nearby, and he veered from his beeline march to wet his face with cold water and maybe wake up a little bit. Oh, how he'd love to sit down in the shade for maybe five minutes. NO, he would not stop!

Kneeling at the edge of the water, he scooped up a handful, splashing it against his face. He took off his straw hat and sloshed his hair and the back of his neck. The bracing coolness of it made him feel better already. He was hungry, but with no gun, there was nothing that could be done about that.

As he climbed up the bank, he saw a patch of wild turnips. Pulling three, he swished them in the stream and went away, gnawing at their peppery globes. It was when he tossed away the green top of the last turnip that it hit him full-force.

He had his own land. He and his brothers indeed had their own land. Until now, it had not been possible to absorb the enormity of it, but now, after the refreshing splash and the spicy turnip, the realization was kicking in.

With land, one could do many things. They could farm it. They could raise cattle and maybe have a dairy. They could... Chester stopped, his left foot in midair as his whole future downloaded into his brain. The Kendall brothers would go into the freighting business.

What with the new territory and everything so raw, there would be more freighting than anyone could ever attend to. Just look around! Everybody needed everything!

They'd need a name. Kendall Brothers, Freighters. Kendall Haulers. Kendall, Heavy Hauling.

They'd need the whole section of land to quarter and care for the excellent horses they would breed and raise. There would be heavy Percherons and Clydesdales, as well as lighter breeds. They would have wagons and sleds. Anything that needed moving, they, the Kendall Brothers, would do it.

Breathing deeply and stepping quickly, he broke into the clearing and saw a sea of tents and covered wagons right where the Guthrie land office should be. Crowds of people swarmed about. Salesmen with everything from land to food to newspapers shouted their wares. How could he see the land office for the milling mass of people?

Well, he'd just have to add his own body to the mix and start looking. Weariness was put behind him, and apprehension took over in its place. There wasn't a whole lot of day left. Something to eat would be nice, but one look at the prices made him leave his coins in his pocket. He had a use for that money, for Kendall Brothers, whatever name it turned out to be.

He saw people in line for this and in line for that, and one line seemed to be going his direction. He began to follow along, as it seemed to be going in the general direction he was aimed. Someone would know where the land office was, and he'd just start asking.

He heard his name called, and he startled around.

"CHET! CHET KENDALL!"

It seemed to be a familiar voice… a woman's voice? A girl's voice…? A familiar voice?

"Chester!"

He located the owner of the voice. "Ellie Gunther! What're you doin' in that line?"

"They got me markin' a place. I been standin' here all day, creepin' forward. Done been to the front twice."

"Couldn't get no service?"

"Didn't have no claim. Ma and Margie, they been spellin' me. We got Wayne on up to the front."

"Wayne! He ain't but twelve years old! He can't do nothin'."

"Neither can I, but we can hold a place for whoever comes in first."

"Nobody from the town here yet?"

Ellie grinned her dimpled grin, which totally decorated her fifteen-year-old face. "'Course not, silly. Else I wouldn't'a had to be standin' here, getting' a cramp in my legs."

"I'm the first?"

"Yep."

"Anybody here over 21?"

"Only Ma."

"Whereat is she?"

"Wagon. Got it parked up in that row. The town said we was to leave it there to be the headquarters. Ma's there."

"I need to see 'er. Bye, Ellie."

Chester followed the pointing finger and found the wagon row and also the Gunther wagon.

"Miz Gunther? Hey, I got'a see you about somethin'. I'm needin' some help to hold my tract, someone over 21."

"Chet! You made it back!"

"Yeah, and I need help fast, like I said. I'm needin' a body over 21 to sign for the town site."

"Reckon that'd be me. But likely they'd let you, bein' only days from 21 yourself."

"No, Miz Gunther. I got my own, and you need to sign for the town."

"You got two!"

"Yeah, and Doug, he's back guardin' 'em. Let's hurry."

"Come on. Seem's it'd be Wayne farther up the line that'd have the best place. That'll cut down a heap'a waitin', and we'll take his place. You got two claims, fer sure?"

"Sure as I stand here. Got the stakes right here. I'm wantin' to get signed and get headed back. Doug'll likely need help with the guardin'."

Wayne was indeed near the front of the snakey line of exhausted runners. At the end of an impossibly long day, they were waiting in an impossibly long line. The excited Wayne bounced around in his excitement.

"Is it far? Is it a good'n? Trees? When can we go, Ma?"

"Hush up an let me think."

Then they were at the front of the line.

"Name?"

"Nettie Gunther."

"Over 21?"

"Law, yeah."

"Sign here, Mrs. Gunther."

Nettie signed and picked up the list of printed requirements.

"Next?"

Chester stepped up.

"Name?"

"Kendall Brothers." He figured that would be safe, whatever they decided to do.

"Over 21?"

Chester grinned slightly through his tiredness. Why, sure they were over 21. In a few days, he would be 21 all by himself, and all together they were closer to 50!

"Sure are, mister."

"Sign here, Mister Brothers."

"Huh?"

"Ain't your name Brothers?" The clerk had experienced a long, hot day facing this endless line, and it was not odd, actually, that his hearing was failing.

"Name's Kendall. Chester Kendall, like I said."

"Sign here, Mr. Kendall."

Chester signed, picked up the sheet, and followed the Gunther family back to the wagon.

"You ain't waitin' in line no more?"

"What for? We got us a place!"

"But the others...?"

"Don't matter about them. All we was needin' was one and we got it. The rest of 'em can stand in their own line," Ellie decided callously.

Nettie Gunther advised, "Now, Chet, you'd be needin' to rest a mite 'afore you trek back. Dark comin' on 'n you in a strange place; chance you'd get lost."

"Naw, Doug, he's back there alone. I got'a go."

"Well, leastwise, you'll be eatin' somethin'. We got beans cooked in bacon, keepin' it ready for whoever comes in. Got a little cornbread but it's cold."

"Cold don't matter to me. Sounds good."

Nettie handed him a bowl and a spoon. "This here is the beatinest place for not havin' food. I could'a sold that pot'a beans a hunnerd times over. You eat up, son."

Chester filled the bowl with food and devoured it, intending to have seconds, but when he leaned against the bedding in the wagon, his eyes closed. Ellie reached out to toward him to wake him.

"Back off and let 'im be," Nettie instructed. "Plum tuckered out, but he got us a place to put the town in. You youngens quiet down and let 'im sleep."

Thirty-Five

Danny Dunbar followed the Deep Fork until he reached the Indian Meridian. There were signs of a lot of people having been there, but all that was left was six wagons populated by women and children. Also near the camp were the newlyweds who had staked out the claim immediately over the line. They were still trying to decide on the best place to put their cabin but making very little headway as they spent a lot of time noticing each other.

Danny asked about the Carliles. A young woman with a little girl and an older man. A caravan of two wagons and a buggy. A green covered wagon.

No, no one could remember anything that looked like that. You see, fellow, there were so many folks, there was no way to get a clear look at anybody. You know how it is.

As Danny walked away, they looked at each other and nodded. They did the right thing. Maybe that pretty young lady in the green wagon wanted that young man to know where she was, and maybe she didn't. There were more than a few in the camp who would just as soon not be known.

The first plan that came to Danny's mind was to criss-cross the tracts, asking everyone for information. He should have remembered from the hill country that correct information was seldom acquired from strangers and that he may have just as well saved his breath to cool his broth.

In addition to that, it was not surprising the settlers were so antsy with strangers after the warnings they had about claim jumpers. Any slight movement brought out a rifle. After facing down the first two, Danny began to approach the campsites with both hands lifted, calling, "Hello. I'm a friend, just passin' through."

Even then, he was never welcomed. Well, there was another way.

Securing permission to sleep the night at one campsite, he arose early and headed for the land office at Guthrie. If they had managed to get a claim, he could trace them that way. If not, he could headquarter out of Guthrie to do his looking. If it meant he spent the summer looking, so be it. Also the winter, if necessary.

Picturing Guthrie as a station with a few official buildings and a few campsites, he was overwhelmed to see, at a distance, its rolling knolls spread with white tents appearing to be a cupful of large, white dice tossed across the landscape.

A "hotel" had been set up, consisting of 200 tents, each with four bedrolls. Several of the tents were kitchens where a meal could be had for fifty cents. They were doing a very good business.

The bank and the post office were in tents. Several lawyers worked out of wagons or tents, and a brisk business was going on in the selling and re-selling of lots. Due to the fact of two surveying companies working over the same town, many lots were registered to two parties and many were sold by those who did not own them. Lawyers were also doing very good business.

Two things were in short supply: food and water. Especially water. Thirsty crowds soon drank up the water in the tower that had been meant for the locomotives on the Santa Fe Railroad, and those with containers were hauling water from nearby Cottonwood Creek, selling the muddy liquid for a nickel a cup as fast as they could haul it.

The locomotives that had brought boxcar-loads of people into the territory left and returned with the same cars loaded with building material. Lumber was sold by the board and used as a frame for a shelter made of cardboard boxes, if they could only find the boxes. Cloth tents were constructed in wagon beds using sheets and blankets.

And the noise! Angry fights broke out over boundaries and animal food, over water and building material. Business was conducted on the street as there was no other place to conduct it, and the way to be heard was to shout louder than anyone else.

Lines were everywhere. People were quick to join any queue because whatever was being sold was surely something they needed or something to trade for what they needed. One wagon contained a small wood-burning cookstove, its chimney belching smoke out across the crowd. There were no complaints, however, because, for a nickel, one could buy a generous cup of brown beans, temptingly flavored with bacon grease. It was well if the buyer had his own bowl, however, as the bowls belonging to the bean seller had limited rental. Any beans not eaten at the end of five minutes were forfeited so the bowl could be rinsed and rented to the next customer. Most buyers were able to eat in the prescribed length of time, and if not, plenty of help was available.

Danny Dunbar had his own bowl, so he could eat in leisure, crumbling the single piece of cornbread into the broth of the beans.

Walking about in the crowd with two horses and two dogs brought a fair amount of scowls his way, but Danny paid them no mind. It was after dark that he found the land office, and the tired clerks had gone home. Six men stood in line, waiting for morning, and Danny joined them.

The horses and the dogs presented a small problem. Every one of the animals needed to be fed. Every blade of grass had been tromped down long ago, and every rabbit had been eaten or scared away.

Danny stood in the line, watching the men in front of him. They were exhausted and footsore, sitting on the ground. Shoes were off, and aching fingers massaged weary feet.

"Fellows?"

Drooping eyes looked up into his.

"Fellows? I got a deal to offer. I got me these animals that's got'a be fed and watered, and I see you are all dead tired. If'n one of you, or all six, could see your way to hold me a place till I tend to my livestock, I'll be back and stand watch so's you fellows could get some sleep. I ain't that tired."

A moment passed. "How'd we know we could trust you?"

"You thinkin' you can stay awake all night, tired as you are?"

"Ya got a point. I'll do it."

"Me, too."

"Thanks, men. I'll be right back."

He wasn't right back. It took over an hour before he located a wagon with a load of corn, selling it whole kernel or chopped. Ten cents a cup full. A woman stood at a stove beside the wagon making pans of cornbread… twenty-five cents for a skillet full.

Danny sighed, knowing he could do no better, and bought a skillet of bread for himself and the dogs, retaining one piece for his breakfast, and four cups of corn for the horses.

"Sorry, girls, but that'll have to hold you for tonight."

Back in line, he saw that fifteen more runners had joined the line to wait till morning opening. He took his place as seventh, and the men before him stretched out on the bare and dusty ground and were instantly asleep. Danny, weary himself, set himself firmly toward staying awake and alert as promised.

It was not all a waste, either, as he had thinking to do. He removed the saddles and drove a stake in the ground, tying the horses close by. The dogs stretched their long bodies over the barren, dusty ground and slept.

As soon as it was permitted, Danny's mind went back to the question. *What happens when I find her?* If she had chosen to answer his letters, he would be assured of a welcome, but there had been no word. Of course, a lot of things could happen to letters mailed from remote places, but what were the chances of something happening to every one of them? It was possible, he guessed.

And then, maybe they were not successful in getting land? Not that he cared, particularly, because if he could only find her, there would be a way to take care of her. The problem was, if they did not get land, where would they be by now? As each set of questions lined themselves up in his mind, and he worried about them equally, each in its turn. It helped him stay awake.

About midnight, he was terribly conscious of the piece of cornbread carefully protected in his shirt pocket. He had thought of it for breakfast, but his stomach growled and rolled from emptiness, and he finally relented. Both dogs alerted, raising their heads in the moonlight, watching as he ate. He broke apart the last bite and gave them each a taste. They licked his fingers and sighed, settling back on the dry ground. He was sorely tempted to join them, but he had promised he would watch out for the six spaces ahead of him.

Resisting the temptation to sit down (he was far too tired and sleepy for that), he walked a short sentry: three steps this way, three steps that way. Swinging his arms then holding them over his head.

Back down the line, a fistfight broke out over a place in the line. Those nearby joined in the fight, anxious to save their own places. A uniformed officer from the 5th Cavalry broke up the fight with the handle grip of his pistol. Someone would wake up with a fierce headache tomorrow.

Those who could settled down to rest, but there was constant milling about. Weary and footsore, they wandered in, eager to get registered before someone stole their claim. By dawn, the end of the line was out of sight. Danny had been wise to strike this deal, as he could get his business done and sleep today if he had to.

At six o'clock, the land office was opened by the registrar. It was still somewhat dark, but, by the light of a lantern, his papers and books were set out, and he let the first part of the line enter the building. A hard-faced Cavalry officer stood by the door to keep others from crowding in.

The routine was the same.

"Name?"

"Nathan Jones."

"Over 21?"

"Yes."

The registrar copied the numbers in the book.

"Sign here, Mr. Jones."

"Thank you, sir."

"Next? Name?"

"Ogilvie. Clarence Ogilvie."

"Over 21?"

"Yes, sir."

"Sign here, Mr. Ogilvie."

And it was Danny's turn.

"Name?"

"Daniel Dunbar. Sir, I wanted…."

"I ask the questions. Over 21?"

"Yes, sir. If I could just ask…."

"Gimme your tract number."

"Sir, I don't…."

"You don't have a claim? Then get on out and don't waste my time. Next?"

Danny was not that easily dismissed. "Sir, if I could just ask about someone. I need to find someone, and I think they registered a claim."

"Now see here, this ain't no bureau of information. Look at them books stacked over there. Full'a names, all of 'em. Now get on out!"

"Sir, it's important. An emergency. If I could just look in the books, it wouldn't take your time."

"What kind of'a emergency?"

"Would a death in the family qualify?" It wasn't a lie. If Robert had not died, he would have known where Roberta was.

"Death, huh?" The registrar was not entirely without heart. "You think they was in yesterday?"

Danny nodded. He had no earthly idea when they were in, or if they were in, but it could have been yesterday. "I could look."

"Well, that one on the top, that was the last one. If it was me, I'd start there and go backward. Now take the book and get on back by the winder, out'a the way. Next?"

Danny eased behind the desk into the cramped corner and picked up the first book. Running his finger down the page, his grainy, burning, sleep-weary eyes sought the name. Car... no, it was Cartwright. Carlile. He needed to find Carlile. One part of his mind worried about what was happening to his animals still staked outside. Those horses were valuable. He tried to comfort himself that the Cavalry officer had known they were his and surely would not let them be stolen. Then, too, the dogs might put up a fuss. The four animals had traveled a fair piece together and likely considered themselves a family.

Cam... Campbell. Ca... Caldwell. His finger slid down the names, those printed by the registrar, and the signature afterward.

Then he found it. Carlile, Roberta. And right beneath it was Carlile, Ebenezer. He blinked his burning eyes! Two tracts! But there were no signatures. Should he bother the registrar to find out? If he didn't, how would he know?

"Sir...."

"I ain't got time to help you."

"Ain't needin' help. Just need to know what it means when there ain't no signature."

"Oh. That'd mean somebody else registered a declaration. Likely they'll be in here in a day or two, makin' it legal."

"Who'd'a done it?"

"Likely whatever name is above theirs. Or maybe below."

The name above theirs was James Kelvey.

"Thank you, sir. Know where I can get me a map?"

The registrar pointed with his elbow to a pile of platted, numbered maps.

"Help yerself. Next?"

The Cavalry officer let another group into the building, and Danny Dunbar slipped out. He sighed with relief when he saw the animals' four pairs of eyes trained on the door.

Saddles back on the horses and dogs alert, they headed out of town. Passing the corn seller's wagon, he saw that the price for a cup of corn was now fifteen cents. He bought two cups chopped and two cups ground into flour. As soon as he cleared the noisy, dusty crowd, breakfast would be served. It would be nice to have an egg for the cornbread, but as he looked around, he knew he might as easily get the moon as an egg in Guthrie.

Three miles away, where the sight of the town was just a memory, he gathered sticks and built a fire. The chopped corn he spread on two fairly smooth stones. The horses licked up the grains, crunching hungrily, working every grain from the crevasses of the rock. The dogs waited, watching every move as the cornmeal batter was stirred. They knew where their meal would be.

Breakfast over, Danny tied the horses near fresh grass and stretched out for a nap. The dogs moved protectively about him as he slept.

Thirty-Six

With his hatchet, Eben Carlile walked among the trees, marking with a blaze those he would cut down. There must be a place for a garden, and if the roots could not be grubbed out for this crop, at least the trees could be cut down, furnishing sunlight to the plants. Beans, peas, potatoes and turnips. Not the variety he would like, but he would do the best he could. Next year would be better.

Hitching the black horse to the plow, he stepped on the crossbar, pushing his weight against the point, forcing it into ground that had never known a plow. Ignoring the pain in his side, he yelled to the horse, encouraging him to pull. The web of grass roots, even in shaded ground, had interwoven themselves into a solid mat. In two hours, Eben was tired, but the black horse was exhausted.

Enough for today, and someone else would pull the plow tomorrow. He estimated it would have to be gone over at least four times to break up the clods enough to get sufficient loose dirt to cover the seeds.

After turning the black horse onto the grass, Eben leaned against a wagon wheel as he watched Roberta and Alecia, pail in hand, go into the woods in search of wild greens. So beautiful they were, the two of them. Brought tears to his eyes, it did, watching them walking under the trees of their own land, the dappled sun shining down on the caramel-golden curls of his lass and the butter-yellow locks of Robert's little girl. *I'll take care of her for ye, Robert, laddie. Long as the Good Lord gives me down the strength.*

The two of them disappeared through the leafy pathway, and Eben added to himself, "Son, I'm reckonin' there'll be another comin' along to take care'a your sister."

He stood by the wagon wheel, resting, trying, without much success, to will the pain to go away. Next thing to do would be to get them trees down, he told himself, and he was just lifting the sharpened broad axe from the wagon as the girls returned, their bucket overflowing with green leaves.

"Papa, there's all kinds'a greens out there. Poke, dock, chickweed, wild lettuce… all kinds! I been so hungry for greens, I almost dreamed about 'em at night." Seeing the axe in his hand, she exclaimed, "Papa, what're you doin'?"

"Thought I'd get the axe out and have it ready come time I can get some'a these trees down."

"You weren't neither! You were aimin' to have a go at 'em while I was in the woods. You got'a let that side heal!"

"Bertie, lass, they's things to do. Why, you don't even have no outhouse."

"Now, Papa, it'd be good to have a outhouse, but you mess up them ribs and you might not be able to get them trees down all summer. If'n Mama was here, what'd she say? You know she'd say two weeks, bound up tight, and another week with liniment. And not one day sooner. You hurtin' yourself, that'd not be fair to me and the girl." Roberta knew she had him when she said those last few words.

Eben sighed and returned the axe to the wagon. He had promised her that he had made the last important decision that affected her, and his physical ability was certainly one of those things. Somehow, he was going to have to show improvement on both tracts of land until the soldier could take over his own. But she was right. If her mama was here, she would know just exactly how long it would take for rib bones to knit. Some women just simply knew those things.

One thing he could do, though, was to get the little bucksaw out and saw off some of the low limbs around the camp. The lower limbs of the blackjack always grew down instead of out; the twigs were catching their faces and poking into their eyes. Not only that, but the sawed-off limbs would be good for the fires.

Even moving the saw back and forth took its toll on the sprung ribs, so after trimming two trees, he put it back.

"Think I'll do some lookin' about, seein' what's here."

"Good idea, Papa. If you see any garlic or wild onions, could you bring 'em?"

"Sure thing." It was only April, but winter was always only a few months away. It was time to see to provisions for the stock. If he could find a suitable place, one he could guard, he would sow some of his precious hayseed. It would easily make a crop, but he would have to guard it until it made its own seed for replanting.

While Big Papa roamed about admiring the claim and while Roberta arranged the camp, Alecia learned:

"'S' is for soup. It's hot, and I blow it.
If I don't cool it, my tummy will know it!"

"'T' is for teacup, for drinking my tea.
I'll fill up a teacup for you and for me."

"'U' is for umbrella. It spreads like a tree.
It helps keep the sun or the raindrops from me."

"'V' is for vase, for flowers and plants.
After I wash off the bugs and the ants!"

"Bertie, what if I didn't wash off the ants? Would they crawl up my nose?"

"They might...."

Thirty-Seven

Chester Kendall awoke with a start and found himself looking into the bonny blue eyes of fifteen-year-old Ellie Gunther. Her pink lips worked themselves into a smile.

"Thought ya didn't have no time to rest 'afore ya set out! You been there sleepin' like the dead for nigh onto six hours, Ma makin' us shush to keep from wakin' ya. She says we got'a take care'a you, 'cause you found the town site."

All the attention was well and good, but truth be told, that wasn't the whole of it. "Now, Ellie, you're knowin' good and well them others likely found places, and it's a fair thought that they'd be better'n the one me and Doug found."

The pink lips pressed firmly together, and the lovely head moved from side to side. The blue eyes danced merrily. "No, sirree! Ma said!" Ma's word was law and gospel, and if you didn't believe that, just ask Ma!

"Where is yer ma?"

"She's out talkin' to folks. She don't like bein' shut up here, and she's wantin' everyone'a y'all to get on in here so's we can go out there to the land."

"None back yet?"

"Just Pa. He drew the stick sayin' he had'a go straight south, and he done run into another town a'formin' 'afore he got clear'a this'n. Saw what he was up agin and headed on back. Didn't hurry like you done, knowin' there weren't no use, bein' he didn't get no claim nohow. Others likely had to go farther, but Ma says they'll be back today. You gonna go back with us."

"Naw. Quick as I get a bite to eat, I'm a'leavin'."

"Oh, I forgot. Ma said I was to break out the biscuits'n honey, and you was to eat all you wanted. She made up two sandwiches with biscuit and fatback she wants you to take to eat on the road. And another'n for Doug."

Chester settled back in a state of euphoria. Food was in front of him, food was ready to go with him, a pretty girl beside him hanging on his every word, and her ma favoring him with special things like the honey. Then, lightly spread over his wonderful mood was the fact that he was not only first to report back, but Nettie Gunther was planning to lend her considerable weight behind his tract for the town site. Could things get any better?

Shouldering his gun and heading out, compass in hand, Chester allowed his mind to wander into its dreams. There were no if's and but's now. The land beside the town belonged to the Kendall brothers.

A freighting company. That would be best. There was the land for the horses, his pa knew how to build the best wagons, and one look at the town of Guthrie told him there would be freighting for longer than he had to live, even if he lived to be a hundred.

With the three of them, all capable of handling horses... well, shucks, even the girls were good with horseflesh. His sisters might just want to help. Why, business could get so good, they... Well, anyway, it would be fun.

The timbered woods rang with the notes of Chester's whistling as he headed beeline back to his land. He swung along with his distance-eating stride, not bothering to go down the section lines. Camping here and there were those who had won that quarter section in the race. Occasionally, someone would hear his approach and shoulder a gun, yelling, "Who's there?"

Chester would stop his joyful song long enough to shout back, "Just a neighbor a'passin' through," and the song would be resumed. He was spoken to and waved to, and he finally saw the corner stake of his land clearly dead ahead. Stretched out across the grass beside it was his brother, his rifle across his chest.

Quietly, he slipped up, and as he stood over him, he said, "Good way to get shot!"

In a sudden fluid movement, his brother was on his feet, looking down the rifle sights.

"Back off, it's just me."

"Lucky you didn't get yerself shot. Did ya get it done?"

A wide grin answered for him. "That place where yer standin' belongs to the Kendall brothers. Spent the night in the Gunther's wagon. Didn't aim to, but I went to sleep eatin'. How'd you get along?"

"Good. The Cavalry come by lookin' fer sooners."

"I reckon you told 'em we wasn't."

"Sure did. Told 'em we was what you'd call "laters" but considered ourselves blest by the Good Lord that these two good tracts was passed over."

Chester nodded. "That was good. Pa'd never let it go if he thought we was lawbreakers a'slippin' in and jumpin' the gun. That'd be bad, too, him a'livin' next door to us like he will be."

"Chet, I been walkin' all over, guardin' this whilst you was gone, and you know what? They's a stream 'bout midway back. Not big, and it might be from a wet-weather spring, but you know them's better'n nothin', and most times they mean the water is high underground. I was a'wonderin' what'd be best to do first; bring down some trees or see if maybe we can scoop out a basin to hold water."

Chester nodded. "Seein' we got no axe or saw, I reckon that leaves scoopin'. How hard's the ground?"

"It ain't so hard as it is full'a weed roots. We need a sharpshooter shovel."

"You checked with the neighbors to see if we could get the loan of one?"

"Now, Chet, just put your mind to thinkin'. I was left here to guard the claim jumpers off these two quarter sections, and you think I got time to go see the neighbors? Could be you thought I had time to write a letter to Ma, too."

"No offense. I wasn't thinkin', just puttin' no thoughts to my words. I'm here now, and I could shoulder that gun and let you go, or I could go. It was a good thing, you findin' that water, whatever kind it is."

"That's what I was a'thinkin'."

"You thought any more on what we ought'a do with this place?"

"Truth be told, I ain't hardly thought on nothin' else. I can't get past horses and wagons, that bein' what we know best. You thinkin' for sure there'll be haulin' to be done?"

"Well, I can tell you one thing. If there ain't haulin' here, there's for sure haulin' in Guthrie. They ain't got nothin' over there that they need. Why, if it weren't so far to haul 'em, we could sell every log on this place. 'Course, we'd not want to do that. It's the truth; they ain't got nothin' down there. Folks come on this run not thinkin' what they'd eat, even. Nettie Gunther cooked up beans and like to'a had to beat folks away with a stick, keepin' 'em from takin' her food."

Doug laughed at the joke. "You don't mean it!"

"Every word of it's true. I saw beans bein' sold a nickel a cup and folks standin' in line to get the chance to get at 'em. If'n I had a load'a hay, I could'a sold it for a winter bill'a groceries. They's gonna be haulin' like you ain't got no idea. You and me and Manny, we'll be goin' six ways from Sunday with all the work. Might even have to put the girls to work."

Now Doug really laughed. Imagine Pa letting the girls hire out as drivers. What a picture, fourteen and thirteen-year-old girls driving the team! Not that they couldn't do it. Why, he'd put them girls up against any fellow their age and half again.

Chester wasn't laughing. "I wasn't tellin' no joke. You thinkin' Caroline'd not jump at a chance to drive a team...?"

147

Doug built a mental picture of his black haired, black eyed sister seated on the buckboard of the wagon, fully in control. The picture did not seem in the least out of focus. "I reckon I see what you mean…."

Chester continued, "And put Evie up there on the seat long side'a her."

Doug nodded. It was still a clear picture.

"Well, like you said, we could scoop out a basin. You know what? I saw muddy water bein' sold a nickel a cup."

Now Douglas doubled over with laughter. "If you're tellin' the truth, the whole world's gone daft."

"It's the truth, man. Now which you want? You go borrow the shovel or man the gun?"

"I'll take the gun. Feels like that gunstock done took root in my hands."

Nodding, Chester took off in the direction of the camp with the two wagons, the green one and the grey one.

Thirty-Eight

Roberta looked around on the ground for the right size of rock. Back in Tennessee, or even in Arkansas, it would have been a job of a few minutes, but it was different here. No rocks. And a lot of what appeared to be rocks were just a lump of hard-packed sand, and when picked up, it crumbled at the edges or broke in the middle.

Finding two she thought would work, she rolled them over and over until she reached the gray wagon. If the wagon bed was going to be her home for a while, and it seemed it was, she needed a doorstep to make it easier to get in and out instead of walking down the sloping tongue.

Papa had planted a few rows of a garden and had cut the limbs off most of the trees in the camp. She could see the grimace on his face when a sharp pain hit, but keeping him still was impossible. Finally she set the limit on the use of the chopping axe and let him attempt any other thing he felt up to.

He had cut the small ends from the bigger limbs until he had enough of the straight ones to build three walls of a roofless outhouse. Roberta had been glad to get it. Papa had always been one to think of little things like that.

He also carried water. Back among the trees was a tiny brook, maybe the headwaters of Redbud Creek where James Kelvey had seen the mark to lead them to their lot. Papa took it on himself to keep the buckets full, occasionally toying with how he could rig up a yoke on the horses and bring more water at a time. They'd need a well, but that was only one of the many things they needed. What they faced, now, was the trip into Guthrie to validate the declaration made by their neighbor.

Roberta shoved the rocks in place and sat on them for a minute to rest. So much to do.

Inside the wagon, Alecia slept on the pile of quilts. She looked so peaceful that Roberta stepped up on her rocky front porch and stretched out beside her. The pressure of the quilts against her tired body seemed to pull her away, closing her eyes and claiming her thoughts, taking her into peaceful oblivion. Into another world.

It was spring. The bed was soft and she was so tired. Had she been working in the garden? In a half-dream state, she wondered. Maybe it was canning. There was canning to do all summer long, and it was one of the most tiring jobs expected of a woman. There was the preparation of whatever was ripe in the garden, the carrying of water, the building of the fire, and the heat of the summer. There was the difficulty of maintaining a constant temperature under the boiler or the right pressure in the cooker. Canning was a lot of work. She must have been canning to be so tired, but she couldn't remember what it was. But that didn't really matter. Apparently, she had reached a point at which she could lie down for a few minutes, and it felt so good. Her breath came steadily and peacefully.

Small Alecia opened her eyes and saw her aunt lying beside her. That meant no one would be watching her but Big Papa, and it was easier to slip away from him than it was from Aunt Bertie.

Easing herself away so as not to wake Roberta, the little girl tiptoed to the wagon front and walked down the tongue, balancing herself with her widespread arms. Maybe she could see a bunny rabbit, and maybe she could catch it. It was funny how they stayed just out of her reach.

At the end of the tongue, she jumped off. There was Big Papa walking up and down where he made the horses plow. He wouldn't be looking this way.

Around the wagon she came. If she was behind the wagon, Big Papa would not know she had woken up. She heard the sound of someone coming and stopped to watch. She didn't see many people now, but a few days ago, a lot of people came by, and sometimes Big Papa got his gun and pretended he was going hunting, even if he just shot a squirrel. Also, Aunt Bertie sometimes went to her food box so she would be close to the gun she kept there.

But Big Papa was busy, and Aunt Bertie was asleep, and someone was coming, so she watched through the trees.

Dogs. Big dogs. Whoever was coming had dogs, and she liked dogs. Maybe they would let her pet them. There were horses, too. There were two of them, and she held up two fingers the way Aunt Bertie showed her, and counted, "One. Two." A man was on one of the horses.

The dogs came closer, and they looked like big, friendly dogs. They looked like the dogs Big Papa gave away that she wished he had brought along. She really wanted to pet these dogs, so she walked toward them.

Then, with a yip, the two big doggies ran toward her, knocking her down on the ground, covering her with their warm, wet tongues. She laughed and giggled as their tongues tickled her face and neck, and when they finally let her sit up, she hugged their necks and kissed their floppy ears.

"Pete and Pokey! You found us! I'm glad you found us."

The man riding one of the horses came closer and stepped off the horse. "Is your name Alecia?" he asked her.

Aunt Bertie had told her not to talk to strange people, but she looked at this man, and he did not look strange at all. He looked like all the other men, only maybe he had a nicer smile. Besides, he knew her name, so it was probably all right to answer.

Smiling at him, she nodded.

"Do you have a grandpa?"

Alecia's face clouded, and she clasped her hands behind her back. Hmmmmm.

At this moment, Eben had left his garden and come to the wagon for a drink and maybe a trip to the creek. As he cleared the corner of the gray wagon, he startled back as two familiar-looking dogs came running to him, and someone who looked very familiar stood behind them.

"Danny… ?"

"In the flesh. Eben, how are you?"

"But you… where have…?"

"Later. I'm here now. Where is she?"

In the few seconds it took Eben to answer, Danny's heart did not beat.

"In the wagon." He motioned with his elbow.

Roberta heard voices, but her weariness tried to pull her back into sleep. Just a few minutes longer, but the voices continued. Her mind engaged. Alecia! Where was the girl? She was gone!

Sitting bolt upright, Roberta rubbed her eyes and stared into the strong, weathered face before her and the open smile she knew so well. Sunlight filtered through the trees onto his sun-bleached hair. Not again!

"GET OUT!" she screamed at the face. "I TOLD YOU AND TOLD YOU TO GET OUT AND NEVER BOTHER ME NO MORE! NOW, GO AWAY!" Hadn't she been tormented enough?

"GET OUT!" she screamed once more and turned and buried her face in the pillow.

Startled, Danny backed away from the wagon, his eyes pleading with Eben for an explanation.

"Wait here," Eben cautioned and stepped up into the wagon.

"Bertie, lass, you been asleep, and you just woke up."

"Papa?"

"I'm here, and I'm tellin' the truth. You ain't asleep no more, and we got company."

"Company…?"

"Special company." Eben reached out his hand toward his daughter, and she took it, accepting help to step out of the wagon. And there he stood.

"Danny."

"Ain't nobody else," the smiling face told her.

"It's really you? How did you…?"

"Later. I know there's talkin' to do, but right now I want to come closer. Will it be all right?"

Finally awake, she walked into his arms.

A tug at her skirt. "Aunt Bertie?"

Another tug. "Aunt Bertie? We got Pete and Pokey. They come to play with me."

"That's good."

Later, she explained, "It's just that old dream, over and over, and there weren't no getting' shut of it."

"I know. I had 'em, too, only mine were nightmares. Pa had a round'a bad luck, and I let 'im make me think I had to fix it for 'im. That was my nightmare and maybe losin' you 'cause'a my own makin'. I'm a'hopin' it's over and done."

"The nightmare?"

"Yeah, but I found you now, and you ain't getting' away agin. I'm wantin' to court you like I was plannin' to do, takin' you to picnics and Saturday night doins'. Trouble is, I don't see none of them things a'goin' on. I'd'a heap rather have us get married and me get busy with the broad axe on them trees. Then maybe string out a fence to keep livestock in. We could do our courtin' later. We could be in the dry in a month, but if you was wantin' courtin', the Good Lord knows you got it comin'. You let me know."

"I, uh… well…."

"What'll it be? I know I sprung it on you, like. But I had me two years'a worry and more'n 500 miles a'bein' scairt spitless thinkin' you wouldn't have me. But if you ain't wantin' to give no answer yet, I'll wait."

She nodded. "You see a preacher while you was down there in Guthrie? Me and Papa, we got'a be there…."

"Girl, they's everything in Guthrie. Cows in the streets, folks livin' in packin' boxes, and that's the lucky ones. Beans is sellin' a nickel a cup, and they's so many lawyers you couldn't stir 'em with a stick. For a fact, there'll be a preacher."

Posey and Babe had two days rest before the trip to Guthrie. Dancer reared and whirled in her eagerness to be on the go. With Danny at her reins, she led the other two fillies to the city. Roberta, in her overalls, rode beside Danny, and Alecia sat on the saddle with her Big Papa. Horseback would be much faster than a wagon where no roads had yet been cut.

By the time they got to Guthrie, beans were selling fifteen cents a cup, but that would not last long. The trains that had first brought people now brought goods. Train load after load. Food, wood for fires, lumber and animal feed.

The preacher had opened business in a giant tent. He had two rows of benches, each six feet long, and a squeeze box accordion for music. A sign in front of the tent proclaimed he would do weddings and funerals, and there would be services on Sunday. He was glad to pronounce the words for Danny and Roberta.

"Wait, 'afore we leave town, I got'a mail a letter to my ma."

"I didn't see you write no letter."

"Nope, 'cause I wrote it down in Fort Smith, crossin' the ferry. Got me a stamp and all, and it's got only three words in it. Read it."

Roberta unfolded the frayed letter from the dog-eared envelope and read, "Dear Ma. I FOUND HER. Danny."

The post office in Guthrie had been constructed from an old farm chicken house, but no self-respecting chicken from Tennessee would have roosted in it.

On the return trip, Dancer and Posey walked closely, side by side, and Babe brought up the rear.

"Big Papa, you want'a hear me read out'a my head?"

"Why not?"

"I can read, 'A' is for apple that grows on a tree. Some are for…" And the little girl amused herself for six miles before she went to sleep against Big Papa's sore ribs.

Voices were low as Dancer and Posey walked side by side.

"Roberta, honey, this ain't gonna be no fair honeymoon for you. I wanted to have a place ready for you to move into with all your own things ready. I want you to know this wasn't the way I planned it."

"I know. But we didn't get to make no plans, did we? I wasn't aimin' to lose Robert and make this trip and didn't know nothin' till Papa had me on the way. Now I see it was for the best. If'n I'd stayed, and we had our place in the mountains, there'd always be the fight with the Doughertys over Alecia. Besides, you got here, and that's all I wanted."

Back at the claim, Danny lifted the sleeping little girl down from the saddle and carried her to her new bed in the grasshopper wagon with Big Papa. He moved aside the ABC book and covered her with her sheet. It had been a long, hard trip for a little girl.

Dusk had fallen by the time Roberta had heated the beans and baked fresh cornbread to serve under the blackjack oak.

Twenty-eight miles on horseback with a bound rib made along day for Eben, also, and he retired early.

Roberta put away the food as Danny watched. Then he went to her and wrapped his strong arms around her, easily lifting her into the gray wagon.

The cicada crickets and the Whip-Will's-Widow birds conversed in the trees. A small, bandit-faced raccoon scavenged for crumbs around the campsite. Then the song of the night birds was exchanged for the mockingbird's many-faceted morning song and the chatter and raucous calls of the crows.

It was morning under the sycamore and blackjack trees.

Alecia's hand felt around in the dim light, locating her book. Slipping quietly from her bed, she walked down the sloping tongue of the wagon to her favorite rock beneath the whispering leaves of the cottonwood tree. Turning to the back of the book, she moved forward three pages and recited her last three verses.

"'W' is for water, for rinsing and rubbing.
I get so dirty, it takes lots of scrubbing."
"'X' is for xylophone. Just hear it playing!
Do, mi, so, do, the hammers are saying!"
"'Z' is for zipper. It runs on a track.
Just like a choo-choo, forward and back."

On either side of her, just like a pair of bookends, sat Pete and Posey, lolling out their tongues companionably and watching for movement in the surrounding woodland.

"You know what I saw yesterday?" she asked the two dogs. "I saw a choo-choo, running back and forth, just like a zipper!"

The mockingbirds trilled, and the meadowlarks whistled. A redtailed hawl burst through the limbs and closed talons on a cottontail that moved too slow. A rosy sun rose into the sky, and it was morning.

The morning of the rest of her life

Caravan

One

It had been just fireside talk from the beginning, born in the frustrated minds of snow-bound Nebraska landowners as they warmed around the pot-bellied stove in the general store. But, as sometimes happens to frustrated talk, the words took legs.

All that was left to do was a lot of work, a long summer ahead and maybe a harder winter, but no one was ready to back out. Like a snowball on a hill, there comes a time that the weight of it is too great to stop.

It all started back in January when Clyde Kendall and Clancy Harper ducked into Hewett's General Store to thaw out from the blue norther that had swept across southern Nebraska and headed to all points north.

They huddled over the monster stove that had been forged from solid iron and was now the source of heat for the store. The monster occupied the center of the store and gobbled three-foot logs like a king snake downing a bullfrog.

James Hewett, owner and proprietor, had just bent over the stove to poke the spent coals down into the ash bin below the firebox in order to make more room above. It was time to feed another pine log into the stove's yawning mouth, and at that exact moment, Ed Gunther happened in.

"Cold 'nuff fer ya?" came the standard winter greeting of Providence Falls, Nebraska.

"Pretty near," came the standard and expected answer.

Formalities over, the subject under current discussion was resurrected. "Still seems strange to me, havin' a foot race to get free land. Whatever'd the government be thinkin' on, lettin' land go for nuthin' that'a'way?"

"Ain't exactly fer nothin'. Got'a win it in a foot race. That's somethin'."

Another voice. "Ain't exactly to be a foot race. A body could ride a horse or a mule or even a jackrabbit if he was a'mind to. Seems like it don't matter long as he pounds his claim stake in the ground sooner'n somebody else."

"'Speck anybody'll show up? The whole thing looks chancy to me."

"They'll show up all right. If ya was to try fer it and lose out, ya ain't lost nuthin' but time and aggravation. If ya was to win, now, that'd be a different matter."

"What'd it be like down in Oklahoma territory?"

"Reckon it'd be a sight warmer, bein' farther south. That'd be somethin' to think on. My Nettie don't do nuthin' but complain all winter for the chill blains on 'er feet. It'd be a relief to me just not to have to listen."

Then a voice from the farm just south of the falls. "I could do without the floods. I know it don't bother most'a you fellows, but down where I am, that river backs up and floods over the field, takin' out a crop'a somethin' or other most every year."

Now Clancy Harper. "Yeah, well, they's times I find myself wantin' to be down south at that run just for the excitement of it all. Likely I ain't all growed up yet."

"Same with me. Ain't nothin happened here in Poverty Flats since that wagon train honcho passed on to his reward and left his string'a wagons out here. Seems strange to me that one of them men on that train didn't have the moxie to pick up and go on to the coast. Then we'd all be livin' in Californie."

Clancy agreed. "You'd'a thought so. My pa, he was twelve and may not remember it like it actual was, but it seemed to him when the wagonmaster passed on, it flat let the air out'a their sails, and they was likely tired and sore a'movin'. Named it Providence Falls, unanimous consent."

"Name didn't stick though. Been Poverty Flats ever since I can recall."

The door to the general store opened, and a blast of wind-driven snow swirled inside, practically obscuring a fur-clad figure. Stephen Tullius shivered dramatically, patting off the snow and stomping his ice-coated boots.

"Cold 'nuff fer ya?"

"Pretty near."

Clyde Kendall cleared his throat and began, "Get yerself on in here, Tull, and help us out. Got us a talk a'goin'. The bunch'a us, we got it in our head to trek on down to the Oklahoma territory and get us some'a that free land."

Steven Tullius perked up with decided interest. "Ya don't say! Had the same thought myself whilst I was a'wadin' snow up to my armpits tryin' to take care'a the livestock. Been carryin' around that flyer for a week now; 'bout to wear all the writin' off it."

The four men huddled around the stove, looking at each other, and then they stared at the newcomer. Was he serious? He sounded that way.

James Hewett poked the three-foot log into place, sending a spray of sparks up into the room. "You thinkin' serious, fer a fact?"

Without a pause came the reply. "You bet your sweet life I'm talkin' serious. It was so cold out my place, the milk froze in solid streams 'afore it hit the pail. Hard on livestock, out in weather like this. You know, fer a fact, the snow in the draw got so deep it was over the fence. Had half'a herd'a sheep walk out right over the fence on the ice. Wouldn't'a know'd they was out 'cept I saw we had a buffalo calf walk into my field over the same fence. That calf's ma was a'havin' herself a hissy fit, bellerin' at 'im to cross back over."

The assembled men considered that strange occurance. The fact was, it didn't sound unreasonable. Likely wasn't.

"Figure it'd be that much warmer down there in the territory?"

"It'd be farther south, ain't it? The way I figure it, movin' anywhere south'a town'd be an improvement. Yep, anywhere south'a here, I'd say it'd be an improvement."

"Hmmmm. Truth be told, I ain't been too crazy about this place myself. Town ain't hardly big enough for me to make a livin' as a wheelwright, buildin' wagons on the side. Just ain't enough call for 'em. Them wagons we build just last too bloomin' long and when ya got a good wagon, with good wheels and underpinnin' like I put on 'em, it just don't wear out. Then if it don't wear out, they don't need to buy another one. It bears on my mind that I got them three grown sons under my roof with no place to go."

Clyde Kendall sighed as the problem that had weighted him down for the past year was now out in the open. A man with grown sons, ages sixteen, eighteen and twenty, had better act fast, or there was the chance they'd pack up and go off on their own.

Clancy Harper, blacksmith, faced the same problem. "I'm with ya, fellow, only I got a few more years 'fore it hits me full in the face." His sons were thirteen, ten and eight.

James Hewett opened the heavy cast iron door of the stove once more and poked at the log, settling it farther down into the bed of redhot coals. "Wouldn't take too much to make me pick up stakes and move, goin' through winters like this'n. Don't have no strangers comin' through town to buy things, and the locals can't get their doors open fer the snow. A fellow could go broke 'afore spring."

There was long pause, during which time the huge, wind-up, 8-day clock, which sat on the letter-drop box, tick-tocked rhythmically. The snowfall had totally absorbed all outside noises, and the crackling of the wood in the stove was the only other sound as the big hand made four complete sweeps.

"Hewett, was you talkin' serious on what you said, just now?"

There was a pause as the storekeeper brushed an accumulation of ash off the nail keg that served as a stool. "I was a talkin' dead serious; if'n I could for sure get me a good place in some town, I'd go. Way I read that flyer, them runs they're havin' is for quarter section plots, and that'd not work for me. In the sellin' business like I am, I need to be where folks are, them that need to buy things. That'd be all that was a'keepin' me here. Fact is, I might even start shovelin' the snow out'a the road and take off fer the south right now, the way I feel this minute."

"Yeah, it says quarter section, all right. I wouldn't want that much land neither. I see they got six towns platted, with lots and everything. Ain't big lots, though, and I don't know if I'd like a town the size them's gonna be. Too many strangers livin' too close."

Ed Gunther propped his feet onto the foot-warming rail of the stove and leaned back, a clear signal that he had something important to say.

"Well, Ed…?" Stephen Tullius invited.

Ed complied. "Way I see it is this. Ain't no problem a'tall. We'll jist move the whole bloomin' town down there. We'll move lock, stock and barrel and find us a better place."

"The whole town, huh? All of us together?"

"Yep. All that wants to go," Ed Gunther refined.

"'Course they'd be some that likes it here and wants to stay. Wouldn't want them along no how."

"Just for the sound of it, Hewett, how big of a town would you want if you had the choice?"

"How big?"

"Yeah, like, how many folks'd you need to trade with you? If the town was to go, and you went along, how many households would it take to keep your shelves stocked?"

James Hewett pulled up a cane-bottom chair and sat down, propping his feet on the warming rail. Reaching behind him, he picked up one of the many flyers describing the run and blew off the coating of fly ash from the stove.

This would take a little thought, and there certainly weren't any customers out in this storm to be waited on, nor were there likely to be. He picked up a pencil stub and tapped his teeth with the lead. The other four men waited in respectful silence, each considering what his own answer would be.

"Well, now this here ain't writ in stone, and it's only words off the top'a my head. But if I was to put down a bottom number, it'd likely be twelve, maybe fifteen. 'Course, now, if there was to be twenty or more, that'd be a sure thing."

A moment of silence followed as each man digested this fact.

After further thought, he added, "Now, if we was to get one of them tracts, they'd have all kinds'a other folks livin' outside the town. That'd add to the number. The thing of it is, though, them tracts so big there'd not be many homesites within walking distance."

Clancy Harper added, "For my part, blacksmithin' don't take up much room, and I'd mainly want a house and garden, a place to grow my own animal fodder, and my shop. I got two acres here, and I make out. With my boys a'comin' on, I'd want close to five acres, I calculate."

"Five acres'd be a good size for me, too," Tullius agreed. "That there gristmill'a mine, it don't use up more'n a half acre, all told."

"You'd take it along?"

Tullius looked at Clyde Kendall in surprise. "Why'd I not? It's what I do, and folks is always needin' somethin' ground up. My grandpappy freighted them parts in from the east, across the Mississippi, and my pa, rest his soul, made good use of 'em. I wouldn't no more think'a leavin' that mill behind than you'd leave the tools'a your trade."

The minute hand of the clock on the letter-drop box made five more turns, at which time the door burst open again, and from the swirling snow evolved two fur-clad figures.

"Cold enough fer ya?"

"Pretty near."

"Drag up a couple'a chairs and help us out. We're 'bout to get us a deal to move the whole town down the Oklahoma territory."

"The whole town?"

"Them as wants to go. We been settin' here thinkin' of first this and that of the things we'd like to change, and we allow this'd give us the chance to get it done."

"You'all serious?"

"Yep. Seem to be."

"Hewett says he could be up to it."

"Yeah. Says we'll need at least a dozen families to go along. Ain't that what you said, Hewett?"

"Well, I...."

Hamp, the elder of the Baker brothers, cut in. "'Cause the reason I asked, me'n Bart, here, we put our heads on our problem, havin' nothin' else to do, and we put two and two together. First, there ain't much well-diggin' goin' on in the winter, makin' summer too busy and winter too long. And the thing is, summers ain't been too good of late. Not enough new people."

Bart nodded. "Interestin' hearin' you fellows been talkin' on leavin', 'cause we done decided."

"Decided? You mean you're gonna do it, fer a fact?"

"Sure as the goose flies right side up."

Hamp propped his feet onto the warming rail and leaned back in his cane-bottom chair. All eyes turned toward him.

"Way I see it, folks'll be goin' down there in droves and herds, and every single one of 'em'll have to have a well. If me and Bart was to get land, that'd be good, but if we didn't, there'd be a place for us to stay somewhere, and when we worked a while, we could come back for the wives. Seems there'd be all the work a well-digger'd want for the next ten years and then some."

Clyde Kendall, wheelwright, cleared his throat. "We could put you down for a five acre tract, then?"

The propped-back chair landed with its four legs back on the floor, and Hamp Baker stared, frowning at the group. "You meanin' to tell me you fellows got so far as talkin' about the lot size, and not a word was leaked to Bart'n me? What kind'a friend'd that be?"

"Keep yer shirt on, Hamp. Subject didn't come up till less'n a hour ago. Barely got ourselves waded out into the talkin', and here you come in. Good thing, too. You'd be the one to help us sign up families enough, you bein' able to guarantee a well."

"How many lots you thinkin' there'll be?"

"Ain't set pen to paper, but I'd wager 25 to 30."

"Tell you what, me'n Bart, we'll sign you up a dozen families, and we'll make the run. What we got'a have out'a the deal is the guarantee to put a well on every lot. That'd be enough to get us started, and folks'd need a well anyway."

"Yeah…."

"Well, let's talk cost. There'd need to be 'start up' money. Say twenty-five dollars a lot."

"Twenty-five dollars a lot for free land? How do ya get that?"

"Way I see it, not all the lots'd be sold right off. Quick as the next folks bought lots, the first twelve of us, we'd get our money back. A town got'a have money to run on, ya know, for the school and church'n all the stuff a town got'a pay for."

A long pause followed. Talk was getting serious. It would be too easy for snowbound men in a warm store building to say too much and be sorry later. Picking up and moving a business and a family, well, now, that was a serious thing, and there were wives at home to be consulted.

Clancy Harper picked up a circular and turned it over to its clean side. "One quarter section of land, that'd be 160 acres. Divided by 5 acres, that'd make thirty-two lots, but they'd have the street easement took out'a that. What's left'd be enough for me. I'd hand over my twenty five dollars this minute if the thing was set in concrete, and I could start plannin' toward goin' down there in the spring."

More silence. Clancy putting solid figures to the abstract words put finality to the venture. Thoughts of how to approach their wives began running through their heads.

"Hey, fellows, back up."

"What'd'ya mean, Hamp?"

"Think what we're doin'. We're sittin' here by Hewett's fire, talkin' like it was a done deal. First off, we ain't got that quarter section, and even us goin' down to the run, that'll not guarantee we'll get somethin'. Folks'll be gathered round them borders worser'n Coxie's army a'raidin' the southern plantations. 'Afore we start plantin' beans, we got'a get the land."

"What'd'ya suggest?"

"Well, for starters, me and Bart, we're goin'. Done made up our minds. For what we do, we'd rather have a town lot than a quarter section and have it stuck out a long way from nowhere. Now if there was to be several more wantin' to make the run, we could take fast horses'n head on out, and likely one of us'd get one."

"Maybe more'n one?"

"Could be."

"That'd be good."

"Yeah, then we'd have a thing to sell, all them extra tracts we get, and we'd all get our twenty-five dollars back right away, wouldn't we?"

Ed Gunther was making mental calculations. Talking his Nettie into the trip would be no challenge. Nettie was ready for anything and everything. A right stand-up kind'a girl was his Nettie, and even after birthing four youngens, ages twelve to fifteen, she could still stir up the pride in him, causing tickle feelings on his neck just to look at her. Yep, Nettie'd be right in there, but, if he could, he'd like to get a little extra for her.

He stood up, the better to gain their attention. "Got a deal for ya. I'll add my name in with Hamp and Bart, and I'll go a step farther. I'll go on ahead and I'll take my wagon on down there with me to be a headquarters for food'n water. My Nettie, she'll drive it and stay where we think we'll need it most."

"Now that'd be good. That'd let the riders travel light."

Clancy again. "One thing I'd want, though."

"What'd that be?"

"I'd want my Nettie to get first choice of any lot she wanted, me thinkin' she earned it by makin' the trip and operatin' the headquarters."

"Sounds reasonable enough."

"So now we need four more, to make six for the run."

Kendall, the wheelwright, took a deep breath and began bravely, "I can send two'a my boys, if they can be let to stay together like a team. Seems there'd need to be pairs, chance somebody needed help."

"That makes three. Shouldn't be no trick to get three more."

After the serious offer of his sons, Clyde Kendall knew he had even more difficult work to do. Putting his four chair legs back on the floor, he stood and reached for his heavy coat that he had pitched on the floor behind him. "Fellows, I can't stay here gum-bumpin' all day. Got things to do."

"Got'a go home and convince the missus?"

"That'n a few other things. Look, fellows, ya'll are serious, ain't ya?"

"Me and Bart's a'goin'. Ya'll got'a do whatever yer big enough to do."

Put like that, all the men became brave.

"Count me in."

"Me, too."

Tommy McClure had also come in through the snow to Hewett's store, but he had no time to sit and talk. He had been sent for a can of baking soda, or there would be no biscuits for lunch.

James Hewett had not been able to wait on him, as he had been busy with the stove, rattling the ash grate and readjusting the massive log he had just put into it. It didn't matter to Tommy, though, because he well knew where the baking powder was kept and how much it cost.

He picked the can off the shelf and dropped it in the pocket of his parka, laying the correct number of coins on the top of the cash register. It would not be the first time the storeowner had found loose change on his register and did not bother to determine what it was for.

Tommy turned and left, but not before he had heard the gist of the conversation around the stove. With a hint of a grin, he plunged once more into the Nebraska winter, allowing only a minor whirlwind of snowflakes to enter the store behind him.

The grin widened as he trudged along the stomped-down path toward the house of his brother-in-law, Samuel Littletree. He had interesting things to pass on to him and his other brother-in-law, Jacob. His wife's two brothers lived side by side, not far from the store, so he was soon in a warm house again.

Part of the luck he had when he had met and married his wife was the friendship he formed with her two brothers. He found them both at Samuel's house, as he had thought he would, and he knew where to get the cup for the coffee that always brewed on the iron stove.

The brothers looked up as Tommy sat down. "Well, you're lookin' like the cat that got the canary," Samuel greeted him. "Wouldn't'a thought you'd be so happy-lookin' havin' to go on an errand in this storm."

Tommy sat down at his accustomed place at his brother-in-law's table, dipped his usual 2 spoons of sugar in his coffee and stirred in the cream. Two pairs of eyes watched expectantly.

"Well, out with it!" demanded Jacob. If there was news to be had or any goings-on in the town, the deputy sheriff could use an update.

Tommy took his time. It was not often he was in such an enviable position with news of such far-reaching consequence. It was certainly to be savored, but when he felt he had drawn it out long enough, he began. "Those plans we're hatchin', they could be takin' a new turn."

"Plans?" wondered Samuel.

"You don't mean those about the territory, do you? I'm not open to any changes. I got no wife or family like you fellows, and I see no chance to better myself here any time soon. Especially with a sheriff no more'n two years older'n me that may live longer'n me. Top'a that, it don't pay enough here for me to have a family if I was to have a chance at one." Jacob stared at his two table companions and then picked up his coffee.

Samuel looked at Tommy. "Out with it, man. Let's hear the news 'afore Jake blows a gasket."

Tommy decided it was time. "Could be good news, leastwise it is for me. I come by the store, and Ed and all the fellows were talkin' and lookin' at the flyer from the territory. They were so into it they didn't even know I came and left."

"The flyer? You mean our flyer?"

"Yeah. 'Course I guess it isn't entirely ours, bein' it's been spread out all over town. But the thing is, it looks like they're fixin' up to have the whole town a'goin'."

164

"Whole town…?"

"What'd ya mean, the whole town?"

"Well, I didn't stay for the whole of the talk. Figured I'd get on out here with the news'a what might be goin' on. They sure sounded serious, and if they are, it'll get around pretty fast. If they ain't, then we'll hear nothin', and we can go on with our plans. I'm thinkin' I'm with Jake, figurin' on goin' on anyway."

Samuel sighed and stared soberly into his coffee. He added two more spoons of sugar. "Then it looks like the goat's in my yard, waitin' to see if I'll feed it. There's Jake with no family and you with that little fellow. It'd seem easier for you. Me… I got Nellie and the girl, and neither one of 'em are gonna be an easy sell. Trouble with women and girl children is they tend to get themselves tied to places and things, and it gets hard to move 'em. I'm thinkin' you'll have an easier time with my sister than I'll have with my women folks. For a youngen of 13, that Taffy can be downright hard-nosed about what she don't want to do, and she's got a passel'a friends she'll not want to leave."

A moment of silence as the men looked at each other considering what to do next. The 13-year-old "youngen with the hard nose" opened the kitchen door and came in, took the lid off the cookie jar, extracted two cookies and left with a toss of her black braids.

Her father commented. "That'n there could be my trouble, but right now I'm bigger'n she is, so I 'spect what I say'll go."

"Nellie'll not be a problem?"

"Hopin' not."

"Then it's soundin' like you've decided."

Another pause. "Could be. The buildin' trade here is zero to none in the winter. Fellow with a family can't afford the idle time. Should be a lot of buildin' goin' on down in the territory with so many new people comin' in at one time."

Nods all around. "Could be another thing, though."

"What's that?"

"Our pa. He seems to be goin' downhill fast. Wish't he was a little younger, and he'd be a help on the plannin'. Always talked on goin' into business together but didn't seem to get it firmed up, and then Jake joined up with the law. Sort'a left me hangin'. What I'd like to do is set myself up with a little business, like maybe a café, the way Nellie can cook, and then when business is slow, there'd be something to fall back on."

"Hmmm, well… Any reason why that couldn't happen?"

Samuel sighed a weary sigh. "Well, no… I do have a little money put by. Likely could start somethin'."

Jake fiddled with his coffee cup then got up and poured its contents in the slop jar. He refilled it from the pot and explained, "Done sat there dreamin' and let it get cold. Can't do serious plannin' on cold coffee."

"Well, what's the plan?"

"I'm jist gonna toss this out as a maybe. I got a little money, too, and I'm with Sam on thinkin' there'll be a sight'a buildin' goin' on. Now I still remember how to pound a nail the way Pa made us learn, and I could help at the beginnin' for a share of the business. That'd get us goin' quick."

Tommy tossed in a comment. "You thinkin' a café'd be enough to take care'a two families?"

Samuel brightened with an idea. "Maybe not, but I'm thinkin' a boardin' house could do the trick if Jake was wantin' to be part of it. 'Course, there'd come a time I'd be able to buy him out if he was wantin' to go back with the law. Could be there's as much need for a law man down there in the new territory as there'd ever be up here."

Tommy again. "Think your pa'd be able to make the trip? If he could take it easy in a wagon… or somethin'?"

Jake ignored the question. "You know, Sam may'a got the right idea. That boardin' house, that'd bring in cash right along if it was bein' run proper. That's a good thought; let's work on it."

"Yeah, let's think on that and about Pa. Bein' all he's got wrong with 'im, the plannin' is gonna fall on us."

Two

Those around the stove had begun to thin out, each going his own way.

Ed Gunther also thought it was time to go. He so seldom had anything to say to make Nettie happy that he was pulled along the snow-packed road by the very thought of it and felt neither the cold of the snow nor the force of the wind.

He closed the door quickly to keep from cooling off the kitchen. "Nettie, my little plum cake, I got good news for you."

"What?" her gruff voice demanded.

"I'm fixin' to take you where you won't never get cold feet no more… leastways, hardly ever!"

"Don't you be funnin' me, Ed Gunther, jist 'cause I set here with my feet in hot water all winter. Them chill blisters ain't no fun."

"I know they ain't. That's why I'm gonna take you down south to the Oklahoma territory. Got decent weather down there."

"You ain't serious…."

"Serious as the sun a'comin' up of a mornin'." He now stood behind her, wrapping his bear-like arms around her and around the back of the cane-bottom chair. Leaning down, he nuzzled his face into her neck.

"Ed! Get yerself on out'a here, you with grown daughters lookin' on!"

"More the better. That'll teach 'em what a husband's supposed to be like. It'll send 'em out lookin' for a man like their old pa."

Giggles came from across the room as fifteen-year-old Ellie and thirteen-year-old Margie looked on with great interest.

Margie wondered. "You sayin' the truth, Pa?"

Ellie backed her up. "True as the blue'a the sky? I can go?"

"No, little Margie. I'm leavin' you up here for the prairie dogs."

"Aw, Pa! When'll it be?"

"Middle'a April."

Nettie lifted her feet from the pan of water. It was getting cold, anyway. "Now, Ed, are you just teasin' them girls, 'cause if you are…."

As an answer, Ed pulled the crisp, newly-folded flyer from his pocket and handed it to her. Oklahoma territory… quarter section… free land….

"Now, Ed, you thought this through? Livin' here, doin' for city folks like you do, that makes us a good livin'. Ain't that quarter section a lot'a land? What're you thinkin' to do on it… farm?"

Ed grinned his handsome grin, eyes sparkling. "You ain't heard the best part. The whole town's a'goin', leastwise them that wants to. Likely about twelve families, anyway."

"For sure?"

"And they's more. You and me and them youngens, we'll be goin' on the first round so's to have food and water handy and not have to be carryin' it on the saddle horses. And you, my pet, get first pick'a the lots in the new town."

"Me? Why?"

"'Cause I got it for ya. Now ya owe me." Ed leaned down and sniffed appreciatiavely at Nettie's hair and nibbled at her ear.

"Aw, Ed, get on away! Them girls is watchin'!"

Clyde Kendall was not in such a hurry to get home. He knew what he had to do, so it had just as well be this snowy day when everyone was tied up indoors and needed something to think on. He tried to form words, but none seemed right, and then he was stepping through his front door.

"That you?"

"Yep."

"Wait. 'Afore you knock off the snow, I need you to get me a couple pails'a water."

Clyde took the two buckets that were thrust at him and walked to the well in the yard. The activity gave him a few more minutes to think. Maude usually came around, but it was always on her own terms. In these two dozen years he had been married to her, he had developed the plan that sometimes worked. His plan had one important feature, and that was never to put out his best plan first, because she would always change it.

Back in the house with the water pails, he wandered over to the window and gazed out at the falling snow.

"Maude, honey, I got bad news."

"Somebody died?"

"Almost. The whole town's fixin' to pick up and move itself down to Indian territory."

"Clyde! You gone daft?"

"Nope. Just come from Hewett's, and it was talked about. Seems there's them that're makin' serious plans. Didn't want you to hear it from nobody but me. So I come on home."

"Town a'movin'? Never heard'a such'a thing."

"Reckon not, this bein' the only town either of us has ever know'd."

"Why'd it move?"

"Everyone got his own reasons. First one thing and then the other. The Baker boys and Ed Gunther, they're gonna be a part'a the run."

"Run…?"

"That's what they call it when folks line up and listen for the gun. Then they take off and try to get the best place. A body'd need guts'n fast horses, but some of 'em'll get free land."

"The Baker boys'n Ed, huh?"

"Yeah. The town—what's left of it, that is—is a'gonna miss 'em. Them and Tullius and likely Hewett's Store."

"The store, too?"

"Yeah. We'll be havin' to stock up good 'afore they leave. He'll likely have good bargains."

Clyde knew it was time to walk away, and he opened the warming oven over the cast iron cook stove. Sure enough, there was a leftover piece of berry pie. Lifting it out carefully, because of the tender, flaky crust, he balanced it on two fingers and a thumb and took a bite.

"Clyde Kendall, you're gonna ruin your supper, eatin' that pie."

"Never have yet."

He sat down at the table and leisurely munched the pie, sprinkling a fair amount of crumbs on the table. Finally, chewing the last bite, he jabbed his finger at each of the crumbs, gathering them on the end of his finger to put in his mouth. Maude always did make a good pie.

"What's it like, this Oklahoma territory?"

Clyde sighed, as though hardly interested. "Well, some says it's a lot warmer. Likely got things that'll grow down there where it don't get so cold of a winter." Then, as though he had just thought of it, "You know, Hamp and Bart, they think there'll be more year 'round work with all the new people wantin' wells...'n things."

"A lot'a folks there, you think?"

"They'll be sproutin' up like hairs on a dog's back. Good land... water... trees... and free. That'll attract a fair number'a folks. Can't see why there'd not be right smart of a crowd around that piece'a land."

"Everyone think they'll get a lot?"

"No, but it ain't necessary for 'em to. They was sayin' there'd be several in the run, and it'd be likely that one or maybe more'n one'd get land. Whoever got the best land, that's what they'd take and sell the other'ns."

Maude Kendall glanced at the clock and reached into the cupboard for her bread-mixing pan. The stomping of feet on the snowy porch heralded the arrival of the oldest boys.

"Clyde, tell them boys to each bring in a load'a stove wood."

Clyde Kendall slipped on his coat and stepped out onto the porch.

"Boys, your ma wants you each to bring in a load'a stove wood, then leave your coats on. I want you to meet me out in the shed."

Telling Maude had been a carefully orchestrated performance, but telling the boys would be a pure pleasure.

James Hewett pushed back from the table. Lacey was not the world's best cook, but she made sure there was plenty, and she made up for any small lack in a lot of other ways. He knew he was lucky to have Lacey.

He began. "Been a bad year so far."

No answer.

"The sellin' business ain't like it was when my pa started it. Folks got to livin too far out'a town, 'n new stores been settin' up that takes away the trade."

Lacey Hewett swished the clean dish in the rinse water and dried it on the tea towel that had been embroidered "Monday is wash day." She set the dish in the cupboard and reached for another.

"James, if you're workin' up to tell me we're movin' down to Oklahoma territory, just spit it out. I done got past that and got to wonderin' how much I was gonna get to take with me."

James sighed and pushed back his chair. Reaching out for a handful of her apron, he pulled Lacey into his lap where she was a perfect fit and wrapped his arms around her. This was one of those times that made up for there being a little too much salt in the gravy. "Lacey, honey, you can take anything you want to take if we can find wagons to haul it in."

And speaking of wagons, he'd better start trying to buy some. He would certainly try to take most of the store

And there was the matter of drivers. Lacey was afraid of horses and would never let their girls around them, possibly also considering it an unladylike thing for a girl to do.

Not so with Clyde Kendall's two oldest girls, the same ages as his Mary Lou and Beth. Those girls of Clyde's could ride anything that could be ridden and drive anything that couldn't. Hey! It was a thought... No, it was more than a thought; it was a plan. He'd just have to figure how to put in into action.

Stephen Tullius had no wife to tell. He would be leaving her in the Nebraska soil, buried beneath the willows by the stock pond. He had only his two boys, six and eight. Of course, there was also his sister who might want to come. In fact, she probably would.

So Steven Tullius had his own planning to do.

Three

The flyer about the land giveaway said those who wished to participate in the run and those who chose to come down from places north of Oklahoma territory would be obliged to wait on the Kansas border until three days before the run. Then they would be permitted to cross the Cherokee Outlet, which lay between the Kansas border and the Unassigned Lands, to reach the subject of the run.

In this way, it was assumed that a three-day crossing would put them at the border of the Unassigned Lands in time for the shotgun start of the run.

On the tenth of April, 1889, the first entourage, those from Providence Falls who would be participating in the run, were prepared to leave.

So confident they now were of success that they had begun calling the town by its new name. At first, there had not much thought been given to the name of the town, what with trying to make plans for something that might or might not happen. There was still a chance that none of their runners would be fortunate enough to win a tract of land.

So it was that in the middle of March, the minister of the church decided, for certain, that he would stay in Nebraska with those of his flock who were remaining. He did, however, call the town together for an evening of fellowship and farewell, after which he would give his blessing on the trip.

It had been a long evening at the church, and little six-year-old Jimmy Hewett became tired. He ate a lot at the fellowship dinner and played in and out of the benches with his friends, and when the dull talking part started, he crawled under his parent's bench and stretched out on a quilt provided for that purpose.

He had slept peacefully through the words about father Abraham being called out to a new land and about Joshua's conquests after he crossed Jordan. He was now becoming restlessly awake as the old minister pronounced his benediction.

171

"…and we ask You, Lord, to go with these people and guide them, because we know You want them to prosper."

Jimmy's sleep-drugged mind caught the last two words, and the next day he asked his mother, "Are we really going to prosper when we leave here?"

"I surely hope so, Jimmy." Lacey wondered why her son would be concerned about that. Nothing of a serious nature had ever concerned him up to now. And how did he know what the word meant?

"I just wondered. The preacher said God wanted us to go."

"Huh? To go where?"

"To Prosper."

"Are you sure?"

"Yeah, Ma. He said he knew God wanted us at Prosper… or to Prosper, or something like that. I heard 'im say it."

"Oh, of course! When he prayed for God to bless our trip, he said he knew God wanted us to prosper. That means God wanted good things to happen."

"Then they will."

"I hope so."

"He said God wanted them to, so whatever God wants, He can have, can't he? Preacher wouldn't say anything that wasn't true, would he?"

"No, Jimmy. You're absolutely right. I'm certain God wants us to prosper."

The next day it buzzed through town.

"Little Jimmy Hewett said God was sending us to Prosper, like that was the name of the town!"

Then, "The little Hewett boy thinks God said we should go to Prosper."

By the end of the week, no one called the new and unformed town by any other name. And now it was the twelfth of April, and the runners must be on the way.

The Gunther wagon took off first, at least an hour before daylight. Loaded aboard was a hundred-pound sack of beans, two slabs of fat back for seasoning, a keg of cornmeal and a fifty-pound sack of flour, along with two gallons of bee tree honey. If anyone on the trip wanted anything other than beans, cornbread or pancakes, he could see to his own provisions. The rest of the wagon space was needed for necessities of living for Nettie and the four children. An empty barrel rode along to be filled at the last watering place.

Following behind the wagon, attached to tethers, were a saddle horse for Ed to ride in the run and a mule, just in case its strength was needed to help pull something. Ed would ride along in the wagon with his family until they reached the Kansas border, then Nettie and the children would go on alone after the run started.

In addition to Hamp and Bart Baker, there were Chester and Douglas Kendall, eighteen and almost 21, sons of Clyde. With them was Bernard Campbell and Winford Stanley, the young farmers who lived down by the river and were regularly flooded out.

There was Josh Fields, a newlywed who was persuaded by his bride to join up. And lastly, there was a father and son pair who did custom farming around the neighborhood, furnishing themselves and a plow to work by the day. They allowed there would be plenty of need for their services in a new place.

In southern Kansas, one of the Kendall horses went lame, so Douglas Kendall rode the wagon with the Gunther children, contemplating making use of the mule. He didn't like the feel of it, mules being too slow and stubborn, and then his mind was made up for him when the newlywed, with his mind wandering (who knew where), allowed his horse to wander off in the night.

This meant the colony from Nebraska reached the border two horses short.

So it was decided they would spread out across the northern border of the land so as not to compete with each other. They were to try to find something within twenty miles of Guthrie or Edmond Station, though they would take what they could get.

The Kendall brothers drew the short straw, sentencing them to the far eastern border where penciled notes on the map indicated timbered woodlands, streams and gullies. It would be a good place to live, but a hard place to run through.

Chester and Douglas, tall and long-legged and accustomed to walking, nodded together in unspoken agreement and said they'd just walk and give their remaining saddle horse to the dingle-headed newlywed. Ed Gunther could ride the mule.

The Kendall brothers deduced that for crawling under limbs and jumping gullies, maybe the horse could do it or maybe not, but the mule would only slow them down. Bent over the map, they studied distances and divided by their ability to make time and knew they had made the best decision. Feet and legs were reliable. Horseflesh was not always so dependable and sometimes a bit of trouble.

Nettie Gunther, in the wagon, took the two young men eastward along the border to a place due north of the Indian Meridian, marking the eastern border of the Unassigned Lands. Capable with a compass, they would walk south over rivers and streams to the north border and be in position there, ready for the run.

The Baker brothers would take the next strip west, Ed Gunther would go south from Guthrie, and the other two pairs had positions farther west.

On the 22 of April, a beautiful Oklahoma morning, the singing birds and light breezes welcomed them as the gunshot sent them flying south. Nettie Gunther wisely held back until the first rush had left the border.

In the first quarter of a mile, wagon wheels broke, horses bolted, riders were thrown and one eager runner fired a gun to spur his horses forward, hitting a runner in his water canteen. He succeeded in creating a fountain of drinking water from the canteen, overbalancing the rider and knocking him off his galloping horse.

One confused horse turned and ran back and was shot by an oncoming runner.

Some tried to make the run in lightweight buggies only to have the wheels crumble beneath them at the first washed-out gully. When Nettie finally got on the road, there were so many on foot that she was offered astounding prices for her horses, and several times someone tried to take her wagon by force.

Then there were those who tried to hitch a ride on her wagon or take her provisions away from her. Nettie knew what to do. She broke out the guns and handed them to her three daughters and her eleven-year-old son, Wayne.

Stationing them two at the front and two at the back of her wagon, she instructed them to let off a shot every mile or so just to show everyone the guns were loaded.

By dark, she pulled up beside the land office in Guthrie and lifted her metal tripod out onto the ground. With wood she had gathered along the way, she set the stove to blazing and put on the beans she had been soaking for the last two hours.

174

She kept the guns handy, because she knew she would need them to defend the beans. Her third daughter, twelve-year-old Anne, sat in the wagon behind her mother, gun pointed.

If an unidentified person approached the wagon, Anne would innocently ask, as the pistol wavered about in her little-girl wrist, "Mama, if I squeeze this thing, does it make the gun go 'pop'?"

How could the intruder know that any of Nettie's children could shoot the eyebrows off a gnat?

Nettie stirred the beans and waited, and late in the afternoon she put her children into the line already forming at the door of the land office, spacing them 20 feet or so apart. As each child worked up in the line and reached the door of the land office, he went to the end of the line. This way, she knew that when her first runner came in, he wouldn't have to wait long before he could register. He would simply take the place of whoever was closest to the door.

First in was Chester Kendall, totally exhausted and starving hungry. He had staked a claim on a good quarter section only fourteen miles to the southeast of Guthrie. What more could the town want?

The townsite was registered in Nettie's name, and Chester registered another quarter section for himself and his brothers. So as soon as Chester registered, Nettie took her children from the line and settled back to wait.

Ed Gunther was next to get back, and the office was closed, but it didn't matter. Going south the direction he did, he had run into another town and never did get a chance at a quarter section. He ate his beans and went to sleep.

The Baker brothers were successful, but the tract they claimed was far to the south and bordered on a river. That would be a good place for a lot of purposes, but bad for a town. The town of Prosper needed room to grow in each direction, so it was certain that the riverside tract would later be sold.

The two young farmers from the Nebraska flood zone were also successful, but their claim was more than twenty miles from town. The father and son had not been successful. Neither had the newlywed.

Chester Kendall ate and rested and headed back to the townsite claim the first thing in the morning to help his brother guard it from claim jumpers and also to guard their own quarter section, which lay beside the town site. The Bakers and the two farmers registered their claims, ate beans at the Gunther wagon, fed their animals and stretched out on the bare dusty ground, exhausted from their ride of more than 30 miles.

At the telegraph office, late on 23rd of April, the telegraph wire was sent to Providence Falls, Nebraska: "SUCCESS stop START PACKING stop BRING EVERYTHING stop."

A crowd had gathered at the telegraph office in Providence Falls. Never had one small turn of events affected so many people, and even those who were not involved were pulled into the drama of it all.

The telegraph keys clicked and the yellow paper in the machine rolled forward in its jerky way as the words appeared on it. Excited faces peered at the paper.

Then came the excited cry. "They got one! They got one!"

"What do they mean 'start packing'? I've been packed for a month."

"What does that mean, 'bring everything'?"

"I don't know…."

The excited crowd hovered over the yellow paper of the wire, staring at the words that would drastically change their lives.

"Wire 'em back and see what they mean, 'bring everything'."

Keys clicked out the message that was sent across the wires.

"EXPLAIN BRING EVERYTHING stop."

Two hours later the second message came to Providence Falls. "THINGS WORTH MORE THAN CASH stop GUTHRIE GOT NOTHING FOR SALE stop."

"Hmmm… Guess we may need to repack."

The gathering in Nebraska bent over the message, each concentrating on his own problem, mentally re-prioritizing their selection of what to take… and where would they get wagons?

"Wire 'em back and tell 'em when we're leavin'."

"When'd that be?"

"Well, this here's the twenty third. Who all can be ready in a week?"

"We all got' a go at one time?"

"No law says so. But I was thinkin' it'd be good to have several together. 'Speck you could go on whenever you got ready."

"I reckon my bunch could be ready in a week. We're pretty well tore up, anyway."

"We'll need to wire back. How about the third' a May?"

"Good."

"Fine with me."

The telegraph office in Guthrie, Oklahoma Territory clicked out a yellow paper that read, "EXPECT DEPARTURE THIRD MAY stop."

At the office in Guthrie, the Gunther family read the message and nodded. No more need to wait around the crowded, smelly office with all the others needing to send and receive messages.

"That done it," Ed Gunther decided, circling his arm around Nettie's waist. "Now, we got'a get you out there on the claim."

They trekked the fourteen miles out to the site of the town of Prosper. Wagon ruts marked the section lines that would eventually be roads, and trees had been cut to make the traveling easier. The new settlers had begun to mark the trees along their property, encouraging traffic to stay in the roads. Already deep ruts were forming.

Across the section line from the town site, a family was busy settling in, plowing and felling trees and scratching a place for the garden. They were living out of their wagons, a gray one and a green one.

Nettie Gunther looked about her and smiled with satisfaction.

"See there, Ed? Like I told you, me and them youngens'll make out just fine. Got neighbors right over there and the Kendall boys ain't far. You go on ahead back up there to Providence. There'll be them that needs help, and with you comin' back with 'em, we won't be havin' to send someone to the land office to meet 'em."

Ed nodded and looked around. Everyone they had seen along the way had been too busy getting settled in to have their mind on mischief. The only trouble would be from claim jumpers, and in a battle of arms, his sympathy would be with the intruder. Any of his five were wicked with a gun.

With a hug and a wave, he was gone. His head and shoulders and the rump of the horse disappeared into the blackjack shrubs.

Maude Kendall had made her plans in her head, but now they must be enacted. "I ain't a'drivin' one of them wagons," she announced to her husband. "You got Manford and yourself and you'll see to gettin' them girls took care of. I got cares of my own to attend to."

Clyde nodded and said nothing. All this he knew.

Maude continued, "I want stronger springleafs in my buggy. Don't need no jouncin' around. You'll be wantin' to eat, and that wagon'll have the food. Get on and do it and leave the rest of it to me, and I got a list'a what else goes. You got'a trip to Hewett's to make. Remember that."

Clyde remembered.

Manny Kendall, age sixteen, waited to see what other requirement would be put on him. Seemed that nothing good had happened to him for days, or at least since his brothers got to go to the run without him. Driving the wagon down to the territory was nothing. Having five sisters as passengers would... well, he'd do what he had to do. Sixteen was an unhandy age... big enough to work but not old enough to have a say on what was done to him.

Clyde motioned to his son. "Manny, come help me."

Caroline Kendall, age fourteen, had her own concerns. She was trying to think how best to broach an important subject and could think of none. Best to just come out with it.

"Ma, me and Evie, we got invited to ride with the Hewett's."

Maude turned to her daughter with a puzzled frown. "Who was it done the invitin'? Mary Lou and Beth?"

"No, Ma. It was Mister Hewett. He said it for sure, didn't he, Evie?"

Evie Kendall nodded vigorously in affirmation.

Maude considered the matter. It was puzzling how anyone could be so daft as to invite two more youngens into those little old wagons when he had four youngens of his own, not to mention a whole store he had to move.

Of course, there was no accounting for what some folks did. She'd have Clyde ask, though, to be sure they were invited. If it was true, that would take away two of her responsibilities. It could, yet, be a good day.

"Can we, Ma?" Caroline prodded.

"We'll see," she told her daughters. "Now you see you get them quilts washed out. Ain't no knowin' what'll be down there where we're goin' or what'll happen on the way, but we're a'gonna start out clean."

Caroline and Evie exchanged a knowing look. Everything was going well on the surface. What had actually transpired was somewhat more involved.

James Hewett, with a legion of details on his mind, had watched the Kendall girls giggling and discussing the trip with his own two. Overlaying the picture of the girls was the sights and sounds of Clyde's girls at the reins of wagon or buggy and being sent here or there on errands for their father.

"Caroline, you and Evie can drive a team, can't you?" Mister Hewett had asked.

"Sure enough," Caroline, the elder, answered agreeably. "You want one moved somewhere?"

"Not right now, but I heard you'll be riding south with your brother. If you girls will ride with my girls and help drive a wagon down to Prosper, you can have enough yard goods from the store to make three new dresses.

"Three dresses each or for both of us?" He had their interest, but Caroline was a negotiator.

"Each."

"Lace and buttons?" Evie made her own inquiry. She had learned from the best. James Hewett almost smiled. Smart girls. Learning to bargain.

"Certainly," he told them.

"Any kind of yard goods we want?"

"Any kind."

"We want to do it."

He had been sure they would, but he wanted to get the matter sewed up air-tight before the shortage of drivers triggered Clyde's mind to the value of his daughter's skills.

"Good. Now girls, I wouldn't want to have you keep nothing from your folks, so you got'a tell em the plans we made. I'll say, though, the way you tell them is your business." Actually, he was proud of the girls for driving a bargain, and he already planned to make it four dresses.

Caroline didn't have to think very long. "Mister Hewett, how'd it be if we said you was invitin' us to keep Mary Lou and Beth company?"

"Sounds good." Who would be daft enough to believe that to be the reason, but, by the same token, who would believe he was hiring two girls as drivers, one thirteen and one fourteen? These were strange times.

Now, if he could just find a couple more wagons. He figured he needed six, all told. At least.

Tommy McClure sat at the kitchen table of his brother-in-law, Samuel Littletree. There had been no words from either of them or from Jake Littletree for the last five minutes.

"You can always count on a snag to hold up plans that took so long to make."

"Yeah, though I hate to refer to our pa as a 'snag', much as he's done for us."

More silence, then Tommy, "No better, huh?"

"Don't seem to be, but I got'a say this. Tommy, you go on ahead. Don't you be lettin' this stop you. Jake and me, we'll do what's got'a be done, then we can come on."

"Now, wait a minute. That's Nancy's pa, too, and I'm a part'a this family. Seems like it'd be my 'snag' along with yours."

"No," came Sam's voice with a sound of finality. "You got'a go on. We paid our money, and you've got your brother from Illinois a'comin'. Someone ought'a be down there to look out after our interest and yours and your brother's. Your Nancy, she's took care'a Pa all this time and done her part for the last year and more. Like I said, Jake and me, we'll do what needs to be done."

"But it could be...."

"Yeah, and probably will. The thing is, we'll not rest easy till it's over. You goin' on, that'll mean we for sure have somethin' to come down there to. You'll be able to look around and let us know how it'll be. That could be a help. You got sis ready and lookin' forward to it, and I know you're packed and all."

Tommy looked from one to the other of his brothers-in-law. For a fellow who likely didn't deserve to have such good luck, he sure stepped into it when he found this family. Nancy being the way she was, and her two brothers... But then, if they thought it would be a help to them for him to go on, then who was he to argue? It was true that Nancy had done her part for her ailing pa, and there was Tommy's brother, Willie, and his Aunt Sadie who had practically raised him. They both counted on him to be there.

Tommy commented, "Well, if it'd be help. And it could be that it won't be too long... I mean, now I didn't mean..." He groped for an apology.

Samuel to the rescue. "That's all right, Tommy. You didn't say nothin' that ain't been thought on by the both of us. Pa's not had much joy since Ma went on and even less since he got down with whatever's wrong with him."

Then Jake, "Yeah, Tommy, you got no cause to be concerned. You take care'a Nancy, and we'll take care'a Pa. He's always been so strong with nothin' wrong with him, it almost seems he let himself get down so he could go on to be with Ma. Could be that it won't be long."

Four

And plans went on.

Clyde took his remaining son, Manny, to the wagon shed. "Now what we're gonna do is this. I got these metal cleats made over at Clancy's, and we got'a put 'em on the wagon sides. Gonna make up sort of a shelf that'll set out over the wheels to carry the light stuff. A two-foot-wide shelf down each side'll turn a four-foot-wide wagon bed into an eight-foot-wide floorspace. I ain't quite figured out the dimensions an' all, but you set yerself to work on it while I tend to somethin' I got'a do."

Clyde Kendall walked away, a small smile on his face. He knew exactly how the shelf could be made, and if Manny worked out a better plan, he'd change to that one. Otherwise, he would instruct Manny. It did good to give a son a responsibility once in a while. Especially Manny. He'd done enough bad things to Manny, not letting him go on the run with his brothers, and this might help make it up to him. Besides, there wasn't nothing that Manny couldn't repair or build.

What Clyde himself had to do was go contact some of his usual customers and sell them on the idea that they needed the shelves. When wagons were your business, you had to use whatever trick you could think of. Also, it would use up the scraps of lumber that he would have to leave behind anyway.

Stephen Tullius, the miller, walked yet another circle around the separated parts of his gristmill. He could see right off that he could not get everything in his two wagons. The mill parts themselves weighed so much he couldn't fill the wagon bed with them before the weight became too much for the axles and wheel, to say nothing of the strain on the horses.

Well, he could handle that. He'd put part of the mill in each wagon, filling in with lighter items. He'd need another driver. Could an eight-year-old boy handle a team? Maybe not. Then it hit him: with all of the out-of-work old men sitting around the town, how much would he need to pay them to get them to use their own wagons to freight the household goods and then come back home?

Three more wagons should do it. He himself would carry the grinding plates for the mill and also the big wheels. They absolutely must all get there together.

So now, it was time to tell Greta and get her checked out on driving. He'd tell her she could take anything she wanted to take, as long as it didn't weigh much and she could get it in her wagon.

Clancy Harper, the blacksmith, circled his heavy cast iron anvil several times, trying to figure a way to get along without it, but there was no way. How could he shape metal with no anvil, and how could he be a blacksmith if he could not shape metal? And the telegraph had said bring everything. But it took a ramp and three strong men just to load it.

Now, if he could get ahold of a really strong-built cart or small wagon, maybe a couple of mules…? Yeah, that would work. He'd have Kendall strengthen up the springs… hey, no… he'd just take them out! Whoever heard of a hunk of cast iron complaining that the riding was too rough!

Having gotten past his concern for the anvil itself, he could now think about other things. He had those two wagons, and with himself and his thirteen-year-old son, they could handle that. The mule cart would be hooked on behind the wagon he drove.

Right this minute, his Mellie was walking the floor, trying to decide what would have to be left behind. It was enough to drive her crazy.

Clancy had just about gotten his thoughts together when Clyde Kendall rode up, dismounted and tied his horse.

"Lookin' serious, there," came the greeting.

"Yeah, tryin' to think how to tell Mellie she's got more'n a load just in her kitchen alone."

"Know what you mean. That's why I had'a do what I'm doin'."

"What'd that be?"

"You know them metal cleats you made me?"

"Yeah, what did ya do with 'em?"

"Gonna make 'em take the place of another wagon to haul light stuff. Manny, he's back at the shed makin' extensions down the side'a the wagon… both sides. Gonna add two feet, each side. Had'a do somethin' to take care'a all the light, bulky stuff in the kitchen plunder."

"Extensions, huh? What'd they look like?"

Truthfully, Clyde didn't know just yet, but he was certain Manny had one made by now. "Tell ya what I'll do… I got me some errands to do, but I'll bring one on over sometime 'afore dark. 'Speck Manny'll have several made, case someone needs a set and ain't got the time to make it hisself."

"Shelf, huh? It'd be solid?"

"Well, not for some things. More like for kitchen chairs and quilts and stuff that takes up room but don't weigh too much. That'd be what I'd think."

Having planted the seed, Clyde rode away. He stopped in at the store, but Hewett did not have time to talk.

"Just one thing, Hewett. Won't take a minute. My Maude says our biggest girls got an invite to ride with your girls. Figured there was a mistake, knowin' how girls is, getting' things twisted."

James Hewett stopped what he was doing. True, he was busy, but he had time for this answer. He stroked his chin thoughtfully and answered, "Well, like you said, you know how girls is, and them two'a mine, they can be right bothersome. If yours was to be along, that'd give 'em somethin' to do."

"Well, if that'd be a help to you…."

"Sure would, Kendall."

Clyde Kendall turned to leave, and James Hewett watched with a sly smile of satisfaction playing about his mouth. It would be fun to see Kendall's face when he figured it all out a few miles down the road. He'd be spittin' mad he didn't think of hiring the girls out and collecting the money for himself!

Clyde, having made the query Maude had demanded, set his mind to other things. He reckoned he'd spent enough time away from the shed, so he'd go see how Manny was coming on. The sound of hammering and sawing met his ears as he approached the wagon shed. Stacks of boards were spread out, and Manny was bent over a tri-square, marking a measurement.

"How're ya doin'?"

"Look it over. See what ya think."

There it was, its bracing legs fitted through the metal cleats. They held up the shelf on both ends and the middle. The whole thing consisted of a flat shelf that ran eight feet down each side. By dingle, it wasn't what he had in mind, but there wasn't no reason it why wouldn't work… maybe even better than his own idea!

"What I was thinkin', Pa, was if we was to have a rope or a strap and fasten it on the edge'a the shelf, we could loop it over the plunder and hook it inside the wagon bed. It'd help on the strength."

Clyde looked it over, visualizing the strap. "Believe I'd make it two straps, son, about three feet apart." One would have been aplenty, but it wasn't good to let a kid get too cocky without having a last-minute refinement of instructions.

"Sure, Pa," answered Manny agreeably.

"And, Manny, you get that done, and we'll take this'n over to Clancy's. Chances are he'll want some made. Try to use up all this lumber makin' shelves. Time folks start loadin' their plunder, they're gonna see just how little them wagon beds is, and we'll be ready for 'em."

"Sure, Pa."

On the twenty-sixth of April, 1889, a dusty and weary Ed Gunther rode his horse into Providence Falls. It had been a long haul north from Guthrie. Representatives of twelve families crowded around him to hear every detail.

"They's stuff we got'a do to get this operation off to a good start. First off, we got'a have a temporary mayor. Got'a have a treasurer, too. Got'a have someone in charge, makin' the decisions."

"Hewett," was the first suggestion.

James Hewett was quick to shake his head. "No, not me. I got'a good safe you can use, but I ain't handlin' the money. I ain't a'gonna have time. I ain't gonna make town decisions, neither. I got enough'a my own."

That settled, Clancy Harper suggested, "Why not everybody think on who you'd want? Then we'll vote."

"Yeah, good idea."

Ed Gunther again. "Now folks, them boys'a Clyde's done us a good job on pickin' that town site. The place has got trees, good ground for plantin', water-table high. But there ain't no way to get nothin' that you ain't already got and brought in with ya. Everything's scarce. 'Course, that'll change. The Santa Fe line goes right down through Guthrie."

"Hey, we could ship our stuff and not have to take these wagons."

"Hold it. Won't work. You'll need wagons to get yer stuff home from the depot, and any wagon you don't want later on, it'll be money in your pocket to sell. Never saw the beat'a folks with money and no sense about what they was gettin' into. A smart fellow brought in 200 tents and rented out bedrolls, four to the tent. Served beans and cornbread in some of them tents, along with canned peaches. Made 'imself fifteen thousand dollars in two days and nights. Don't know what the tents cost 'em, but he made 'im a bundle on 'em. Later on, he'll likely sell 'em for ten times what he paid. That'll tell you how it is there. Gonna be a great place some day, but that ain't today. Or even tomorrow."

"Got neighbors?"

"On every quarter section tract."

"Nettie like it?"

Ed grinned and nodded. "You seen me come in town alone, didn't ya? If'n she hadn't liked it, she'd'a not stayed there. Her and her youngens, they'd'a been right along with me."

"Then it's got'a be all right."

Ed nodded and repeated, "Remember to take everything you can. Nothin' ain't no good bein' left here for the rats, and I'd guess there'd be a market for anything you didn't need. Now I got'a go load up my wagon."

Clyde caught Ed by the sleeve. "Afore you go, let me show you what I put on my wagon. Goes along with what you said about takin' everything."

Ed studied the shelves on the Kendall wagon. That would take care of a nagging problem of his own. There was no way he could load onto one wagon all the plunder that Nettie had laid out for him to bring.

Clyde knew he had made a sale. "Got'a spare set over at the shed. Manny'll put 'em on for you for time and cost."

"I'll be over in the morning."

On the twenty-eighth of April, it was time for a final meeting. Up-front money was to be collected. Ed, again, found himself presiding.

"All right! All right! I'll be temporary mayor, but I WILL NOT be permanent. I heard words said about Tull to be treasurer, and if I don't hear no protest, it'll be him."

Silence.

"Hewett, send the safe on over to Tull. Let's get down to business. Them lots is five acres minus easement for roads. Folks on the corners may have easement down two sides. Now you see the plat I drawed, and Nettie was to get first choice, only she says she wants next door to the church, and that ain't been decided. That and the school. Want 'em in the middle'a town?"

Several nods.

"So they'll be there and there. Any objections? All right. Now, there's Nettie's lot right next to the church. I got thirteen scraps'a paper, got numbers on 'em. Everyone'll draw one, and that'll say the order you choose."

"Ed, what about them that wants two lots?"

"There'll be lots enough. You want 'em side by side, you pick where they's two together." Ed pitched the paper scraps into his hat and passed it around.

The Kendall's and the Hewett's took two lots each. So did the McClure's. Fourteen families were going, so 17 lots were chosen. The school and the church took two more, making 19. That left thirteen lots to sell.

"Now I want $25.00 from each of you for each lot you want. They's a more'n even chance you'll get most of it back. For your money, you get guaranteed help on the way down there if you leave on the 3rd of May. We'll pay someone to cut the trees in the roadway front'a your lot, and every lot gets a well dug by Hamp and Bart."

"What about them as has two lots?"

"They pay twice; they get two wells. Only fair. Later on there'll be a fee collected to pay the preacher and the schoolteacher when we get one, and it'll be voted on then. As mayor'a this movin' town, I say it gets on the road at first light, 3rd of May. I'm appointin' Clancy as wagonmaster. You tell him how many vehicles you'll be takin', and he'll say the order you go in. He'll say when we stop and for how long. Any objections?"

Silence.

"So now you step right up and hand your money over to Tull. Nuther thing, there might be huntin' along the line, and there might not be. Make sure you got beans enough and count on cookin' 'em at night."

"How long'll it take to get there?"

"Three weeks, outside. Hope to make it sooner."

Clancy Harper, the newly-appointed wagonmaster, wrote down names and the number of wagons. There were thirty-eight for absolute certain but likely closer to fifty eventually. He did a mental calculation of the length of a wagon and team, multiplying by fifty. The string of wagons would likely stretch halfway across the whole state of Kansas.

Then he sighed, deeply and wearily, noting mentally how a harmless little conversation in a warm store during a snowstorm could mushroom into a vicious rolling snake fifty wagons long. Well, they had been told to take everything, and Hewett, by himself, had 6 of the wagons.

The Littletree brothers and Tommy McClure met for the last time before the train would leave. Nancy had paid a call to her father to say last words, though it was doubtful that he heard them. He seemed to be already in another world, lying there with a peaceful expression on his pale and wrinkled face.

Tommy made a last offer. "You fellows still all right with me goin' on? You think you need Nancy and me to stay, you just speak up. Your pa was certainly good to me when he was up and around…" The offer hung in the air.

"No, Tommy. You go on." Samuel's words were firm. "We done decided, and there'll be enough of us goin' later that we won't be travelin' alone. It'll be a help to us knowin' you and Nancy are already there."

Jake nodded and echoed his brother. "Yeah, he's right. You go on. Everything's closed down here, and we're just waitin'. Be no reason for you to stay. I'm thinkin' it'll be less'a a month, at the longest."

Jake's guess was on the mark. It turned out to be three weeks later that their pa drew in a breath, sighed, and breathed no more. He was put to rest beside his wife of many years. Their graves were in a meadow of wild flowers, and after a last look, Jake, the lawman, and Samuel, the builder, turned their faces toward the Oklahoma territory. Thirteen-year-old Taffy Littletree set her dimpled chin with resigned indignation. How could her indulgent parents do this terrible thing to her?

What was a territory… anyway? Whatever it was, who in their right mind would want to go there?

But all of that happened later.

Five

Nettie Gunther wandered about under the trees in the new town of Prosper. Redbud trees. There were trees of many kinds, but the redbuds that grew short and stubby in the north were tall and spreading here in the new land. Instead of single stems, they grew in bunches, sprouted from the many seeds in each of the bean-like pods that covered the trees. In the spring, it must be a sight to look at the blooms. It would be nice to know where her lot would be, but the church had to be decided first.

She'd been over to the green wagon to visit that nice young lady from Tennessee. They were right busy over there, so she didn't stay long. Her own girls enjoyed hunting for their supper to vary their diet. It would be nice to get a garden going, and when Ed got here with her seeds…! Making plans was such fun!

Now what in the world was that stopping along the road? As a reflex, she put her hand on her gun and kept still. The children were out… somewhere?

The black horse worked its way through the trees toward her. She eased the gun into position and leveled it.

"Stop or I'll shoot!"

A startled male voice shouted back, "I'LL STOP! DON'T SHOOT!"

"Put your hands up and come in slow."

After a pause and a silence, the male voice queried, "Can I get off the horse?"

"Be slow about it."

The overalled young man wearing a weathered straw hat moved slowly off his saddle and advanced toward her, his hands in the air.

"Close enough. Stop and speak your piece."

"Don't blame ya for bein' careful, ma'am. Name's Hamilton. I was in the run and weren't too lucky. Wasn't surprised. Never been overmuch lucky in my whole life. Reason for botherin' you now was, we heard this tract was to be a town, and we was needin' a place to stay for a bit. Hoped there'd be a lot for sale, but if there wasn't, could be you'd let us stay somewhere close by? I ain't got much, but I always pay my way.

"Thing is, back at the camp on the border, I got my wife and she's in… well, in a family way, not doin' too good. I was hopin' to be on our land when 'er time came, but she got to thinkin' there was reason to… well, we heard… anyway…" and his voice trailed off into indecision.

Nettie lowered the gun. "How far away is she?"

"Eight, maybe ten miles over. Maybe not that much. Hard to tell in all these trees. You thinkin' we could stay here a while… maybe?"

"Well, it'd not be for me to say, but the rest'a the town'll be here first part'a May. I reckon I'm boss till then." Nettie chuckled at the idea of being boss. "Say, was you wantin' a town lot, five acres big?"

The man's eyes brightened. "You got some as ain't sold?"

"Could be. Won't know till they get here, but there was a few left last I heard. Price was $50.00 and a dug well comes with it. If you'd just want to camp over, it'd be $10.00. If there's a lot and if you'd want to stay, it'd be $5.00 a month till it gets paid for. Them as don't pay regular gets run off."

"Ma'am, I'd be grateful to have a lot in your town. I'll run on back to the missus to get 'er back here by dark. Thank you, ma'am."

Nettie watched him go, thinking she should have told him her name. Her second thought was what the town would say when they heard she sold a lot on a mortgage. Whatever made her do that… telling him how much to pay down and such? Well, he was only one person and one lot. If the town didn't like him, they could give him his money back.

Basil Hamilton galloped excitedly back to the camp on the Indian Meridian, the eastern boundary of the Unassigned Lands. Perhaps one thing in his life was going right. The two and a half weeks he had spent on the border had seemed like an eternity. First, there had been the wait before the run happened, then the disappointment of not getting land.

Then he had come back, disappointed, and Goldie had seemed worse. Of course, they knew it was risky to start out like they did, with her so far along with her first, but it had seemed their only chance. Now they had nothing.

He had heard, the way things get heard, of the town somewhere in this wilderness of trees.

A town? Maybe there was help in a town. Then he had found where the town would be, only it wasn't there yet… but maybe there would still be some help. Anyway, the whole plan seemed good to him. Much better than nothing.

There were six other families still camped on the banks of the Deep Fork where they had waited so hopefully. Then, like himself, they had been unsuccessful, and for various reasons of their own, they had not found the courage or the wherewithal of strength to go on their way.

The black horse trotted into the forlorn camp, and Basil went to his wagon, all eyes watching him. Weariness and frustration looked out of every eye of every person, even the children. Especially the children. No laughing and no playing. Only downcast eyes and quiet mouths.

Goldie was exactly how he had left her. He was eager to give her the good news. "Darling, we have land and we're gonna go to it."

"When?"

"Right now, if you feel up to it."

"I ain't feelin' no better here. I still got pain, but I ain't knowin' if it's the right pain. All the women here have somethin' different to say about what the pain feels like. You say they's a place we can stay?" Her voice was hesitant with hope.

"Darling, we…" and he stopped himself. Now was not the time to tell her the whole of the good news; she was happy with just a place to camp. He could tell her more about that later.

"You just rest yourself, and I'll be drivin' easy as I can."

That was when Basil Hamilton looked out over the pathetic camp. He wanted nothing more than to drive speedily away from the sad sight, but he reasoned that he could stay one more minute and relieve his mind that he had done his best for them… the ones he would leave.

"Folks, we're leavin' and goin' over into the territory. We bought ourselves a lot in a new town that's bein' built. I hear they's more lots, and if'n you'd be interested, I could show you where."

"A town? Not a quarter section?"

"A town lot. Five acres."

"For free?"

"No. They're fifty dollars."

"Fifty dollars! For five acres!"

Basil Hamilton sighed in exasperation. How could folks have such twisted thoughts when they were at the point of desperation, as he had been? Here they were, parked in the middle of nowhere with no place to go, and they were concerned about the price of the lot! Either they wanted it or they didn't; either way, it meant nothing to him. He began again, with a stern voice.

"Now look, I ain't up to arguin'. I'm a'fixin' to head on out…."

"Wait. What'd ya get for the fifty bucks? A gold mine?"

190

"You get five acres 'n a well. That's more'n you got right now." His weary voice was now caustic with sarcasm.

"Yeah, well, some folks may not have fifty dollars just layin' around gettin' moldy."

Basil sighed impatiently. *Try one more time.* "You can talk to them, and if they'll accept you, they'll take ten dollars now and five dollars a month till it's paid for. You don't pay, you get kicked off. I took a look at them fine trees on that lot, and I thought about the well that'll be dug for me. They'll be a school close by for my baby to walk to and a church to go to of a Sunday. Them folks didn't even ask if I had fifty dollars on me, figurin' I'd need whatever I got for start-up money.

"Now it's no hair off my nose if you don't even want to go look. I just told you about it 'cause I'm that kind of a fellow, and I wanted to share good news. Now you do what you want'a do. In twenty minutes, quick as I get harnessed up, I'm movin' over to my land. You follow after, if you want, or you can stay here with nothin'."

Whereupon, Basil Hamilton hitched his black horse beside his gray one and clicked them into motion. It only took ten minutes. He flinched as the wagon rolled over grass clumps and stones, knowing how it pitched Goldie about, but, for himself, he felt like a sailor on a stormy sea who had just had a glimpse of the harbor. The cold waves of panic striking him in the face had no more force, and his weariness meant nothing now that he saw a safe harbor ahead.

Nettie had walked over to the camp with the green wagon. "Roberta? Roberta, honey, I just wanted to say we got someone comin' over here, almost due I think. Her man says she was painin', and it's a first baby. Could be you'll be needed."

Roberta Carlile Dunbar paused and straightened her weary shoulders. "You just call me if you need me. My papa'll go get some water right now. Water'll be needed for somethin'. I'll set it on to boil for tea and whatever else we need it for."

At a commotion down the section line, Nettie looked up. "Here they come now. I'll hurry on back and meet 'em."

Nettie hurried away, and Roberta Dunbar watched as a wagon turned the corner and moved toward them. As the first wagon cleared the corner, another team of horses appeared, pulling a second wagon. Then another… and another.

When Basil Hamilton finally pulled his wagon up near Nettie's camp, six others took their places beyond him. To answer her puzzled look, he suggested, "Reckon they might be wantin' to talk to you about movin' into your town."

To herself, Nettie exclaimed, *Great Merciful Lord, what have I done? I done brought down all the leftovers from the run right on top of our heads!*

Then she found her wits. "You folks're welcome to park somewhere. I can't talk now. I got a sick woman to tend to."

To Basil, she asked, "What's your woman's name?"

"Goldie, and she's painin' bad. It's fair catchin' her breath away. I'd be obliged..." The urgency of his voice hung in the air.

"I'll do what I can."

Nettie climbed into the crowded wagon, crouching under the low canopy. "Miss Goldie, my name's Nettie Gunther. Your man says you're painin'?"

The young woman (girl?) on the bed of quilts, looked up, her features tensing as a pain passed over. Looking at her, Nettie saw that her name was appropriate. Her skin coloring was the pale gold of apple juice, the first straining, and her hair and eyebrows were bleached like wheat straw. Pale hands held the quilt up to her chin, though the April evening was warm.

"Nettie? I get scared, and women tell me things. You got any babies?"

"Honey, I had five, all of 'em healthy as wild goats. If you'd let me... maybe see how you're doin'?"

"You would?"

"The best I can." Experienced hands moved over the swollen abdomen, gently probing. Nettie saw the girl's fingers clutch at the quilt, white-knuckled with tenseness. Her teeth bit into her chapped lips. Scared to death, she was. Not only that, it was evident the girl had a long night ahead of her, and likely she herself and Roberta could expect a long night, as well.

"Am I...?" Her voice was faint but hopeful.

"You're just fine, honey. Ridin' this old wagon's got you all tensed up like a ball'a yarn the cat's been at, all twisted up. Nerves can do that, you not knowin' what you got comin' up." She sat on the pile of quilts and took the girl hands. "I can say this to ya: all of us that's ever been born come to this earth the same way. Ain't nothin' a'happenin' to you

192

that ain't happened 'afore. I'm wantin' you to think about somethin' you like and try to rest. We got some special tea a'comin' 'n that'll help."

The girl sighed a long sigh, watching Nettie with her tired eyes, playing Nettie's comforting words through her mind. Ain't nothin' happenin' that ain't happened before. Then she wasn't to worry, was she?

"Nettie?" came a voice from outside the wagon.

"In here, Roberta. You bringin' the tea?"

"Got it right here." Roberta climbed into the crowded wagon, crouching down to work her way among the heaped household plunder. "It'd be good if she could sit up a little."

"Here, I'll roll up this afghan for her back. Her name's Goldie."

"Now watch the tea, Miss Goldie. It's a mite hot."

Goldie reached for the heavy mug of steaming liquid. Wrapping her cold and trembling fingers around the cup, she felt its warmth and strength before she even took a sip. Here were two strangers sitting with her, taking up their time with her, talking to her and handing her tea. Maybe she could push away this feeling of total, desperate aloneness.

The tea warmed her throat, and the aroma soothed her head as the steam swirled around her face. Weariness settled over her like a smothering blanket.

"Peppermint?" Nettie asked Roberta.

"That and some chamomile. If it was me layin' there, I'd figure I'd need somethin' to make me relax."

Nettie nodded approval. "I was sayin' to her that sleep'd be best. That'd be a way'a savin' up her strength for later."

So the birth was not imminent, Roberta noted. She backed out of her cramped position. "That'd be good. I'll go and be back in a little while."

Nettie moved her position so she could push Goldie's tangled hair back from her forehead. This girl didn't look no older than her Ellie.

"Honey, you got your hairbrush handy? I know you ain't felt like tendin' to your hair, so I figured I'd get that brush, and when you finish your tea, we'll work on getting' rid of them tangles."

A voice came from outside.

"Ma?"

"What, Ellie?"

"Ma, you want me to start cookin'?"

"Yeah, you youngens go on ahead. I'll be there shortly."

Tea finished, Goldie turned to her side, presenting a tangled mass of baby-fine hair. Gently, Nettie pulled the brush across the mess, stroke after stroke, slowly working the snarls away. The girl's eyes drooped, and when she again turned, so Nettie could reach the other side, her eyes closed altogether.

Poor little thing, Nettie thought. *She'd ought to be home with her mama, but that ain't gonna happen.*

Easing the afghan from under her head, Nettie lay the sleeping girl down onto her bed of quilts. Climbing out of the crowded wagon, she came face to face with the young man.

He lifted up his bloodshot eyes from his pale, weary face questioningly.

Nettie gave the best report she could. "She's sleepin'. Labor ain't started real good. Could stop and not be back for a few days. Then agin, she could come on 'afore mornin'. Worst thing I can see is she's scairt, and her muscles and nerves is fightin' each other. Tea helped."

"Thanks, Miss Nettie..." His eyes followed her as she moved away.

"What I think about you is that you need to come with me and eat. My youngens, for sure, got more'n we can eat. Likely got roasted squirrel on the spit right now."

"Oh, I wouldn't...."

"Don't be wastin' time. Come with me." Again noticing the group of wagons, she called out in their general direction, "Make yerselves at home, folks. I ain't got time to talk business today. I'll talk to ya in the mornin'."

After a meal of roast squirrel, Basil Hamilton returned to his wife. Just after midnight, a scream of terror woke up the camp.

Nettie startled upright. "Ellie, run over and get Roberta. Take the lantern. Then come back and light the other lantern and bring me both of 'em. Margie, you get the snakebite kit and get out the scissors and cord. Get all the towels and that old blanket and come sit on the wagon tongue."

In the darkness, Nettie could see the moving lantern and also the blaze as a fire was stirred up. Of course, Roberta had heard the scream and had already begun to poke up the coals.

The lantern was returning, and Margie sat, nodding, on the wagon tongue, the needed items in her hand. Nettie moved into position beside the bed, and Ellie wondered, "What else, Ma?"

"Take that stuff from Margie 'afore she drops it on the ground."

Roberta appeared at the tongue of the wagon with a pan of almost-hot water just as Basil worked his way out of the pile of household goods. He had no words but just looked at the two women and dejectedly walked away into the darkness.

"Roberta, honey, come around here and tell me what you think."

Roberta Dunbar, 22, felt her eyes widen with concern. Twice she had witnessed childbirth, and at one of them, mother and baby were lost. She herself had never even assisted the midwife. Her heart pounding, she nevertheless decided that this was not the time to confess her total ignorance.

"What'd'ya think, honey? Baby's little, I know, but them pains is comin' on hard."

Nettie's words were punctuated by another piercing scream. Roberta could only nod agreement. Any pain that could cause such a hair-raising, heart-rending scream as they had just heard would certainly appear to be hard. She placed her hands beside Nettie's. Muscles hard as bone were beneath her fingers. "Too late for chamomile tea, I'd reckon. Maybe a massage, just to loosen…?" She could only question and guess what to do.

"Good idea. I'll turn 'er to let you get at 'er back. She don't weigh no more'n nuthin'."

Moving a box out of her way, Roberta crouched behind the girl. Why had she suggested a massage? What did she know about massage, anyway? All she had ever done was help her mother ease her shoulders after a long day of canning or that time her mother had slipped on the ice and strained a muscle in her back. Her mother had said she did good, but what did she know about childbirth pains? She looked up at Nettie, who was busy wringing out a cloth in the water, sponging the girl's face.

Do something, Roberta, she commanded herself. Moving her hand along the girl's ribs and across her back, she could feel the rope-like hardness of her back muscles. Too bad she couldn't have more tea; that would help. So here goes. Just as she pressed her thumbs into the hardness, another scream pierced the air, causing Roberta to draw back her hands.

"Keep it up, honey," Nettie encouraged. "Need to get her relaxed, somehow, don't you think?"

Roberta continued, finally feeling that a bit of progress had been made though the screams still came regularly. Women from the other wagons had accumulated at the wagon tongue, and looking at the lantern light reflecting on their faces, she wanted to shout to them, "Someone come do this! I got no idea what I'm doing!"

But she didn't.

Near two o'clock, the screaming stopped, but the pains did not. "Good thing to happen, her lettin' go like that."

"Lettin' go?"

"Yeah, like she decided to let it happen. Girl like this, she gets so scairt she can't get no scairter, and her mind goes numb."

"She fainted?"

"Ya might say."

"Is that good?"

"Could be good and bad. Bad 'cause she can't help none, but good 'cause she finally let her muscles do what they got'a do."

"What can I do?"

"You can bring that blanket on around and some'a them towels. Likely she's got baby things in here somewhere, but we'd never find 'em in time."

"In time…?" Was the birth that imminent?

"I think… Well, you can come and check and tell me what you think."

It was at that moment that Roberta saw what was ahead in her life. There would be times she would be forced to do what she had never done before, and this was one of those times. Now was the time to begin learning how to do what she didn't feel confident of doing. Moving into Nettie's position, she placed her inexperienced hands beside Nettie's. This would be a learning experience, and it was certain that the knowledge learned would be needed in this wilderness, so she had best learn all she could.

Small baby, Nettie had said. All right. The birth was soon to happen, Nettie had said. So this was how it felt. The girl had been more tense than most, and Roberta had already witnessed that. Had she given the right kind of a backrub?

So much to learn, and how did women learn these things? Her frail little mother had not stayed on the earth long enough to tell her very much.

Nettie was looking into her face inquiringly. Roberta remembered the counting she had heard women speak of. "One, two, three." Nettie waited. Now was time for words of wisdom. "Two minutes apart, maybe less? Small babies come quicker, don't they?"

"As a rule. Ellie, hand me up that snakebite box."

Scissors and cord were layed out, and the two women waited, silently, their arms touching in the closeness of the wagon bed.

"Figure it won't be long. You needin' to stretch your legs? Wouldn't want to risk no cramps later when both'a us'll be needed."

Roberta considered the offer. "I feel like I'm all right."

She would, in fact, have liked to step outside the wagon for a minute, but the memory of the drawn and frightened face of the girl's husband was something she did not want to see again.

Nettie dipped the towel into the warm water and carefully wiped her own hands, then handed the towel to Roberta. "Thinkin' we might ought'a get washed up and ready."

A series of low moans attracted Nettie's attention. "Ellie, you awake out there?"

"Yeah, Ma. What needs doin'?"

"Step up here, and pick up the near lantern. Just hold onto the handle, and if I say so, you lift it up to give me'n Roberta better light."

The moans became louder. "Ellie, lift the light."

"Roberta, honey, you move on around there… can you? MARGIE! You there?"

"Yeah, Ma."

"Slip around back and move that crate to give Roberta some room. She's done washed her hands."

The girl squeezed into the small space and slid the wooden crate a scant six inches. "Won't go no farther, Ma."

"That's room enough," Roberta decided and reached for the dry towel Nettie was handing her. What was she supposed to do with it?

The moans were louder and another scream. Nettie's hands were on the swollen abdomen. "Help us, Goldie, honey. Come on now." Nettie's voice was low and soothing.

Roberta remained motionless, holding the towel.

Nettie lifted Goldie's knees. "Put the towel here, will you?" Roberta placed the rolled towel where Nettie had indicated and in minutes it was over. A tiny, beet-red bundle lay on the white towel. The baby.

THE BABY! *Come on, Roberta, you know what to do now!*

Nettie's quick fingers tied off the cord and with a snip, the tiny girl was on her own. Roberta wrapped the towel around the delicate miniature, hardly bigger than a little girl's babydoll. Turning the tiny creature over, she rapidly patted the towel, and an angry yell filled the space under the wagon canopy.

Nettie, still working with the girl, flashed a smile at Roberta, who held the baby with one arm and crawled toward the wagon tongue.

Nettie yelled, "Ellie, take the baby till Roberta gets to the ground. She'll likely have a leg cramp."

"You got yerself a tiny little girl," Roberta told the anxious father. "You got a name picked out?"

Ignoring her, he took the towel-wrapped bundle and cradled it to his chest. His eyes shone in the lantern light, reflecting the unshed moisture. Nettie appeared at the wagon tongue and stepped onto the ground. "Mr. Hamilton, Goldie is fine. Gonna be weak tomorrow and likely another day or two, but it's my guess she won't remember much."

"Won't remember…?" How could one forget an ordeal like this? He would remember every second of it as long as he lived.

"A body knows what it can take, and her's done had enough. Shut down, that's what her body did. That didn't stop the baby, though. Now I'd think you might want me or Roberta, here, to stay 'n watch the baby, though I can't think what could happen."

"Would you?"

"Roberta, honey, if you'd tend that baby, to the washin' and such, I'd grab a wink' a sleep and spell ya 'afore mornin'. Feel up to it?"

"I'm fine," Roberta answered with a smile. Certainly, she was fine! Her first crisis in her new home was successfully behind her. She had been a help… maybe… and certainly she had learned something. Actually, a lot! Taking the baby, she told the father, "Why'n't you take a little rest, too, while you can? Likely you'll be needin' it in the mornin'."

One by one, the other women faded into the darkness. The crisis was past. Ellie and Margie followed their mother, and Roberta was left alone. Alone. Seated as she was on the tongue of a wagon in the

Oklahoma territory, carefully cleaning the tender folds and creases of the tiny red creature in her lap, the first baby born in the town of Prosper.

Roberta felt good. Really good!

Dawn was breaking when Nettie came to relieve her. "Roberta, it'd be good to get her to drink tea if you have plenty. Comin' down here like we did, I didn't have no thought'a bringin' comfort things like tea. Ain't wantin' to run you short, though. Then you'll be needin' to get some rest."

"Oh, I'm not tired. I'll get the tea."

Handing the baby to Nettie, she left and was back in 20 minutes. Nettie was arousing Goldie.

The puzzled girl looked at Nettie. "I had me the strangest dream. Thought I heard a baby cry, and I saw two angels. They was helpin' me to feel better. I still kind'a hurt inside. Am I still all right? Did they take away my baby?"

"Honey, you're more than all right! It's all over and you have a baby girl. She's who you heard crying. She's getting' hungry and wantin' her mama to wake up."

"I have…?" Voice faint with apprehension.

"A baby girl. Your man, he's got 'er and is walkin' with her, but what she wants is her mama. We've got you a cup'a tea, and you need to drink what you can, and then we'll get that little girl for you."

Roberta leaned toward the girl to hand the heavy mug filled with steaming liquid. Taking the cup, Goldie looked squarely into Roberta's face. "I know you! You're one'a them angels, and she's the other one. You got on different clothes. I ain't on earth no longer, am I?"

The sky-blue eyes darted here and there, attempting to place herself. "This ain't heaven…?"

Nettie began to laugh. "Oh, no, honey, it ain't heaven, and you'll be one of 'em that knows that come time you get settled in."

"But you're the…?"

Roberta looked at Nettie, who looked back, puzzled. "You reckon it must'a been them white night dresses we was wearin' that set 'er to dreamin'? Them bein' white and us bein' strange could'a put her in the mind'a…?" How could they possibly have seemed like angels?

Nettie nodded in agreement. "Honey, you didn't see no angels. It was just her and me, and when you feel better, we'll talk about it. Right now, your man's here, and he's got that little girl 'n her whimperin' like a lost puppy. We're gonna let him in here with you while you feed her, and we'll get on about our business. You need anything, you send him to get me." Patting Goldie's shoulder, Nettie crawled from under the canopy and followed Roberta away from the wagon.

"Angels, huh? Been called a lot'a things in my day, and angel ain't never been one of them things!"

Six

The six wagon units that missed out on the run had now widely dispersed. They had paid their $10.00 and were told nothing would be final until the rest of the town arrived.

The Kendall brothers, who had staked the town site claim, went to work clearing trees on their quarter section, preparing to make a shelter cabin and a rail fence.

Josh Fields, the newlywed, hightailed it back to Providence Falls to put his body where his mind had been all along: with his bride. The two young farmers from the flood plain and the father and son who usually hired out for day work saw the opportunities in Guthrie to make hard cash and decided to postpone bringing their families to the town.

The wives and families were still set up back there in Providence, and opportunities to earn the kind of money that could be made in Guthrie right now had to be taken when presented.

The Baker brothers, Hamp and Bart, had done a lot of talking, both in Providence Falls (otherwise known as Poverty Flats) and also on the trek down to the Kansas border. This seemed the time to make the great move forward, the one that they had always hoped to do. They had been guaranteed 32 wells, and, deducting the 2 that would go on their own lots, that was a lot of paid business. Their fee was $10.00 for the first forty feet of the well, as long as they were allowed to dig where they thought was the best place for water. After that, the charge was another dollar for every five feet of dirt removed.

That was a lot of digging, and reason told them that the thirtieth person to get their well was likely to become very impatient for it to be dug long before they got to it. And with good reason.

Over the past year or so, the brothers had dreamed over the colorful brochure advertising the mule-powered well-driller. It worked on the principal of a pounding, dropped weight, and a suction pump removal of mud and water. It could dig a well much faster than a pick and shovel.

To the brothers, being of more than average ability to figure the cost of labor against wages, it was crystal clear that driving a mule on the treadmill and working a pump handle would be easier and quicker than working with the pick and shovel many feet below ground and drawing every bit of removed dirt out with a bucket on a pulley using arm muscles.

They even knew where they could get such a driller for the princely sum of $225.00 plus freight.

The thing that had held them back was the scarcity of both cash and work, but now it seemed both of these obstacles were to be removed. Forming a meeting with their wives over the magic wires of the telegraph office, they made the decision to go for it.

Everything that could be spared and anything that had a monetary value was summarily sold, the cash pooled, and the order was placed for the driller, commonly called a spudder rig. The parts were to be shipped, unassembled, to the Santa Fe rail station in Guthrie.

When the brothers completed the land run, in which they secured a tract on the edge of a river to the south, they had returned to Guthrie, and they saw the golden opportunities right there in town. The lack of water in the town of Guthrie was so acute that even the watering tank that was intended for servicing the train had been emptied by the thirsty residents. Also, muddy water hauled from a nearby creek had sold for a nickel a cup on the day of the run and for a few days afterward.

A wire sent back to Nebraska informed their wives that they would need to wait there in town for at least two months or possibly more and let the fellows earn a bit of cash while there was so much of it was floating around. They would take the spudder rig out to the town first and fulfill their obligation there, then bring it back to Guthrie and work for a month or more. The wells in Prosper might possibly be dug in, maybe, 2 days each, and at an estimated $12.00 per well, that would pay for the rig. It would also take a couple of months of their time unless the rig was faster than they had estimated.

Then, after another month of paid work, if their wives had been in agreement with waiting, they could go get them and bring them down in time to be set up comfortably before winter came on. Anyway, it seemed like a plan. The only thing was, the passenger load was so great from Arkansas City, Kansas down to Guthrie, that freight hauling by rail was suspended for a week in order to bring much needed foodstuffs. The rig parts were marooned in Arkansas City.

Then, also, there was their quarter section claim down by the river that the town would need to sell... the one the brothers had staked. This was probably a good time to go down there and take a better look, since the well-drilling rig would not arrive for a while.

It was quite a distance down to that quarter section, backed up to the river the way it was. It took the greater part of a day to get down there, through the new fences and claims. Following along the riverbank from the west, they could see the claims were filling up fast. Trees were being cut and fence wire was strung. In fact, some of that wire stringing was going on right there on their own land!

Stopping short, they listened to the fencing crew. Four men were cutting trees to use as posts where needed; otherwise, they were attaching the fencing wire to trees.

Approaching as quietly as possible, the brothers from Nebraska slid down from the horses and drew their squirrel guns to their shoulders. Easing along from tree to tree, they came to within fifty feet of the four men, busily working and talking among themselves.

Bursting out into the open, Bart yelled, "Hands in the air or I'll blow your heads off!"

Obediently, hands were raised. "Don't shoot, man!"

Hamp stepped through the trees thirty feet away, gun also drawn, and demanded, "What're you doin', stringin' fence wire on our property?"

"Your property? This here belong to you?"

"You pretendin' you don't know?"

"It's the truth, man. Me and them men, we was just stringing' the wire where we was told. We didn't know whose land it was."

They looked as though they were telling the truth.

"Who'd'ya work for that told you to put a fence here?"

"The boss, over to the 7C ranch."

"Ranch? With cows and things?"

"Yeah, man. It's right there through the trees."

"You know I could shoot you right now for claim jumpin'. I don't see no ranch nor no boss. All I see is you, and you're on my land that's been registered in my name, and I want to see you spread-eagled on the ground where you stand."

He punctuated his statement with a skyward blast from the squirrel gun. The noise momentarily silenced the birds in the trees and influenced the men to throw themselves face down onto the ground.

"Well, Bart, what'd you think we ought'a do with these here lawbreakers?"

Bart surveyed the scene. "Shoot 'em and throw 'em in the river? Bodies'd be a couple miles down stream 'afore suppertime. Or we could string up with for the buzzards. Them birds don't look to be too well-fed. Look like they'd like to peck out a few eyeballs."

"Could do that. Then again, we could divide 'em up, two for you and two for me, and find out where that boss man is that takes a man's land 'thout askin'."

"Yeah, and a nuther thing'd be if you held a pair of 'em on the ground on their faces, while the other two headed out in front'a me, leadin' me to the boss man."

"Could do that. Sounds like a plan to me." He yelled at the men stretched out on the ground, "You two that're closest to me, you crawl over here… No, don't stand, crawl." Bart emphasized his words with another blast from his gun. "Now you turn, one lookin' east and one west, and if you're on a hill'a red ants, you let 'em bite if you don't want your head blowed off. T'other two are yours, Hamp."

Hamp nodded. "You two men march ahead'a me to go get my horse, and then we'll find that fellow you said put you up to breakin' the law."

Leaving Bart with his gun leveled at the two men on the ground, Hamp set his tired horse to walking leisurely after the men before him. "Now, don't you be ziggin' and zaggin' and makin' me nervous. I just fair can't shoot straight if I get nervous. Gun blast'd likely go every which'of'a'way."

The men stumbled ahead of him along the sandy bank of the river. Good-looking stream of water, Hamp noted. The wide channel showed how it could flood if a heavy rain happened to fall on out to the west. Fact is, a whole section of the land was subject to flooding, and it would have been entirely unsuitable for the town.

The men walked in front of Hamp for two miles, and then dead ahead were the buildings that must be the ranch. Barns and bunkhouses were fenced apart, and a number of animals were in corrals. A lot of them were cows. Good-looking cows. What if…? Hmmm… Wouldn't hurt to try.

Hamp pointed his gun toward the sky and fired. A man looked his way and disappeared into the barn.

"That the boss man?"

"No, but he'll bring 'im."

Hamp was getting charged up to the job ahead, and he rammed another shell into the gun and fired, just for the pleasure of hearing the sound.

"Hold your fire!" came an authoritative command, and a tall man with an even taller hat came toward him. "What'd'ya mean comin' on my property, shootin' and scarin' my livestock? And what're you doin' with my men?"

"These here your men? Well, they was just stringin' fence wire on land I registered more'n a week ago. Claim jumpin' is against the law, and I got every right to shoot these thieves. Fact is, my brother may not be as nice as me, and he's got two more'a your men back on the claim holdin' 'em at the point of a gun."

The tall man looked at the two workmen. "That right? You were on this man's property?"

"Boss, we was just doin' what..." He began, but he was cut off.

"Joe, take these men to barn. I'll deal with them later. You sayin' that land borderin' on the river is land you staked? If my men were there, it was 'cause they didn't see no stakes."

Hamp nodded agreeably. He knew a lie when he heard one.

The tall man continued, "You gonna be buildin' there next to us? You note how that land overflows when the floods come?"

"Floods don't bother me. I can swim."

"You sure enough gonna prove up that land?"

"Why'd you think I staked it if I wasn't aimin' to live there, me and my brother?"

"Could be you could find better land if you had money out'a that piece."

"Sure enough, but who'd buy crawfish land the way that there piece is liable to be. Leastwise, that's what you said."

Hamp still sat on his horse, changing his rifle from one hand to the other. It made the tall man nervous, just as it was intended to do.

"Say, man, could you point that gun down? My name's Wilcox and I'm the foreman here. I'm thinkin' you'd best talk to the boss. Could be he could give you a little somethin' for that worthless land, bein' as how it borders up against his'n. Won't ya come along in?"

Hamp continued to fiddle with the gun. "Naw, I got things to do, me and my brother. Got'a get settled in, like the law says. Yer boss man wants to talk, he knows where I'll be. I'll be right where that fence wire is, me and my brother and them two other thieves."

With that, he turned and walked his horse a few feet then whirled and fired another blast at the buzzards overhead. One unfortunate bird fell end over end in a swirl of ebony feathers. Forcing his tired horse into a temporary gallop, just for show, Hamp was soon out of sight.

Hamp felt good. Hmmmm, the ranch wants the land, even if it has to buy it. Likely it was being used by them right up to the run. Hamp could see why: good water and grass, the two things a herd of cows need. An occasionally flooded pasture would mean nothing to them. He was certain the boss would soon be over, wanting to talk business.

But he didn't come that day. Hamp and Bart shot food in the nearby timber and let the two men eat one at a time, but they took turns guarding them at the point of their gun. Night came, and they were just too weary to watch them. Forcing them to climb into a tree, they tied them to the trunk, straddling a limb. Their knives were confiscated, and their shoes were removed. The sandy bank of the river produced a wealth of wickedly large grass burrs, treacherously hiding in the bunch grass and blue stem. If the men managed to get down, they likely wouldn't get far barefooted.

Keeping a small fire to discourage varmints, the brothers hobbled their horses in the good grass and settled down at the base of the tree to sleep until morning.

They were roasting the last of yesterday's meat over the fire when Wilcox and another man approached. The two fence builders were still shoeless and not likely to bolt, and Bart and Hamp had their guns leveled.

"Don't come no farther without a invite," Hamp warned. "You're walkin' into where I live. Might wake up the youngens. You the boss man?"

The two men stopped. "I'm the manager. The boss is not here at the present. We come to make an offer for your place."

"How much?"

"A hundred dollars."

"Well, that ain't a bad start. 'Course, we got us a mite'a talkin' to do. If we was to sell this here, it'd mean we'd be forced to leave, and we'd need us a good, heavy wagon to do it in."

"A wagon! You ain't got nothin' here!"

"You don't know what we got. We came up to within fifty feet'a your fellows yesterday and them not even knowin' it. 'Sides, I ain't here to argue. I'm just relatin' to you what it'd take to buy this here land I won from the government. For starters, a heavy wagon and a team'a strong mules."

The men waited silently.

"Then, it could be that a hunnerd dollars'd be enough, if you was to throw in twenty head'a cows and two bulls, not related to each other."

"Twenty cows? And two bulls? That's robbery!"

"No it ain't. It's the price. I didn't ask you to pay it. This here's good land for cows, deep grass 'n such. I could buy me good stock and raise beef to sell, but if I don't get to keep this here good land, then I'd have to buy somewhere else, and it'd cost a bundle. Yeah, and them cows'd need to be in good shape. Wouldn't want to start a business with no scrawny stuff."

The two men looked at each other and exchanged a few words. "Well, we couldn't make no deal today. We'd have to see...."

Hamp cut in, "Sure thing, man. You take all the time you need. We'll keep these here fellows here, just for the company of 'em. We're feedin' 'em good, as you can see. Now if you was to think you could slip around and gun us down, you'd need to figure we got ways'a getting' even that you ain't never heard about."

Bart added, "And we'd have the law on our side. Plain to see that's true, ain't it?"

The two men walked away, but they were back before noon. "Boss says he'll go for it if you let our two men go."

"Be happy to oblige. All I need is the money and a promise you'll let them cows go. Need it on paper with names on the bottom. And bring that wagon with ya, so's we can see if it's what we wanted."

Dusk was falling, and the brothers were just about ready to send their hostages back up the tree when they heard the wagon coming along the river bank. The mules pulled into sight, drawing behind them a ten-foot long, narrow-gauge wagon. Solidly braced, with heavy wheels.

"Hold it right there. We got'a check out the underside and the axels. Wouldn't want it to fall apart on us."

First Bart, then Hamp crawled under the wagon, ceremoniously checking each joint, bolt and brace.

"Reckon it'll do. Let's see the paper."

The brothers signed on the line and handed one of the papers back. "We'll be back in a couple days fer the cows, and there'll be a gang of us, prepared to take no funny stuff off'a you."

They watched as the wagon driver and the hostages walked away behind the two men on horses. They held their congratulations until the 7C Ranch men were out of earshot.

"Would ya look at that wagon! Couldn't'a got a better one if we'd ordered it special from Kendall!"

"Yeah, but have you thought on how we're gonna get twenty cows and two bulls up to the town?"

"I got a idea." Bart jumped on his horse and galloped after the retreating men.

"Hey, hold up, there. My brother and me, we allowed we'd just take them two bulls now. We'll be by for 'em first light in the mornin'. Have 'em ready."

The brothers slept in the new wagon, exchanging comments on how the town was going to take to the fact that the land was sold without a vote, but they were virtually certain the cows would be welcome.

It was near midnight when Bart sat bolt upright, staring around him in the light of the full moon.

"Hamp, you asleep?"

"Not now with you a'grabbin' my shoulders like you was killin' a bear! What's got into you, here in the middle'a the night?"

"Had a thought. Tilst we get them cows and get gone, this here land'd be still ours. That right?"

"Well, I reckon, but…."

"That's what I thought. You look over there and see that moon a'shinin' on that new fence wire hooked onto them trees. That'd be ours, and we need to be pullin' it down. Now!"

"By crackies, if you ain't got a'hold on to a good idea. I was sure sleepin' good on these smooth boards, up and out'a the way'a the crawlin' critters, but there'll be more nights for sleepin'. We got anything to pull out them staples that's holdin' the fence to the trees?"

Bart grinned at him. "You recall how you never let them fencers up to get their things? Reckon whatever they was workin' with'd still be there, and it'd be ours, too. Come on."

During the next four hours, more than five hundred feet of fence wire had been removed and rolled up. Possibly another two hundred was still attached to the trees.

"We could eat us a bite, and one of us go after them bulls, and t'other'n could be finishin'. Which you want?"

"Don't matter. I'd just as soon keep on pullin' staples."

As promised, the wagon was at the ranch early. Bart sighed as the bulls were presented. The animals had seen their best days, in truth, but it had been quite a demand for any ranch to suddenly produce two bulls that were expendable.

Even then, he couldn't resist a jab. "We're gonna take these here bulls off your hands, but them cows better be a sight younger and in better shape. We'll be back inside'a two days."

The bulls were tethered to the wagon, and they followed along as Bart drove the mule team through the still-grassy section line roads back to Hamp and the fence.

"Reckon they done the best they could on the bulls, bein' short notice like it was. Look like good stock, though. Could put us through a round or two'a calves, and whoever wants to tackle keepin' a bull after that, it'd be his problem."

Rolls of fence wire were piled into the wagon, and the mule team was headed north. By the time they reached the town site, it was late in the evening and too dark to read cornerstones. They trudged along in the semi-darkness, trying to dodge stumps and rocks.

Chester and Douglas Kendall had been cutting logs all day and had fallen asleep under a tree, exhausted. From the campsite of the green wagon, the two bluetick hounds set up in full cry when they heard the intruders. Everyone startled up and reached for their guns.

Claim jumpers!

"Who goes!" demanded Douglas in his most stern and commanding voice.

"That you, Doug?" came a familiar voice.

"Who's that?"

"Hamp Baker. It's me'n Bart."

"Hey, Hamp! Bart! Get on up here! What you doin' out there? What's that you got a'followin' your wagon!"

"Got a couple'a bulls, 'n that ain't all. We need all the help we can get to go get twenty cows tomorrow."

"Twenty cows? Whereat did you get twenty cows?"

"Long story. How many fellows you got around here?

"Well, they's me and Chet. Got seven new people wantin' lots. Could be they'd go if the cows was to be for sale. Got a new fellow to the north. I reckon they's others, but we been too busy fence-buildin' to do a lot'a socializin'."

Bart and Hamp took a day of rest while the Kendall brothers rounded up a crew for the cattle drive. For a chance at a cow, all of the men were willing to give a couple of days.

Before daylight ten men and two teenage girls headed out on the cattle drive. It would clearly take that many to get the cows through the trees without loss and to guard them against theft, but by using all the rope that anyone had, they devised a plan. They decided to form pairs by tying two cows together and assigning them to one person to keep up with. Even in a stampede, two cows running together would not get far before they hooked onto a tree.

It was a long day that got the twenty cows to the new town of Prosper.

A joint effort rolled out the fence wire and stapled it to the trees in what would someday be the schoolyard. That would keep them penned up, and the chore of milking the cows that were fresh would be gratefully offset by those weary of the monotonous diet and the welcome-ness of the milk. Everyone offered to help, and the cows were duly herded through the trees.

Subject to town vote, an auction would be held when the others townspeople arrived. That would distribute the cows. Any extras would be gladly bought by those on surrounding claims.

After a night's sleep, the Baker brothers headed out for the Santa Fe depot with the new ten-foot wagon. Surely their equipment would be there by now.

A well in the school yard was sorely needed, as it was a constant chore taking the cattle, a few at a time, to the scooped-out watering hole on the Kendall Brothers' quarter section.

Roberta's father, Eben Carlile, came for two of the cows, offering to attend to the feeding and watering of them until the town came.

Roberta and Nettie visited with Goldie and her baby.

"So you got that little girl and got 'er named."

"Yeah, there was a time I thought if it was a girl, she'd be named April, after when she was born. But then it got to be May, and I thought that was still all right. Then things happened like they did, and I knowed the name ought'a be Mary Prosper Hamilton. Could be she'll be called Mary, but I think I like Prosper. Seems to me she's got the right to be called that."

"I reckon the right'd be hers if it was anyone's. Could be a name she'll like." Nettie tried to be agreeable.

Goldie continued brightly, "I was thinkin' today I'd move some stuff around, makin' a little more room in this here wagon. For the life'a me, I don't know how you both got in here and did for me the way you did. Seemed like I didn't have no heart to do nothin' to help, but I feel a lot better now. Gonna shove them crates down to...."

"Goldie, honey, I ain't no doctor, but I been a mama, and it'd be my advice for you not to be pushin' and heavin' on stuff just yet. I got me these three girls goin' crazy for somethin' to do. You got somethin' needin' to be pushed, you say what, and they'll do it."

"But I...."

"Shh! Don't talk like that. We're neighbors, and there'll likely come the time when they'll be needin' help from you."

Margie walked up the wagon tongue, balancing herself by waving her arms like rooster wings flapping on the barnyard fence. "What you want shoved?"

Seven

Two states to the north, Clancy Harper, blacksmith and now wagonmaster, went over the finalized list of wagons that would be heading south. After the first 38, two more had been added as the travelers became painfully aware of how small wagons actually were when a houseful of plunder was being piled aboard.

Also, two new couples from down on the flood plains had bought their lots in Prosper. They paid the full $50.00, being anxious for reasons of their own to move south.

Though two wagons were added, plus the four for the newcomers, nine were taken away when the Baker brothers, the two young farmers, and the father and son wired that they had taken on work for cash money and would come for their families later.

That left thirty-five teams and wagons and ten families represented. A driver had been hired for Clancy's own wagon, leaving him free to ride the sidelines, checking for trouble. Trouble, indeed! What did he know about being a wagonmaster? How did he get himself into this mess? Oh, well, likely he'd do as well as anyone else.

So he'd start with Ed Gunther, acting mayor. His wagon would be first, and then he would follow with the six wagons belonging to Hewett's store. So, who was next? The newcomers, maybe, and then his own. He had ended up with three wagons and a mule cart before he got his blacksmith equipment and household plunder aboard.

There were the four wagons belonging to the Littletree brothers that were pulled out. With their pa on the point of leaving this life, they could neither take him along nor leave him with no other folks to see to the burying. They did what good sons were expected to do. They did, however, insist that Tommy McClure, their sister's husband, stay with the train.

Then there was Josh Fields and his bride and their hired wagon. The Malone's and then Steven Tullius and his sister. Tull managed to get everything onto two wagons plus the one for the gristmill.

That left Clyde Kendall and his three vehicles. He wanted Kendall to be last, as he and his son, Manny, were most knowledgeable about wagon repairs.

Thirty-five wagons long, and the only good thing about it was that it was considerably less than the fifty he had thought there might be.

He was determined that Ed Gunther should pull out at first light and the others would flow into line. He estimated an hour would pass between Ed getting on the road and Clyde Kendall finally moving, at least on the first day.

After that, things would go more smoothly. Maybe.

Dawn had barely broken as Ed Gunther clicked his team into motion. James Hewett had hired two young men and a pair of older fellows with wagons to make the trip for wages using their own teams.

He took the first position after Ed Gunther, followed by thirteen-year-old Evie Kendall, with twelve-year-old Beth Hewett by her side. Evie's experienced hands picked up the rein, and the team instantly knew who was boss, pulling out onto the road without incident.

Behind Evie came her sister, fourteen-year-old Caroline Kendall, flanked by Mary Lou Hewett. The three hired wagons followed behind.

The newcomers from the river flats were motioned into line, all four wagons of them, and the sun broke over the horizon. Moving the others along, he finally saw Maude Kendall's large two-seated buggy piled with assorted boxes and baggage setting heavily on the springs and leaving barely room for her to sit.

Next came sixteen-year-old Manford Kendall with his three younger sisters climbing about on the load. Lastly, Clyde Kendall pulled into line.

Clancy waved and fell in behind him, walking his horse slowly. It would likely be best to save the horse's strength as well as his own. Who could guess how many trips from the front of the line to the rear that he and the horse would both make before the first day was over?

There were seven extra horses going along, and the agreement was that they would be used where needed unless the owner of the animal needed it worse. Seven seemed to be a safe number.

Clyde Kendall watched the wagon ahead of him. It was a good thing that the big girls had been invited to ride with the Hewett's, because Manny seemed to be having his hands full. Several times he saw his son turn and talk to his sisters.

He was too far back to hear what was said as ten-year-old Betty yelled, "Manny, you got'a stop. Sophie's got'a weewee."

Manny yelled back, "Sophie's six years old and that's old enough to go when she's told to go. She can wait."

A hundred feet down the road, eight-year-old Ollie announced, "Sophie says she can't wait. What're you gonna do?"

Manny yelled, "Find somethin'. Rummage around in the stuff and find somethin'. I can't be comin' back there. You take care of it."

The girls moved around, poking their hands into this box and that crate. Sophie screamed, "Hurry!"

Manny yelled back to the searchers, "You got somethin' yet?"

"Ma's glass pitcher is all," came the discouraged answer.

"Give it to 'er."

"Ma'll kill us."

"She won't, less'n one of you tell her what happened."

A few minutes passed.

Betty again. "What'll I do with it?"

"Pour it over the endgate."

Betty again. "Ollie, you scoot on back there, and I'll hand you the pitcher."

Now Sophie offered. "I take it."

Manny yelled, "No, Sophie. You done helped enough already."

Clyde Kendall gasped as he saw his eight-year-old lean out over the endgate and pour something. Whatever could she be doing? Whatever it was, however, she got it done without incident.

Then the girls all crawled forward to sit on the buckboard seat with their brother. Four backsides on a five-foot seat was not an easy fit when one of them was a strapping sixteen-year-old. Manny's face turned toward the girls, and something was obviously said, as Sophie was then lifted onto Betty's lap.

In that way, they jogged along ahead of him for a couple of miles.

Manny had thinking to do. If this trip didn't drive him totally crazy, he had his life to plan for. Near as he could make out, the family was moving to a ten-acre plot, and the wheelwright business would continue and be expanded. In the new country, a lot of new business could be had, and likely the wagon-building part of Pa's business would be very good.

It wasn't that Manny minded work, and he even knew how to get along with his father; it was more about something else. He occasionally thought he would really like to try something else. All he had known since he was a toddler was to work in the wagon shed, building this, repairing that, creating wagon spokes, soaking and bending the wood for the wheels, measuring, pounding, drilling… something… something….

He had entertained in his mind for a few days that he would be permitted to make the trip south with Chester and Douglas. It would be fun to make the land run. But no, he couldn't go, because he would be needed to drive a wagon. Likely Pa didn't know there would be a lot of young men who would hire out themselves and their rigs just for the wages and a change of scenery. A lot of the wagons ahead of him were hired. But no, Pa's wagon had to be driven by him.

That wouldn't have been too bad, except he also had the three little girls. At first, Pa had said he would have all five girls, and if that had happened, at least Caroline and Evie could spell him, and he could doze for a few miles. But no, all he got was the little ones.

Working for his pa had been all right. He was given money when he needed it and usually when he asked for it, but a fellow of sixteen should be earning his own money and knowing he would get it without asking for it. Looking ahead, he could see the situation would not soon change.

Chester and Douglas, twenty and eighteen, were under the same restrictions as he, so he knew he could look forward to the same treatment for at least the next four years.

"Manny!"

"What!"

"Sophie dropped her doll overboard. You got'a stop!"

"I can't stop. Can you get it?"

"You mean jump out?"

"Reckon you'd have to, unless you got'a real long arm."

Ollie now. "I'll get it, Manny."

Whereupon Ollie scooted to the endgate and leaped down to the ground. Clyde could not believe it when he saw his eight-year-old jump down to the ground in front of his horses. The team shied away, and Clyde pulled back on the lines.

"Whoa, there! Whoa, up!"

He couldn't see where she had fallen, and he couldn't jump to the ground and still hold onto the horses. In the split second of his indecision, he saw the girl's flowered dresstail flutter past the horses and run alongside the wagon driven by Manny. At the front of the wagon, she reached up, caught her brother's hand, and was drawn up to the buckboard seat.

Clyde felt his heart settle back down into his chest with relief. At the first stop, he was going to have to have a talk with that son of his.

Manny scooped up his little sister and clicked encouragement to the team, keeping them an even distance behind the buggy driven by his mother.

Handling the team was a subconscious action to Manny. It was no longer something he thought about, having been almost ten years on the buckboard seat. Pa believed in early training. Manny had been grateful for that, and it was because of Pa's training that he could do just about anything that needed to be done with a wagon or a house or a lot of things.

Now that he had a lot of time to sit and think, a thought that had occurred to him sometime ago now firmed itself in his mind. Pa was a good man and a good father, and he had wanted and loved his sons. Trouble was, sons eventually became men, and Pa wasn't going to be easy to break away from.

And Manny wasn't blind. There were girls everywhere. It was hard to look away when Ellie Gunther was in his sights, and her sister, Margie… she wasn't far behind in good looks. Mary Lou Hewett was a pretty girl, and her little sister would probably look a lot like her. Maybe even prettier.

It wasn't that he thought about actually having one of the girls to kiss or such, but they certainly improved the scenery.

"Manny, we're hungry."

Aw, ha! Now that was something he could take care of. "Ollie, over back'a you, reach down in there and get the tin'a crackers and peanut butter. That'll hold you till we stop."

Back to his thoughts.

Yeah, and this trip was the turning point. It might not be next week or even next month (he'd likely need to help get the family set up), but he would soon be working toward being on his own. There should be a lot going on in the town of Guthrie, and if he had a little cash… Now, there'd be the trick. Pa'd want to know what he wanted the money for. Well, he had a lot of miles to think things through. Maybe he could help Hamp and Bart dig wells… Now, that's a thought. Those fellows were sure to be up to their armpits in work.

"Manny, we got any water?"

"Bring a cup and come up here. You can't have much 'cause we can't stop, but I know them crackers make you dry."

Behind him, he heard his sisters. "Ollie, catch a'holt on that quilt and spread it out. We can get the dolls and put their clothes there, and dress 'em up for a trip."

Sophie. "All the clothes?"

Betty. "Of course, silly."

Manny turned. "You girls see you don't let them little old doll clothes get worked down in the stuff. We ain't unpackin' them boxes again, not for more'n two weeks. Don't let 'em fall overboard, neither."

Sophie. "How much is two weeks?"

"Too long for me to listen to you a'whinin' and askin' questions."

Ollie. "We'll be careful."

Clancy Harper, wagonmaster, had made two trips from one end of the wagon train to the other. Everything seemed to be well in hand. They were making good time, but it was likely a good thing to pull over. There seemed to be a dense grove of trees up ahead, which should be welcome just about now. Should he tell them it was a lunch stop and have them try to build fires?

What the tarnation did he know about being a wagonmaster? He'd have to think of a way to get even with that Ed Gunther, ridin' lazy and comfortable up front! 'Course, this was Ed's second trip down, and he had even made the run. Likely Ed needed the rest.

Putting his horse into a fast trot, he headed once more to the front of the line.

"Hey, Ed. Slow down and pull over."

"What for? Got trouble?"

"No, but there's some good trees. Likely they'll be appreciated."

"Good thought."

Ed's wagon eased to the edge of the graveled road, and James Hewett pulled in behind him.

"GEE, UP!" Evie Kendall's voice rang out as she gave the right hand reins a light jerk. "GEE UP, THERE!" The horses stepped out of the tracks they had been following. "WHOA! WHOA, THERE!" They stopped, shaking their heads and shoulders to settle the traces.

"GEE, UP!" came her sister's voice from the next wagon.

Clancy shouted toward the first wagons, "Ed, Hewett, you fellows be ready to head on out in 20 minutes. Ladies to the right, fellows to the left."

Trotting back, he contemplated what he had just done. Likely it was not usually done by wagonmasters, but these were people with proper houses, not used to the deprivations of a wagon trip. As long as the bushes came at the right places, stops would be made for their comfort. What was a few extra minutes? They would get to Prosper when they got there.

By the time the Kendall wagons approached the rest stop, Ed Gunther had pulled out. Clyde Kendall took advantage of the stop for an opportunity to speak to his son.

Manny watched his father walk toward him, and something strange and foreign happened inside his chest. He suddenly determined that he would not be pushed, and his father was walking toward him in his best pushy fashion.

"Son, just a word."

Manny waited, silent and motionless.

"Couldn't help notice, bein' right back'a you there. Them girls did a right fair amount'a movin' around in there. 'Course, you lookin' forward, you'd not notice it. Ought'a try and keep Ollie from jumpin' out like she did."

Manny took a deep breath. "Pa, when I drive a wagon, I know what's happenin' in front and in back'a me. I figure myself to be right fair skilled in what I do. Now, I'd like to point somethin' out. I was wantin' to make that run with Chet and Doug, and you saw fit to keep me home to drive this here wagon. You must'a thought me capable'a doin' it, or you wouldn't'a told me I was to haul them girls. Now, if you think I ain't to be trusted to take care'a them girls in proper fashion and get this here wagon down south for you, I can jump out right here and walk. I ain't aimin' to take a lot'a orders. Now, I'm a'goin' to the bushes, and you decide which it is you want to do."

Whereupon, Manny set out across the road to the left.

Clyde Kendall stared, speechless, after his son. Whatever got into him that he couldn't take a word of advice? Never done that before. And there was that different look in his eye that seemed to say he meant what he said. Well, boys go through stages, and this must be one of Manny's.

When Manny returned to the train, his father's buckboard was empty, so he hoisted himself up to the driver's seat to wait. When he saw his father coming, he took in a deep breath, and that new feeling was still inside his chest.

"Pa, I done some thinkin'."

Clyde Kendall nodded agreeably. Likely an apology was coming.

Manny continued, "You do what you want about me takin' that wagon and them little girls on down to Prosper, but I wanted to warn you ahead'a time, just in case you was havin' plans for me after we got there. I may stay in the town, and I may go to Guthrie. Law sakes, I might even come back up to Arkansas City. Plan to look it over when we get there. Ain't sure what it is I'll do for a fact, but I know it ain't doin' what I been doin' all my life. You and them other men seem to be headed south for a change and a fresh start. I'm past sixteen, and I got the same feelings."

Whereupon, he swung himself down to the gravel road and headed toward his wagon. His three sisters lay on their stomachs in the crowded space behind the endgate and watched him. As he reached them, he thumped lightly on each golden-haired head, causing them to break into giggles.

With a flip of the reins and a click of the tongue, Manny Kendall was again headed south. Behind him, Ollie and Sophie curled up in the space behind the endgate and dozed off to sleep. Betty crawled forward and sat beside him.

"Manny?"

"What?"

"What if you was to let me hold onto them reins?"

"You mean, let you drive?"

"Well, I...." She hesitated, her eyes questioning.

"Seems to me ten'd be a good age to learn. You're already a mite older'n I was or your sisters, either. Now, lookie how I hold these reins. They ain't bunched together like I was pickin' posies."

Betty giggled and tapped her brother on the arm. "I know that!"

Manny continued. "Now, see, I got one line 'tween my thumb and finger, and t'other between my fingers. If I was to want to turn both horses to the left, I'd say 'Haw, up there,' and I'd tug on these two top lines, the two 'tween my thumb and fingers."

At this point, Manny yelled, "HAW, UP THERE!" His fingers tugged the top lines, and without hesitation, the two horses headed for the left side of the road, walking out of the ruts and onto the grass.

He continued, "Now watch. GEE, UP THERE! Now I'll tug at the other reins." The horses moved back on the road and continued walking. "These here horses are trained good, and they don't have to be yanked on. Ya don't never yank on the reins of a good horse. It'll make 'im forget all the good trainin' he's had. Now, you move over here in the middle and take these reins, puttin' 'em in your fingers like I do. There, that's right. Now this other hand. That's good."

Betty grinned up at him as she held the lines.

Manny watched a minute. "Doin' good. Now you make 'em gee up. 'Member which lines is to the right? That's right. Now tell 'em."

"Gee, up there."

Nothing happened. Puzzled, she looked up at her brother.

"Now, Betty, trouble is you used your little girl voice, and them horses thought you was playin' with Ollie and Sophie. You got'a let' em know you're a'talkin' to them, and give the lines a little tug."

"GEE, UP THERE!"

The horses moved out of the ruts and started to walk on the grass at the right side of the road.

"Now, move 'em back."

The right words and a gentle tug brought the team back into line. Betty giggled and ducked her chin.

Manny complimented. "You done good! That's the lesson for today, and you can drive till you get tired. Tomorrow we'll learn to start and stop."

Clyde had watched as the wagon had moved to the left, then to the right, and he stroked his chin in puzzlement. Was Manny just trying to aggravate him after threatening to leave? Or was it even a threat? It had sounded more like a promise. Likely it'd be better not to mention anything when they made the next stop.

In wagon number four, Mary Lou Hewett watched as Caroline Kendall expertly fingered the lines. "There don't seem to be too much to it, drivin' this wagon. Strange how my ma never wanted me to learn."

"Naw, drivin' a single team ain't nothin'. Drivin' double is when you get to have more fun."

"Well, I...."

"Slide on over here in the middle. Now you take the lines, and you hold 'em, see? Like this...."

Also, near the front of the line, actually in wagons five and six, were a pair of hired drivers. It seemed like a lark to drive their team and wagon down into Oklahoma territory for $30.00 actual cash money. It sure beat working in the field. Directly behind the wagon containing Caroline Kendall and Mary Lou Hewett were drivers Herbert Bentley and David Hill, respectively. Herbert had the best position, as he occasionally caught a glimpse of the drivers of wagon three, a sight that went far toward relieving the tedium of the day.

Being good friends, the two young men would have had a lot to say to each other if they could ride together, being of the same age (past nineteen) and good friends. As it was, they were forced to save all conversation until the wagons stopped. So far, they had only an opportunity to grin and congratulate themselves on their good fortune being an opportunity to see the country down south, to escape fieldwork and to enjoy the excitement of the trip. The eats that came with it weren't bad, either!

Being hired drivers only, their meals were part of the package. They would eat whatever the Hewetts ate. They would soon see what that was, because the sun was fast headed toward the western horizon.

Clancy, wagonmaster, rode past, and Herb shouted, "When's the grub stop?"

"Three hours," Clancy flung at him.

Three hours! That would be near seven o'clock, fourteen hours since they had started. The buckboard below their backsides was getting hard, and they were getting restless. The monotonous crawl of the canvas-covered vehicles across the plains of northern Kansas seemed to be getting them nowhere. All around them they saw the same scenery they had seen hours ago.

Clancy had answered Herb as a reflex. Fourteen hours was a long day, but it was the first day and presumably everyone started well-rested. It would likely be the longest day and maybe the worst. There would be a lot of sore backsides on those who were not accustomed to riding all day, likely most of the women.

Finally, the sun dropped below the distant horizon, and purple shadows began to form in the east. It was time.

Clancy galloped to the front of the train. "Pull over, Ed. Gonna park 'em three in a row to get bunched up better. Hewett, pull on around a'side'a Ed. Kendall, you pull up outside'a Hewett."

Evie Kendall yelled to the team and tugged them aside, drawing the wagon up even to the west of the Hewett wagon.

Clancy stood in the road. "Next Kendall, pull over back'a Gunther."

By now, the pattern was established, and Herbert Bentley and David Hill drew up beside Caroline Kendall. In groups of three, they were only twelve wagons long, the last group having only two. Maybe tomorrow he'd go four in a row, and that would bunch them nicely, only nine bunches long.

It was a good camp. A nice fringe of privacy trees decorated the almost-treeless plains and a stream of water ran full from the spring rains.

He galloped down the road to the end to see if everyone was in position. As he returned, a group of men stood in the road, blocking his way.

"Yeah?"

"Clancy, you got'a do somethin' about Banner's hogs."

"Why?"

"'Cause they're 'bout to stink us out, that's why!" And there, stuck in the middle of row eight was the offending wagon. The front of the wagon contained panels of fencing that Alvin Banner was removing and hooking together. When he had made a pen about 8 feet-square, he opened the endgate, and three huge hogs walked down a cleated ramp and into the pen.

Clancy watched, fascinated. "Right obedient hogs you got there. Walked right along."

Alvin Banner did not look up but dipped out a generous bucket of grain and poured it into a trough inside the pen. "Aimed for 'em to be," he finally answered. "Didn't aim to be no trouble to nobody with my livestock."

"Special animals you got there, bringin' 'em all the way south?"

"Ya might say so. Been breedin' 'em careful. Them two sows is bred, and one of 'em's nigh due. Hated to leave that boar behind, him in the good shape he is. So I brung 'im."

"I can see that. Well, like I said to everyone at the start, there'd likely be movin' around, once we got goin'."

No answer. The only sound was the grunting of the hogs and the cracking of the golden corn grains in their powerful jaws.

"So, Banner, come mornin', I'm puttin' you back'a the Kendall wagons."

"Getting' complaints, huh?"

"Well, hogs can't help how they smell."

The men of the train grabbed buckets and headed for the stream of water. They'd need to get their water for the meal out of the stream before the animals were taken to get a drink.

The women began to open boxes and crates and set out skillets and pans. Fires were started, some blazing brightly, others fizzling, as the skill of the fire builders was put to the test.

Manny Kendall motioned his sisters to grab up whatever would hold water and come along. "No, Sophie, not the pitcher. Get somethin' else."

Setting the water before his mother, he poked wood at the flame, adding a few dry buffalo chips. His team could wait a few more minutes until the fire got going. His mother adjusted the three-legged metal tripod over the blaze. He admired her tight-lipped fortitude.

Never in her life had she been required to cook a meal out of doors. The kettle over the tripod contained beef stew with vegetables and savory chunks of meat. He could hardly tear himself away from the smell of it. Betty was wielding the serrated knife, slicing the loaves of bread into thick slabs.

Fire started, Manny took his mother's buggy team and his own and headed for the stream. After they drank, the animals were put on a short hobble, tying their front feet so close together they could take only tiny steps. That would assure they would not wander off while the family ate.

The little sisters chattered about this and that as they ate their stew, then ran off to play hide and seek with other children, enjoying the last remaining light. Manny ate with his silent mother and puzzled father and said nothing. What was there to say that he had not already said?

Herbert Bentley and David Hill hung back, watching the food preparation. Loaves of sliced bread were opened, buttered, and made into sandwiches stuffed with sliced beef. A kettle of beans was beginning to bubble over the flame.

The Hewetts set a good table. China bowls (all she had) were used for the beans, and the sandwiches were thick and filling. A box of store-bought cookies was opened, and water was heated for tea.

Besides the family of 6, they had the Kendall girls, the two young men, and the couple of elderly men. The older men had spelled each other at the reins and took naps in between.

The smells of different foods drifted up into the evening air, and a murmur of voices compared the day's events. Clancy, the wagonmaster, rode the length of the train and back, warning, "Pullin' out at sunrise. Have your breakfast ate and cookin' gear put up."

A few groans followed his command. Was he being too hard on them? Everyone wanted to get there as soon as possible, didn't they? Well, if they didn't get there on time, it wouldn't be his fault.

When it became too dark to play games, the little Kendall girls crawled up in the wagon and went to sleep. As Manny prepared to join them, he remembered. "Ma, could we maybe have some bread and jelly tomorrow? The girls…."

"Sure, son. You just tell Betty to see to it at breakfast."

It seemed they had hardly gotten to sleep when they heard the beat of the hooves of Clancy's horse. The shrill sound of the rider's whistle cut through the darkness. Every so often, he yelled, "Just consider me the rooster."

Lanterns were lit, and water was brought. Fires blazed, and smell of bacon and sausage was everywhere. Oatmeal bubbled companionably in kettles.

Alvin Banner's hogs crunched their corn and climbed docilely up the cleated ramp into the wagon, grunting contentedly.

As the sun cracked over the lip of the eastern horizon, the purple shadows changed to golden shafts of sunlight. A beautiful day. This trip was not bad at all.

Eight

As Ed Gunther had turned out to be the mayor of the moving town, his unelected wife had fallen into the same position at the town site. Seven wagons with household plunder now waited anxiously to learn whether there would be lots available or if they had already been sold before the town left Providence Falls.

Twenty cows munched grass and bawled for water. A portion of the wire fencing was removed and made into a pen around the scooped out wet-weather spring on the Kendall Brothers' quarter section, and the cattle were left there overnight. They drank the water as fast as it seeped through the ground. It was decided not to let them into the creek, as that many animals would surely foul the valuable water.

Two of the cows had been farmed out to the camp with the green wagon, the people from Tennessee. They promised to water and tend them in return for the milk, in the hope that they would get to buy them.

The young man there, Daniel Dunbar, had felled trees as fast as he could, dragging them into place for a log cabin. The brushy tops of the bushes he used as a temporary fence for the cows and their own seven horses. He had his new wife Roberta, her little niece, and her pa to think about. They needed to get in the dry by fall, and the days were too short.

Basil and Goldie Hamilton, parents of little Mary Prosper, waited and hoped along with the other six families and walked the town plat, deciding which lot they would like if they were lucky enough to get a choice.

The Kendall brothers, twenty-year-old Chester and eighteen-year-old Douglas, worked their quarter section like ants with winter coming. The first thing they made was a doorless shed twelve feet square from felled blackjack trees.

Stopping to eat was a pure drag on their time. Their flour had long since run out, and most meals consisted of wild game. It was nourishing, strengthening, but totally monotonous.

"Chet, what'd you give for all the biscuits 'n honey you could eat for breakfast?"

"Hush up. We don't need to be tormentin' ourselves, thinkin' on that. I keep tryin' to think on what we can do best with this here land. If we was to'a knowed we'd get a chance at a whole quarter section, just us, we could'a had plans made and all drawed up. Here we come, nothin' but the clothes on our backs and shells for the rifle."

"Yeah, but look, Chet. We could get us a herd'a horses. It'd take time, but this country, it'll need a lot'a animals to get around. I get to thinkin' if we just had us a little hard cash…" His voice trailed off into his dreams.

"Doug, listen at what you said. Whereat is the cash and nothin' to buy?"

"Uh… Guthrie?"

"Yeah, and you and me and Manny, if he wants to, we got'a figure someway to get around. Pa'll get here with six horses; chance we could talk 'em out'a two and a wagon. Folks down in Guthrie needs stuff moved. 'Member how the Baker brothers had that well driller rig shipped out? Other folks'll be doin' that."

"You sayin' hire ourselves out? Well, I…" Ideas were circling his head.

"I know what you're thinkin'. You and me, we can't hardly think on tearin" ourselves away from what we got here, but it'd not be for long."

The fire had died down, but the smoke still smelled of the rich juices from the roasted rabbits. Tree frogs and cicada crickets trilled in the trees.

"How long, would ya think?"

"Reckon it'd depend on what we wanted here. We could raise horses, like we talked on, or maybe cows. It'd take a lot'a thinnin'a trees to get the grass for 'em. Got'a get us a bigger house. With the three of us in there, we'll be wringin' each other's necks come spring."

"Sure enough there'd be money to be made in Guthrie? You think?"

"You heard the Baker brothers. I reckon they'd know, and they was even leavin' their wives up in Poverty Flats jist to get some of it. You know, folks got'a have water, but they got'a have things hauled, too. Folks'll be orderin' out'a the catalogs, and the Santa Fe depot'll be piled full. I don't see hardly how that wouldn't happen."

"Well, haulin'd be one thing we could do. They's three of us, and if it was good enough money, we could hire Caroline and Evie." The darkness hid his grin, but his brother was serious.

"Reckon they'd do 'bout as well as any fellow we could get."

They sat in silence under the cacophony of sounds overhead. The harmony of the insect trills and buzzes was enough to put a fellow to sleep. Then a stick broke under a foot. The sound was unmistakable.

Doug was closest to the rifle, and in an instant, it was leveled toward the sound.

"Who goes!" he demanded.

"Aw, put down yer squirrel gun, it's only me."

"Ellie, what're you doin' out in the dark?"

"I ain't afraid'a the dark. Only what's in the dark."

"Come on over 'n set spell."

"Aim to. I brung you somethin'."

"What?"

"Me and Margie tried to make cookies in a skillet. I come to see if we done anything right."

Ellie Gunther sat down between Chester and Douglas and handed each of them a cookie from the bowl in her lap. The cookies were large, heavy and moist and smelled of cinnamon and raisins. The rim was a bit crunchy, but the center of the cookie was so tender it fairly broke apart in their hands.

"Eat 'em," she commanded. "They ain't to look at."

"I was fixin' to, quick as I convinced myself they was real. Been so long since I had a cookie, I thought they was likely agin the law."

Douglas looked at Ellie, the last of the fire lighting her face and glistening on her pink lips. If he hadn't been so hungry for something different, he would have had trouble concentrating on the food.

There she sat, her knees pulled up under her skirt, her elbows propped, holding the bowl high. The light of the fire caught every golden strand of her hair, appearing to create a halo.

"You fellows eat 'em, and I got two more here." She looked at Douglas, pinching small bites off his cookie, making it last longer. The features of his tan face in the semi darkness appeared to be carved from mahogany. His squarish chin balanced his broad nose, and his shaggy brows were a silhouette against the starry sky. His eyes were hazel, she knew, though it was far too dark to see them.

"Here's your other cookie." Instead of taking what she offered, he held his palm open for it, carefully drawing it toward him as if it was a precious gift, and began again to break off small bites.

"Right good cookies, Ellie. I can't think how you made them with no stove."

"I got a secret way'a doin' it." The mischievous grin was barely visible in the light of the coals. "Here, Chet. You got'a eat another one, too."

She watched as he reached both hands for the cookie and held it in both hands while he ate, also taking small bites. Chester's profile was somewhat like Douglas', though his nose was a little longer. His eyes were darker, sort of a greenish brown, and his hair was also darker. It would be hard to find two fellows as pleasing to look at.

After the activity of the town site, it seemed nice to sit by the dying fire and listen to the insects, but her mother had told her not to linger. "You leave them young fellows alone to get some sleep. They don't need you over there chatterin', keepin' 'em up. I know they ain't been half eatin', workin' like they're doin'. A couple'a them cookies, that'd remind 'em they ain't alone down here in these woods. Don't you be stayin', hear?"

Remembering, Ellie sighed. "I got'a get on back. You want'a hear my secret way'a cookin' them cookies with no stove? I took 'em over and used Roberta Dunbar's little iron box that her pa bought for their trip. Works good, don't it? I got'a go."

"I'll walk with you." Douglas was quick to offer.

"You don't need to. I come by myself."

"But it weren't so dark then. You ain't got no lantern, so I'll walk ya till you see your ma's light."

The two walked away, and Chester watched them. That Ellie, now, she was one pretty girl. Always was, even when she was a little squirt. He sighed with contentment. Those cookies, they just hit the spot. He was going to miss Ma's cooking when he was in Guthrie, but when a fellow moved away from home, things changed. Some things for the good and some not so good.

Douglas came back through the trees, and the fire was only a bed of blackening coals. "Reckon I'll go on in and go to bed. Mornin's a'comin'."

"Yeah. Always does."

The coals blackened, and a prairie rattler moved closer to the fire, warming himself in the last of the heat from the coals. Before morning, he would move on away, but sometimes the heat attracted insects, a pleasant addition to his diet.

The young men did not bother to light a lantern but removed their clothes and stretched out on the floor, falling instantly into sleep. Nothing moved in the tiny cabin until well after midnight.

"Chet, you asleep? CHET!"

"NO, I AIN'T ASLEEP! I was till you whacked me in the gut. I wish't you wouldn't do that!"

"Couldn't help myself! I got a idea!"

"Won't it keep till mornin'?"

"No. It was about what you said about Guthrie."

"What about Guthrie?" May as well let him get it out of his system so they could both get some sleep. "What was your idea?"

"Goin' in to get day work, haulin'."

"I know. That's what I said."

"But you said it'd be just till we get money. What if we keep on goin'?"

"Goin' where?"

"Keep on makin' money over in the city. Ain't you got ears?"

"You mean, if we would..." A half-formed idea was tantalizingly close.

"Yeah! We don't have to stay here all the time just 'cause it's ours. We could build us a horse barn, startin' with a pair we'd get from Pa. He'd likely let us use a wagon, too. We could put us a sign on the side'a the wagon: 'KENDALL BROTHERS. We can haul it.' And we wouldn't have to come out here 'cept when we wanted to, but we could build a place, later on, and maybe we could..." His ideas trailed off.

"Wait a minute." Chester was sitting up, totally interested. "You're sayin' we could have a business, like the Baker brothers, just doin' haulin' and not doin' farm work. Hmmm."

"Reckon it'd take some thought 'n maybe some jawin' 'afore we got it settled. There'd be Manny to consider, but he ain't never been too hard to get on with."

"And we'd buy more horses and wagons. We could tell 'em at the depot that we'd be there a certain day to do whatever haulin' was needed."

"If Pa was the one that put them wagons together, they'd stand the strain'a bad roads, like there's gonna be aplenty."

"Reckon what Pa'll say? He was thinkin' to expand on account'a us."

"This'd call for different thinkin'. If we got us an actual plan, then we'd be better at knowin' what to do with all this land and these trees."

"Know what, Doug? We been flounderin' around like a worm on a hook, lookin' for a way to go, then all of a sudden we got the idea."

"It was my idea."

"Yeah, but I got whacked in the gut, so it's part my idea, too."

"I know what done it, actual. It was Ellie's cookies. They felt so good in my gut, I flat dreamed up that idea. It'll work, won't it?"

"Why won't it? If there's a thing we know how to do, it'd be drivin' a team and wagon. By crackies, I wish Manny'd get on down here."

So did Manny!

Nine

The fourth day out of Nebraska, the sun did not come up. The air was thick and moist, and the morning fires fizzled and sputtered. Then the drops began to fall.

Clancy rode the length of the train as it was parked. Most of the wagons were on grass and not on the packed roadbed. If it rained, he was not sure which would be worse than the other, the roadbed or the grass, but the Kendalls and Alvin Banner and his hogs were extended down into a draw, clearly in danger if there was very much water.

He charged ahead to the front of the train. This was clearly a matter on which to consult the mayor, acting or not.

"Ed, look at them clouds."

"Been lookin' at 'em."

"Any chance'a pullin' on out of the way, if we start now?"

"With them getting' lower and movin' south?"

"That's what I thought. Just needed to hear it from you." He turned and galloped to the rear under a pelting shower.

"KENDALL! BANNER! Hitch up and pull on up higher. They's a spot across the road looks solid enough."

"How far up?" Alvin Banner wanted to know. "Need to move my pigs."

"How far can they walk?"

"Fer piece, most times."

"You pile the pen on the wagon and I'll get help to move the livestock. Manny, you pull your wagon up first, right over there in the clear. Then you bring me the first three men you see not holdin' onto their own reins. Kendall, you pull up by Manny and bring up your buggy. Miz Banner, you follow in after 'em."

The panels of the pen were stowed, and the four drafted pig drivers appeared.

Alvin explained, "You fellows take these here buckets and rattle them corn grains, and them hogs'll trot right along after you." His voice was loud, yelling against the roaring wind.

The pen had been reconstructed by the time the animals had crossed the road and had walked the short distance. By now, the rain was sheeting across the plains and had soaked everyone not under canvas and many who were.

The sky had become pitch black, and lightning pierced the clouds with fiery, jagged incisions, sending flaming balls before it and growling thunder afterward, spreading the storm over the grassy miles.

A gust of wind whirled under the canvas cover of the McClure wagon, popping it loose from the cleats and sending the sheet of canvas sailing into the sky. A wind shift, causing a down draft, caught the canvas sail and tucked it into the top limbs of a cottonwood tree.

The horses, tethered together on the downwind side of the grove, bucked and reared, whinnying pathetically and pulling at their restraints. They became more wild-eyed at every bolt of lightning.

The panels of the hog pens rattled and shook but remained in place while the hogs turned their rounded rumps to the wind and settled flat to the ground, water puddling around their snouts. They grunted with pleasure as the raindrops peppered onto their broad backs.

One of Josh Fields' wagons lost its end flaps, and the driving rain blew in, thoroughly soaking everything in the back half of the wagon.

His bride, Sarah, wept bitterly as her wedding gifts were pelted and soaked.

It didn't take much to make Sarah cry. The fellows assured Josh that a lot of crying was to be expected at this stage of her life. That and a lot of upchucking. At least with the first one.

By mid-morning the worst of the storm had passed, and by noon the sun shot through the clouds with shafts of golden yellow melting them into vapor.

The young two Tullius boys and Clancy's thirteen-year-old climbed the cottonwood and retrieved the canvas cover with only a few rips caused from the tree limbs, but the end flap to the Fields' wagon was gone forever. More tears.

The horses had stomped a mudhole with their rearing and dancing, but as soon as the cloudburst passed, they were contentedly munching the moist spring grass.

Clancy and Ed Gunther walked along the road, studying the condition.

"Good road, but that rain softened it right smart. What'd'ya think?"

"Soft. I figure the first five or six wagons'd be fine, then the bottom'd drop out, and by ten or twelve, we'd be pullin' through puddin'."

"That was my thought. Sandy ground, though. Road could harden up in a'couple'a hours."

"Yeah, and if we hitched up to go, we'd have to drive into the dark to make use'a the time. 'Member, these folks ain't used to hard road travel, and this trip ain't long enough to get 'em used to it."

Clancy looked at the wagons and the people milling about looking for damage. "Well, I " And he stared at Ed.

Ed countered, "Don't look at me. You're the wagonmaster. You got'a tell 'em what to do."

"Yeah, and you don't need to remind me'a that!"

Swinging onto his horse, he galloped to the back of the train, whistling shrilly through his teeth. On the return trip, he yelled. "We're stayin' here for the day. Dry out what you can, cook up what you need to, and let your animals graze the grass. We're on the road at first light."

Sarah Fields dried her eyes and demanded that Josh find her a clothesline and pins. A line strung between their wagons would allow her to dry her fancy things in the bright sun.

Ed dropped by the Hewett wagons that contained the contents of the general store. "Hewett, you bring along any of them little cans'a sardines? One's them'd sure be good if they ain't too far down in the heap."

Before he had repacked the box, James Hewett had sold seventeen cans of sardines and four cans of salmon. Also nine tins of crackers.

Beans were put to soak, and wood and buffalo chips were set in the sun to dry. Sarah Fields' pretty things were admired by the women as they wafted in the breeze.

Manny approached Clancy, squirrel gun in hand, surrounded by a handful of younger boys. "Clancy? Be all right if me'n these youngens went out to scare up some pheasants? We'd not be gettin' where we couldn't see the train, so's you'd not think we might get lost."

"Sounds good. Bring me back a bird."

The Banner hogs rooted and snorted, enjoying the day of mud after three days of trying to stand up on the jiggly, wood-cleated floor of the wagon.

First light found the caravan moving south again. The road was still wet but not soggy. Though it might be said that the 35 wagons did the gravel of it no good at all.

On the twelfth day, they reached Arkansas City on the southern border of Kansas. Ed, the mayor, called a meeting.

"We'll be campin' on yon side'a town. You got a day to spend here, tryin' to find what you got'a have that you ain't got with you, and I advise you to go do it. Don't you be dependin' on getting' a thing in Guthrie. If'n it ain't better'n it was when I left it, you'll be pullin' a gun to defend your plunder while we drive through, and anything you want to sell, you can get rid of for a profit.

"Think about if you got plantin' seed, like beans and taters. Think about tools. Hewett's store'll have to have a few weeks to get geared up, so ya can't just run in and get what you wanted like when you was in Poverty.

"'Nother thing. Come mornin', we ain't lookin' for nobody. I move out, and you follow on. You ain't there, you get left."

Clancy Harper took over the meeting. "Now, we ain't a'goin' through town and messin' up their streets. We'll swing out around, and they's a field where Ed says they waited before. Reckon we can still use it.

"You men see to your wheels and axels. Get 'em greased good. Check your harness lines. If you don't have repair leather with you, get it now. Day after tomorrow, we'll be in Cherokee country, and they ain't got no stores. We plan to move fast as we can and make up time. We're all of us wantin' to get there."

James Hewett talked with his drivers on wagons two and three. "Now you girls go to the store and look over what they got. I been watchin' the way you came on behind me, and you done as good as any drivers could. Caroline and Evie, you pick out four dresses you'd like; the extra one is for the drivin' lessons you handed out. Mary Lou and Beth, you get the same thing for applyin' yourselves and learnin'. Go pick 'em out and I'll be there to pay the bill."

"Pa, we can get any dress goods we want? No matter what it costs?"

"Yes, Mary Lou. That's what I promised."

The four girls hurried away, silent and dumbstruck by the wonderful thing that had just happened. Four new dresses, all at the same time! Unheard-of riches. James Hewett smiled after them. The Kendall girls would have been better off to hold out for the wages earned by the hired drivers. As smart as they were, it was surprising they hadn't figured that out. Well, watch out for next time!

Manny Kendall asked his mother, "Ma, you mind if I take the girls downtown to look around? They may not get to see a town for a while."

"That'd be good, Manny."

Ten

The Baker brothers picked up the spudder rig from the depot and loaded it aboard the wagon. By double-teaming with the horses, the mules were able to get it to Prosper, but it was evident it would eventually take two wagons to transport it for any distance. Too hard on the wagon and too hard on the mules otherwise.

Nettie Gunther was first to get a well. That piece of machinery was the best entertainment the town had, and even the Kendall brothers left their work to see the mules walk the treadmill circle, raising and lowering the weight. The pointed weight dropped heavily into the muddy slush at the bottom of the hole, plunging deeper with each thud, and the muddy water they had poured in the hole was sucked up, bringing dirt and small rocks.

Large rocks took considerable pounding to convert them to sand, but the town was lucky and the underground water was reached at forty-five feet.

Hamp and Bart decided two things. They needed a better way to haul the water they required to flush out the tailings, and they were going to limit a day's work to ten hours, no matter how impatient the customer got.

Other than the Gunther lot and the church and the school, the owners of the town lots were not in place and could not tell the drillers where they wanted the wells located. So, after drilling for the Kendall brothers and three of the quarter sections nearby, they headed back to Guthrie.

They borrowed a wagon and a pair of strong bays from the Dunbars. That was a stroke of luck. Drill them a well, and get the use of the wagon and animals for a month or so. Things were working out.

Basil Hamilton, father of baby Prosper, gathered the waiting hopefuls together, and the seven of them measured and marked out the thirty two lots. Maybe that would save a day or two when the town got there and when it would be determined what would be available to buy.

Each of the seven newcomers waited with seeds practically in their hands ready to plant. It was already into May. The older fellow from Tennessee, Eben Carlile, had potato vines poking through the ground and beans six inches high. He had herbs, peach tree sprouts, and a lot of varmints trying to eat them. He was currently battling the raccoons away from his corn and sweet potatoes. Several of the masked robbers had landed in the stew pot.

Chester and Douglas Kendall talked for a night and a day, then they plunged into the work again. They needed a wagon shed and a place for the horses. They needed more room, especially when Manny moved in. They needed a garden that first year, didn't they? Or would they be away too much to take care of it?

So many things to consider. No matter which way they went, it required trees being cut, so the sound of the borrowed axe rang out, and the rasp of the saw teeth rivaled the grating trill of the cicada crickets. They were on their own claim!

Around their fire, roasting their supper, they dreamed. "KENDALL BROTHERS. You have it, we haul it."

There were many wonderful ways to say it, and they had to decide which to use before the painting was done. First off, they could make regular trips to Guthrie. Most folks would be ordering from the catalog, and the trip into town to pick up the stuff would kill a whole day. Regular, ordinary people couldn't afford to lay off a day of work to pick up merchandise, but the KENDALL BROTHERS, HAULING, they could do it.

Twice a week, maybe oftener, the KENDALL BROTHERS, DRAY SERVICE could stop over at the Santa Fe depot to see if anything was in.

Or it might be KENDALL BROTHERS, Freight Service, or maybe KENDALL BROTHERS, Hauling for Hire. Yes, there were many beautiful ways of saying it.

Back at Arkansas City, the moving town looked at the shops.

From his meager pocket money, Manny Kendall bought three shiny ribbons, pink, yellow and blue, and his sisters tied them in their hair. He spent some time looking at the knives and selected a large, pearl-handled model that looked like it meant business. It suited his current mood.

He took the girls to look at the dolls and admire their shiny painted faces and ruffled dresses, then he bought a picture book with poems and bright colors. Betty could read well, and the book would help pass the time now and also later when they got to Prosper.

Back at the wagon train, Maude Kendall was cooking beans. Her bread pan of dough was rising under the tea towel and a fire was blazing in the cook stove.

THE COOK STOVE? Sure enough, there it was, its slim iron legs poking themselves into the Kansas soil. Greased loaf pans were full and ready for the oven.

Manny smiled to himself. Ma was a trooper! Even so, he was glad he had missed the words and the effort it must have taken to get that stove out of the wagon… wait! All around him were women with their bread rising.

This was apparently a community effort, and there would have been plenty of hands to help lift the stove out and back into the wagon bed!

Then he noticed the pail of soapy water his mother was using to wash out the pots. From the back of his own wagon, he took the glass pitcher and dipped up a little water, swishing it around and pitching it away. Then he swabbed out the interior.

"What're you doin', son? We ain't needin' to get that pitcher out. You don't have to be washin' it."

"That's all right, Ma. The girls let somethin' fall into it. It's clean now, so I'll just put it back."

The two young drivers of Hewett wagons, Herbert and David, had followed afar off as the girls did their shopping. Standing at a distance, they watched as the excited girls scurried around, choosing their favorite patterns and trimming. The boys decided it had been their best entertainment of the trip.

James Hewett, on the other hand, restocked his grocery provisions at retail cost. He'd have to raise the prices, but if he was the only store in town…? Well…?

Sarah Fields bought a new pair of shoes totally impractical for the place she was headed, but Josh let her be happy while she could. He had spent the last few miles wondering if he had done the right thing by moving his wife to the new town, even though it had been her idea.

The Banner hogs rooted for acorns in their pen under the oak tree, and the horses gorged on the fresh grass. Tomorrow, they would pull the wagons into the Cherokee Strip.

Eleven

Eben Carlile had been almost three weeks on his claim. It had been the last of February, less than three months ago, that he had left his Tennessee farm to trek west with the hope of winning a quarter section of free land in Oklahoma Territory. Sometimes it seemed more like years, and sometimes it seemed just like yesterday.

During the trip, he hardly had time to mourn the loss of his second son to the mine cave-in. The death of his youngest had necessitated quick action to avoid the further loss of his granddaughter. So the trip had been quickly made.

He, his 22-year-old daughter, and his now-dead son's child, the almost five-year-old Alecia, had moved quickly across the Mississippi

River, through the hills and valleys of Arkansas, onto the rolling knolls of Oklahoma.

He had been fortunate beyond belief and now had a quarter section of trees.

His daughter's childhood boyfriend had been delayed but now had arrived, and they were married. A new family in a raw, new country. Daniel Dunbar, the sturdy-muscled boyfriend, was built for strength and trained with a sense of responsibility. He took over the family, and he was, at this moment, felling trees for the buildings he would need to begin the homestead.

Eben himself was older and not in the best of health. He had been gently relegated to the sidelines by his son-in-law. He was given necessary duties, animal care, water carrying, and fire building. It was not a bad job. There always came the time when a man would expect to turn over his responsibilities to a younger man, preferably his son.

If this could not be, then a daughter's husband was a good second choice. And if this was to be the way of his life, then Danny Dunbar would be his first choice in a son-in-law.

Eben had even loaned his second axe (Danny was using the first one) to the pair of young men whose property joined theirs. Eben was intrigued by these two young men... brothers, they were.

In addition to staking the claim for the town site, they had managed to snag a quarter section for themselves. If either of his sons had lived, he would have hoped they would have the courage and foresight of these two.

He had been glad to loan them the use of his axe, and off and on all day, the sound of it could be heard from within the trees of their claim. That is, until yesterday.

Both yesterday and today, however, he had heard not one lick of work being done, not one chop or one cry of 'TIMBER' as the tree fell to the earth. Eben began to be concerned about them, having no other family around them until the town arrived. It was a good May morning, so he thought he'd just walk on over and relieve his anxiety.

As he neared the location of their tiny 12-foot square cabin, he called out, "Hello, the camp!" It was always safer to give a warning, especially with everyone still antsy about claim jumpers. The woods and timber were filled with able-bodied shooters with their weapons at the ready.

"Come in," came the invitation.

As Eben entered the clearing in the trees, there they sat, looking at each other and talking. This was unusual.

"How're you fellows doin'?"

"Right tolerable, Mr. Carlile. You come needin' your axe?"

"Nope, wasn't thinkin'a that a'tall. But since you mentioned it, I ain't been hearin' no sound'a trees fallin' and got concerned one'a you might'a got hurt… or somethin'."

"No, sir. We're both of us fine. We just got behind on our talkin', I reckon. We talked all night for the past two nights and all day yesterday and seem to be headed that'a'way, today." Chet Kendall sat on the ground, his knees bent before him. His muscled arms rested on his knees, and his head leaned dejectedly forward.

His brother was stretched out on his back under the blackjack oak, blinking as the sunshine shone through the new leaves onto his face. "Come sit a spell, Mr. Carlile. Add a word or two, if'n you can find a place fer it. We was talkin' on how we could get to where we wanted to go."

"You leavin'?"

"Oh, we ain't a'leavin' here, for certain. It's just that this here land sort'a fell on us like a ripe peach, and us with no knife to peel and eat it with."

"How so?"

"Well, all we could think on to do with this land was to farm it, or raise animals. We was a'choppin' and a'draggin', tryin' to keep busy till we got us a plan, but it ain't easy to get a plan when you don't know where you're goin'." Douglas Kendall arose from his prone position and joined his brother in the elbows-on-knees position.

Chester took up the explanation. "Then Doug here hit on the idea'a us bein' drivers, haulin' freight. It'd be a thing we know how to do, and we got the land here for the animals and vehicles. The thing we ain't got is money or a wagon. Our pa, he'll be here, and we can likely get a wagon off him, and that'll let us go to Guthrie to earn some 'a the money that's goin' around. Then we'd be able to buy another wagon or two."

Interesting. Eben was pleased that his assessment of the young men had been accurate. They certainly had vision.

"Waitin' for your pa, huh?"

"Yeah, and that'd be likely another week and a few days to help 'im get started. We got another brother and five sisters a'comin'. Some of them girls is little and won't be no help a'tall. And our pa'll be needin' them wagons for a while."

Then Doug, "Yeah, and that'll make us later on what we want, but we ain't figured no other way."

Eben nodded. "You was thinkin' to maybe make trips to Guthrie and other places, haulin' what folks need for wages? Good thinkin'."

"Yeah, we got that far in our thinkin', but we got no wagon."

"Yeah, we was thinkin'a that gray one you loaned to the Baker brothers. If that one was to be not used, it'd be good. That'd be if you'd let us borrow it for a few weeks, just to let us get our start."

Eben's head was whirling with thought. "Wasn't thinkin'a that one. I was thinkin' in terms'a my green one. It's built on the Conestoga style, heavier, with better axels. It'd be better for what you want. And I let them bays go on loan, and they ain't back yet, but I got the black and paint, and them gettin' fat and lazy on that grass."

"Oh, Mr. Carlile, you ain't a'sayin' they was for loan, are you?"

"No, they ain't for loan, but I'll sell 'em."

The Kendall brothers jerked toward Eben like two mules in a harness. "You'd be sellin'? Fer sure?"

"'Course, we ain't got money, yet, but the end'a the summer, that'd see us with the cash to be talkin'. What'd you want for 'em?"

"Well, son, it'd not be the paint and the black to be sold. It'd be the bays, them better suited for that wagon and that work, and the price'd not be cheap. I'd be needin' $60.00 for the pair and the wagon."

"Well, we'd..." The brothers breathed deeply, their minds searching.

"Mister Carlile, we ain't sayin' they ain't worth it, but it'd be right smart of a while to get 'em paid off. You'd be willin' to wait?"

Eben's thoughts continued to whirl. "You fellows listen, and if I say somethin' you like, then you stop me, and we'll talk about it. If you was to be makin' regular trips to Guthrie and back, say once a week, workin' it around your other jobs. Over at my place, we'd be needin' a lot'a delivery out here. My daughter spends a bit'a time lookin' at the wish book, plannin' on orderin', and I got in mind a few things we could use. My son-in-law, Danny, he ain't got the time to drop his work-a-day and make trips in town."

As Eben paused for breath, Chester and Douglas Kendall hitched themselves a bit closer and their attention became more rapt.

The older man continued, "So if we was to make a deal, you takin' that green wagon we call the grasshopper, on account'a the color, and take the paint and the black till the bays come in, you could make a trip on down to Guthrie and see what you could round up.

"Then if you was to see things was gonna line up the way you think you want 'em to, we could work out a deal. I ain't needin' that wagon right now, but I will need considerable haulin' done. They's a good possibility there'd be a trip every week, maybe till fall. Now, I'd expect you to set a price on your haulin', and we'd keep a record and when my haulin' bill got the same size'a your wagon bill, we'd call that wagon bought and paid for.

"Now I generally wouldn't be wantin' no trip made special just for me. It'd be like if you was to let the folks here know when you'd go, likely most'a the men'd be like our Danny and rather pay a small amount and not lose a day'a work, leastwise till they've got a crop in."

Chester and Douglas hitched themselves even closer and forgot to blink their eyes. "Then the wagon'd be ours with no cash money movin'…?"

Eben nodded. "You ain't heard what all I got in mind to order. Likely you'll be free'a the payment, come fall. First 'a the year, for sure. Right off, I'm wantin' you to find out where the catalog store is and bring back a new wish book for my daughter. The one she's got is worn out from her and the lassie a'lookin' at it so much. Top'a that, it's a year old. You go in and stay a while, lookin' around at what work there is to be had. In a few days, come on back and bring that wish book, and we'll talk."

Eben looked from one to the other of the speechless young men. "Well, what'd you think?"

"Mr. Carlile, you sayin' we could maybe go on to Guthrie today, usin' your wagon? You sayin' we're that close to makin' a deal?"

The older man nodded. "Like I been tellin' you, my daughter wants a catalog so she can order baby chickens, a proper table and cook stove, and I got a list'a things I want. I'll leave now and let you talk it over. Come on over when you're ready."

"Sure, Mr. Carlile. We sure thank ya!"

"Yes, sir. We'll be right on over."

The two young men stood statue-motionless as Eben walked away. It was as though they had been handed heaven and a couple of store-bought ice cream cones and didn't know which to take first.

"You reckon he meant it?"

"Don't know why he'd not."

"What'll Pa say, us goin' on and makin' a deal on our own?"

"Doug, workin' like we been doin', you'd likely not remember yesterday was my birthday. I'm twenty-one now, and it ain't fittin' for a man of twenty-one to be askin' fer his pa's go-ahead on every little thing. You and me, we're fixin' to have a freightin' business, just like we planned. It's just scary that it seemed to come on sooner and easier'n we thought."

"Reckon we ought'a go on over a'fore he changes his...?" Douglas was practically breathless from anticipation.

"Naw, we better think on eatin'. You wasn't over there in Guthrie, but I remember what it was like: people everywhere and nothin' to buy, and we ain't all that flushed on havin' money. It could be long and hungry 'afore we get a paid job or two. You go shoot dinner, and I'll stir up the fire. Leastwise, we'll leave on a full stomach."

It was an hour and a half later, maybe a trifle more, that Chester and Douglas sat on the buckboard of the solid green wagon with its oversized wheels and the cross-braced Conestoga-type body. It was a bit hard riding due to the bulk and solidness of it, and it held two well-muscled young men on the buckboard without bowing the springs of it at all.

The horses, glad of activity, worked their way around holes where stumps had been removed, following the beginnings of a section line road.

"Chet, you havin' trouble believin' this is happenin'? My thinkin' is so hung up on how it come about, I can't get no further."

"That's all right. I'm done past ya. I'm wonderin' if we got cash enough to buy some yellow paint and put our name on the side."

"Yellow?"

"Yeah, that or black... somethin' that'll show up. We ain't decided on what to write. 'KENDALL BROTHERS We Haul Everything'?"

"Maybe. Or that would mean we think we can get everything on at once? We could write, 'KENDALL BROTHERS We Haul Anything'."

"Or, 'We Haul for Hire'."

"Or, 'We Haul Anywhere'."

"Or, 'We Haul...? Whatever You Have'."

"That'd be the same as 'We Haul Anything', like I said a minute ago."

"You're right. 'We Haul Freight'?"

"That'd sound like we draw the line on animals and folks."

They rode in silence for a while.

All the way into town, there were trees falling before the axe, cabins going up, cook fires being tended and children running about. For the entire fourteen miles, there were at last two campsites to the mile on each side of the road. Every half mile or less, someone would lift an arm in a wave, or call out "Good day to ya."

"Doug, just look at all them folks, and they don't even know there'll be a freightin' route goin' right in the front'a their doors. We come back by, a'goin' back to the claim; we need to be sayin' somethin' to plant the idea in their minds."

"Could do that. 'Course, they'll see the yellow paint on the side'a the wagon."

"Hard as it is to buy somethin', you think there'll be paint?"

"This mornin' when we got up, would you'a thought we'd be ridin' along on our first business trip?"

"Well, no, but…?"

"See there?"

In the three weeks since Chester had been to Guthrie, so many changes had been made that he was temporarily lost. The Santa Fe depot that had been on the east edge of town was no longer there. The entire east edge of town was a sea of tents, shacks and lean-tos made of packing crates and boxes. The streets swarmed with people like a bumble bee hole swarms with bees.

"I got'a be getting' my bearin's. Now, that track a'goin' north and south, and us a'goin' west, we'll cross it. Can't keep from it."

"Look, Chet. Folks is openin' stores! There's a food store!"

"Yeah, and I hate to think on the prices. We need paint."

"Well, keep a'goin'. They're sellin' tents there. Look there, at that fellow sellin' beans! Still a nickel a cup. I know where we are. Land Office to the right, and the track ain't far."

"I could'a told you that. I hear the train."

"Look! Sellin' nails. All bent."

"Where? Maybe he's got paint."

"Well, pull over and whoa. Hey, fellow! You got paint?"

"I got everything. Come on!"

Looping the reins over the hitching rail, they stepped into the merchant's tent. Kegs were everywhere; boxes, bottles and canvas bags covered the floor.

"Paint? You got yellow paint?"

"No, but I got white."

Chester shrugged. Why did it have to be yellow, anyway? "How much?"

"Got a whole gallon."

"I mean, how much money?"

"Oh. It'd be fifteen dollars."

"FIFTEEN DOLLARS? I wasn't wantin' to buy the whole store!"

"How much paint was you wantin'?"

"Enough to put letters on my wagon."

"Oh, I'll sell ya that for fifty cents."

"I'll take it."

"That's fifty cents a side. Your wagon got two sides, don't it?"

Chester looked at Doug, who shrugged wearily and hauled two quarters from his pocket. Chester matched them.

The merchant opened the can of paint and handed them a brush. "Use my brush for free, and when you're in business, remember who done you a favor."

Daubing the brush carefully into the thick white paint, Chester began with solid white strokes on the grasshopper green of the wagon.

"KENDALL BROTHERS We...."

"Wait. Look what you done."

"What?"

"You done made the letters too big."

"They got'a be seen."

"Yeah, but...."

"But what?"

"Look at it! You ain't gonna have room for it all."

"Hmmm. Well, it's too late now. I'll go as far as I can."

Twenty minutes later, they stood back and gazed the startling white on the green of the wagon. It read: 'KENDALL BROTHERS We Haul.' They looked at each other and nodded. That pretty well said it all anyway.

Chet carefully cleaned the can and the brush and handed it back to the merchant, who put it in the shelf. When they turned to leave, a man came to the door of the tent, peering into the darker interior.

"You got white paint?"

"I got everything, buddy!"

"How much a gallon?"

"Twenty bucks, and a brush comes with it."

"Robbery!" he announced, but he handed over the money.

The merchant handed the man the gallon can that Chet had just finished wiping. And the brush, still smelling of cleaning fluid.

Chester and Douglas looked at each other, shaking their heads in disbelief.

Back in the wagon with Douglas on the reins, Chet observed, "Well, we're in business like everybody else in town. Reckon we'll head on up the street to the Santa Fe depot."

After a few minutes of milling around with the crowd, they located a man whose cap matched his uniform.

"Hey, buddy! You the boss, here?"

The man looked them up and down and pointed toward a cage blocked off with chicken wire. Inside was a desk piled with paper and a man in a shirt that had been, at sometime in the past, white.

"Sir! Could I ask a question?"

White Shirt looked up, then pointed to a counter marked 'INFORMATION'.

"Not that kind'a question. We was lookin' for work, haulin' freight."

"Haulin'? You got a team and wagon for hire?"

"Got it right here."

"Start to work now?"

"You bet, man."

"Well, step back here and look at th… say, can either one of you read?"

"Read? Like out of a book? Sure, what you want read to you?"

The weary, coal-dust-lined face broke into a half smile. "I was just wanting to know if you could read this map. It shows where the freight has got to go. You have to read the streets and the names on the address. You can do that?"

"Don't sound too hard."

"Now, we got two things we can do. We got freight that the depot has to deliver, and we pay for that. Then things come in for folks that's got no wagon to take 'em in, and they pay to get it done. Then you get whatever you can get folks to pay. Us, we pay a dollar an hour for a team, wagon and two men. What'd'ya want?"

"A dollar an hour…" Chester cut his eyes toward his brother, who was too dumbstruck to blink.

"All right, make it a dollar and a half. We got stuff so piled up we can't even sneeze proper. Here, take a map… take two, in case one gets messed up. Follow me out here to these bins. When you get to knowin' the street better, it'll be easier, but with the two'a you, and you both read…?"

They followed him to the bin piled with packages and boxes higher than their heads. White Shirt continued.

"So, you just load on what you think you can carry. Where at's your rig?"

Douglas pointed, "Pulled up to the dock there."

"That green one? Ought'a do the job. I'm Murphy, and you're… the KENDALL BROTHERS?"

"Chester and Douglas," and they extended hands.

"You can work long as you can see. When you stop, check in with the timekeeper over there to get your money."

It was three o'clock in the afternoon, and they began loading packages.

At seven o'clock they had to give it up. The poorly marked streets were hard enough to find in the daylight. They turned in four hours and collected six dollars. It was far more than they had in their combined pockets when they came to Guthrie that morning. Walking away, their feeling was akin to guilt, as though they had gotten the money by robbery.

They found the bean seller and bought three cups of beans each and a pan of buttered cornbread. Sixty cents. They found a grain seller and paid fifty cents a quart for two quarts of chopped corn for the horses.

Both they and the horses could have eaten more. They had $4.40 left.

By nine o'clock, they still had not found a place to park for the night. Every square foot of space belonged to someone who didn't want an oversized wagon and two horses in the way. Finally, they went back to the depot and backed the wagon into a corner of the freight yard. Unharnessing the horses, they tied them to the endgate and stretched out in the wagon to sleep.

They had not come prepared with bedding or pillows, and every hour another engine chugged in, whistling and blowing steam. The first time or two, the horses shied back, straining on their leads, but finally the animals settled down and ignored the train, drooping their eyes in sleep.

Chester and Douglas twisted and turned in a mixture of weary exhaustion and heady elation with the knowledge of the money in their pockets. Surely this wonderful thing could not happen again tomorrow, but if it did, something would have to be done about a place to sleep.

The next day they worked from seven until six. During the course of the day, they had passed the catalog store.

They were told, "Well, ya see, we don't usually let these books out'a here. Folks come in and look and order. If we let them go, we wouldn't have none here to look at."

After assurance that the book would be serving a whole town (Prosper), they reluctantly released a wish book.

Also, the brothers found the livery stable. Four large tents, it was, and a number of outdoor stalls. Grain and hay could be bought and animals boarded overnight and fed for two dollars each animal. Wagons could be parked in the open yard for one dollar and under a tent for two dollars.

After a quick consultation, they decided on the tent. That way, if it rained, they would, for certain, have a place to sleep dry. Four dollars for the horses and two dollars for themselves, plus the price of their food. In the darkness of the wagon bed, they spread out their coins and decided the next purchase would be a blanket to sleep on. And maybe some clothes. What they were wearing was fast needing attention.

Over four dollars left over from yesterday added to the nine something from today? Man, this was living! It surely couldn't last long, but it would be good while it did!

Back in the town of Prosper, Eben Carlile slept well, feeling he had done the right thing for the two young men who reminded him so well of the one he had lost… hardly four months back.

In his pocket, Eben still held the price of his Tennessee farm in addition to his life savings. All he had left in the world was Bertie (his daughter) and Robert's little girl. And Danny was here to take care of Bertie.

"Robert, my son," he told the night breeze that blew through his tent. "I'm gonna do my best for your sister and that little girl you left us. We got us Danny, now, and there ain't no reason your little girl can't grow up in a store-bought house. I just got'a set my head on how to get it."

Twelve

Clancy Harper, wagonmaster, called out to Ed Gunther, temporary mayor, at the head of the wagon train, "Pull out in twenty minutes."

Galloping his horse down the road, he alternately whistled through his teeth and yelled, "PULL OUT IN TWENTY MINUTES." At the end of the train, he pulled up short. "Banner, you need help with your livestock?"

"No, sir, Clancy. They're in and we're ready!"

The day at Arkansas City had been a welcome one with interesting trips into the town and a chance to replenish supplies and do some cooking and baking for the next few days. Tomorrow, they should be in the Oklahoma Territory, and maybe in a week, they would be in Prosper. It had taken a little longer than they had expected, but that was not surprising.

At the appointed minute, Ed Gunther clicked his horses into motion and pulled his heavily loaded wagon onto the badly rutted road. James Hewett drew in behind him, followed by twelve-year-old Beth Hewett under the capable supervision of Evie Kendall. Beth's sister, Mary Lou, followed behind.

The wagons had been pulled aside in rows of four abreast, making nine rows. Without incident, all thirty-five wagons rolled over the Oklahoma line. They were now in the Cherokee Strip, with the Cimarron River being their next obstacle.

"Don't know how it'll be now, but it was a mess at the run. The dinky ferryboats the government had out there wouldn't hold no weight, and they was only two of 'em when they needed two hundred. Folks took wagons apart and floated stuff over in boxes, swimmin' the horses. Lost one whole wagon with folks in it, likely drowned.

"Could be the river'll be run down some. What we finally did was stop the Santa Fe and use the tracks. Took Nettie over an hour to get to take her wagon over, and she was close to the front'a the line. Seems they's no good way to look at it. Reckon we'll figure out what to do when we get there."

Clancy mulled the words over in his mind, and they gave him no comfort at all. He never had liked surprises. Well, he was only the wagonmaster; the mayor was responsible for the safety of the town.

Wasn't he? Certainly he was!

They traveled the morning, and by noon the air began to be heavy and muggy. Even the most delicate fern gave no movement at all. The stillness was oppressive, and there seemed to be no air for the lungs.

The sky took on a yellowish haze and an ominous stillness settled around the crunch and grind of the wheels on the rutted track. There seemed to be an echo as the sound of the wheels was bounced back by the wall of stillness.

"What'd'ya think, Ed? A storm a'brewin'?"

"Ain't been wantin' to think about it. We're hard put for cover if somethin' was to blow in. Best to keep movin'. Leastwise, as long as we can."

By three o'clock, a black cloudbank grew up out of the western horizon, extending from due west on around to the north into Kansas. A breeze came in from the south, and puffs of wind began to billow up small dust devils. Warmer air joined the dust devils, whirling them to spiral up into the sky. Anxious glances were turned toward the west.

By four o'clock, it seemed a decision should be made. Clancy rode forward. "Ed? How about them trees up ahead? Might have time to eat a bite 'afore it hits."

Ed Gunther nodded. "That'd be the best thing, I reckon."

"Well, you pull on in there and I'll tell 'em."

By four thirty, the four abreast rows were made, and a scramble was taking place for the fastest thing to eat. The row of blackness was climbing into the sky, darkening the late afternoon sun. The puffs of wind were rapidly becoming a steady gale beating down on them first from the south and then from the west.

Clancy whistled sharply through his teeth and shouted, "BRING THE HORSES, AND LET'S GET 'EM TIED IN THE GROVE!"

There really wasn't room enough to give all of them protection, but they couldn't be tied near the wagons. A frightened horse could cause considerable damage. Tossing heads and rearing feet could cause injury to a child.

A storm on the prairies was not a total surprise. Clancy and Ed had discussed the sudden prairie storms and what was best to do, hoping the plan would not be necessary. It did not appear they would be so fortunate. It came down to doing the best they could at the time.

With Ed starting at one end, and Clancy at the other, everyone was advised, "On signal, you crawl under your wagon. Everyone. Lay flat to the ground, face to the west. You see stuff start to fly, put your face down and cover your head with your arms. That's the best we can do."

The men gathered in concerned groups, staring westward. Mothers rounded up their frightened-faced children. The horses tossed their heads and whickered nervously. Alvin Banner's pigs planted themselves against the ground and grunted sociability together.

The black band of clouds was now rimmed with violet, and they extended the length of the western horizon. The band grew steadily upward until it was overhead, thick and roiling, turning over within itself.

Torn shreds of clouds blowing in one direction momentarily parted to show layers of clouds above them, blowing their blackness the opposite way. The air between the cloud layers began to circle and roll.

Clancy looked at Ed, who nodded. It was now five-thirty. It was clearly time.

Swinging onto his horse, Ed circled his train, his whistle cutting shrilly above the roar of the wind. Silently, the terrified travelers knelt and crawled under their wagons, their faces flat in the dusty grass.

The dark cloud lifted from the horizon, showing a band of clear sky on the lower horizon, definitely a good sign. This storm would be a fast one. Dozens of eyes watched the strip of clear sky, willing it to spread.

The sky above them was a mural of black, gray and charcoal, ever-changing, twisting and turning. Then, with the roar of the strength of a rockslide, a pale gray rope formed within the clouds, looping and snaking like a wild thing. The whirling, twisting rope was rising into the sky, then falling toward the prairie, again pulling itself back again into the clouds.

Lightning bolts shot toward the ground, and the horses reared and whinnied, pulling at their leads, their manes and tails whipping in the wind gusts.

A massive dust cloud sailed by, and when it was gone, the gray rope in the sky had broken in two, one of its tails falling to the ground. The broken end of the upper tail was sucked higher again, turned around and spit out, joining the one on the ground.

The grayness of it turned black and then blacker, and the deafening roar descended with ear-splitting volume, causing small children to clamp their hands over their ears and scream, huddling against their frightened parents.

Caroline Kendall and Mary Lou Hewett occupied the southwest corner of the block of wagons, putting them in the first row to receive the strongest blow. Seeing the double-tailed twister and knowing what it meant, the girls buried their faces in the Oklahoma soil, forcing themselves to continue to breathe as the air seemed to be sucked out of their lungs.

Something slammed against their wagon… in the distance a horse screamed, and suddenly the wind was all around them. Dirt and grass clods came raining down on their heads. A gush of water fell on their backs, and they were forced to lift their faces from the ground or risk drowning. Looking up, they saw only muddy rain above them where the wagon should have been.

Voices behind them screamed, "Crawl under here," and they dragged their sodden skirts behind them as they crawled under the wagon with their sisters.

Suddenly as it had appeared, the clouds and the roar began to die away. The bright band from low on the horizon was now practically overhead, and the entire sky was lighting up.

As suddenly as it had started, the rain stopped. The band of blackness had moved to the east with its twisting gray ropes of debris-filled air and streaks of fire.

Clancy untied his horse and swung into the saddle. It was time to assess the damage.

A quick gallop to the end of the train showed all wagons accounted for except Caroline's, and all four girls were present and unhurt. Dripping people were crawling from under their wagons.

Two canvas covers had blown away and three others had been damaged by flying debris. Ed circled at the end of the train and galloped back, afraid to look at the Hewett family.

With a sigh of relief, he assured himself that he had been right. All the girls and James now stood looking at the place where his number three wagon had been. All that remained of it was a gouge in the sod where the wagon tongue had been.

Clancy headed for the grove to check on the horses, and a quick count showed two missing and an injured mule to be put down. His own. The unfortunate animal had been hit with flying debris and his neck was broken. Drawing his pistol from his pocket, he fired, using a bullet to save the animal from the pain of its last few minutes of life.

Of the Hewett wagon, there was still no visible trace.

"What did ya have on that one, James?"

"Mainly tools and wire. Lot'a axes, hoes and shovels. Let 'em go." He looked at Clancy with moist eyes then turned to look at the four silent girls and the rest of his family. He moved his gaze back to Clancy, finally being forced to drag his sleeve across his tear-wet face. "Them things don't matter. They don't matter a'tall," he stated in a cracked voice.

"No, James, they don't." Clancy moved away, allowing James Hewett his privacy. A fleeting thought tugged at his brain to think how he would feel if it had been his sons under the wagon…? Dear Lord! It was impossible to imagine.

He forced himself to pull his wits together. He was, for whatever reason, still the wagonmaster, and certain duties were still his.

His whistle sounded out for attention. "I want all the men to come with me and grab a horse. We're gonna fan out to the east, lookin' for what might'a dropped out'a Hewett's wagon. He had tools in there that we're likely gonna need. Look for tools, wire or anything you wouldn't expect to find on the prairie. You women settle in for the night. Do the best ya can."

By seven o'clock, it was too dark to see anything, and the men returned with a couple dozen items, hardly a sampling of what had been lost. The items were stowed in James Hewett's other wagons, and Caroline and Mary Lou moved in with their sisters.

Clyde Kendall had tried to retrieve his daughters, but his wife had agreed with the girls. They might as well be crowded up with the

Hewett girls rather than be crowded up on Manny. The sixteen-year-old had his hands full with the girls he had.

The next morning, Clancy gave his train an extra hour, hoping the presence of the sun would help the mood. In the manner of Oklahoma storms, when the twister was gone, it was gone, and the gush of rain had washed the air to crystal clarity. The sky was robin's egg blue from horizon to horizon. Pink and peach rays across the sky promised a perfect May morning.

The wagonmaster made his last circling before heading out. Then he glanced to the west at a curious sight. Dozens of curious eyes watched as he circled out into the green clumps to see what it was and came back grinning from ear to ear.

"Saddle up, men. Don't know how them tools blowed into the wind the way they did, but we got a hour or two to gather 'em up. Get with it so we can make some time today. All you youngens and my three boys, you get them near things and bring 'em to Mr. Hewett. We're gonna need all them things."

The men on horseback fanned out, coming back armed with tools, some with cracked handles. Several of the boys rolled a wooden keg of nails, still intact and unbroken, bumping across the grass to be stowed aboard.

At twelve o'clock, the caravan was on the move again.

A horse was hitched with the mule on Clancy's cart. The huge blacksmith's anvil rode heavily, pushing the cartwheels into the soft soil. He watched a while, saddened by the loss of the mule. It was hard to beat a mule for steady pulling, and a horse just didn't do the job. Tomorrow, he'd put two horses on the load. Mules and horses did not work together very well as a rule. Rather like some people, he noted with a wry grin.

Like so much of the Kansas soil, the gravel roadbed contained a lot of sand... washed sand with rounded edges rather like miniature ball bearings. They rolled about when stepped on, fitting themselves together the best way they could. The rolling about of the sand particles did not make for a solidly compacted roadbed.

The first four rows of wagons, 15 in all, moved ahead on the soggy road without incident. Another 5 passed by before the bottom began to drop off the roadbed.

By the 25th wagon, the rutted trail had become a loblolly of sticky mud. Horses buried up to their knees in the goo and had no traction to pull.

Riding out around the train, Clancy sped to the lead wagon. "Hold up, Ed! The bottom dropped out'a the road!"

Ed pulled over, followed by James Hewett and the rest, forming the pattern of their regular camp.

"THE LAST SIX WAGONS IS STUCK!" he shouted. "Likely have to triple team to get 'em movin'."

Back out around the sea of mud he rode, his whistle shrieking above the excited voices.

"You women set up night camp. Men, grab a horse and come on back."

The Banner wagons, the Kendall wagons, and the Hausfield wagons, 6 in all, were hopelessly stuck in the mud all the way up to the bottoms of the wagons. Maude Kendall's buggy, being lighter and high-wheeled, eased on out with only two men wading the mud and pushing on it from the rear.

The Banner wagon with the hogs was first to be moved, and a double team of horses slid it along, practically floating the wagon bed on the top of the muck, until the wheels could get a grip on the ground.

The hogs themselves rooted playfully at the edge of the muddy wallow, snorting and grunting their pleasure.

The other five wagons were manually unloaded, each item being carried to higher ground. Tandem teams were attached to the wagon fronts, and the outside teams were kept on solid ground.

Their pulling power was severely reduced by their distance from the wagon, but with much yelling and physical encouragement with the lines, they were influenced to pull the wagon along on top of the sea of mud.

At four o'clock all wagons were back on grassy ground. All were mud-covered. For all the mud and wetness, there was no water for clean-ups. The water in the barrels and kegs must be saved for drinking, as Ed was not certain where the next clear water would be reached.

Clancy looked at the sea of mud, blaming himself. "I should'a know'd better. It ain't like I don't know about quickie sand. This here dirt is half sand that's been under water and got its corners rubbed off. Hangs together when it's dry and separates like a million marbles when it gets soaked. I should'a stomped on the road to test it. That kind'a dirt always brings water to the top when it's stomped on. That's what them wagon wheels did."

The men stood in their mud-soaked shoes, staring dejectedly at the mess. Josh Fields expressed what was on everyone's mind. "When d'ya estimate we'll be getting' out'a here?"

Clancy sighed. "Can't say till mornin'. Only good thing to say about this kind'a mud, it usually drains quick. Could be we could get out'a here by mid-mornin' tomorrow."

It seemed that was a good guess, and by morning, the soil had drained, but Clancy was in no hurry. "Take your time with breakfast. Aim for pullin' out at ten."

By that time, there was no longer a doubt about the roads, and Ed Gunther headed out once more, the entire train following along.

Yesterday's loblolly was gone, and spirits began to rise with the climbing of the May sunshine.

Thirteen

The wagon train made good time that first day after the twister, despite the late start. Clancy had kept them moving until it was too dark to safely continue. When he finally allowed them to pull over, he rode down the line with the warning, "SHORT NIGHT! SLEEP HARD AS YOU CAN!"

An hour before first light, he called out to Ed Gunther, the head of the train, "Pull out in 20 minutes. Ed, tell me more about that Cimarron River. You sayin' it ain't able to be fjorded a'tall?"

"Not and get your wagons free'a the quickie sand. It'd take more horses'n we got to slide a loaded wagon up out'a the water. Too deep, anyway. I wouldn't go to worryin' just yet. There'll be a way to get through when we get there."

Clancy tried to take heart but was unable.

All that day, and all of the next, his thoughts of the river ran concurrent with his other worries. The crusted mud left over from the loblolly after the storm was an irritation to the men. Every little brook or rivulet was an occasion to try to persuade Ed to stop and let them clean up a bit, but when he finally did let them pause, he told them, "This stop is ten minutes only. Fill your water jugs and bring your dirt on along."

It was mid-afternoon of the next day that they saw the bank of tall trees up ahead, along with a colorful assortment of waiting travelers. The rutted trail that had been serving as a road had been following the Santa Fe Railway line for the last few hours, and a succession of trains had rumbled this way and that.

It was not surprising that the familiar sound of a train also served to lift spirits. It had seemed, for days, that the forlorn string of wagons had been totally alone and forgotten in the world. Now, there seemed at least to be a semblance of civilization.

The trail they had been using moved straight ahead and disappeared into the river. THE RIVER! They had reached the Cimmaron River.

At the edge of the waiting crowd, Clancy stopped the train, and he and Ed galloped on ahead to check out the current situation. It was just as Ed had secretly suspected and Clancy had feared. Nothing had been done at the crossing, and the only way to get across the river was on the train bridge.

The two men stood and stared at what they would be facing.

An accumulation of wide planks had been assembled to be placed end to end across the railroad ties parallel to the tracks. The horses were unhitched from the wagons, and a number of strong men pulled on the tongue, guiding the wagon across the string of boards. Other men walked along the side of the moving wagon to keep the loose boards adjusted so they would be in correct position under the wheels of the wagons.

Only one wagon at a time was laboriously hand-maneuvered to the opposite bank. A small ferryboat operated in the water below, carrying passengers if they didn't want to walk the rails, or, more importantly, they would tether a group of horses to the ferry and guide them across. This kept the animals from straying or being swept downstream with the current.

A good dozen wagons were grouped on the north bank, waiting to be taken across. Clancy finally found someone to talk to.

"How much time does it take to get them wagons over the river?"

"Depends. Twenty minutes mostly, at times a mite longer."

"For just one wagon?"

The man looked puzzled. "Sure, man. We only take one wagon at a time. Charge a dollar."

"Well, we need to use the bridge when you get these over."

"Just sit tight, mister. We'll get to ya when we can."

"Oh, we won't need to bother you. We can pull 'em over ourselves. We got a lot'a help and thirty five wagons and carts."

"THIRTY FIVE WAGONS?"

"Yeah, but we'll move 'em right along once we get started. We'll not hold ya up no longer than we can help."

The man motioned them to wait and signaled to a uniformed man with a whistle around his neck. "These here fellows got a wagon train thirty five long. Say they'll take 'em on over, pullin' 'em themselves."

The uniform approached Clancy and Ed. With shoulders reared back with importance, he informed them, "Can't let you do that, men. We got the transportation contract here, and it's us that's got the right to stop the train. You comin' across on your own, that'd violate the contract, and you got no flagman rights. It's a dollar a wagon, and you wait your turn. Likely be all day tomorrow gettin' you over."

"All day!"

"Most likely. Say you got a train? Loaded heavy? Likely be a dollar and a quarter, loaded like you'll be."

Clancy and Ed looked at each other and sighed. "Might as well get in line. Don't seem to be no other way," Clancy decided.

Most of the moving town of Prosper took the news with silent acceptance, though one slightly sarcastic male voice requested permission to finally clean the dried mud off his shoes in the Cimarron River. Permission was given.

A dollar and a quarter! Highway robbery! Paying a price like that for something they could do for themselves, if just given the chance! By the end of the day, the aggravation level was high. Night fell with the entire train still on the north side of the river.

At nine o'clock the following day, Ed Gunther's wagon was hand-pulled up the grading to the entrance of the train bridge.

"Now you fellows stay out'a the way," they were told. "You can walk across after your wagon, but don't get in the way'a the workmen."

Ed stalked behind his loaded wagon, glaring at the board straightener men as they almost let his wheels slide off the planks. When his wagon was safely pulled aside, he returned to the other side and walked with James Hewett behind his own. It was now nine thirty.

As the pullers lifted the tongue of the wagon driven by the Kendall girls, Ed told them to begin to attach the horses to the ferry and get them across, and he'd hold them on the other side.

By noon, nine wagons were across. They were making better time than they thought they would. Likely because there were several buggies in that number, and they were easier to move. By mid-afternoon, the pulling crew was getting tired.

Clancy suggested, "You fellows let us help, and we'll get this done quicker. You can still get your dollar and a quarter."

"Can't let you do that, man. You ain't authorized to flag the train."

In his most polite and friendly voice, Clancy suggested, "Can't see that'd be a problem. You can flag the train. All we'd do is help."

"Can't do it. We got us a contract."

It was while this argument was going on that Stephen Tullius' grinding mill was being prepared be pulled across.

With careful planning, Tullius had been able to fit the entire mill, wheels, grinding plates and all into one highly-fortified wagon, and it was fairly heavy. Actually, it was extremely heavy.

The wagon was finally maneuvered onto the ties, straddling the rails. The exhausted pulling crew had rested twice, and the men adjusting the planks crawled along tiredly on their knees.

On the third go, a front wheel chunked off the edge of the plank and bumped down onto the railroad ties, settling a wheel down between two of the ties.

Hand-pulling it back onto the planks was an obvious and utter impossibility. Anyone with two eyes could see that. Actually, one eye would have been enough to see it. The workmen sighed and stared at the problem as though their continued staring would somehow solve the dilemma.

A pry plank to raise the wheel so a block could be put under it might be a possibility, except there was no place for the person on the pry plank to stand. The end of the plank would be extending out over the river with its rolling brown water, and no one was fool enough to agree to do that.

The railroad ties were fourteen inches apart, and between each of them, one could look down into the flowing waters of the Cimarron River. Anything dropped from the bridge would sink into the sand at the bottom of the river or float away in the current.

The pulling crew stood staring hopelessly at the problem as Tullius, the miller, became madder and madder.

"You sloppy, fiddlefingered apes! Look what you done to my wagon!"

The "apes" were silent, seeming to find no words appropriate for a response.

Looking under the loaded wagon, the pulling crew saw the problem was even worse than they had at first imagined. The weight of the mill equipment falling from the plank to the ties, a good foot or more, forced a kink in the axel that had been holding the wheels together.

Tullius had known the axel problem existed without bending over to look under. Words were boiling up into his head, and he chose to allow them to escape.

"Me and these fellows here, we could'a had that wagon across and all the rest of 'em, and your stinkin' train could'a been long gone. I want'a know what you think you can do? I see smoke now. You reckon that train'll wait till you grow new brains to get this took care of?"

Sure enough, a plume of dark smoke snaked along the rolling knolls and the groves of trees. With screeching of metal against metal, the train halted, puffing and chugging.

Ordinarily, the wait would be not more than twenty minutes, so they just waited, chugging impatiently. It was easier to keep the fire going than to raise the steam again.

One of the men leaned over the high sideboards into the bed of the wagon to assess the possibility of unloading, whereupon he found himself with a squirrel gun against his ear.

"Don't you never even think'a puttin' a grubby paw on one piece'a that machinery. You clumsy oafs done helped me enough, 'thout droppin' my valuable machinery in the river. There ain't one piece'a that metal that ain't got its place, and there ain't spare parts' fer none of it. You start thinkin'a what you can do, and then ask me if'n it'll be all right fer ya to do it."

The man at the edge of the wagon eased himself away and thought he would avoid looking into the wagon.

By now, Ed, Clancy and several of the drivers were standing, shoulder to shoulder, with Tull. Clyde Kendall joined them.

Clyde Kendall, the wheelwright, felt he was now in position to step forward. The problem had entered his sphere of expertise. "Now,

I know it ain't no help this minute, but you might want to know, when we get them fool apes off'a the bridge, I got an axel that'll fit under that wagon."

"Well, at least that's good news. Look yonder, at what's comin'."

The usual twenty minutes must have been used up, because a uniformed man in a conductor's cap was walking the rails toward them.

"What's the hold-up?" As he came closer, he saw it was a useless question. The problem was plain to see. The pulling crew with the "contract" waited as the conductor looked over the problem.

"Fellows, I ain't got no answer, but I got a hand car on board I can offer. Could be it'd help get the wagon unloaded. If you want, I'll ask the engineer to let us get it on the track."

The pulling crew, somewhat humbled, readily agreed. The uniformed boss approached Steven Tullius. "The only way I see to go is to let us get the wagon unloaded. We'll lift the pieces out, one at a time to the handcar, and…."

The red-faced and angry Tull cut in, "Hold it there. You done helped me enough, like I said. Any unloadin' that gets done'll be by the members'a this train, the way we help each other. I got me a tarp on my other wagon. It'll get spread out under this here wagon and under that handcar I see a'comin'. These fellows and me, we'll see to the transfer. I want your men far enough back so's if I get tempted to use my squirrel gun, the bullet won't hurt any of 'em too bad."

The handcar, operated by the two men on the pump handle, brought the little car as close as they could, working their way around the wagon tongue that angled out over the water. Tull now dragged his sheet of canvas across the ties.

"Clyde, your youngen around? Oh, there he is. Manny, son, could I get you to scoot under the wagon, bein' skinnier in the middle and younger'n than most of us? Now, if you'd just drag this along 'tween them wheels… there, that's good. Now, pull it on around the tongue, good job! Now, if I could get two'a you men that's got a steady hand to stand with Manny Kendall, here, we'll hand-over-hand each piece to the car. That'a'way, you can get solid footin' on them ties and not have to step around."

"Tull, how about them big pieces, the wheels and plates?"

The miller was still trying to work out that problem. "Let's get the little'ns out first."

Stephen Tullius heaved himself into the wagon. Lifting out a gear chain, he handed it to Manny, who passed it on. The chain traveled hand over hand until it reached the safety of the handcar. Small pulley wheels came next, gears and axels, bands and clamps.

The conductor watched the operation. "Hold it, men. I got'a back up and empty the car." With that, the pump hands reversed the handcar and moved to the south bank, where it was unloaded on a tarpaulin spread on the bare ground under the strict supervision of Ed and Clancy.

Clyde Kendall climbed onto a rear wheel and studied the contents of the wagon while another handcar was loaded.

"Now, Tull, we'll do what you want, but I want'a say this. I been lookin' at what you got left in here, and if you and me was to lean them plates the other way, shiftin' the weight, I'd get me them three liftin' jacks I got and bring 'em over. Fixin' them planks solid, they'd hold the jacks. 'Course, it'd take some men with strong hands, but it could be done. I would'a said my son Manny'd be one of them men, but I got somethin' special for him to do.

"My thought'd be to raise that corner of the wagon with two'a the jacks and put the other'n at the other side. Most'a the weight inside the wagon'd be on the back, see? The front'd be lighter, and me and Manny, we could pull them wheels off and put in the new axel. That wheel that's up agin the ties, ya see how it's cracked? I got two wheels, but I don't think that right one got damaged, bein' up in the air. Now, that's what me and Manny could do, less someone's got a better way." Clyde stood back, respectfully. Axels and wheels were his skill, but the valuable mill equipment belonged to Steven Tullius.

Clancy looked at Tull, who contemplated the offered solution. "Sounds good, Kendall. Let's you and me get in there and move them wheels. Got one thing to say, though. Someone'll have to man my gun, keepin' them webfingered fumblebums backed away so's we can get somethin' done."

"I'll keep 'em back, Tull," Clancy promised. "My gun'll shoot farther'n yours anyway."

Considerable huffing and groaning was required to shift the wheels and plates, rolling them against the endgate.

"Reckon the endgate'll hold 'em?"

"Yeah, till the axel gets changed. Then we'll roll 'em back. It'll work, Tull." Slowly, as the weight shifted, the rear right wheel lowered to the planks, and the left front wheel raised itself from between the ties.

Manny, standing by, had heard his indirect orders. Sorting among the items in his father's wagon, he had located the wheel and the axel and put them aside. The three lifting jacks were set out, and willing bystanders carried them to the north bank and set them down. Something as valuable as a lifting jack should be handled only by its owner. Bringing a heavy steel mallet with him, Manny tapped the planks into position and set the heavy jack under the edge of the wagon front, wedging it under the bracing. Another jack was placed 14 inches away, on the next tie.

"Say when, Pa."

"Hold a second, son. This here tongue needs a mite' a straightenin'. There, now. Let 'er rip."

Pumping the lever on the first jack, Manny produced a few creaks and groans from the tortured wood of the wagon bed. Then a few strokes on the second jack to secure up the lift. Again on the first... more creaks... then the second. The cracked wheel was now moving free.

"Hold up, son. Let's get this other'n in place and raise 'em together."

"You want me to do it, Pa?"

"Reckon not. It's a squeeze for me, and you'd be better, but you got'a take both'a them on that side." Clyde worked the jack in place and pumped the lever a few times, creating more creaks.

"You again, son."

First, then second, then first, then....

"You free-wheelin' yet, Pa?"

"One more round. There. Don't want'a take 'er no higher'n we have to."

Removing the bolts, Manny slipped them into his pockets. Then, tapping the giant cotter pin from the hub, he freed the cracked wheel from the bent axel and carried it carefully to the north bank.

Sidling along the right side of the wagon, stepping carefully on the ties, he removed the right wheel and carried it away. It would be too risky to lay it on the ties while they changed the axel.

Back on the left side, he tapped the axel, threading it through the ball-bearing clamps.

"That thing's heavy, Pa. I'll be around there to help." And together they drew the oversized axel from its clamps.

"Pa, let's put it in the wagon. The weight of it won't matter."

Father and son slid the bent axel through the boards of the wagon, then walked on the railroad ties to the north bank and brought back the new axel. Working together, they threaded it through the clamps. Manny was stretched out across the ties under the wagon. "Pa, it's a little tight. It ain't been greased."

"That's all right, son. We'll tend to the greasin' on the other side."

The right wheel was reattached and the new one put on the left. Tull had sat on the edge of the handcar and watched the proceedings.

"Clyde, you and Manny need this here handcar no more?"

"Reckon not. Gonna need about eight sure-footed fellows on the tongue, though, when we start to pullin'. Need a couple more to tend to the straightenin' of them planks. Couple'a more turns of the wrench and we'll be ready."

Clyde and Manny stood back as the men from the wagon train eased past them to the front of the wagon. Lining up four to the side, they lifted the tongue.

"You fellows handle the guidin' of it?" They thought they could.

"Well, you move on, goin' slow. Me'n Tull and Manny, we'll lean on the endgate. They's still a lot'a weight in the wagon."

Slowly across the canvas tarp the wagon moved. Eight pairs of eyes watched the progress of the wheels on the planks, waiting until they could be tapped into a straight line.

The handcar moved back to the south bank, and the pumpers watched with admiration as the loaded wagon was maneuvered off the tracks and onto the ground beside the rest of its load.

Clancy approached the pumpers on the car. "Much obliged to you fellows for the help. We'd'a been a week doin' what you did. Quick as Tull there gets his tarp off the bridge, we'll stand back and let you pass. We got a dozen more wagons to bring across."

With a wave, the pumpers were gone, and the Santa Fe coughed and belched black smoke then sputtered white steam. When the pressure of the steam was sufficient, the whistle shrilled and the steel drivers clawed against the rails, pulling the weight of the train along the steel runners.

There was "kthug… kthug… kthug… kthug… kthug…" The blasts of sound from the drivers became closer as it gained speed. The huge engine called out an even-spaced chug... chug... chug... as it crossed the river, and within minutes, it was only a pillar of smoke in the distance.

Clancy marched onto the bridge and addressed his work crew. "You fellows done good. We got twelve vehicles more to go, and we can do it today. Anybody get tired, say so, and we got men that's rested that'll take your place."

The leader of the puller crew made a motion to move toward Clancy and thought better of it as the wagonmaster lowered his squirrel gun at his face and stared at him with cold, ice-blue eyes.

The men from Nebraska worked together as they had from the time they were toddlers, each knowing what the other could and would do best. Weariness was put aside, as it always had been in times of emergency, and they worked together as one.

It was then four o'clock. By five o'clock, only the Banner hog wagon remained. The puller crew with the contract was eager to quit for the day and get away from the scornful gaze of the wagon train travelers. Tomorrow's work had already built up on both sides of the river, at least ten wagons on each side.

"We'll just hook onto this last wagon and bring it along behind you," the crew chief offered, directing his men to hold to the tongue of the wagon.

Clancy Harper was also tired. The hog wagon was small and sturdily built. He watched critically as the pullers attached themselves to the last of the wagon train's vehicles. Surely they could handle it.

Up the grade they came, the three huge duroc hogs bracing their hoofs as best they could against the cleats Alvin had nailed to the wagon floor. Lining the hog wagon up with the planks, the puller crew followed along after the other Banner wagon.

"Wait, fellows. Plank's crooked." With his mallet, the plank straightener whacked against the offending board, sliding it against the rails with a bump, sending a shiver trembling through the wagon and catching the duroc boar off guard.

His hoof slipped over the cleat, throwing his considerable weight against the endgate. The braced boards would have easily held his weight, except for the crimping of the sideboards caused by the bump of the mallet. The sideboards, now out-of-square, released the catches that held it in place.

At that moment the tongue of the endgate popped loose from the groove of the sideboards, sending it down to the rails with a crash and then tumbling it over the edge of the bridge.

Alvin Banner, adding his weight to the rear of his first wagon, did not realize the pulling crew had taken charge of his hogs until he heard the yells and saw his endgate go sailing into the water.

He stopped, staring after it with horror only to see his prize boar sailing through the air, ineffectually flailing his short legs and squealing with terror.

The pulling crew stopped and drew back, watching with wide eyes as the panel of wood and the hog splashed into the river's swirling, brown liquid.

In a mound of foam and spray, the hog disappeared beneath the muddy water of the Cimarron River. Alvin Banner's tongue was loosened.

"Of all the knuckle-headed, feather-brained things to do! Didn't you numbskulls never have no dealings with movin' live weight? Who told you to be puttin' your grubby hands on my wagon, anyway?"

The pulling crew thought it best to retreat to the north bank once more.

Tullius removed himself from the pushing and joined Alvin Banner in the word fight. "You empty headed imbeciles! You ain't got the smarts God give a caterpillar! Would'a thought you'a learned to stay out'a the way by now."

Alvin again. "A body with a brain in his head'd know live weight, like a hog, shifts to brace hisself. These here hogs come all the way across Kansas and half of Oklahoma 'thout no trouble. They even weathered a twister a couple'a days back, and all it takes is two minutes with you puddin'-headed morons, and you lost my valuable hog."

Tull looked down to the dark water of the river. "Hey, Banner, look down there!"

Alvin turned to see his hog digging its short legs into the sand of a river island, pulling his rotund body onto the bank.

"I got'a go get 'em."

"You gonna leave these sows this'a'way?"

The two female durocs leaned against the panel farthest from the gaping rear of the wagon where the endgate should have been.

Clancy and two other men were now on the scene, having pulled the other Banner wagon across. Alvin Banner dispatched one man to bring ropes, lots of ropes.

"Banner, you do what you need to do here. Me and these men, we'll get that hog."

"Well, I…" Alvin Banner hesitated with the decision.

"Man, you can't be two places. You stay where you still got two hogs and let us deal with the one."

Manny Kendall joined the problem on the bridge.

"Alvin, I know where to lay hands on my pa's brace and bit. If you was to drill holes two or three inches apart, all down the edges, we could thread ropes back and forth tight enough to get these girls on across."

Alvin had crawled into the wagon, putting himself between the sows and the open end. "Manny, you got a plan! I'll stay here, keepin' 'em calm, and trust you to drill them holes."

For once more of the many times he had stepped across the Cimarron River on the railroad ties, Manny again walked to the south bank.

"Need ropes," he announced. "Gonna make a rope endgate. Need to get the drill."

Clyde Kendall nodded. "You go on with the drill, son. I'll tend to the rope gettin'."

Clancy led the pig rescuers down the bank to the river. The current rippled the water as it whirled round a sandbar, lodging sticks and other debris against the roots of the willow sprouts. The sandy island was a good thirty feet out into the stream.

Otto Hausfield came forward. "Clancy, I ain't been too much of a help along the way, but they's one thing I can do. I can swim. Me and Alvin out on the river the way we was, we was rescuin' somethin' or a'nuther from the river all the time. Could'a even been a time that I helped rescue that there hog. I'll be the one to go…."

"Wait, that water's movin' right along. You can do it, but you're gonna have a rope attached. We ain't riskin' losin' you."

Otto had stripped down to his underwear and submitted to a rope looped around his chest. Over his shoulder, he looped two more ropes. He apparently had a plan.

Backing up-stream a good way, he swan-dived a perfect arc into the water and came up, pulling strongly for the island, fighting against the pull of the current. The men on the shore loosely held the rope attached to his chest.

Scrambling up the bank, he began to talk to the frightened hog, working his way nearer and nearer.

Forming the rope into a double noose, he worked it under the hog's front feet, making a loop on his chest and one on his neck tied together behind his head to keep from choking the animal. The other rope was fastened securely in front of his hind quarters, just past his round belly.

Still talking and scratching the hog's floppy ears, he coaxed the animal to the edge of the island.

"Tighten up on the slack!" he yelled to the men on the bank, and when the hog felt the pull, he stubbornly dug all four stubby legs into the sandbar.

"Keep the slack took up!" Otto instructed. "I'm fixin' to push 'im in."

With a splash, man and hog landed in the water together. Paddling into the current, they were swept rapidly downward but were hauled out by the pull of the men on the ropes. The hog clawed its way up the bank, grunting and squealing with indignation at the crowd around him.

"Come on, pig, we made it. Quit yer complainin'," Otto commanded, grabbing the knot of the halter noose. "Will somebody grab onto my clothes?"

The huge hog with muddy sides and the man in the soggy, muddy underwear trudged along the sandy bank and up to the railroad grade. With the pulling crew looking on, Otto stepped into his clothes and pulled on his shoes, then turned to face the enemy of the day.

He said not a word but stared meaningfully at the pulling crew for a full minute.

The wagon train crew had backed the hog wagon to the north bank to collect the battered boar, then the lengths of rope were threaded and woven to make a secure net at the end of the wagon. It would not be as convenient as the endgate when it came to making a night pen, but one dealt with what one had.

Setting out once more across the train bridge with the animals, the weary travelers sighed with relief and weariness as the Banner hog wagon cleared the train grade and rolled onto solid ground.

Clancy waved toward the pulling crew, and they lifted the signal. With a snort and a belch, the steel drivers moved the iron wheels of the next train across the bridge. It puffed its white steam and snorted in the distance, finally disappearing into the landscape.

Clancy slumped wearily against a nearby wagon and addressed the moving mayor. "Ed, there ain't no more rivers 'tween here and there, are there?"

"Yep."

"You're pullin' my leg…" he suggested hopefully.

"Nope. One more. It's called Cottonwood Creek, and on a good day, you could jump it in places. We'll wade across the others. Good little stream, that Cottonwood, but it gets fat and frisky in the rainy season, I heard tell."

Clancy turned to the re-assembling of wagons and animals. It was now dusky dark and after seven o'clock.

He whistled loudly through his teeth and announced, "Late start tomorrow. We pull out a hour after sunrise. Get some rest, fellows."

Manny rounded up his little sisters and sent them to their mother, who was preparing their supper. Clyde leaned against his wagon and watched his son. "Good work you done today, son. It'd been hard to get along without you, but I know I'll need to learn how."

Manny knew he had heard the nearest thing to an apology that he would ever hear from his father. He accepted it. "Sure, Pa."

They walked along together, father and son, toward the fire crackling under Maude Kendall's bean pot. Manny sought to soften his words.

"Pa, them things I said, they was all true, but I didn't have no call to dump 'em on you sudden-like. I know that everything you ever said to me, you meant it for the best, and I'll be a long time thankin' you for the things you taught me to do. Today, you treated me like a man, equal to the rest'a you, and I appreciated it. I got'a do what I said I'd do, but I don't want it to be with no hard feelin's either way."

"I know, son. You do what you got'a do."

"No hard feelin's."

Fourteen

At ten minutes until nine, Clancy called out to Ed, "Pull out in ten minutes."

Ed Gunther grinned to himself, congratulating himself on his choice of a wagonmaster. One thing about Clancy: he kept to a schedule and he thought ahead. He did a lot better job than Ed himself would have done. Clancy hadn't wanted the job, and he didn't like doing the job, but the job had to be done by someone, so Clancy did it. Just as Ed had known he would do. Truth be told, he wouldn't make a bad mayor, once they got set up.

At nine twenty, the Banner hog wagon pulled out onto the rutted trail, its netting of rope holding the boar and the rotund girls safely inside. They grunted and snubbed conversationally to each other, bracing their short legs against the jiggle and sway of the wagon just as they had done for the past two and a half weeks.

It was a little after eleven when Alvin Banner felt the first creak in his wagon bed. He jumped down to the ground and walked along beside it for a little way, looking for what had made the noise. Nothing visible. He jumped back aboard, and ten minutes later another creak happened, and another. Then a lurch, and the right front wheel raised, twisting the wagon tongue against the right side horse, who shied and whinnied loudly.

Patrice Banner heard her husband's difficulty and pulled over. Clyde Kendall heard the whinny, an unusual sound for a calm horse. He looked back, and seeing Patrice pull over, he yelled, "Gee, up there!"

His horses moved to the grass beside the track. Manny pulled over and stopped.

Alvin was bent down over the left rear wheel. The wagon bed shook with the movement of the animals, and the tame hogs, seeing their beloved master, came over to greet him.

Their weight concentrated in the left rear corner of the wagon bed, and the wagon began to settle, crunching and splintering as it lowered.

"Got a problem?" Clyde wanted to know.

"Yep. Them fool-headed nincompoops cracked my wheel, bangin' on it with the mallet. I heard the creakin' but didn't look to see that a chunk'a wheel was gone. Purely come apart on me, splinterin' into kindlin' wood." He stood and stared at the corner of the wagon resting on the heap of splintered spokes and broken wheel pieces. The excited durocs were fighting to keep their hooves under their bodies.

Manny came past his father's wagon and reached in for the lifting jack. His father was now bent over the problem. "Axel looks to be still good. Glad about that. We got a spare wheel, but no more axels."

Seeing Manny approach with the jack, he nodded, "Good job. I'll get the wheel."

One by one, as the wagon drivers realized there was no one behind them, they stopped. By the time Clancy realized there had been a problem at the rear, it had been repaired, and the hog wagon was again moving.

Wheeling his horse around, he headed back to the front, "Move 'em out!" One by one, the wagons crawled back into the line.

The trail had become much more crowded in the last few hours. Where they had formerly gone for an hour and more without seeing another traveler, now were several traveling along with them.

"Getting' close to somethin', are we, Ed?"

"Yeah, Guthrie up ahead. I know everybody's tired, but if you make it a long day today, chance you'll make it on in tomorrow."

Clancy slumped wearily into his saddle. Could it be? Could it actually be almost over? There are many sweet words to enter the human ear, but to Clancy, 'Guthrie up ahead' ranked among the sweetest.

Turning back to the north, he whistled. "Keep a'rollin'. We got'a make up a little time." By galloping rapidly, he missed hearing the weary groans and the colorful epithets laid upon him.

From the fires of their night camp, they could look ahead and see the night lights of the city of Guthrie, Oklahoma Territory. Young and old, they stood on their sideboards and stared. Small children climbed onto wagon seats for a better look.

Clancy made his rounds. "Short night, folks. Gonna try to make it on in tomorrow."

"Tomorrow? Really tomorrow?"

"Gonna try."

Smoke had begun to curl up from the many cook fires. What had taken an hour or more three weeks ago now was done in a manner of minutes. Amid the constant aroma of beans came the pungent fragrance of cooked greens, gathered from along the roadside during that day.

The very smell of the woodsmoke had a relaxing quality for the weary travelers, promising a night of rest very soon.

Clancy Harper breathed in the aroma of the smoke and walked his tired animal back to where he knew his beloved wife would have his food ready.

All in all, life wasn't half bad.

But all of "life" was not conveniently camped just outside of Guthrie. Some of it lay far to the north. It was not even daylight, but Taffy Littletree was awake. Most of Providence Falls, Nebraska, was still asleep, but a small assemblage of wagons waited at the southern edge of town.

The departure was scheduled for five o'clock. Any person wishing to be part of the caravan and not making the deadline would be on his own to catch up, hopefully, somewhere down the line.

It had been only yesterday that Taffy had stood in the meadow sunshine beside the hole someone had dug. There was the box, and inside it, Big Papa lay asleep, just as he had been for the last couple of weeks. They said he didn't ever wake up, and she hoped they were right. There comes a time when one was only thirteen years old that one must trust the grownups to know what they were doing.

She had stood there with her notebook. It was unthinkable to be somewhere without it. A sharpened pencil was pressed between the pages, and she had stood quietly while the preacher was saying words about Big Papa that everyone already knew. Then her own special words came to her.

> *"Big Papa, he was lots of fun until he had to go.*
> *He went to be with Grandma. The grownups told me so.*
> *When people get so tired and old, there isn't any fun.*
> *They look around for things to do and find there isn't none*
> *And then you don't have things to do and have no place to go,*
> *Big Papa didn't tell me this, so how am I to know*
> *If he decided he would leave, 'cause he loved Grandma so?"*

She was relieved that she had brought her notebook along. That way she could write the words down and not have to remember them. One never knew when a new poem would creep in and crowd out the old one. She had learned that the poems that were crowded out never really came back as good as they once were. They just stood outside her mind trying to get back in… mixing up their words so they didn't make sense.

So now, this morning, she sat in the dark wagon on a pile of quilts. The grownups were standing around talking, because there seemed to be a few minutes left before time to leave.

This trip was going to be a bummer. If Pa and Uncle Jake were going to go to that somewhere place called the territory, they should have gone with the others, and there would have been someone to be with. Who knew how many days it would be until they saw a person again?

Oh, sure, she knew why they had to wait and that three other families waited with them. The only trouble was they were only babies and old people like her parents. And she had fifty million friends back in the city, sleeping away, with no idea of how much she would miss them.

"The town is dark, so very dark, black as a wicked witch's heart.
If we're ever going to have to go, I wish they'd let it start."

It was really hard to see the notebook, but still she had the scribblings down. She could re-copy them later. It seemed that she would get her wish, because she heard the grinding of wagon wheels on the gravel and the shuffle and jingle of harnesses as the horses became restless.

The grownups with their lanterns began to separate from the group where they had been standing, and the lights of the lanterns spread out like a string of beads in the blackness of the world.

Her pa, Samuel Littletree, went back to talk to whoever came in the last wagon, and then he came back. He stepped up into the wagon bed, jiggling it slightly, and then he tapped the reins on the backside of the team of horses.

Taffy, however, did not see him return, nor did she feel the jiggle of the wagon.

"The grownups stand around and talk,
and each one has a light.
Their lanterns make a necklace
on the black neck of the night.
I heard a sound, a crunching sound.
I couldn't see a thing.
The horses stomped and jiggled
and they made their harness ring.

I saw the necklace come apart.
The lights all moved away."

… now what rhymes with "away"?

Then Taffy felt the movement of the wagon, and the loneliness she had tried to ignore settled down on her like a wet blanket that she was trying to hang on the clothesline on a windy day. Ah, there was the last line.

"I saw the necklace come apart.
The lights all moved away.
I left my life behind me.
Now, what more is there to say?"

There! She got that written down. It was so worrisome to have a line with no rhyme. If the next line didn't come to her quickly, she just as well throw away the last one, because they would never fit together. It all had to be done at the right time.

Taffy sighed and reached beside her for the new doll. She was really too old for dolls, maybe, but Pa had seen this one for sale at Hewett's store when they were trying to sell off or pack everything they had. She guessed he thought it would help make up for all she was leaving behind.

It didn't, really, but it was a pretty doll. If she ever had a room again, it would look very nice on the pillow or even hanging on the wall. Well, anyway, she had it, so she wrapped the doll blanket snuggly around its cold arms and legs and cuddled it under the quilt with her. She might as well sleep. There was nothing else to do.

The wagon rolled along. Samuel and Nellie Littletree had the first wagon. Next came a hired driver and the accumulation of carpentry tools used by Sam and his pa. Pa wouldn't need them anymore.

Next came Jake, who easily got all of his plunder in one wagon. A single guy did not accumulate much. Next was Marvin Hausfield, whose brother, Otto, had gone with the first group. His brother had hardly cleared the edge of town when Marvin began to wish he'd gone. Now he was on the way.

The Falleys had the next two wagons. It took two of them to transport their five boys. Then came the Morehouse family. They had five girls.

That made ten in all, a very sizeable train when all stretched out on the Kansas prairie.

Taffy roused when the rays of the sun shone in under the cover of the wagon, but there was nothing to get up for, so she pushed herself back under the quilt and into sleep.

Sam Littletree seemed to be the unofficial wagonmaster. As everyone had eaten before they pulled out, he decided the first morning should be a long one. Every mile they put behind them was one more mile behind them.

The sun was directly overhead when he pulled to the side of the road for a lunch stop. Taffy was beginning to have an empty place in her stomach and was glad to see some activity toward correcting the problem.

She sat up in the pile of quilts and set her doll aside. Picking up her notebook she wrote:

> *"I do not know where I am now.*
> *I know it's not for good,*
> *But now I'm really hungry and*
> *I wish they'd stop for food."*

At that moment her pa stuck his head under the wagon cover. "Taff…? Out with you. Stretch your legs a little, and go pick up some of these dry sticks so we can start a fire."

She had felt the stirrings of another line of poetry and really wanted to write it down. "But, Pa…?"

Dad's voice became a little louder. "TAFF… I SAID 'NOW'…!"

Taffy put her notebook aside and shoved the line of poetry back into her mind. Sometimes, when it was not quite ready to be written down, she could make it wait for a little while.

Small sticks, Pa had said. Well, that might take some looking in this land of no trees. Would really big weeds do? She knelt down on the ground and gathered those closest to her and crawled a little way to get some more.

She reached out for a thick branch of weed and saw a shoe beside her fingers. The shoe covered a sock and a foot, and there was something familiar about that shoe. How many people in the world had pink Mary Janes? And pink socks?

She jumped up and screamed in her excitement. Her bundle of weed stalks was flung away! "Junebug! You're here! How did you get here?"

June Morehouse was inclined to be a jokester. "Likely got here the same way you did, in a wagon."

"But I thought…?"

"I did, too. It was 'go' and then 'no go' and then 'go' again till I was about dizzy. Dad wanted to come on, and Ma wanted to stay until the Baker ladies left. Finally Dad said we were ready now, and we wouldn't be no more ready if we waited another month. So here we are."

Taffy just stared at June. It was truly unbelievable. The long, lonely trip would now be a 2 or 3 week adventure. There were only days worth of difference in their ages. Taffy, born Tiffany, had a birthday in May, and June Morehouse was born less than a month later. She had been expected in May and was going to be named "May," but it was change to "June" when she turned out to be late. The name "June" turned itself into "Junebug" in the mouths of most of her friends.

Taffy remembered her errand. "Look, I got'a pick up little sticks for the fire. I'll hurry."

"No need to hurry. I'm picking up sticks, too. That is, I'm supposed to be."

Junebug spent the rest of the day in Taffy's wagon. When it was time for her to leave, Taffy picked up her notebook.

> *"I thought I'd left my life behind.*
> *I thought I saw it end.*
> *I was sad and lonesome, but wait!*
> *'Cause then I saw my friend!*
> *To see a friend you thought you'd lost,*
> *Especially like Junebug,*
> *Is just like…"*

What was it like? There had to be a special word, and she had to get the word RIGHT NOW, while there was enough light to write it down. Bug, rug, mug, dug, where was it? Come on, rhyme! Ah, there it is!

> *"To see a friend you thought you'd lost,*
> *Especially like Junebug,*

Is just like if your eyes had arms
To give your heart a hug."
Yes, that was it. Was there more…?
"We walked together, side by side,
Beside the wagon bed.
Sometimes we talked, and sometimes not,
But lots of things were said.
When you're not a grownup,
They can tell you what to do.
They can make you do some things
That make you sad and blue.
Life can make you lonely
Like the days will never end,
Then it can give a present,
Like the times it brings a friend."

With a satisfied sigh, Taffy put aside her notebook and picked up her doll. Pa and Ma were just outside the wagon. She could hear them talking in low voices with Uncle Jake and with some of the folks from other wagons.

She couldn't hear the words of the grownups over the calling of the night birds and the crickets. That was all right. She couldn't think of a thing that any of them could be saying that would interest her. She'd just go to sleep. and when she woke up, there would be another day of fun with Junebug Morehouse.

The very next sound she heard was Pa's voice. "Taff…? Out of bed, now, and eat. We're going to be on the road."

Fifteen

Many miles south, other wagons were surrounded with activity. The smell of woodsmoke and bacon, of baking biscuits and brewing coffee had filled the air for the last hour. By now, most of the cooking equipment had been stored under the buckboards.

Clancy Harper swung into his saddle and whistled loudly between his teeth, then yelled, "Ed, pull out in ten minutes."

It was still darkish at 6:30 when Ed Gunther pulled onto the well-worn, rutted trail. It would soon be crowded, but they had the road to themselves for a little while. By straight up seven o'clock, Patrice Banner pulled in behind Clyde Kendall, and the hog wagon brought up the rear.

Ed motioned Clancy off his horse, and he rode for a ways seated beside Ed in the wagon and leading his own horse on a tether.

"Been thinkin'," Ed began. "These fellows been takin' orders, not havin' to think, for the last three weeks. We're fixin' to dump 'em on their own land, and most of 'em'll need to know where the city is. I was thinkin', we could halt the wagon and take the men on a jaunt around by the Santa Fe depot. You'll need to know where it is and so will they, and Guthrie is bound to be crawlin' alive with folks not knowin' what they're doin'. I do remember where the depot is, and if I could take the men in and show 'em, I'd feel my work was done."

Clancy nodded. "That'd be a good thing. You're thinkin' there'd be a place to leave our train?"

"Easy. Right before we head east, just park 'em. We got saddle horses to use as far as they go, and we can unhook what we need for the rest'a the men. Be good for the men to know where they're at in relation to the town."

A mile east of Guthrie, the wagons stopped. Manny called to his father, "Pa, we can take my horses. They ain't been carryin' the load like yours. Bring along a saddle, and I'll have your mount ready."

A band of seventeen men left the train and headed east toward the constant hum of sound and cloud of dust.

Mechanical and human noises, after the quiet and the crunch of wagon wheels, sounded strange and alien. Manny reined in his horse to trot companionable beside his father. Actually, it would have been fairly easy to find the depot, with the trains huffing noisily through it so often, but still, it was good to get a glimpse of the big city.

People were everywhere. They were living in tents and in shacks made of wood and cardboard boxes, but they seemed excited and alive.

Stacks of lumber waited beside some of the shacks, indicating a proper house was soon to be built. Some lots had only a covered wagon serving as a house. Children played joyfully in the yards and washings hung on the improvised lines. Life had settled in.

The Santa Fe engine huffed its way down the track and halted with a screech and a cloud of steam beside a long building surrounded by a loading platform.

Manny Kendall looked this way and that. It was a wonderful sight. Truly this was where he would come, just as soon as he…? His thoughts stopped amid sentence.

"Pa, lookie over there! Somebody's got our name. See that green wagon with the white letters? KENDALL BROTHERS We Haul. I wonder if we're kin."

"Likely they's a lot'a Kendall's in this world, son."

"Yeah, Pa, but I'm a'gonna see where they hail from."

Leaving his father, Manny rode toward the green wagon. The driver was gone, but the wagon bed was partially filled with boxes and packages. Someone came from the depot loaded with even more boxes, the heap piled so high he could hardly see where he was going.

There was something about…? Manny jumped down from his horse and found himself face to face with his brother.

"Chet!"

"Manny? Manny, how'd you get here? I mean, hey, Doug, look what just drug in!"

Manny turned to shout toward the assembled men, "Hey, Pa, it's Chet and Doug!"

Clyde Kendall came riding over to the wagon, staring from the boys to the wagon and back. "How you boys… doin'…? Is this…?" His hesitant words hung in the air.

"It's a long story, Pa, and we ain't got time right now. We got us a job and we're on the clock. But, sakes alive, have we got things to say! We'll be on out come Sunday. Manny, have we ever got somethin' to tell you! Don't reckon you could stay over…? Right now?"

Manny shook his head. "Got a wagon and three girls to deliver, and likely Pa'll need help. But you'll be there Sunday. That's two days, ain't it? Sort'a lost track'a time on the road. That rig sure enough yours?"

"Ours, Manny! Yours and ours. It belongs to the three of us. You think about that till Sunday. We got'a get back to work. So long."

Chester and Douglas disappeared into the depot, and Manny stood for a minute staring at the white letters on the green wagon. Good wagon. He could tell instantly it was one of the best. What could his brother mean, saying it was his and theirs?

Manny turned his horse and followed the men back to the wagon train. As they were hitching the animals to the wagon, Clyde asked, "Manny, what was that Chet was a'tryin' to say?"

"Danged if I know, Pa. Didn't seem to be makin' no sense to me."

But the words echoed within his head, bouncing back and forth against his weary brain. "YOURS and ours! YOURS and ours!" Couldn't be no truth in it. Then again, Chet was taught never to lie, just like all of Pa's youngens.

Sixteen

Herbert and David, the young Hewett drivers, sat in the wagon and watched the girls. No one had invited them to go see the town. They were only along for their driving skills.

"Truth be told, this was quite a trip. It's getting' to seem like fun, movin' halfway across the country. Sort'a found myself wishin' my pa'd decided to come."

"Yeah, me, too."

"Reckon a body'd find a job quick enough to keep from starvin'? I ain't expected back till Hewett says I can go. That'd give me, or us, time to be lookin' around. Wish't I'd'a gone on over to that town, just to see what was goin' on. Look at Manny; he'll be livin' in a new town with all them girls, and even Ellie Gunther's done got down here. Wouldn't think he'd run short'a somethin' to look at."

"Yeah. You know, Dave, we could take the horses and come over here while they're getting' the wagons emptied. They're our horses, and they said it was only fourteen miles."

"We could. If jobs was real good, we could maybe stay the summer. Pa ain't needin' this wagon back. No time soon, anyway."

"Aw, here comes the fellows back. See ya, later." Herbert stepped down from the buckboard seat and took his place in the line.

The wagon train turned east, and with every step, the idea became more ingrained in his fertile mind. *I'm almost twenty years old,* he reminded himself several times. *Ain't no reason to go back north less'n I don't like it here.*

Ahead of him, David turned his thoughts over in his mind. *I seen more in the last three weeks than I'd'a seen in a year'a Sundays back in the Flats. By crackies, I could spend the summer in that Guthrie town. The winter, too, if I was a'mind.*

The wheel of his wagon climbed over a small stump, finishing with a four-inch drop, bouncing the springs of the buckboard seat.

David jerked his head erect from the bump just as an idea dropped, fully blossomed, into his head. *I don't have to go home! I been sittin' around campfires, listenin' to these folks talk about their lots and how they was 5 acres big with a well and trees. Said they cost $50.00. Never thought of it till now, but I want me one of them lots. If I got me a good job, I could save $50.00 in one year. Maybe less.*

Now that the thought had fully blossomed, he couldn't wait to tell Herbert. Together, they could pay for a lot a far sight sooner. No, he didn't want to share with Herb. He wanted something was totally his. Likely, so would Herb.

Manny Kendall steered around the stumps and uneven ruts as best he could. The wagon waved and wobbled, and he couldn't see how the three girls lying down in the back managed to sleep, but boredom had made lazybones out of them.

He looked down beside the wagon. Good land. Grass popped up wherever it could get the sun. Flowers everywhere. Look at the size of those redbud trees! Blossoms almost gone, but if the girls were awake, they'd still like to pick them. That other thought crept in… the green wagon… part his? Of course not; he had simply misunderstood Chet.

Suddenly, the semi-quiet was shattered by an ear-rending buzzzzz. The noise seemed to be almost on top of him.

Jerking around, he saw, between the trees, what looked like a pile of logs, a contraption of wheels and gears, and a stack of new lumber, its ivory color standing out in the green shade of the trees.

BUZZZZZ! The steel blade ripped through a log, sending chips and sawdust skyward in a yellow cloud. BUZZZZ! Unmistakable! That was a sawmill making lumber! Say, there might be a job there!

About every half mile along the road, a new camp was set up. Trees were cut, log cabins were under construction. Some of the residents lived in tents.

A lot of people were living in the wagon that had brought them there, working feverishly on their fence… or garden… or house… or… A rush of activity was going on all around him.

BUZZZZ! Another log was sliced into dimension lumber.

Nearer the front of the train, Herb leaned out of the wagon, looking back long after there was anything to see. He shook his head in disbelief. *As I live and breathe,* as his granny would have said, *there was a sawmill, going full blast. Right out there in the middle of nowhere yet! Now, that was a job to have! Reckon they wanted to put somebody on steady for the summer? Or for life?*

Dusk had fallen when the front wagon pulled over and halted. James Hewett drew up beside it, out of habit, and Mary Lou Hewett, now at the reins, pulled in beside him. Herb and Dave took their places as they would for any night camp.

Clancy rode by. "Turn to the right and pull in anywhere. Just anywhere! Could be you'd be pullin' into your own yard!"

Maude Kendall reined her team to the right, and Manny drew in beside her. "This is it, Ma!" he called cheerily. "You don't got to go no farther!"

"You mean we're there already? My, my, where did the time go?" she grinned. Didn't Ma ever get tired and cranky anymore?

Yep, Ma was a trooper! She had been in a fairly good humor during the whole trip, turned out plenty of good food and never complained. Of course, she didn't have the three little girls to contend with. Like he did.

"Wake up, girls. Betty, Ollie, Sophie? We're there."

Darkness was closing in fast. "Let 'em sleep," suggested his mother. Manny sighed with relief. They had reached the end of the journey, and Ma was in charge once again. Good old Ma!

With those three words from his mother, he knew he had been released from his responsibilities. Tomorrow, he'd make a trip down to that sawmill. Or the next day, for certain.

Clyde stepped down from the buckboard, stiffly stretching the kinks from his shoulders and back. Striking a match to the lantern, he walked into the trees surrounded by the small circle of light. It felt like home already.

Josh Fields lifted his bride down from her buggy. "Darling, we made it." She had almost enough strength to return his kiss.

Nettie Gunther rushed from one wagon to the other, ever the concerned hostess. "We got fresh water, right there through the trees. The girls'll help you find it. You need somethin' tonight, let me know. It sure is good to see everybody!"

She might have said more, except her words were smothered against Ed's shoulders.

Lacey Hewett checked briefly on the whereabouts of her four children, the two Kendall girls and her four drivers. All seemed to be well, so she stretched out on the small space she had for a bed. Get to sleep, she told herself. Tomorrow is another day.

Patrice Banner moved slowly to limber her stiff joints just a little after the long day, disturbing five-year-old Marcie, who was pillowed against her arm.

Marcie yawned and blinked her eyes, then stretched out on the buggy seat with a sigh. Patrice smoothed back Marcie's raven-black hair and stepped down from the buggy. She walked on ride-stiffened legs back to her husband's wagon.

Alvin enclosed her briefly in a shoulder hug. "We made it, honey. I got'a let the boar and the girls out. Make up our bed and I'll join you."

Removing the portable panels from their slot, he constructed the usual night pen. The three animals walked capably down the cleated ramp and into the enclosure positioned under an acorn tree.

Sensing the acorns on the ground, the hogs sniffed and grunted their recognition of the smell, experimentally crunching a few in their strong jaws.

The boar, as was his habit, circled the enclosure to determine if he was, indeed, penned in. He was. With that chore behind him, he settled down to munching the acorns. One of the girls joined him.

The other sow walked back and forth along the enclosure panels, circling and rooting half-heartedly. She aimlessly picked up small sticks and carried them a little way, then dropped them.

When one of the other animals happened to move too close to her, she warned them away with a series of low, short grunts. They moved away quickly, giving her the space she wanted. And needed.

By midnight, her breathing came in short bursts, and at one o'clock she threw herself onto the bed of grass and old acorn husks, her long body fully occupying the only patch of moonlight within the pen.

At one thirty, the concentrated heaving began, and before two o'clock, her work was done. Nine squeaking pink duroc piglets nudged against her warm belly, searching for her nipples. The sow's grunts turned into long, purring sighs, and she heaved her body around to make her nipples more easily accessible.

She lay there, grunting contentedly, until daylight began to filter through the trees.

A few hundred feet away from the hog pen, a small, almost-five-year-old girl lay asleep on her pallet in the tent with her grandfather. She had been kept awake very late by a lot of sounds and moving lights in the woods south of her house.

Big Papa had explained to her that the people who would live in the town with them had arrived, and she must go to sleep and not worry about them. But how could she not worry when there were many wagons, so many snorting horses, jiggling their harness rings, and such a lot of people talking all at the same time? She had sneaked a peek when she could, but the trees and the darkness were in the way.

When the muted sounds of the night birds faded and were replaced by the trill of the mockingbird, and the chee-chee of the wrens, the little girl again opened her eyes. Big Papa was still asleep. That was good.

She pulled herself from her cover sheet and stepped outside the tent. No, it had not been a funny dream. Horses were tied to trees and wagons were everywhere. She would like to go closer, but, even though no one had told her she mustn't, she knew she should stay in her own yard.

The large bluetick hound dogs saw her leave the tent and roused themselves to watch after her. As she moved toward the strange wagons, they joined her, wagging their tails and bumping against her with their heads. "Pete… Pokey…" she greeted them.

At the edge of the trees, Alecia stopped, but the dogs continued on.

"Pete! Pokey! You come back," she whispered loudly. They did not obey. She repeated the command a bit louder.

Marcie Banner turned over and sighed, and she heard a loud whisper. What was that, and where was Mama? Sitting up suddenly, she looked about her at the trees and animals, and then at a little girl wearing a white nightdress. Looking down at herself, she saw that she had slept in her day dress. Strange, but that must mean she could get up and walk about.

Slipping down from the buggy seat, she walked toward the other girl, who smiled and held to the neck of a big doggy.

"My name's Marcie. What's your name?"

"My name is Alecia, but sometimes they call me Alec. I got two doggies and their names are Pete and Pokey."

Marcie Banner sought for something she had that was as mentionable as the dogs. Then she remembered.

"I got three big piggies. You want'a see 'em?"

Alecia nodded and, forgetting the rule about wandering off, followed Marcie to the white panels of the hog pen, showing plainly in the growing daylight. Peeping between the boards of the panels, the girls inspected the hogs still sleeping quietly.

A pink pile of lumpy things lay close to one of the hogs, and something squeaked from within the pile. A snort and a wiggle and the 'pink something' tried to climb back into the pile, waking its littermates in the process. Many high-pitched squeals came from the pen, and one of the big "piggies" stood up and grunted scary noises. All the little pink things came running toward the big one.

It all looked so funny that the two little girls began to giggle and then to laugh. Look at all those funny pink things!

Patrice Banner startled awake at the sound of the little girls' laughter. "Wake up, Alvin! Marcie's up!"

Alvin, in his nightshirt, pulled himself from his cramped sleeping quarters and stepped to the ground.

"Marcie! What are you...?"

"Piggies, Papa! Look at the piggies!"

Alvin Banner leaned over the fence panel and smiled. The old girl had barely made it! He had been afraid every night that her time would come, and he would have to figure some way to care for the litter of pigs, but she had made it all the way to the town before giving birth.

A call came from the woods, "Alecia! Where are you?"

"That's Bertie! I got'a go," and she moved away. Then she turned back, "I got an ABC book. We can look at it. Goodbye."

Marcie waved, and Alecia ran through the trees to her Aunt Roberta.

Seventeen

Farther to the north, the ten-wagon caravan cleared Arkansas City with no mishaps. A quick two-hour stop was planned, but it was more like four hours that it took to restock on supplies and get on the road again. All in all, though, they had made excellent time.

The next landmark was to be the Cimmeron River. They had no guess as to how wide it was or how they would get across. Surely it was possible, though, because others were making it. No reason to worry, they kept telling themselves.

They also kept telling themselves there was no reason to worry, but they had trouble making each other believe it. And then they were there.

A group of four or five wagons waited by the bank where the railroad bridge spanned the river. Sam Littletree talked with the men in the waiting wagons.

"Not much worry," they told him. "They's a pullin' crew here to get us acrost on the railroad tracks, but you got'a swim your animals. Cost a half a dollar to the ferry for the horses, and a buck and a half on the wagon."

Jake scratched his head. "Could be we could get our own wagons across for nothin'."

"Naw, it's been suggested. Seems like these fellows have a contract or somethin', and they're the only ones who can stop the train."

"Hmmm… Well, if that's the way it had to be."

Taffy and Junebug stood on the muddy bank and stared at the brown water. The ferry platform was attached to the trees on both banks to keep it from washing down the river on its brown-water current. The horses snorted and whinnied, but in the end, they plunged into the water and swam behind the ferryboat. Junebug's pa went with them to see after them till the rest of the family got across.

The pulling crew lined up on each side of the wagon tongue and pulled, hauling the wagon onto the train tracks. They were hardly in position when a whistle in the distance told of an oncoming train. The crew pushed the wagon back down the grade to allow the train to pass, then pulled it up again. Slowly they pulled, keeping the wheels on flat boards laid down for that purpose.

One by one the wagons reached the other side, and it was time for the people to cross.

Pa told Taffy, "You girls make sure your shoes are tied or buckled tight, and don't carry anything in your hands. You're gonna have this rope tied around your waists, and you are going to walk between Uncle Jake and me."

"But, Pa…?"

"Don't 'But, Pa,' me. Do as I say. I've been to enough expense and aggravation with you that I don't aim to lose you." He smiled, but she knew he meant it. "Now, get on up here, and let's get this over with."

As exciting as it was to step on the ties that were more than a foot apart with brown water showing between them, the girls were glad to be across. They really couldn't have fallen down between the ties... could they? That would have been too awful for words... or thoughts!

It was too late to go on that day, so they let the animals graze and went to bed early. It was still light enough for Taffy to spend time with her notebook.

> "Pa was worried, I could see,
> and Uncle Jake, he wore a frown.
> They talked about a river
> and I wondered if we'd drown.
> They called the river Cimmaron,
> it sounded like a song.
> I stood and watched the water, brown,
> and saw it move along.
> My pa unhooked the horses
> and he made them swim across.
> They tied the ferry to the trees,
> afraid it would be lost.
> We saw the train go chugging by,
> across the railroad track.
> We looked both ways and saw
> the train was never coming back.
> Men pulled our wagon on the track
> just like they were 2 teams.
> Our horses stood and watched them pull,
> as crazy as that seems.
> They put the harness on the team,
> the bit into their mouths.
> We climbed aboard the wagon and
> again we headed south."

This was a long part of her poem, and her hand cramped a bit from the tension of it all. It was a relief to put the notebook aside and reach for the doll. She was too old for a doll, of course, but there was no one to see her, and it felt kind of good snuggled under the quilt with her.

After an early breakfast, they were on the road again with a long way to go. It was now Saturday.

A lot of miles to the south, it was morning in the town of Prosper. It was also the 21st of May, 1889.

Basil Hamilton, who had missed out on getting land in the run, had moved to the town in the hope of being permitted to buy one of the lots. Six other households had come with him, and the seven had been forced to wait until the town arrived to see if land was still available. It was.

There was much consultation of the numbered plat and corner stakes, as the members of the train moved onto their own land and the seven families who had waited were finally permitted to select from those lots that were left.

The Kendall's were so busy all day that Manny did not have time to go to the sawmill to talk about a job, but he would go the first thing Monday morning for certain.

Dave and Herb, their responsibilities done, walked back down the road. It felt good to be using feet and legs after the miles of the jiggle and bump of the road.

"You sure enough gonna stay here? And buy land?"

Dave had battled with it in the night. What a crazy idea he had in his head! Buying land in a strange place, just because he got acquainted with this bunch of people.

But why not? There would come a time that he would want a place to live… maybe get married… have a family? Wouldn't he? But here he was, without even a steady girlfriend, and he just didn't know anyone who had ever had such crazy thought that a man (boy?) not yet 21 could, or even want to, own his own land. Most of the night, he had pitched the idea from one side of his mind to the other just like a ping-pong ball. But now, when he heard the questions coming out of Herb's mouth, he had no doubts.

"'Course I am. I like it here, and I'm over twenty years old. If I can get me a good job, that's what I'm gonna do. First off, I got that

$30.00 comin' for makin' the trip down here. I got the wagon and the horses, and Pa'll let me have them."

Herb walked along beside him, his thoughts racing. Why not? It sounded like a great adventure! He, for sure, wanted to stay the summer. And if Guthrie was the way folks said it was, well...? And he'd soon see about that.

Dave again. "Hey, you could stay, too. We could each buy us a place, side by side. How'd that be?"

Work was proceeding hot and heavy at the sawmill. Stacks of logs were heaped all around, and sweaty men with their shirts off worked among the flying sawdust and chips of bark.

"You want jobs? You bet your life! Rollin' logs and stackin' lumber. Twenty-five cents an hour, seven days a week, long as you last. Ready to start?"

Dave and Herb worked until hunger forced them to stop. Tomorrow, they'd bring something along to eat.

They walked back to the town more slowly than they had come. "Man, that's hard work after sittin' for so long!"

"Yeah, but look at them wages! Two dollars and fifty cents a day, for a ten hour day!"

On Sunday morning, the two young men ignored their protesting muscles and headed for the sawmill, this time riding a horse.

The Baker brothers, Hamp and Bart, showed up Saturday morning, ready to drill waterwells.

They had been able to locate another team of strong mules and a wagon that would do until Clyde Kendall was set up to make them one like the one they got from the 7C Ranch. The borrowed gray wagon and the pair of bays were returned to Eben Carlile.

The green wagon came rolling into town shortly after daylight. Heads turned to stare at the grasshopper green wagon with the stark white letters proclaiming its owners as "KENDALL BROTHERS, We Haul."

By the time Chester and Douglas had found their family, most of the town had read the intriguing words.

"Hey, Ma! Pa! You made it!"

After the first catching up, Chester began, "Pa, we didn't have no way to tell you, but we kind'a went out on our own since we got down here. We saw us a chance at a quarter section, and 'afore we knew it, it was ours, and we was walkin' the section lines with the gun. Then Nettie Gunther got here and…" He hesitated.

Clyde butted in, "Yeah, Ed was sayin' somethin', but he didn't seem to have it clear in his mind what."

"Well, we thought we'd see what the job situation was in the city, and we made a deal for this rig. That's what we was doin' down at the Santa Fe where you saw us. We had a job deliverin' stuff folks ordered."

"But that wagon…?"

"We had to put our names on it. Folks wouldn't know we was for hire if we didn't. We need another wagon."

"Another one…?"

"Yeah, Pa. We was hopin' you'd let us borrow…" Their new need to face their father as equals took away their words.

"Son, it's packed full, and I ain't got no place to…."

"Listen, Pa. Me and Doug, we got a 12-foot square shack over on our place. You could pack it full, or tarp the stuff and sleep in the shack, or…."

"Shack on your place? Where is your place?"

"Jump on, Pa, and we'll take you. You, too, Manny."

"Boys, I'm still scratchin' my head over you with a quarter section'a land. I would'a thought… well, I got them two lots, a'thinkin'… but you two…?"

"It's all right, Pa. It'll come to ya. We done a lot'a head scratchin' ourselves."

Manny had wandered away from all the excited exuberance. That settled it. He'd go to the sawmill, just like Dave and Herb.

Moving the plunder into the shack took a good long while. Clyde had to see to the family lots, leaving Manny, Chester and Douglas to tend to the unloading.

"Good to see you, Manny. We was anxious for you to get here."

"Not as anxious as me. But I know what I'm a'gonna do come Monday. I'll be down there at the sawmill. They're payin' $2.50 a day rollin' logs."

Chester and Douglas had stopped, stock-still, their arms loaded with plunder. They stared at Manny, solemnly shaking their heads. "No, Manny. You ain't gonna do that. We need you to come to the city with us. We got'a find two more wagons. We can make money, a lot more'n that, haulin' for the Santa Fe depot."

"I could…? You mean…?"

"You got'a. When we got a chance to get this land, we know'd you'd be a part of what we did. If'n it weren't for you, one of us'd been kept back there to bring down that wagon and the girls. Could'a been one of us, same as you. So we figgered that made you part'a what we got goin'. We made us a deal for this wagon, and we was hopin' to get to use the one you drove down. Still need one more."

"Yeah, and we'll paint 'em alike, and we'll be seen so many places down there in Guthrie, them folks'll think we're the only ones in the haulin' business."

"The Santa Fe'll let me work…? I'm only 16!"

Chet announced, "Yeah, and right now, I speck they'd hire the devil hisself if he had a good wagon. 'Sides, you're an owner in our business, and it'd be up to you to say if you worked or if you didn't. They got thousands'a folks movin' in all of a sudden, everybody needin' everything, 'cause they left stuff behind the way we did. Only way to get stuff now is to order it in on the train."

Doug filled in, "And the train people wouldn't bother to deliver it till the stacks'a stuff filled up the depot so nobody can get around. The train folks is getting' so much business they can hire us to deliver and still make a killin'. 'Course, the thing is, this here job won't last too long. A few months, then folks'll get their stuff bought…,"

Chet interrupted. "But there'll still be a job, only we'll be chargin' the folks that ordered, 'stead'a bein' paid by the train folks. 'Sides that, they's all kind'a haulin' just around town. And that saw mill…."

"Yeah?"

"We hauled part of it out here. Time they want'a move, could be we'll haul part of it agin. Maybe all of it."

Momentarily out of words, the young men resumed the unloading.

Manny stopped and stared at the green wagon. "I ain't hardly knowin' what to say…."

"About what?"

"Well, after the trip down here and all…."

"Had a bad time?"

"Parts of it was bad. Some of it wasn't."

"Girls give you trouble."

"Not the girls… actually."

"Pa…?"

"Yeah, but it got evened out back up the line. Still, I was knowin' things'd not be like they was no more. You talkin' about this here wagon I brought down, it's my thinkin' that I earned it."

"Trip that bad, huh?"

"Not just the trip…" Manny seemed unable to voice his thoughts.

The unloading continued, but Manny remained thoughtful. "This here land is really yours? A whole piece, big as the whole town put together?"

"You got it a little bit wrong, little brother. It's ours. Yours, Chet's and mine. Kendall Brothers. Pa's name ain't on it nowhere. He's got his place over in the town."

"You don't reckon he'll want'a move over here?"

"Could be. Chances are, if he did, we'd let 'em, wouldn't we? 'Course, that wouldn't change a thing. It's still our land: yours, Chet's and mine. We got the whole say over what's done. Us with a business, we got'a have a place to come to, to raise our hoof stock… repair our wagons….. don't you think?"

The sound of a gun rang through the woods. Chester decided, "It'd be the thing to do to tell Pa, if he was wantin' to shoot a little food, our place'd be where he could do it."

"Yeah, we could. We're 'bout unloaded, anyway."

Manny looked around at the trees and the rolling green carpet. "This here really belongs to us three! That's what you said?"

"It ain't just what we say. That's what it says at the land office. Kendall Brothers, and that means Manford, Chester and Douglas. Wrote it down myself. 'Speck we could go show it to you, chance you have trouble believin' it."

Manny nodded, finally satisfied.

Sometimes things even out.

Eighteen

The ten-wagon caravan cleared a small hill and looked ahead to a sea of tents. Must be the town of Guthrie. Nothing else could be that big. Weary travelers were refreshed by the sight of the town, and they urged the horses to go faster.

They could be in the town early enough in the day to do a little looking around. That would be necessary, wouldn't it… if they were to live nearby?

The noisy Santa Fe depot was a good landmark. Their map said to go due east and follow the marked trail to Prosper. If they thought they might be lost, ask anyone. It was not a usual thing to have a laid-out town with a name. It was so close to Guthrie, so it was likely already known.

They chose two wagons, those that were most lightly loaded, to make the tour through the city. Uncle Jake's and Marvin Hausfield's were chosen. Everyone who wished could climb aboard.

The girls crawled into Uncle Jake's wagon, crouching down in front of the buckboard at the feet of their pa and uncle. They had a good view.

There were people everywhere, even in the place that was supposed to be a street. They hardly even got out of the way of the horses. Taffy turned to ask her pa something and forgot what it was when she saw her pa's face. He was smiling like it was Christmas morning and the town was old Santa himself. Uncle Jake was just about as bad.

Taffy had a lot of experience at reading faces of grownups. Pa had not even seen the land he had bought and was looking around him like the city of Guthrie already belonged to him. The realization drenched over the little girl like the water of a summer shower. Her pa and Uncle Jake would be moving the family to the city… this city, and it didn't matter how nice the little town was.

Just when she thought she and Junebug would be catching up with the other girls, the Kendalls and the Hewetts and all, she would be leaving them behind again. And for certain she wouldn't even have Junebug, either.

The very thought of it took all the words from her mouth and the thought from her head. She leaned her elbows onto the side of the wagon and let the scenery go by. She didn't even try to respond to Junebug's excited comment.

Unbidden, the next line to her story came into her head.

"The city was a noisy place.
My ears could hardly hear it.
We saw…."

Go away, she told the words. *I can't write you down now. I'm getting sick to my stomach.*

But when they had made the tour, she told her friend she was sick to her stomach and had to go lie down in her wagon.

Junebug was sympathetic. "Somethin' you ate?"

Taffy shook her head and sighed as she walked away. More likely something she saw. In the darkness of the wagon, she reached for her notebook, and while the grownups kept standing around, talking, she wrote:

> *"The city was a noisy place.*
> *My ears could hardly hear it.*
> *We saw a cloud of dirt go up*
> *when we were very near it.*
> *We went to see the city,*
> *and it was on our thirteenth day.*
> *I looked at Pa and Uncle Jake*
> *and knew they wished to stay.*
> *Uncle Jake would like to have*
> *a uniform and gun.*
> *My pa would like a bit of land,*
> *'cause he thinks building's fun.*
> *Me? I only want to go*
> *and see my other friends.*
> *And Ma, I think she's tired now*
> *and hopes her journey ends."*

As Taffy applied her final period, she heard Uncle Jake say to Pa, "Ain't that the strangest thing, seein' that green wagon with the Kendall boys name on it? If those young sprouts can be in business in no more time than they've been down here, you and me, we shouldn't have no trouble at all."

And Pa had answered, "My thoughts exactly. You still of a mind to help out with the hammer till we get started?"

"Might as well. I figure it'll be a little while till I can get on with the sheriff's place. With the letter I got from Providence, though, I think it'll be just a matter'a time."

Taffy still had her pencil in her hand. She turned to a clean page and began to write, even though the wagon was shaky and wobbly as it went over grass clumps and loose rocks.

> *"The thing I feared has happened.*
> *I can see it in Pa's face.*
> *He and Uncle Jake would like*
> *to be some other place.*
> *Very soon, I'll have to leave*
> *my friends and go away.*
> *My pa knows what he wants to build*
> *and where he wants to stay.*
> *Uncle Jake would like to wear*
> *a uniform and gun.*
> *He'd like to catch the bad guys,*
> *'cause that's how he has his fun.*
> *I have to go where Papa goes.*
> *I go where he think's best.*
> *I'll leave my friends in Prosper,*
> *Junebug and all the rest."*

She closed the pencil inside the notebook and put it beside her pillow. No, it was not yet time to stop. Balancing the notebook on her knee once more, she tapped the pencil lead against her teeth.

> *"But it won't be forever,*
> *I'll just wait for it to pass.*
> *'Till then, the only face I know*
> *will be my looking glass.*
> *And in that town of Guthrie,*
> *just as crowded as the sea,*
> *I'll look around and then I'll find*
> *the perfect friend for me."*

There! That just about said it all. And with the last words, the stomachache went away. When you were just thirteen, you did what the grownups said. But it wouldn't be forever! Someday...!

Activities went on in the new town of Prosper. The green wagon came rolling in right behind the ten-wagon caravan of newcomers.

Chet studied them for a familiar face and then decided, "I'd bet a dollar to a donut that's Tommy McClure's folks. What's their name?"

Manny answered, "Man, you must be tired to forget that! That's the Littletrees."

"Yeah, that's what I thought. Tommy McClure's folks."

Eben Carlile delivered the team of bays to Kendall Brothers and retrieved his other horses, the black and the paint. "Glad to see you fellas come in. I got a load'a dimension lumber ordered from down at the sawmill, and my son-in-law, he's got logs cut to be took down there. I was hopin' you could work it in."

"Sure thing, Mr. Carlile. Us three, we'll be on over there."

"But your folks just got here, and…" Ed wanted to be thoughtful of his neighbor's family obligations.

"They'll still be there after we got your lumber hauled. We got us a business to run and equipment to pay for." Chester grinned widely. "This here's our brother, Manny. We was sure needin' him to get on down here. We got two wagons now. Figure that'll take those logs down to the mill?"

Doug cut in, "If'n it don't, we can make two trips."

Chet again. "Tell me, sir, how it was you got in on the front part of the lumber cuttin'? They said they was stacked up in work for all summer, and it was all sold. Here you got yours already. How'd you work that?"

Eben Carlile grinned. This was one sharp young man with a good question in his head. "Money, son. The fellow that offers the most money, he's the one to get the first stuff or sometimes the best stuff. Somebody's got'a be first, and this time it was me. I'm fair anxious for my son-in-law to make a good house for my daughter and the little one."

"That's pretty smart, Mr. Carlile. We'll just go tell Pa we got'a use his wagon, and we'll be right over."

Maude Kendall was cooking. A family of nine always had someone hungry. "You boys got'a eat first. The meal'll be ready in a little while."

Doug sniffed appreciatively. It was an aroma he had not smelled in a long time. "Can't stay, Ma. We got a job."

Chester turned to his surprised father, "Pa, we got'a have this wagon for the day. Got a job…."

"Today? We just got here…."

"So did the job, Pa, and it's our job. We'll be back late tonight. Come on, Manny."

"Manny, too?"

"Yeah, it's his job, too, Pa."

The job was finished earlier than expected. Tired and dirty, they pulled into the yard. The food was cold, but tasted better than anything they had eaten for weeks.

"Pa, you want to hunt, our place'd be best. They's a hundred and sixty acres over there with all kinds'a varmints to shoot. We got us a good place. And, Pa, we need to use the wagon all week. We're a little short'a money right now, but we'll be able to get one soon, and…" He waited hesitantly.

"Son, you take the wagon."

"Thanks."

Clyde nodded his response. "And we was thinkin', yer ma and me, if'n it'd be alright with you, we'd just pull our things on over to your place and set up there for a while. The girls was wantin' to sleep in the little shack… like you said… we could?" It was Pa's turn to be hesitant, covering the new ground of their relationship.

"Sure, Pa. That'd be a good idea. We got us a well over there, and you ain't got one yet. There's the pond we scooped out, not too big, but it'll water the horses. You just make yerself at home. Manny and us, we'll be gone a lot for a while. We'll be workin' on our jobs."

Maude watched her sons eat. "You getting' enough to eat over there in the city? You're lookin' a little peaked to me."

"Sure, Ma. Ain't as good as what you cook, but we make out. They's a place that sells good beans and cornbread. 'Nuther place has ham sandwiches."

Maude nodded, not thoroughly convinced. "Well, you'll be comin' on in on Sundays, you think?"

Chester nodded, his mouth full. "Most Sundays, anyway."

Doug amended, "Some Sundays, likely." Then he picked up the courage to say something he thought needed to be said. "About the gardenin', Pa? Won't need to plant so much, us boys bein' gone. Caroline and Evie, they'll be a help to ya on the weedin'."

Clyde looked away into the green of the surrounding timber. "'Speck so. Needs to be some tree cuttin' done first. I'll get started in on that in the mornin'."

"Well, you see anything you want over on our quarter section, you just go and get it."

The sun was down behind the trees as the boys set out, Douglas in the green wagon and Manny behind the lines on the other one. It was the same buckboard seat, the same lines and the same animals that he had known for the last month, but it was not the same Manny.

He drove along, whistling a tune through his teeth. He was going to the city where he would work with his brothers in a hauling business.

"Chet, reckon we could buy green paint?"

"To make the wagons match? Likely we'd have to order it special. 'Course, Pa ain't outright give us that wagon... yet."

Manny took a breath. His mind had put a few things together, and it was time to let it out. "I earned this here wagon. It's my part'a what it takes to start this business. It's my wagon and horses. If'n I wasn't drivin' the girls down here, I could'a hired on in a minute for $30.00 cash money. I took care'a them girls, wiped noses and such, for the whole trip. Ma and Pa didn't have to do nothin' for 'em 'cept feed 'em. I ain't settin' a price on that, bein' family, but I figure I earned this here wagon." He paused and added, "Bein' family."

"Sure, Manny." It sounded right to his brothers.

Back at the Guthrie livery stable, in the light of the kerosene lantern, Douglas spread the map on the floor of the green wagon. "Now, see here, this is Harrison Street, goin' east and west. We been kind'a usin' it as a dividin' line. North side packages went in the front'a the wagon, and south side in the back. Now that we got two wagons, we need another map, and I can take the south by myself. North side's bigger, and ridin' with Chet, that'll teach you the way the streets go and the places where the numbers got all mixed up."

"Numbers mixed up?"

"Yeah, but they're fixin' it. When they was surveyin' the streets, they was two companies workin' at it. One of 'em worked true north and south, and t'other one lined up with the Santa Fe line. It all looks north and south, but it ain't true. Got some streets and numbers mixed up."

"And you, I mean we, really make a dollar and a half an hour?"

"Sure do. Now, by rights, they could cut the wages on me, bein' only one. We're on the clock, and two is faster'n one. Could be they'll think I ain't worth as much as two, but it'll still be good pay, even if I get cut back to a dollar."

Chet put in, "And then, if they's somethin' else goin' the same way, that'd be extra and we charge the person it's goin' to."

"And we get to sleep in here? Under the tent?"

"Yep. Costs extra, but I like bein' under a tent."

Manny let his thoughts drift. "I been three weeks under a tarp with them three girls. Hardly found a place to stretch out. I'd'a laid on the ground if it weren't for the rattlers."

"Girls give you a hard time?"

"Nope. They was just bein' little girls, fidgety and worrisome. I got 'em a book in Arkansas City, and Betty read out loud a lot. Ollie was learnin' the words, and Sophie knows the poems by memory. To be three weeks in a wagon, they done good. Fer little girls."

"Well, we thought about you a mite, knowin' if it weren't for you, it'd been one of us."

Manny sighed with satisfaction. It was a relief to know his brothers had an idea of what he had been through. The owners of KENDALL BROTHERS We Haul had worked a hard day and were glad to stretch out on the quilt-covered wagon bed and sleep.

On Monday morning, Clyde Kendall, accustomed to being on the road at first light, now roamed among the trees of the quarter section. He found a small clearing where a lightning fire had removed the trees. That would save a lot of root grubbing if he was to make a place there to plant a garden.

He sorted through his equipment for the plowshares and points and bolted them together. Sunrise found him sinkin' his shiny-sharp breaking plow into the sod of the Oklahoma territory.

By noon, corn, beans and peas were planted. Not enough, of course, but some needed to be in the ground as soon as possible. He'd have liked to prepare the ground a little better, but the soil looked deep and fertile, and he'd take his chances.

The tomato plants brought down from Providence were set in among the beans in Prosper.

It would be up to the girls to help tend the crop if he was to expect to set up his shop again. He was forced to keep reminding himself his sons were gone. For all intents and purposes, they were gone. All three of them. All of a sudden. Gone! The knowin' of it left a bit of an empty space in the region of his ample stomach.

Eben Carlile watched through the trees as Clyde Kendall made row after row, calling to the horse that drew the plow, directing him... encouraging him. While deep and rich, the soil, having never been worked, was very tough with roots, but the man's hand was steady while he guided the plow as it made the furrows.

A short distance from him, Eben called out, "Hello, neighbor."

Clyde looked around and instructed the horse, "Whoa, up there." The tired horse hung his head and blew his breath, refreshing his lungs.

"Didn't mean to be stoppin ya... friend."

"That's all right, neighbor. Horse needed a breather. I could use one, too. This is good ground, but it's tighter'n the hide on a flea."

Eben grinned. "Found that out myself a couple weeks back. Reckon we'll make a crop this year?"

"Wouldn't see why not. Got four months a'summer yet."

"Your boys left last night, didn't they? Right nice job they done on deliverin' my lumber. My son-in-law reckons he'll set the foundation today. If you was to be needin' dimension lumber, that sawmill down the way, they'll put you on the list."

Clyde mopped the perspiration from his forehead. "Reckon I'll do that. Or I could send my girls to do it. 'Speck I'll find myself missin' them boys bein' here to help."

Ed thought it was time to put in a word for the young men. "Right good boys you got, neighbor."

"Call me Clyde. Yep, them's good boys. I aimed for 'em to be."

"I'm Eben Carlile. Yeah, I was in position to observe... them bein' right here so close. You got all kinds'a reasons to be proud."

"Thank ya kindly. They was sayin' they made a deal with you for that green wagon. What sort of a..." He hesitated, searching for information.

His neighbor cut into the question. "Your boys 'n me, we come up with a plan that suited us both. It's a good thing when friends can work together." Eben decided if those boys wanted their pa to know the particulars of the deal, they could tell him. His own business was with the boys.

"Yeah, I reckon they didn't need my help. Comes a time when a man's boys... well, you know...."

Caravan

"Yep, that time comes if we're lucky. They remind me'a my two boys that I lost in the mine cave-ins. Good Scottish laddies they were. Good boys, just like them'a yours. Then comes the time they get to be men and make their own way. All I have left is my lass, married now, and my youngest son's lassie."

Clyde nodded and sighed. "Yeah, them boys'a mine was good boys. Only thing was, I forgot to look and see they wasn't actual boys no longer. I liked havin' sons to teach to do things the way I do 'em, thinkin' I'd have 'em forever, I reckon. Makin' plans for 'em like they was little tykes. Guess I was wrong there."

Eben looked at the sadness on the other man's face. It was a hard and painful sight to look at. "Well, I'll move on out and let you get on. Wanted to say somethin', though. Of a evenin' and you got time, come on over. You'll find me right through the trees, there. Likely we got a lot to talk on."

"I'll do that, Eben."

Eben Carlile stepped back through the trees, and Clyde Kendall tapped the reins on the horses' flank. "Git on up, there!"

At the end of their first week of work, the green wagon pulled away from the depot, and the brown one was loading. "Hey, Kendall! Got a box here that's got'a go today. Won't last over Sunday."

Manny picked up the light-weight box with holes around the sides and a chorus of cheeping sounds coming from within. "Baby chicks again! Reckon these'll need to go first."

"Whereat are they goin'?"

"It says Daniel Dunbar, town of Prosper. Prosper? That'd be by us!"

"Yeah, that'd be the people up north'a us. Ones we got the wagon from. We'll be headed on out in an hour. Mr. Carlile said his daughter was wantin' chickens."

"If they ain't got a pen, them chickens'll be fox and possum food."

"Yeah, he's got a chicken house; they're livin' in it."

Nineteen

It was dusky dark when the three saddle horses trotted along the rutted road to the town of Prosper. The cheeping box of chicks had

298

been tied to the saddlebags, and the trotting of the horse kept their tiny feet scrambling for footing.

Chester led the way on one of the bays, and Manny, with the chicks, rode the other. Douglas brought up the rear, and as they neared the townsite, he turned his eyes this way and that, searching. Maybe? Where was she?

Ellie Gunther had found things to do outside the hastily-constructed shack that was their temporary home. She had wandered along what was to be Main Street, avoiding the rocks and stumps that had not yet been removed.

At the sound of horse hoofs and snorts, she looked around, but it was only the Baker Brothers bringing in their tired mules. In the dim light, far down the trail, she could see figures on horseback coming her way. She stepped over into the cover of bushes and waited.

Douglas, slumping wearily in his saddle, suddenly straightened his back and lifted his chin. Maybe?

Chester passed by the bushes, then Manny. Douglas was riding a short way behind his brothers. After Manny passed by, Ellie found a reason to step out into the rutted roadway and pause.

Douglas drew up the rein, silently halting his horse. Sliding from the saddle, he smiled into the darkness. The filmy lightness of Ellie's yellow hair was hardly visible, but he knew exactly how it looked. He knew how her mouth would turn up at the corners when she smiled.

"Ellie! I'm glad to see you."

"You're gonna be gladder when you see what I got. I'll bet you're hungry enough to eat a horse."

"Just about. Have you got one?"

"Got somethin' better! A cookie. A big one. I'll walk along with you while you eat it. I know you got'a get on in, bein' tired. But I wanted to see how… you was?"

Doug took a delightful mouthful. "I ain't that tired. You'll be around after I clean up?" Another bite of the moist cinnamon cookie was gone. "You still bakin' on the stove up north of ya?"

"Naw. We got ours set up. You comin' on over later, you say?"

"Sure enough will!"

Twenty

Samuel Littletree pulled up into his own, paid-for lot. It was nice to be home, and he sighed a long sigh. If he hadn't seen the town of Guthrie, this place would look very good. If he just had the money back that he had tied up in this lot... he'd....

Jake came strolling over to him. "Not bad lookin' lots."

"Yeah, better'n I expected...."

"But...?" His brother seemed to want to say more.

Samuel sighed. "Sorta wish I'd'a know'd more about Guthrie."

Jake, the optimist, looked out across the groups of residents of the new town. "I'm bettin' there's more money wantin' to find our land here than there is ground to put it on. We hold onto this for a couple'a weeks or a month, and we'll double what we paid. Maybe more'n that."

"So you done made up your mind?"

"Does smoke rise upward?"

"That sure, huh!"

"Just waitin' for you to say the word. You got the family."

Samuel looked at his wife, struggling once more with a campfire and cooking utensils. "I give Nellie about a week more, and she'll be ready to go along, and the little'n goes where I go till she figures out a better way."

Taffy was asleep with her head on her notebook and did not hear her pa pronounce the fulfillment of her poetic prophesy.

The Kendall brothers took stock of the changes made on their land.

Clyde Kendall had his tent set up near the 12-foot-square cabin, just past the well. A four-legged teepee stood over the well, now, with a rope and pulley wheel attached to make the water drawing easier. A rope line was stretched between two trees, and a sprinkling of laundry hung to dry.

The smell of Ma's food was carried on the breeze, erasing the memory of cold canned fish with crackers, pork and beans eaten from the can and even the nickel-a-cup beans with ham. What was it that made Ma's beans smell so much better?

Ma's drop dumplings were ladled out, biscuits (with butter) passed around. Wild greens, picked from their woodlands came next, and the meal was topped off with supper cake covered over with wild berries and top milk.

After supper, Caroline and Evie had places to go, Betty and Ollie had company, and they played games in the trees.

Sophie's head drooped over with half-shut eyes, and Maude led her to the cabin.

Clyde Kendall cleared his throat, a signal he had something to say. "Was waitin' till you boys got here to make final plans, but I had a deal I thought you might be interested in, if you got time."

Douglas nodded. "Got a little time. After that, I'm a'fixin' to go over to the Gunther's."

Chet and Manny turned his way. "Ellie, huh?"

"Could be."

Clyde again. "Well, what I was sayin', you fellows bein' old enough to make your own deals, I thought I'd offer this. Seein' you got so much land here and bein' a bit cash shy on what you was a'wantin' to do, your ma and me, we thought there'd be room for us here, along side'a the well. I could go ahead with the house like I got laid out, quick as my turn comes to get dimension lumber. That'd leave them two lots I bargained for.

"It was always our thought, your ma's and mine, that we'd have them two lots for a place for you boys to work out of and them girls to come home to, time and agin, but if you won't be needin' 'em for that, likely you'd be needin' the money more'n the land.

"If we was to agree on it, you three and your ma and me, that this here place'a yours, this quarter section, would be a place for your ma and me for the rest'a our lives and for the girls to come to if there was a need, then we could give you them two lots to sell for the money you need right now. The goin' price'a the lots right now is $50.00 each, makin' $100.00, total. Could be that'd be the money you need to get started in your own business.

"Now I'm figurin' another good wagon'd be part'a what you need now, and I'd like to be the one to build it for ya, only it'll be likely another year or two 'afore I'd get the chance with the house buildin', the gardenin' and getting' my shop set up. 'Course, with me settin' up on your land, that'd be quicker'n if I had to start from scratch over there. Done got in beans, peas, tomatoes and sweet taters over by the pond. Staked out the foundation for the house, if you was to agree on it bein' put here. Talked to a couple'a the fellows over on the town lots that said they'd rather get their lumber logs from here and save their own trees. Told 'em they'd have to talk to you three, but they's a chance you'd sell 'em what they want. So that'd be cash money.

"Is anything I'm a'sayin' fittin' in with your plans?"

A quick three-way of glances passed among the tired young men. Chester became the spokesman. "Yeah, Pa. Seems you been doin' some schemin' and plannin'. 'Course, we'd have to talk it over, us three, and you'd be right that cash money was what we needed right how. Sellin' some trees'd be good, but it'd not likely cover what we need. Now them two lots, they...."

Clyde cut in. "Got a nibble on a sale on them lots. Couple'a fellows got their eye on them, bein' side by side the way they are, and they got $20.00 each to put down, makin' $40.00 right now. The rest'a the money, they could pay you at $5.00 a month each."

Chester turned to Douglas. "What'd'ya think? Forty dollars'd buy a rig. Not as good as the green one, but it'd be one that'd do. Think we need to sleep on it?"

Clyde again. "Nuther thing. That wagon you took in to use? I got no use for it, and by rights, Manny earned it and them horses. That'd go in on the deal. Wasn't meanin' to butt in that'a'way, but I neglected to say that at the start. So that cash money, that'd let you get your business goin' right now, while the money's there to be made."

Manny now. "That wagon, you thinkin' that's my pay for the trip down here?"

"Well, son, if you ain't gonna live at my place and be part'a my business, then you earned it, fair and square. I just never thought'a you, bein' only sixteen, as wantin' to be on your own just yet. That does free me up in my thinkin', though. These girls, they'll be married and gone in sight'a ten years, and all I'll need is a business the size that'll take care'a your ma and me. Be a sight easier on me when the years start comin' on. This here little corner'a your land, how'd I ever need any more'n that?

"Now, your ma and me, we thought to take a little walk down by the pond to see how the horses is getting' on and if that patch'a sand plums is about ripe. We'll talk again later."

Whereupon, Clyde Kendall waited at the door of the tiny cabin until Maude appeared, and they walked, arm in arm, into the trees.

The sight of the pair retreating in the distance was totally startling to the three young men finishing up their berry shortcake. They were even more startled to hear their mother laugh at something that was said.

That was our ma? Walking in the woods laughing?

Douglas was first. "What Pa was sayin', that sounds good to me. That'd make three wagons, right off, and we'd clear... what? At least five dollars a day, each wagon. 'Course, that'd mean workin' hard and sleepin' rough for the summer and not comin' to town till Sunday, and..." He hesitated.

"And not seein' Ellie but once a week," his brother reminded him. "It'd mean leavin' her here with other fellows."

"Yeah, and the town'd be hot in the summer, and we'd have to live on what we could buy to eat."

"And May, it's 'bout gone, leavin' June, July and August, if the good haulin' lasts that long."

"But, even allowin' for trouble, that'd come to maybe fifteen dollars a day, mostly clear. I ain't got the paper to figure on, but it seems like that'd let us build a wagon shed out here come winter, and maybe..." The words seemed too encouraging to utter.

Douglas again. "Too much to figure, and I got'a go, but it looks like a plan. That'd mean Pa'd always live on our land, but..." He needed agreement. He got it from Chet.

"It's still our land, and Pa'd never do anything that'd hurt us. 'Sides, when him and Ma got old, who'd there be to take care'a 'em but us, anyway?"

Then Doug. "He'll be buildin' his own place. See how he's got it laid out? Us three, we could pick where we'd like. A hunnerd and sixty acres, that's a lot'a land. 'Nuff for everyone, seems like."

Chester again. "Doug, you take on off. I see your gut's gettin' antsy to go find Ellie. Manny and me, we'll bat a few ideas around. We won't settle nothin' till mornin', anyway. Don't look like we'll see too much'a Pa and Ma till then, either."

Douglas disappeared through the trees.

"What'd'ya think, Manny? Think you can handle two or three month's of what you had this week? Drivin' them streets alone and it getting' hot and hungry down there in Guthrie? That there's good haulin' at the Santa Fe, but it's like a store-bought ice cream cone; we eat it now or we don't eat it at all."

Manny scooped the last of the berries over the last sliver of cake and settled back. "Now, Chet, I don't mind tellin' ya. This here week wasn't no picnic in the park, but it weren't no hangin' by my heels over the river, changin' out a wheel and axel with gears and grindin' plates a'leanin' heavy over my head or tryin' to keep them giant durocs in the wagon bed and them not slidin' down on top'a Alvin Banner.

"If you think ten hours'a hoppin' in and out'a the wagon carryin' packages is bad, try ten hours of the buckboard grindin' on yer backside and nothin' to see but dirt and sky and nothin' to think on except what was I gonna do when the trip was over. Got so boring, I took to wakin' up the little girls, just to hear 'em argue over doll dresses. I listened to them poems so long, I can recite the book by heart, cover to cover." He grinned as he talked around the last bite of cake. "You stack what I just said over the ten hours in the city, and add in the fact that I can stretch out in the wagon bed at night 'stead'a curlin' up in front'a the buckboard to sleep."

Chester again. "Reckon that puts you down for a 'yes'?"

Twenty-One

The boys fell silent, comforted by the closeness of their dreams and their shared difficulties. Mulled over the change in their parents and the easy acceptance of their plans by their pa. Almost like he was glad to be shut of the three of them.

They sat on the ground outside the tent, resting in the quiet. The only sounds were the cicadas and a school of treefrogs from the direction of the pond. Murmured voices and an occasional laugh came from the direction of the pond. A lot of puzzling changes had happened during the last week.

Darkness fell, and a three-quarter moon hung over the trees. Chester and Manny stretched out on the ground in companionable silence, and Douglas and Ellie were silhouettes, too far away to see.

From down past the pond, a faint yipping of a coyote floated out on the air. An answering call came from over on the Dunbar spread. In due time, Douglas returned, but his brothers were asleep. He stretched out on the ground, and weariness claimed him until the song of the night birds faded and the mockingbird began to sing the scales.

Sounds! They were all around.

The wrens called each other with their 'chee-chee'. Coal black crows fluttered about in the trees, squawking and scolding.

It was Sunday in Prospect.

Little Alecia Carlile awoke from her bed in her Big Papa's tent and slipped quietly out the door. The blueticks greeted her with wagging tail and lolling tongue, bumping their heads against her in companionable greeting. Under her arm was a thick book.

The little girl sat down in the morning light and began to turn the pages, pointing to the words.

"'A' is for apple that grows on a tree.
Some are for piggie, and some are for me."
"'B' is for ball, for the baby to play with.
'B' is for ball that the dog runs away with."

"Come back here, doggie, and bring that ball back to the baby," Alecia told the book. But the doggie in the picture still ran away with the ball.

"Hi, Alecia!"

"Hi, Marcie! Come read my book with me."

The dark-haired five-year-old came and sat down beside Alecia.

"I know the next one," she said. "'C' is for chicken with flappity wings. It scratches for worms and wiggly things."

Both girls giggled at the picture of the worms and wiggly things. A twig snapped, and they looked up. "Here comes Sophie. Come on, Sophie."

The six-year-old with the yellow curls came through the bushes. "I got my book, and I can read. See here it says, 'Mary... had... a... little... lamb. Its... fleece... was... white... as... snow... and everywhere... that... Mary... went....'"

It was Sunday in the new town of Prosper.

- Bonus Excerpt -

The Sheltering Stones Series

Book 2
Prairie Flowers

Prairie Flowers

It was in the year of 1896 that the best picture she could think of to describe her life's work was the few lines of verse written by a 13 year old student in her class.

> Look Up! A vast expanse of skies
> As blue as Scottish lassie's eyes.
> Around! Windswept trees and grass are seen,
> A necklace strip in shades of green.
> Look Down! Beside the footpath as you pass
> Are blossoms growing in the grass
> Like tiny chips of painted glass.
> By Miss Francine Canfield.

She stood in the stony shelter of the Prairie Academy and watched the four young girls who were concentrating on the sheets of paper before them.

Carmelita Wilson, age 13, tapped her pencil against her teeth in deep and careful thought. The teacher was watching, even as she was teaching math to the next class. Miss Josie Wheeler, the teacher, could always see two places at once, and maybe three if she needed to.

The thirteen year old girl buried her dimpled chin into her hand and propped her elbow against the table. Time to get down to business.

The class of four girls had just spent the last month working on sentences, parts of speech and capitalization, and now they were studying stories and narrations. A story… they all knew… had three parts: a situation, problem and a solution. A narration was the chronological enumeration of events.

It was now near the end of their study year, and they were being tested. They would write a narration consisting of their own lives from birth until today. That would be the whole of their Grammar/English final test from the Academy. It was to be written in third person.

She began:

"Carmelita did not remember being born in New York, but her parents insisted that she had been. She kind of remembered being a tiny girl, carried on shoulders, and of being swung in a swing where other children played. Most of what she remembered was the time of looking at the big river."

The thirteen year old girl with the pencil was sorely tempted to say "I remembered..." but she knew she must not. This was not an autobiography, told in first person. It must be in third person... like she was writing about someone else. She wanted a shorter name for the little girl, so she decided to make it "Lita".

She continued, "Lita remembered the big river very clearly, the way it was the color of chocolate milk, and how it turned itself over and over and up and down like the water that made boiled eggs. She remembered the river because it was so easy to see.

"It had seemed a long time ago that the family had moved from the house on the quiet street with the playground at the end of the block. She wished they had not moved, because everything was so different now. She had liked the playground.

"Now she lived in the tall house with two staircases up to the little room where she stayed with her brother Jeff and the baby, Darrell. She had her six-year-old birthday in that house.

"Her brother, Jeff, was nine years old, and he was a big boy who could go to the store to buy milk, bread, potatoes and beans. Sometimes Lita got to go with him and they could each spend a penny on candy sticks.

"The worst thing about the tall house was that they were all the time waiting. Papa and her two older brothers had gone across the river to run. Why did they do that? There was a nice place to run in the park where they lived before they moved. The playground was big and people could run all the way around it. It was a puzzle to Lita, but they moved anyway.

"When Papa and the boys came back, everyone would leave the tall house and maybe move to a playground house again. But then they might have to go a long way in the wagon pulled by a horse. It depended on the place where Papa ran and if they were able to win the race. It was all terribly confusing.

"The only thing not confusing was the river of chocolate milk and the tiny ships that moved up and down on it. Lita could see it plainly from the window of the tall house, and if she blew her breath on the glass of the window, she could make marks with her fingers. She could make rounds and squares and count them. She could count all the way to twenty. Her big brother, Jeff, had helped her learn.

"Sometimes she wrote her ABC's but there wasn't room on the window for them all and the breath dried out before she got through.

"Mama hummed a lot, and wandered around in the room. When baby Darrell was asleep, she watched out the window with Lita, and sometimes told stories.

"Lita's big brother Jefferson complained a lot because he couldn't go places and was tired of waiting, and Mama made him read books he had already read. Lita didn't care, though, because she liked the stories even if she knew how everything would turn out."

Sharing the table with Carmelita were three other girls: Rosalie, Francine and Carlotta. The four had listened with open-mouthed horror at Miss Josie's words when she told them that part (actually, all) of their Grammar Test would be a 2,000 word narration of their lives, up to now. Everything would be true to the best of their memories.

They would attend to sentence structure, punctuation, paragraphs, capitalization and paragraph indentation. All of these things would be on their Certification Test so this was part of getting ready for it next year.

The teacher, Miss Josie, came and stood by the round table where the girls were at work. It usually paid off to have students remember they were being watched. As she looked at the girls, what she experienced was pure pride.

These girls had come into her class at ages barely 10 to almost 12 with scant formal education. Multiplication and division were a foreign language; the whole world consisted of New York, St Louis, the Mississippi and Arkansas rivers and the Oklahoma Territory. History was made up of what they could remember of their short lifetimes and their poetry was Mary had a Little Lamb and others like it.

For the last two years these girls had crammed. No four girls had worked harder to press into their minds what they could before returning to their duties at home, as they were well aware of the family sacrifice that permitted them this treat. After all, how much education did a girl need… just to get married, cook and have babies?

As in every one-room school, older students hardly learned a concept before they must assist in the teaching it to those behind them, and these girls had spent hours with the 5, 6 and 7 year olds. These hours helped to cement their own recently acquired knowledge.

Miss Josie smiled to herself wondering, with pride, if she herself could have done so well. There was Carmelita, called Mellie, with her red-blond curls tight around her face, her delicate bone structure (how could she hope to stand up to the work required of a pioneer woman in the Territory?) and dainty hands.

There was her complexion as pale as milk and her pink tinted lips and cheeks. Eyelashes pale as the fuzz on a dandelion puff and eyes as blue as the sky in October. Delicate chin possessing a deep dimple, identical to Josie's own.She was a beautiful girl and would only become more so. All of this wondrous beauty belonged to her own cousin and any education that Josie could give her, Josie knew, would not have come to this girl if her own tragic circumstances had not brought her to the Territory.

On either side of Carmelita were the sisters, Rosalie and Francine Canfield, less than a year apart in ages. Both girls took their coloring from their Italian mother, but that was their only similarity. Rosalie, age 11, almost 12, was round faced and dimpled. Her fingers delicately pointed and her hands small. Tan complexion and abundant coal black hair in a dutch cut... short with bangs. A style requiring very little care after a quick comb.

She sister, Francine, was less than a year younger and two inches taller. Face slim, with dark brows growing straight across over her eyes and well pronounced. Cheekbones that would become more pronounced, and shining black hair that reached her shoulder blades. Today it was tied back with a strip of flowered fabric. Arms long and shapely and fingers smooth with blunted ends. Josie had heard that the blunt finger shape was called artist's hands. Well, time would tell. At this moment, Francine sat tall and straight and stared at her paper in intense concentration.

Last at the table was Carlotta. One could say that most of nature's bounty had been settled upon this eleven and a half year old. Her complexion was purely English, pale cream and deep rose. A sprinkling of tan freckles were on their way to fading out. Light brown brows in a classic arch, and face shape as oval as a smooth almond kernel. A face that dimpled deeply when she smiled. From the time she could walk, Carlotta's beauty had turned eyes, and it was a certainty that the attention would only increase with her age. The girl, an only child, had been so carefully reared, that she had never considered herself prettier than any other, and was forever alertly eager to please. She loved just being included.

Eighteen year old Josie had plans for these four. She had never considered herself a teacher, but only a person favored with an education that was not usually given to girls and a desire to pass it on. Perhaps these girls would choose marriage and a home life, and that was good, but it should be of their own choosing and at a time they chose. On that, Josie was adamant. An option. They should have a choice. Most girls in the Territory in the late 1800's did not have, or expect to have, that choice.

Of the three commonly offered directions open to girls were kitchen help, sewing, or school teaching. Of the first two, Josie was not qualified to help, but the third was a definite possibility if these girls chose to avail themselves.

Josie had already procured a copy of the Certification Test for school teacher and learned that the state minimum hiring age was 14. She was determined to have these girls ready with certificate in hand if that was their choice.

She had issued 10 sheets of paper (more if they needed it) and an assignment to write a narration of at least 2,000 words covering the remembered experiences of their short life. This would require an in-depth memory search to fill that word requirement, and that, also, was part of the education. As her own teacher had told her, "The mind of a child was not a bucket to be filled, but a muscle to be stretched."

Not much stretching happened in the homes on the frontier, especially for girls. There was just too much work that descended upon everyone, all of it necessary just to exist.

Carmelita, of the strawberry blond curls, tapped her teeth with her pencil, touched her tongue to the lead, then applied it to the paper as a newly remembered experience inspired her.

"Mama must not have known at first that Papa was home because when he knocked at the door, she shivered and would not go to open the lock. Then Papa said, "Nettie? Are you in there?" Then Mama started to cry as she ran to open the door.

"Papa and the boys were grinning happily, but Lita had no idea what that meant. Would they be going to a house by the park, or to the wagon crossing over the chocolate milk river? No one asked her what she would rather do. If they had, she wouldn't have known what to answer.

"She had never been across the chocolate milk river but it sounded as though that was where they would go.

"Something really bad could happen. That was when the little girl shivered with fright. How would they keep the chocolate milk from seeping into the wagon, and would the horses be able to swim when the milk boiled and turned itself over and over like it was full of ropes? She tried to ask someone, but no one seemed to care what she said. Even though she spoke plainly and said each word carefully.

"It was that very same day that everything in the room in the tall house was put into two wagons that had a tent over them like a little house. Papa, Mama, Lita and the baby crawled into the tent house on the first wagon, and Junior, Douglas and Jefferson got in the other one. Junior sat on the driver's seat and looked so small after watching Papa, but he knew what he was doing. So did Douglas, and he sat right up there beside Junior as their wagon moved along behind Papa's. Jefferson was standing up behind Douglas.

"Lita had been scared so long she was no longer frightened by thoughts of the Hot Chocolate river. If she drowned??? Well. She's just drown, but it would be with her family, and why would she want to live without her family? She looked out the back of the tent on the wagon, and stared right into the faces of her brothers. They were laughing and talking, and her other brother, Jeff, was laughing and talking with them.

"So... if her brothers were not afraid, then she would not be afraid, either. She was still looking back when the wagon beneath her began to rumble and rock, and when she crawled to the front beside Papa and Mama, she saw that she was on a BIG, BIG boat and the Hot Chocolate was all around her.

"She grinned with relief, and began to laugh with sheer happiness. Papa turned to look at her and asked what was funny. Lita stopped laughing long enough to say, "Papa! We aren't going to drown in the Hot Chocolate!"

"Papa said, "Hot Chocolate?" It was just like he didn't know what was in the river.

"Yes, Papa," she answered, pointing. "Just look out there. See all the Hot Chocolate boiling?"

"Then Papa said, 'Look out there, Mama. Doesn't that look like chocolate? This girl of ours is going to be a writer. Just you wait and see.'

"Mama was too busy to look. She was cleaning up where Baby Darrell upchucked. That was all right. Lita would tell her about it after a while.

"At night they all went to sleep beside the road. Next to them was another wagon and people were sleeping in it. Lita wondered if they were going to the race to run like Papa and the big boys had. She could have told them that it was no use to go because her Papa had already won the race.

"For breakfast, the family had huge bowls of oatmeal with yellow lakes of butter melting all over it. There was even brown sugar to sprinkle on top but Baby Darrell didn't get any sugar. He only got butter. He wouldn't have gotten butter if Jeff had watched him like Mama said, and grabbed his hand. He made a real mess with the butter. "

Miss Josie had told the girls they might stay after school for a while and write if they wanted to. She had also told them that the first copy… the rough draft, she called it… must be done at school while she could watch. They could make notes if they thought of something at home that they wanted to include, but it would be written at school.

Then, after they finished, they would be given brand new clean sheets of paper to copy their essay in their best penmanship. They could make any changes they wanted to make. Miss Josie told them she would also want the rough draft as well as the finished copy. It was all a part of the test.

She told them that these biographies, along with the memorization of the nine rules of capitalization would be their final test before taking the Certification Test that would enable them to be a teacher.

Rosalie Canfield, the almost 13-year-old girl, quick thinking and quick moving, had finished several pages filled with her sloping cursive words.

…."One of the nicest things was the gifts Grandma Nicolo gave the three children. Rosalie and Francine received such darling little chests, or maybe they were like suitcases. Inside the case, Rosalie came eye to eye with the most beautiful doll in the world. She wore a dress that was all pink lace and there were pink crocheted stockings. She wore the most precious little shoes made of white felt and tied with a shiny white ribbon.

"A peek at Francine's case showed the same doll dressed in yellow.

"The girls' brother, Raymond, didn't get a suitcase. He got a box with a hinged lid. When he peeked in, he was too excited to talk, and he crawled to the back of the wagon hugging the box, and then opened it so he could take everything out. From where she sat, Rosalie thought it was a lot of wooden animals and boy things that were painted in bright colors. He seemed to like them and that was good. Maybe it would keep him from whining.

"Rosalie lifted out the doll and beneath it there were six more dresses. They were made in all different colors with stockings to match, and there was another pair of shoes made of brown felt and a pair of boots made in black. There was a pink flowered night grown made in soft, fuzzy flannel and it had a cute little nightcap knitted with pink yarn.

"The girl could see below the dresses that there was a blanket pieced like a real quilt, and when she lifted it out to wrap the doll, she saw that in the bottom of the case there were four picture books with stories and they all said 'For My Sweet Rosalie from Grandma Nicolo' written in pretty blue ink.

"Under the picture books were a color book and two boxes of crayons with six different colors in each box.

"Mama had watched as the girls looked at their presents, and she smiled as they squealed with excitement at each new thing. She said she was glad that the dolls were different and that none of the dresses were alike so they wouldn't get mixed up, because it was going to be a long trip and she didn't want any problems.

The girls weren't really sure where they were going. Mama tried to tell them, but they still didn't know. They only knew that Papa was happy all the time, and in his loud voice he sang all the songs he knew. It was fun to see Papa so happy. He sat up on a high bench while he drove the horses, and Mama could sit beside him if she wanted, but she mostly didn't want to. When she didn't want to, the girls could take turns on the high bench but they couldn't take all the gift toys with them if they did. Rosalie took the first turn and wrapped the doll in the quilt and left the rest of the suitcase full of gifts under the bench.

"There wasn't much to see. She saw one little hill after the other, and watched the horses as they waded through one little stream after the other. Papa watched with her and they saw a lot of birds and Papa pointed out the different ones and told her their names. The birds wouldn't stay still so she could get a good look at them and know them later. Maybe they didn't want anyone to know them, all except the crows. Papa didn't have to tell her about the crows because she already knew about them."

The children of the Prairie Academy had trooped out at the end of the day, and after a last look around, the helper, Miss Janine, rounded up her little brother, Tray, and headed home. It was amazing how much she could find to do to help out so she could earn the time it took for her brother to learn.

The four remaining girls nibbled cookies and scribbled on their paper. Francine sat straight and tall, her long fingers easily moving the pencil. She always insisted that the lead be sharp, so she was more often working with the whittling knife.She examined the point of the lead and deemed it satisfactory.

Her story was now three pages long, and she continued to write as her memory directed.

"Francine, often called Francy, took her doll from the little wooden box and set her aside so she could lay all the dresses in a row. There were seven of them, including the one on the doll, and each one was made very differently with special trimming and darling little buttons that really worked.

"Her brother, Raymond, was a year younger and he had a different kind of box. It contained the most painted animals in all the world! It had some little boards that fit together to make a barn and a shed, and some painted blocks of hay. The wagons had wheels that really worked, and the horses could really pull the wagons when he pushed with his finger.

"Raymond wanted to take everything out at once, but Mama wouldn't let him. She gave him a board and she said he could play with only what he could put on that board. She said if they lost those little animals in the quilts, they'd never find them, and maybe they'd get broke.

"She told him that would be terrible because as long as we were going to be living in the wagon, he would need all the toys to play with.

"Raymond got something else that looked fun. Mama wouldn't let him open the can until we stopped for supper. It was full of little sticks that fit together, and there was a sheet that showed how to build cabins and barns and other things. The sticks had a name called Lincoln Logs. Mama said they were named after a president, whatever that was.

"The Logs looked interesting and Francy asked him if she could play with them with him. He said she could if she'd stay in the back of the wagon the next day so he would have someone to talk to. She didn't mind that, but he mostly talked to his horses and cows. That was all right, because she was busy looking at her doll's dresses.

"It seemed as though she just couldn't get her eyes full enough of the lace and ruffles, and the tiny buttons. She looked at the dresses and was happy for each one of them, but she'd really like to have a whole lot more. She didn't say that to her Mama, though, because she knew Mama would say she was being greedy. Mama thought that Grandma Nicolo had been generous enough with the presents so the children would have something to play with while they traveled."

The teacher watched. So different… these four girls. She watched as they bent industriously over their work. She had seen them almost daily for over two years. One learns a lot that way.

There was Carlotta. Sometimes called Lottie. So many of the gifts from heaven were piled on this one little girl. Almost twelve years old, now, and she exhibited every indication that she would be a knock out beauty and that her parents had resisted spoiling her. Good natured, helpful when she assisted the Level Three boys with their math games and sang number songs with the 5 and 6 year olds.

She had a naturally giving spirit, and seemed to want only to be part of the group. What would she be when she noticed every head at Carlile Corners turn her way?

She studied as hard as she could, succeeded superbly, and all this with parents who wished only that she be happy. They faithfully saw that she attended every day… though they may wonder why would she need all that learning just to cook, clean and produce a family? They didn't say that, exactly, but that was the attitude of so many of the adults. The girls studied math "just like a boy" and… why? For what end? But how were the needs of boys so different from girls? Miss Josie could only shake her head and wonder.

At this moment Carlotta tapped the eraser end of the pencil against the frowns on her forehead as she concentrated on a thought. Then suddenly as a spring shower, a small smile appeared and the pencil began scribbling furiously. It was a good thing this essay was to be re-copied. Josie did, however, have a teacher's curiosity to see their rough draft and note the changes they would make on the final copy.

Carlotta, her teacher decided, could go either way. Her parents were not exactly the pioneer type, though they tried hard to be. Their only daughter also tried very hard. She now had three friends who accepted each other for what they all were, girls of a near equal age living in the newness of the Territory. Carlotta might actually have been just as eager for friendship with the girls a year or two younger. It will be interesting to watch her grow up, her teacher decided.

Josie, herself, had her own work to do. Having been reminded by her former tutor that she must concentrate on HAVING A LITTLE FUN, she did not permit her lesson preparation to occupy so much of her time as at the beginning.

She was startlingly surprised when neighbor Brad Cullen had invited her, together with his sister, Janine, and Josie's cousin, Jefferson, (the fellow with the head full of tight red curls), to an outing.

It seemed the small village of Argyle five miles away had managed to acquire a machine that made "store-bought" ice cream. So much better than having to wait until the weather snowed to make that popular confection, and then consume the delicacy while hovering over the potbelly stove to keep warm.

The four young people, Josie and her cousin, Jeff, with Brad Cullen, the young blacksmith and his sister Janine, sat around the tiny ice cream table on delicate looking wire chairs, so close that their knees almost touched. How did they ever find so many things to talk about, and why were so many things terribly funny?

They chatted and laughed and spooned the favored dessert. So much was said and laughed about, but later the serious-minded Josie could hardly remember a thing that that had been uttered. Certainly nothing of importance passed any set of lips.

Maybe this was fun…??

Maybe it was just a waste of time, but it didn't seem like it. The foursome went again to the Sweet Shop, and on Saturday's every two weeks or so after that.

Brad Cullen was four and five years older than the others, and so interestingly persuasive that it was easy to let him direct the festivities.

Brad, himself, had a purpose. Back at the school, and with the children around, he had been unable to get any attention from the teacher. She treated him as though he was just one of the community, one who was helpful and solved problems for her, as he had promised to do, so his little brother could attend the classes. Now, however, here at the ice cream table, he could see Josie in a different light. And she, at last, saw him.

Having seated himself across the table rather than beside her, he took full advantage of his position. Josie, he noted, had finally relaxed her squarish shoulders… a little. The chin that was carefully held level was allowed to lower… a bit… and her laughter managed to define her single dimple… right in the middle of her chin. Her well-formed mouth became mobile and even mirthful as she and her cousin teased, and when she batted playful verbal barbs with his sister, Janine.

And his sister, growing up as she did with no mother, was just as verbally proficient especially in the company others.

Back to Josie through Brad's eyes. Tall, for a girl. Shoulders broader, perhaps, than would be considered fashionable. Strongly formed hands, and feet that would not be considered dainty… if shoe size was the measure. She wore nice clothes, better than most in the territory, but wore them so naturally and with ease, and not as something to be noticed. Measured steps. Her whole manner exuded confidence, and that was without doubt valuable when teaching children. She knew what she was doing, and intended that her instruction be the final word.

Even with the hyperactive five-year-old brother of Brad's. Josie had somehow intrigued him, giving him no opportunity to argue. Firm, but fair. Stern, but with a smile.

Brad valued this opportunity to evaluate Josie from the social angle. This was because he had already decided, firmly, that she would eventually be his. It might take a while, as she had her own aims, plans and concerns, but he was patient. From the first glimpse, she had attracted him as no other girl had been able, and here she was, living less than a half a mile away.

In the school room, Josie, watching her Level Four girls with their essays, moved a bit to avoid staring and making them nervous. They had all four opted to stay a while to work after the other students had gone. Quieter. Easier to concentrate.

Carlotta was bent over her paper, her hair, fair and honey-streaked, wavy and curled at the end, hung down over her ears and hid her face, but her hand guiding the pencil moved furiously.

"Lottie, almost five years old, rode along the bumpy road, and her thoughts twisted themselves around in her head like tiny ropes. When she asked where they were going, her Mama said 'just down the road a ways.' That was not true, because they had been riding all day. That was longer than 'a ways'. That told her that Mama didn't know the answer, either, so she didn't bother her again. No use to make her feel bad just because she didn't know.

"Papa whistled a tune like he was happy, but then he yelled at the horses. Sometimes he yelled at 'Gee' and sometimes at 'Haw' so that must be the names of the horses, though she noticed he couldn't tell which was which.

"Finally it seemed better to wrap her stuffed bear in his blanket and watch out the back of the tent that was over the wagon. Sometimes both she and the bear leaned over on the pillow and went to sleep. But just about the time she got to sleep, the wagon stopped and Mama woke her up to go into the bushes and wee wee. Even if she didn't have to.

"When it got dark, Papa tied the horses to a tree. The animals moved around in the dark and they ate grass all night jingling the straps around their necks.

"Mama made a bed in the tent and everybody went to sleep right beside the road. The girl heard chirpy sounds all around her so she whispered to the bear not to be scared. She would take care of him. To prove it, she hugged him tighter.

"Then one day Papa had to keep stopping so Mama could upchuck, and she tried really hard to, but sometimes she couldn't. Then she cried when she got back in the wagon. Papa hugged her and said it would all be worth it, but that didn't help Mama to upchuck when she wanted to. Lottie didn't like to upchuck, but she thought everyone should get to do what they wanted to, if they could. And it surely seemed that Mama really wanted to.

"Just when Lottie began to think she would be riding the rest of her life, Papa told the Gee horse to turn off the road. He was whistling and happy and he unfolded a tent and helped Mama make a bed in it. He opened the tin box of crackers and slices of cheese and they all ate.

- END OF EXCERPT -

Additional Book Series
by Joann Klusmeyer

The Great I Am Bible Story Series for Kids
6 books

The Young Pioneers Adventure Series for Kids
5 books

The Wentworth Triplets Mystery Series for Young Teens
3 books

Footsteps in the Canyon Adventure Series for Young Teens
4 books

Burnt Tree Junction Historical Fiction Series for Adults
6 books

Ozark Mountains Historical Fiction Series for Adults
7 books

Taming the Wilderness Historical Fiction Series for Adults
4 books

The Sheltering Stone Historical Fiction Series for Adults
5 books

The Trilogy of Wishbone Hollow Historicial Fiction Series for Adults
3 books

www.ingramcontent.com/pod-product-compliance
Lightning Source LLC
Chambersburg PA
CBHW071845020726
47502CB00003B/602